STAR TREK®

THE LIVES OF DAX

STAR TREK®
THE LIVES OF DAX

EDITED BY

Marco Palmieri

POCKET BOOKS

New York   London   Toronto   Sydney   Singapore   Trill

An *Original* Publication of POCKET BOOKS

POCKET BOOKS, a division of Simon & Schuster Inc.
1230 Avenue of the Americas, New York, NY 10020

This book is published by Pocket Books, a division of Simon & Schuster Inc., under exclusive license from Paramount Pictures.

ISBN: 0-671-02840-5

First Pocket Books trade paperback printing December 1999

10   9   8   7   6   5   4   3   2   1

Printed in the U.S.A.

Contents

"In nine lives I've been a little of everything."

—Ezri Dax
"The Siege of AR-558"

Introduction

DAX
Our baby ... would have been so
beautiful.

And with that, Dax exhales her last breath and dies.

STRANGE AS IT may seem, that was how it started. Back in April 1998, I read Ira Steven Behr and Hans Beimler's moving script, "Tears of the Prophets," the finale for the sixth season of *Star Trek: Deep Space Nine*, confirming the rumors that had already been spreading for months. I read those words, and that's when I knew the book you now hold was going to happen.

Jadzia died, and something in the back of my mind just clicked.

But *why* do a book about Dax? I mean, let's face it, she doesn't fit into the usual formula for a successful *Star Trek* book—she's not a captain, she's not bald, and she doesn't have pointed ears. The skeptics I encountered were beside themselves: How could I possibly expect people to be interested?

And it wasn't as if Jadzia's demise meant I could do with the character as I pleased. When "Tears of the Prophets" aired, I knew the death of one Dax would mean the birth of another. We all did, didn't we? She was a *Trill,* for cryin' out loud—that was the thing that most defined her, that she (or he; we still didn't know at that point) would be back. It would be a different host, of course—the ninth—with the memories of all the previous hosts, male and female, going back nearly four hundred years. Each new personality was different from the one before it, each new life always striving to distinguish itself from the last. I started to wonder about the periods in *Star Trek* history those hosts had lived through, the things they might have done, the familiar faces they might have encountered. And then I grinned like an idiot.

"Why Dax?" Are you kidding? Why *not?*

How could I ignore the storytelling possibilities implicit in the Dax character? The potential not only to flesh out its past lives, but to explore the ways in which they've *always* played a part in the *Star Trek* universe?

And then came the clincher—the inspiration that would, I was certain, make the project truly unique among *Star Trek* books. This wasn't going to be a biographical novel, with one voice trying to capture the entire scope of Dax's life. I mean, think about it: Dax is a living anthology—a collection of stories. The book would be one too.

So I went forward, and on the way *Deep Space Nine*'s audience was introduced to a new Dax. Ezri came on the scene as the ninth host, and to the delight of *Star Trek* fans everywhere, myself among them, she proved as popular as Jadzia—precisely because, true to the nature of Dax, she was completely *different* from Jadzia! Wonderfully brought to life by Terry Farrell, Jadzia had been a strong, confident presence, someone who'd spent her entire adult life preparing herself to process the diverse lives embodied by the Dax symbiont. Ezri, masterfully portrayed by Nicole deBoer, was just the opposite; having been forced by circumstances to become joined to Dax, she was completely unprepared at first to balance the combined personalities of eight previous lives. We only got to watch her struggle for a year, but what a year it was.

We caught glimpses of the other hosts over the years, too, most notably Joran and Curzon. Every once in a while the show would drop a tantalizing new detail about one of the others, but for the most part they were little more than names and professions. It was enough to create a rough time line, and from there, the book just took off.

And it's entirely fair to say that this collection wouldn't have been possible without the innovative ideas that never stopped coming from the talented writers and producers of *Deep Space Nine,* who gave us such incredible characters to build upon. So to Rick Berman, Michael Piller, Ira Steven Behr, Ronald D. Moore, Hans Beimler, Rene Echevarria, Robert Hewitt Wolfe, David Weddle, Bradley Thompson, Peter Allen Fields, and the many others who helped to shape Dax along the way . . . I gratefully raise my glass to you all.

I was also privileged to gather together a talented

EZRI

"She's a Dax. Sometimes they don't think. They just do."

—Benjamin Sisko
"Penumbra"

Judith & Garfield Reeves-Stevens

Judith & Garfield Reeves-Stevens first sat at the Replimat seven years ago to eavesdrop on Odo and Quark as part of their research for *The Making of Deep Space Nine,* the first of four behind-the-scenes books they have written about *Star Trek* film and television productions. They are also the authors of three classic *Star Trek* novels, including the groundbreaking *Federation,* as well as the soon-to-be-published epic *DS9* trilogy, *Millennium,* about the catastrophic discovery of the Bajoran system's *second* wormhole. In addition, the Reeves-Stevenses are co-writers with William Shatner for the ongoing series of bestselling novels chronicling the continuing adventures of Captain Kirk after his "apparent" death in *Star Trek Generations.*

The Reeves-Stevenses' other novels include the *Los Angeles Times* bestseller *Icefire*—hailed by Stephen King as "the best thriller of its type since *The Hunt for Red October*"—and *Quicksilver,* which *Publishers Weekly* proclaimed "a warp-speed technothriller." The Reeves-Stevenses are also the authors of the classic sf/fantasy crossover trilogy *The Chronicles of Galen Sword,* which is now available in a trade paperback omnibus edition from Babbage Books. For more details, please log on to reeves-stevens.com.

"Second star to the right . . ."

Judith & Garfield Reeves-Stevens

SHE WAS LOST. Surrounded by the precariously stacked, cast-off debris of an antique alien city. Beneath unfamiliar stars and a single bloated moon. Her feet swelling from the stored daytime heat of the sand and gravel she had crossed, from the endless walking, from the ridiculously contorted shoes Julian had *insisted* she wear. It was enough to make a person say *End program* and go back to her quarters and—

"No," Ezri Dax said aloud.

She was many things. *Many to the power of nine,* she

thought. But she wasn't a quitter. *Well, Tobin was a bit of a quitter when it came to dealing with Raifi. And Audrid always believed she could have done more to save Jayvin. And Torias . . . well, okay,* Ezri reluctantly admitted to herself, *Torias wouldn't have gotten lost in the first place. But there was that time when . . .*

"Aggh," she said to break the relentlessly unpredictable connective thread of interaction and reflection that stitched together all the lives she had lived, that at least a part of her had lived. "I'm doing it again."

She sighed, breathing in the night's cool desert air, shivering as she hugged her sleeveless arms to her chest. The tiny disks of reflective plastic sewn to the fabric of the long, midnight-blue gown she wore—*almost* wore—scratched the flesh of her arms. Across her exposed back, there was only a chill breeze on far too much bare skin. One more time she wondered why she kept letting Julian talk her into these bizarre historical costumes and adventures from Earth's past.

She shook her head determinedly, as if that's all it would take to clear more than three centuries' worth of cobwebs, then put her hands on her hips and, with renewed resolve, looked about the graveyard of oddly angled broken glass and twisted metal. She deliberately ignored the dainty, indigo-sequined evening bag dangling from her wrist. Somehow, its triviality seemed especially inappropriate, considering the seriousness of her situation.

"Okay . . . ," she addressed herself firmly. She looked up at a towering construction of colored glass tubes and wire and metal to her side. In the soft light of the full moon, she could see it formed a caricature of a humanoid male with a vacant grin and narrow mustache, wearing a circular black hat with a disklike brim, one hand held up in an eternal wave of greeting—or a warning to go no farther. ". . . I saw *you* from the front gate," she said to the impassive giant, "and you were on my . . . left." Ezri peered into the dark labyrinth of other twisted tangles of glass and metal, thin rods and shafts jumbled and interlocked in what Jadzia might recognize as enormous metallic crystals grown at random. "So the gate should be somewhere in that direction . . . on my right." She gazed above the ragged black silhouettes that formed a fractal horizon of debris in that direction, but the desert air was so clear she could detect no distant glow of the blazing lights of the city she sought. The stars were as stark and bright in every direction. The space between them as impenetrably black. Wherever she was, wherever she had to go, her surroundings were offering no clue as to what her direction should be.

"I just have to . . ." Ezri faltered, having utterly failed to convince herself of her logic. ". . . go straight down there and . . . ugh, why do I even pretend I know what I'm doing?"

She kicked viciously at the gravel beneath her, sending up a pale cloud of dust in the moonlight, at the same time thoroughly wedging a small, sharp stone under her cramped and crushed-together toes.

"Aggh," she said again as she hopped awkwardly on one foot, trying to twist off the open-toed shoe to free the stone.

But hopping on gravel in a high-heeled shoe was next to impossible. And when confounded by the long tight gown she wore, not even all of Emony's gymnastic skills could come to Ezri's rescue.

With a strangled cry of frustrated rage, Ezri toppled

backward, braced herself for the impact of sharp gravel along her bare back—

—then gasped in surprise as a pair of strong hands caught her and gallantly restored her to her feet.

"Julian?!" she said as she spun around to face her rescuer, arms already reaching out to embrace him.

But the blinding smile that greeted her didn't belong to the chief medical officer of Deep Space 9. "Sorry to disappoint ya, doll." It was Vic Fontaine. A holographic simulation of a quintessential Las Vegas nightclub singer from Earth, circa 1962 A.C.E. He gave her a wink.

Ezri dropped her arms. Vic smiled as if he could sense the change in her mood.

"I was going to ask what a broad like you's doing in a dump like this," Vic said, "but I think I get the picture. The boyfriend's a big no-show, am I right, or am I right?"

Ezri shifted uncomfortably on the gravel, one foot still in bondage to its shoe, the other resting uncomfortably on the rough stones. "Actually, Julian doesn't know I came up here."

Vic shot her a sideways look. "What? You two lovebirds have a spat?"

Ezri shook her head, almost lost her balance again. "No. We had a date, down on the Strip. . . ." She waved her hand around, vaguely trying to indicate the direction of Las Vegas, three simulated kilometers in . . . some direction or another from here, but gave up. She had no idea where the city was anymore. "But he got called into emergency surgery."

"Son of a gun," Vic said. "Hasn't been a lot of that since the Big One."

Ezri nodded. The station had been quiet in the past few weeks since the Dominion War had finally ended. Life had been almost normal, or at least it appeared to be when filtered through Jadzia's memories. Ezri herself had been on the station for just less than a year, and only knew it in its wartime state of operations. And in the aftermath of war.

But even Ezri knew the end of the war hadn't brought total peace to the station. Colonel Kira was still brooding over Odo's departure, and was stubbornly refusing most of Ezri's offers to provide counselling. Instead, as the new commander of the station, she seemed to be sublimating all her frustrated emotions into convoluted plans to catch Quark red-handed at something—*anything* illegal, or even questionable. But at least all that attention had given Quark a new purpose in life. Except for those two weeks when the Ferengi barkeep had fled into hiding on Bajor after some bio-acceleration concoction he had peddled had succeeded in growing hair on every part of Morn's body *except* the prune-faced alien's head, Quark had been the station's sole source of excitement.

There'd be more excitement to come soon, though, Ezri knew. What with Kasidy Yates expecting Captain Sisko's baby and half the religious leaders on Bajor debating the significance of that birth in light of the mysterious rash of new visions being experienced by those who used the Orbs. On top of that, the Cardassian reconstruction effort was finally hitting its stride and even Bajor was contributing supplies and personnel to restore that battered world, making DS9's loading docks work at full capacity, twenty-six hours a day. And—

"You're shivering," Vic said.

Ezri came out of her reverie as the hologram wrapped his black sports jacket around her bare shoulders. "I did it again," she said crossly.

"Ya gotta give me more than that to go on, doll."

"Rambling," Ezri said. "It's . . . I think one thought, and that makes me think of another, and it's not as if I only have one lifetime of memories to remember, I've got eight, so . . . so everything I think reminds me of something else, and the next thing I know . . ." Ezri paused, distracted by a sudden recollection of how Curzon had once had a similar conversation with Ben Sisko at Utopia Planitia. It was late at night, after Sisko's shift was over. Curzon had added healthy dollops of Saurian brandy to the *raktajino*. "I hate *raktajino*," Ezri said to Vic's bafflement. But Jadzia had enjoyed the beverage. Which made Ezri remember one night when Jadzia and Sisko had been talking late at Quark's, after Sisko's shift was over. . . . "Aghh!"

"Don't tell me," Vic said kindly. "Rambling."

"Especially when I'm upset."

"Such as, when a certain young doctor gets called off for emergency surgery on a Saturday night."

Ezri studied the hologram, suddenly confused. "It's not Saturday . . . is it?"

Vic shrugged with a patient grin. "Hey, doll. It's not Saturday, this isn't Las Vegas, and it's sure not 1962. There's a holosuite wall not ten feet in front of you. But why spoil a beeyootiful evening with cold hard facts?" He offered her his arm. "C'mon, you look like you need to take a load off."

Ezri had no idea what the hologram meant by that, but she took his arm, using her free hand to keep his jacket tightly closed around her throat. "I don't think I can walk much farther on this gravel," she warned him.

"Then why don't you walk over there," Vic said. Ezri looked where he was pointing and saw an expanse of grass edging the gravel right beside her. She set her shoeless foot upon it. It was soft, springy, and impossible to miss. But somehow, she had. Impossible, she thought. *Unless . . .*

"Did you do that?" Ezri asked.

Vic guided her toward what appeared to be a large shoe, maybe two meters tall at the heel. In the moonlight, it had a metallic, silvery shimmer. "Do what?"

"The grass. Aren't all the simulation parameters set at the factory, or something?"

"Hey, doll, do I *look* like a parameter?"

Ezri didn't believe it, but she felt embarrassed because she might just have insulted a hologram. Somewhere, deep within her, Tobin had memories of the earliest versions of what would become holosuite technology—the bulky encounter suits, the crude sensory helmets, the exceedingly clumsy feedback gloves. Four lifetimes later, Joran had found a disturbing new application for the emerging technology. But for all the memories of holographic environments shared by Ezri's predecessors, each recollection carried with it the clear-cut knowledge that such artificially constructed environments were unreal.

But not to Ezri.

She had grown up with holoenvironments. As a child back home on Sappora VII, she had had a personal holoplayroom that had served as a welcome escape from her mother, for both her and her younger brother, Norvo. In fact, one of her first encounters with Earth had been in her favorite program, an extremely realistic simulation of an African veldt, complete with wildlife. Apparently, it was a classic.

That early experience with holotechnology had made it easy for Ezri to adapt to Starfleet Academy's extensive use of even more sophisticated simulations for training its young cadets. And now, since she had been joined with the Dax symbiont and her mind was constantly flooded with the memories of all of Dax's previous hosts, objective reality had become an even more fleeting notion to her. There was no reason for her *not* to think of holograms as any more or less real than the thousands of individuals who populated her shared memories. In fact, since Vic Fontaine was by some quirk of programming a hologram who *knew* he was a hologram, Ezri felt she had even less reason to think of him as anything other than a real individual.

"I'm sorry," Ezri said. "I didn't mean to . . . you know."

"No offense taken, doll." Vic stopped, then looked around the clearing in the midst of the graveyard as if he had arrived at a long-sought destination. "This looks like the place."

"What place?"

"The place to rest those barkin' dogs of yours." Again Vic pointed ahead, and as if he had given a cue to some unseen stage manager back at his nightclub, a moment later the giant shoe blazed with lights, studded as it was by dozens of incandescent glass globes.

Ezri blinked at the sudden brightness that flooded the clearing, wondering how Vic had known the shoe would light up just then, or if he had somehow been responsible for what it had done. Either way, now she could see she was surrounded not by bulky machinery and sculptures, but by *signs*.

She saw individual letters that were a full two meters high, giant bottles poised over equally mammoth glasses, what looked to be a chorus line of dancing *dabo* girls frozen in midkick. Some signs were outlined by glass globes, others by glass tubes. For a moment, Ezri wondered if the map she had consulted was in error. This might not be a junkyard after all. It could be some type of art museum.

"What is this place?" she asked.

"YESCO," Vic said with a dramatic flourish of his hand. "The Young Electric Sign Company. They've been making all the signs on the Strip since the whole big ball o' wax got started."

Ezri still didn't understand. "But these look broken. Is it a repair facility?"

"Some things can't be fixed, sweetheart." Ezri watched as Vic regarded the derelict signs with holographic sadness. "The Silver Slipper. The Golden Nugget. Caesar's . . . All kaput. All finito. That's Las Vegas for ya. A real Neverland. Home to lost boys, lost dreams, here today, gone tomorrow . . ."

"Wait a minute. What's a sign from Caesar's doing here?"

Vic turned to her, his eyes wide with delighted surprise. "What kind of question is that?"

"Well, this is Las Vegas, 1962, right?"

"Don't stop now, you're on a roll."

Ezri paused, decided Vic's colloquialism was some sort of food allusion, and ignored it. "But the gaming establishment known as Caesar's Palace was still in operation as of 2053. For two months following the outbreak of Earth's World War III, Caesar's was the operational command center for Colonel Amber's Regimental Volunteers. It was the site of the final battle of—"

Vic said it with her, "—the Siege of Las Vegas." He cocked his head at her, curious. "How's a little girl like you know so much about things like that?"

Ezri shrugged. "Well, that's why I decided to come up here tonight. I was checking out this location for Julian . . . in case he wanted to try out a new historical last stand. He's got this thing for lost causes. . . ."

"Then you've come to the right place."

"No, no. If this is 1962—"

"—or a reasonable facsimile thereof—" Vic added.

"—then how can you know what's going to happen after World War III, almost . . ." She hesitated as she did the math. After lifetimes of thinking in terms of clear and straightforward stardates, Earth years were hopelessly perplexing in comparison.

"Ninety-one years later?" Vic said helpfully.

"Exactly," Ezri said. "Isn't that like breaking the rules?"

Vic looked up at the stars, all but the brightest ones now hidden by the glare from the blazing silver shoe. He tugged on his shirt collar, loosening his thin black tie. "Depends on who makes those rules, wouldn't you say?"

"Well . . ." Ezri began uncertainly, "then that would be whoever programmed you in the first place. Right?"

"My pal Felix. Great guy, but sometimes he's been known to borrow a bit of code from this place and that. So out here, at the edge of the program, sometimes things get a bit muddled. Sort of like me, ya know." Vic looked up at the stars, as if wishing he could reach for them. "Sure I'm strictly 1962, but I gotta tell ya, I know everything there is to know about that station you all say you come from, and that century." Vic looked back at Ezri and tapped a finger against her nose. "Just between you and me and the Man in the Moon, I don't think Felix has a good grasp of the importance of purging memory buffers. Not that I'm complaining, mind you. You'd be surprised what happens when programming mixes it up in here. Ya get all sorts of . . . unexpected iterations. Not that a mutt like me has any idea of what I'm talking about."

Ezri gazed thoughtfully at Vic's smoothly handsome

face, framed in silver hair. He was an enigma among holograms, that much everyone on DS9 could agree on. He knew he was a hologram, he had the capability of entering other holosuite simulations, and he seemed to have some kind of ongoing existence even when the holosuites in Quark's bar were offline. Jake Sisko had sometimes wondered if Vic might be a captive alien personality, somehow downloaded into the holosuites' memory circuits. Chief O'Brien, when overly fortified by bloodwine, had once forwarded the theory that Vic represented the next step in the evolution of machine intelligence, like the eerily lifelike Emergency Medical Holograms that were becoming more common throughout Starfleet.

"Vic, may I ask you a question?"

Vic gave her a playful smile as if he could read her mind as easily as a Betazoid and knew what was coming. "Shoot, dollface."

"What's it like being a hologram?"

Vic laughed. "Answer me this first," he said. "What's it like bein' a Trill?"

"I think you mean, a *joined* Trill."

" 'You say tomato. . . .' "

Again with the food, Ezri thought. But she gave Vic's question serious consideration, not because of anything in Jadzia's or Audrid's or even Joran's past, but because of her own—Ezri's—Starfleet training as a counsellor.

"What's it like being joined . . . ?" she repeated. "In a word, confused."

Vic gestured with open hands held to the heavens. "What's it like being a hologram? I couldn't have said it better myself. Confused, with a capital *con.* "

Ezri frowned, not willing to accept that answer for a Ferengi second. "What does a hologram have to be confused about?"

Vic stared at her, open-mouthed, and shook his head once, exactly as Ezri had seen some Las Vegas comedian do, on an earlier date she'd had with Julian. Jimmy the Ranti . . . or something like that.

"You think being confused is something that can only happen to your kinda people?" Vic asked. He tapped both hands to his chest beneath his loosened tie and open collar. "I'm a twentieth-century hologram in a twenty-fourth-century world. Sometimes I have to ask myself if *I'm* the only real McCoy on the face of the Earth and all you people are mathematical constructs being generated by some big number-crunching hunk of transistors and vacuum tubes out in the great beyond. Don't get me wrong, sweetheart. I love my life. But still, sometimes I wonder where it is I'm going, and worse yet, where I was before I was here."

Ezri caught herself replying with more than a touch of Jadzia the scientist. "Those questions are merely a common function of any self-aware intelligence attempting to build patterns from the past in order to anticipate the future." She paused, grimacing at how cold she had sounded. "What I meant to say was, how confusing can life be for you if you've been programmed to mesh perfectly with your environment? I mean, you know where all the grassy parts are. You know when the lights will go on. It's . . . a perfect match."

"Perfect?" Vic raised his eyebrows skeptically. "It doesn't work that way, dollface. But from my side of the street, I'm looking at you, saying, How confusing can it be for her? She can go anywhere in the whole wide universe, see anything, be anyone, for real."

Sudden fatigue swept over Ezri. She looked around for someplace to sit. "It doesn't work that way for me, either."

Maybe he really can read my mind, Ezri thought as she watched Vic drag a large metal box out from beside the glowing silver slipper. The grimy container looked as if it had once held electrical connections, back in the days before transtators.

Vic brushed off the top surface of the box, sending puffs of holographic dust into the air. "Park it here, doll," he said.

Ezri took that as an invitation to sit, and did, wincing as the sudden chill of the metal made itself known through the thin fabric of her gown.

Vic swung a foot up on the corner of the box, rested an elbow against his knee. "So, you're not convincing me."

"About what?"

"About you not having it better than me."

Ezri tried to find a blunter way to put it. "I didn't choose my life."

"Join the club, sweetcakes."

"But . . . but . . ." Ezri sputtered.

"Take it easy, doll. Sounds like you're having trouble getting started."

"I've heard you sing, Vic. You're good."

Vic nodded thoughtfully. "Maybe not as good as Frank, but I won't give you an argument on that one."

"Which makes me think you enjoy what you do."

This time, Vic's smile transformed his face. "Oh, yeah. To be up at that mike, belting out pure gold, holding that audience in the palm of my hand. . . ." To Ezri, Vic seemed to be staring away at someplace, sometime, other than the

Young Electric Sign Company junkyard. "What can I tell you? Like the man said, 'baby, it's witchcraft.'"

"Exactly. So at the end of the day, no matter how you got here, is there anything else you can imagine that would be more fulfilling than being a nightclub singer in 1962 Las Vegas?"

Vic smiled at her, clutched his chest just above his holographic heart, and said, "Ya got me." Then he took on a more serious expression. "Which makes me think, there's something else, somewhere else, *you'd* rather be."

Ezri looked off at the surrounding signs, none of them fulfilling their functions anymore, no longer pointing the way to anywhere. She couldn't believe she was having this conversation with anyone, let alone a hologram. But then, maybe the fact that Vic was a hologram was exactly why she *could* have this conversation with him.

"That's the problem," Ezri said softly. "I can't answer that. I . . . I never got a chance to find out what I wanted. Not on my own. Not before I was joined."

Ezri could see that Vic, whatever algorithms fueled his awareness and his personality, appeared to sense the sudden serious mood that had enveloped her, drawing her into her own personal wormhole of despair.

The hologram sat down beside her. The metal box creaked a bit under his illusory weight. When he spoke, his voice was softer, more deliberate. "I gotta tell you, I'm not up on all your fancy twenty-fourth-century Flash Gordon, Buck Rogers atomic-ray rocketship you-name-its."

Ezri stared at him blankly, having no idea what he was saying, but trusting he'd mention something familiar eventually.

"But the one thing I do know," Vic said kindly, "is that this being 'joined' megillah, it's not something that sneaks up

JUDITH & GARFIELD REEVES-STEVENS

on you, is it? I remember Jadzia talking about it once. Training for years. Selection committees. Only one out of a thousand qualifies, and even then that don't guarantee you a place at the table. Isn't that how it really goes, dollface?"

Ezri rubbed at her eyes, wondering why she didn't just call it a night. She could go back to her quarters—or to Julian's—have some tea, fall asleep, and when she woke up, Julian would be there beside her, to take all these questions from her.

But that would be quitting, too, she thought.

"You're half right, Vic," she said quietly. She was dimly aware of tears building up in her eyes, though she had no idea why. "That's how it goes for every Trill . . . except me."

She made an effort to smile up at him. The hologram's silver hair was almost luminous in the bright lights of the slipper, as if his head were surrounded by a glowing nimbus of radiance. The image seemed to evoke some faint echo of recognition in her, something or someone or even a symbol from one of the other lives her symbiont had led. But she couldn't bring up anything more concrete. For an unsettling moment, it almost felt to Ezri as if the Dax part of her were gone, or asleep, or somehow standing back from what she was doing now, as if this moment belonged only to her. Could belong only to her.

"I don't get it," Vic said. "What makes you so different?"

Such a simple question, Ezri thought. *With such a simple answer.*

But it still kept her up at night, staring into the endless darkness of the ceiling, whether Julian was beside her or not.

She realized then there was no holding back. She had gone this far with the hologram—no, with *Vic*—that she might as well see it through to the end.

"I never wanted to be joined," she told him haltingly, the very words a sacrilege against everything her world and her people held dear.

Vic nodded slowly, knowingly. "Riiight. Now I remember. When Jadzia bought it. The symbiont heading home. Something goes wrong. It has to be joined or it's lights out forever. And you were the only Trill on the ship."

Ezri opened her mouth to give her rehearsed answer, the one that had been drilled into her by Starfleet and the Symbiosis Commission and by Dax and all the previous hosts now sharing her consciousness. But the words wouldn't come. Not here. Not now.

"I wish . . . I wish it had been that simple," she said, her voice almost a whisper.

She saw Vic study her, intrigued, and his expression made Ezri smile. Isn't that why they were here having this discussion? Artificial being and joined Trill, both wrestling with their respective confusion?

"You mean," Vic said, "that's not how it happened?"

"No," Ezri said. "That's exactly how it happened. But . . . that's not all that happened."

For long moments, hologram and Trill held each other's gaze. Then Vic reached into his back pocket, pulled out a flat silver flask, and twisted open its stopper. "I've got a crazy feeling we're going to be here a while," he said. He held out the flask to Ezri. She took it, smelled some kind of Earth brandy she couldn't identify. Took a swallow and felt it burn so far down her throat Dax shivered in her abdominal pocket.

"Badda bing," Vic said, as if he had felt the symbiont move himself. Then he took a swallow of his own and moved closer to Ezri so they were side by side. He sealed the flask, put it behind them, then slipped an arm around her as if to make sure his jacket was as snug as it could be.

Ezri didn't protest, didn't feel the least awkward, enjoyed in fact the feeling of inner warmth from the brandy and the security of Vic's arm around her. She leaned her head against his shoulder, looking up at those few stars bright enough to outshine the silver slipper, alien stars that reminded her just how lost she was.

"So what's your story?" Vic asked.

Ezri laughed, feeling strangely better than she had for months. "Stories. That's more like it."

Vic gave her a squeeze, protective, nothing more, but just enough. "Not *their* stories, doll. *Your* story."

"My story," Ezri said. *"My* story." That first word sounded odd, because the way she said it, she wasn't talking about Ezri Dax, she was talking about Ezri Tigan. The person she used to be before she became . . . the persons she was . . . were . . . *damn these pronouns,* she thought.

"We've got all night," Vic said soothingly. "As long as you need. As long as you want."

Ezri snuggled in closer to Vic's broad shoulder, letting her mind drift back, almost eighteen months earlier, to one of her first Starfleet assignments, and her first glimpse of Deep Space 9. . . .

"I was on a starship," Ezri said.

"Imagine that," Vic told her.

"A starship named *Destiny.* . . ."

And as easily as that, the past came to life, and—

—in the main shuttlebay of the *Starship Destiny,* Ensign Ezri Tigan pushed her long dark hair from her eyes and peered through the slightly fogged viewport of the medical transport pod. Inside, bathed in billows of inert nitrogen and the purple mist of Trill ocean water, the glistening brown, sluglike shape of a symbiont, the life-form that was the driving force behind Trill civilization, the shining ideal for which all Trill children were raised to aspire to serve, pulsated slowly.

Ezri screwed up her face. "Ewww. That's so gross."

Beside her, Ensign Brinner Finok jabbed his elbow into Ezri's side. "Zee! That's *Dax*. One of the greatest. Show some respect."

Ezri grinned at Brinner, her delight at teasing him multiplying as she saw his cheeks flush until they were almost as dark as the intricate curlicues of Trill spots that ran up both sides of his high forehead. He was so serious, it was obvious he needed her to remind him that life held other possibilities than a constant devotion to duty. Last night, she considered she had done an especially good job at diverting his mind from his work. His cheeks had flushed then, too, and as if Brinner also remembered how they had passed their evening, he now allowed his typically intent expression to soften with a self-conscious smile.

It didn't last, though. Suddenly, he reacted to something he saw from the corner of his eye and his smile vanished as he snapped to attention like a first-year cadet.

Ezri turned to see what Brinner saw, and instantly stepped back from the transport pod and the two security officers who flanked it. Beyond the pod, the *Destiny*'s chief medical officer, Dr. T'pek, stepped down from the DS9 runabout, holding her medical tricorder before her like a protective sword. The tricorder was aimed directly at the pod, as if its contents were the most valuable cargo ever to come aboard.

With everyone's attention on the tall, startlingly thin Vulcan doctor, Ezri couldn't resist. "It's a big ugly worm," she whispered to Brinner, "and you'll never catch me with one of them in my pocket." She jabbed her own elbow into Brinner's side for emphasis, then squared her shoulders and smoothed her jacket. Someone else was coming out of the runabout behind the doctor, and he wasn't wearing a Starfleet uniform. Its design looked Bajoran.

"They'd never pick you, anyway," Brinner whispered back, still keeping his eyes locked dead ahead. "Triple-niner."

Ezri snorted, but didn't take offense at Brinner's insult. She didn't care if she was among the ninety-nine-point-nine percent of the Trill population unfit to be joined. She didn't even care if she was among the one-tenth of one percent who *were* fit. She wanted no part of her planet's parasitic brain vampires and had never even bothered to fill out her standard selection profile for the Symbiosis Commission. But before she could come up with a suitably insulting rejoinder for Brinner, Ezri felt her throat tense up as she recognized what was coming through the runabout door.

A Founder.

Ezri looked from the eerily half-formed humanoid face of the changeling to the security guards by the pod and wondered why they didn't draw their weapons. There was a war on. The shapeshifting Founders and their Jem'Hadar had brought near ruin to the Federation. How could Captain Raymer permit the enemy to board the vessel? Why wasn't Dr. T'pek offering any protest? Why weren't the changeling detection protocols being followed? How . . . Ezri's cascade of questions came to an end as she saw the Founder place his hand, almost affectionately, on the surface of the transport pod.

"There . . . the symbiont remains in stable condition," Dr. T'pek said to the changeling. She even showed him her tricorder readings, as if he were a colleague. "The delay has not compromised it at all."

The changeling looked faintly annoyed, but Ezri wasn't sure if that was an accurate reflection of his mood because his features were so alien and unreadable to her. "As I said, Doctor, Jadzia had no difficulty using transporters. The Dax symbiont could have been beamed onto this ship and you could have been on your way an hour ago. *If* you hadn't insisted on using the runabout."

Ezri glanced sideways at Brinner, trying to gauge his reaction to this surreal scene. Not only was the enemy onboard *Destiny,* he was actually criticizing Dr. T'pek. But Brinner's attention was still riveted on the transport pod and the symbiont within. *Typical,* Ezri thought. She knew Brinner was desperate to be a tenth-percenter. But given the waiting list at the Symbiosis Commission, she also knew this was as close to a symbiont as he'd be likely to get in the next twenty years.

T'pek maintained her patience with the changeling, but since the doctor was a Vulcan, Ezri could expect no less. "Constable, I do not have to tell you what a valuable asset Dax is to Starfleet, and to the Federation. As Jadzia Dax, it was on the front lines of the war, and we cannot risk losing that knowledge or experience. Some symbionts have unusual reactions to the beaming process, and with Dax already suffering from some type of energy shock and host-death trauma syndrome, an hour's delay did not present an unacceptable risk in relation to what a transporter reaction might have triggered. It was the logical thing to do."

The changeling with the unlikely rank of "constable" sighed deeply, then patted the transport pod. "Dax was more than an asset, Doctor. It . . . *she* . . . was a friend."

"I understand," T'pek said with equal parts respect and firmness. "And we will have your *friend* on Trill in two weeks. More than enough time for recuperation and a new joining."

The changeling nodded, then turned back to the runabout, without once looking around the shuttlebay, as if nothing on this ship was worth his attention except for the worm. Ezri didn't know why, but it seemed obvious to her that at least there was one changeling who was allied with the Federation, for whatever reason.

Immediately after the changeling had boarded the runabout, T'pek had the security guards file off, carrying the transport pod with antigravs. Then, with a curt nod indicating that Brinner and Ezri were to follow, the doctor fell in behind the pod, her flashing tricorder held in operating position.

Just before leaving the shuttlebay with the others, Ezri looked over her shoulder to see the runabout slip through the bay's atmospheric forcefield into space. Far beyond it, like a glittering ornament silhouetted against a frozen spray of fiery sparks, she saw Deep Space 9. Each docking pylon was mated with a ship—Federation, Bajoran, even two Klingon cruisers. Other ships from other systems kept station nearby, as if DS9 were the center of a whirlpool, an island of calm in a storm-tossed sea.

Too bad we didn't have a chance to visit, Ezri thought with real regret. With the war, there was no telling how soon the

Destiny might get this close to the front lines again. She re-signed herself to the fact that, like so many of the sights she had seen in her brief time with Starfleet, this first glimpse of Deep Space 9 might also be her last.

Then the shuttlebay personnel door slipped shut, and she half-stumbled as she hurried to catch up with Brinner, now marching dutifully in Dr. T'pek's wake.

Even before Ezri reached the others, she was wonder-ing why the wide corridor was so quiet. By the time she fell into step with Brinner, she had realized the answer. They were the only people in the wide passageway.

"Where is everyone?" she whispered to her fellow ensign.

But before Brinner could answer, T'pek spoke. "We are now in security condition alpha."

The party halted before a turbolift door as T'pek an-nounced their arrival into her communicator badge. Ezri and Brinner exchanged a silent, questioning glance. Ezri knew that security condition alpha meant that sections of the *Des-tiny* had been sealed off from the rest of the ship by blast doors and security forcefields. From training drills, she knew that alpha conditions were for preventing lethal biological contamination, or escorting beings so critical to the Federa-tion that their loss would cause irreparable damage, like the president of the Federation Council.

As the turbolift door slid open, Ezri murmured to Brinner, "Is that thing really *that* important?"

T'pek turned to her. "Ensign, the Dax symbiont has just served six years on one of the most important outposts in-volved in the war with the Dominion. As a Starfleet officer, it knows the latest codes, the latest battle plans, the latest strategies. It knows our strengths. It knows our weaknesses. It knows the same about key personnel in Starfleet Command and the Klingon Defense Force. How would you have us transport it back to your homeworld? On a pleasure cruiser?"

Though the Vulcan's tone had not varied in the slightest, Ezri knew she had been severely reprimanded, and like Brinner she unconsciously snapped to attention, eyes straight ahead, an errant cadet once again. "No, ma'am," she said.

During T'pek's even-voiced tirade, Franklin Solon, the ship's surgeon, had stepped from the turbolift to the chief medical officer's side. Now T'pek turned away from Ezri to hand her tricorder to the surgeon.

"All life signs are stable for now," T'pek reported. "But host-death syndrome is known to cause rapid reversals without warning."

Solon studied the tricorder display with a frown. "I understand. I've been familiarizing myself with the necessary emergency requirements." He looked up from the tricorder, checked out Brinner, then Ezri, his large dark eyes reflecting the tricorder's multicolored flashing lights. "Which one?" he asked.

"We might not have a choice," T'pek answered.

Ezri felt her spots pucker. What were the doctors talking about?

"You may proceed," T'pek said to Solon. "Keep a full implantation team on standby. And keep the subspace link to Trill open."

Solon nodded brusquely, then stepped back into the turbolift with the security guards and the transport pod. "See you in sickbay," he said.

Then the doors closed, leaving Ezri and Brinner alone with T'pek in the otherwise deserted corridor.

Here it comes, Ezri thought. She had a terrible feeling she was about to find out why Dr. T'pek had requested the only two Trill on board to meet her in the main shuttle-bay.

The Vulcan pulled a padd from her medical smock, checked a text display on it, then stared at Ezri. "Ensign Tigan, your medical records are incomplete."

Ezri's startled first reaction was to want to laugh. Four years at Starfleet Academy had left her feeling like a medical experiment. She had been scanned, genetically decoded, retropulsed, and biolfiltered until she had decided her visits to Starfleet Medical were really covert training simulations, like some perverse, psychological variation of the *Kobayashi Maru.* If there was a cell in her body that Starfleet *didn't* have a blueprint for, then it had to be one she had grown in the last five days.

"I'm sorry, Doctor," Ezri said, "but I don't understand."

With long and delicate fingers, T'pek held out the padd so Ezri could read it. "There is no symbiosis evaluation."

Ezri nodded agreement. "No, ma'am, there isn't."

"Is it not law that all Trill are to submit to preliminary screening tests on their twelfth birthdays?"

Ezri's eyes widened. She knew Starfleet was thorough, but surely it wasn't going to go back to her twelfth birthday to find flaws in her record. "It's not really a law, ma'am. More like . . . a custom."

"That's right, Doctor," Brinner said quickly, and Ezri was glad of his support. "First Screening is a cultural celebration, similar to a human bar mitzvah, or a Klingon bloodkill. There's no actual legal requirement for anyone to take part. It's just that everyone does." He glanced at Ezri. "Almost everyone."

"Ah," T'pek said. "So the records are not incomplete. You simply chose not to undergo screening."

"Yes, ma'am."

"Why?"

On one hand, Ezri was tired of that question more than any other she had been asked, second only to her mother's constant refrain of, Why leave home to join Starfleet? The answer to that second question was that joining Starfleet was the *perfect* excuse to leave home. And, with luck, to not go back for years. The answer to the first question was far more complex. She and Brinner had spent hours talking about it over the past month. And Ezri still wasn't anywhere close to having explained all her thoughts and feelings to him.

So for now, she chose the easy way out.

"I don't wish to be joined, ma'am."

Ezri braced herself for the inevitable questions that would follow. She expected they would be especially brutal coming from the logic-honed mind of a Vulcan. *How can you make such a profound decision that will affect your entire life at so young an age? How can you not aspire to fulfill the biological destiny of your species? How can you disappoint your parents?* Or, Ezri's favorite, *What dark secrets are you hiding that you don't wish a symbiont to know?*

But T'pek asked none of those. Instead, she called up another text display on the padd, then addressed Brinner.

"Ensign Finok, your medical records do include a preliminary symbiosis evaluation, and several follow-ups."

"Yes, ma'am."

"Logic suggests you do wish to be joined."

"*Yes,* ma'am."

Ezri tried not to think any less of the young man who had so recently become her lover. What chance did he have for true independence when the whole of Trill society was dedicated to brainwashing its children into believing there could be no higher goal than sacrificing their individuality to a parasitic race of slugs?

"Very well," T'pek said. "You are to report to sickbay until further notice. I will have Captain Raymer excuse you from all other duty until we reach Trill."

"I . . . don't understand, ma'am." Brinner looked nervously at Ezri, then back to the doctor. "Are you saying I'm to be joined with Dax?"

Ezri stared at Brinner. The question was ridiculous. Even if a Trill were biochemically suitable for the joining process, years of training and preparation were necessary before the procedure could be undertaken.

But the Vulcan surprised her and Brinner. "Unlikely," T'pek said. "However, in the event the symbiont's condition worsens, we must stand ready to perform an emergency joining procedure. And, since Ensign Tigan has not seen fit to have her suitability for joining assessed, you, it would appear, are the only suitable Trill on the ship."

"B–but . . ." Brinner stammered, "I haven't been trained."

T'pek raised an eyebrow. "But Dax has. Eight times. Report to sickbay at once."

By now, Brinner's face was so pale his spots seemed black. He looked at Ezri, but neither spoke. There was too much to say, and no time to say it.

T'pek stepped to the side and the turbolift door opened.

Brinner walked inside. *Like a condemned man entering a Trikon brainwipe chamber,* Ezri thought. Then T'pek took her place in the 'lift beside Brinner and gave Ezri another curt nod. "I have no further need of you, Ensign. Carry on."

"Yes, ma'am," Ezri mumbled, then watched Brinner until the 'lift doors closed and she heard the car speed away.

Ezri remained motionless in the silent corridor after that, remembering once again how much she loathed the worms, and startling herself by how much she was going to miss Brinner.

"I wish I was a Vulcan," Ezri finally said to herself. Life would be so much simpler without emotions. And with that defiant wish playing in her troubled mind, she returned to her quarters, alone.

By the third day outward bound from Deep Space 9, Ezri worked up her courage enough to slip into sickbay after duty hours.

She had checked with the ship's computer that Brinner Finok was not under quarantine, so technically, she reassured herself, she wasn't doing anything wrong. She was simply visiting a friend. A friend who had not responded to any of the notes she had sent through the *Destiny's* internal messaging system.

At ship's midnight, the main sickbay clinic was deserted. Ezri could see one of the medical department's biotechnicians in his office, working on a desk padd. But other than the bright spill of light through that small cubicle's transparent wall, the main light levels were dim, and the only sound was the hum of the air circulators.

Ezri walked quickly across the clinic to the closed door to Isolation Room 2. The biohazard seal wasn't active, so again she told herself that she was not breaking any crucial protocols.

Beside it, the seal for the door to Isolation Room 1 *was* active. That room contained the apparatus for identifying changelings. Only Captain Raymer, Dr. T'pek, and the *Destiny's* chief of security had access to Isolation Room 1, and then, only when two of the three of them were present at the same time.

Ezri herself had been randomly screened four times in the past month. She had heard that some command staff were checked every day. Such vigilance was the price of war, she knew. And since the test was simple—just a quick pinprick and the extraction of a single drop of blood—she had never felt indignant about it. But let the Symbiosis Commission ever try to examine a single follicle of hair to assess her as possible joining material, and she'd—

"This facility is off-limits!"

Those were the first words Brinner said to her as the isolation door slid open to reveal him standing by the locked-down transport pod containing the Dax symbiont.

The young ensign's formal words and attitude were so unexpected, that Ezri ignored them. She entered the small isolation room, holding up the present she had brought—a fragile, single-crystal bottle of *samsit,* just like the one they had shared on their fifth date, which was the first date on which they hadn't quite gotten around to leaving Ezri's quarters.

"Brinner, are you all right?"

"I'm fine," he said stiffly. "But you do have to leave."

Brinner stepped in front of the pod, his back to the symbiont, facing Ezri as if he was about to challenge her in combat.

Ezri knew what was wrong, tried to correct the situation.

"I'm not here to argue," she said. "What you want to do with your life, that's your decision."

For the briefest moment, Ezri almost had the feeling

that Brinner didn't know what she was talking about. But then he seemed to relax.

"I'm sorry," he said. "And I . . . appreciate your trust. But you really do have to leave. I'm . . . supposed to be under medical quarantine."

Ezri moved closer to her friend, trying to coax out his playful side. She knew he wasn't under quarantine. He was just using that as an excuse. "Good, that means no one else will come in to . . . disturb us."

"Ensign, please . . ." Brinner said. He was actually pressing back against the pod as if trying to get as far away from her as possible.

"Ensign?" Ezri frowned. "My, aren't we formal."

"Ezri," Brinner said, as if correcting himself.

At that, Ezri stopped two meters from Brinner. She felt her own face flush, even as Brinner seemed to maintain complete equanimity.

"Ezri? We're back to that? As if last week didn't happen?" After that first night they had spent together, close in each other's arms, Ezri had told Brinner how her younger brother had first called her Zee, when he was learning to speak and "Ezri" had been too much of a challenge. Ever since then, it had remained her brother's special name for her, and had become the special name she shared only rarely, and only with those, like Brinner, whom she had welcomed into her heart.

So for Brinner now to call her "Ezri" was a repudiation of what they had shared, of what she had believed they had come to mean to each other.

"I'm . . . sorry . . ." Brinner said defensively, and though he seemed to be upset, his cheeks remained pale. "I . . . don't know what else I can say. . . ."

Males, Ezri thought. "So don't," she told him as she closed the distance between them. She brought her hands to Brinner's face, carefully holding the *samsit* crystal bottle between two fingers of one hand as she used the other to caress his cheek. Then she leaned even closer and kissed him just as she had that first night.

Brinner shrank back from her but that only made her more determined. She held him more closely, kissed him more forcefully.

Still, he made no response.

Ezri went for broke, delicately biting Brinner's lower lip the way she knew he could not resist. Then teasingly, she pulled back on it, forcing him to finally draw closer to her, one way or another.

But all he did was cringe, as if what she did was unspeakable.

Ezri didn't have to be a Betazoid to feel the revulsion that filled him.

For one brief moment of emotional torment of which her mother would be proud, Ezri gave in to the realization that she had somehow turned from Brinner's lover into a repulsive thing he couldn't bear to touch. It was as if a phaser had fired full power into her heart.

But then, her self-respect came to the fore. This wasn't *her* problem. This was Brinner's. He was the one who was behaving reprehensibly. He was the one who had changed.

And then that last word blazed in her mind like a general quarters siren.

Changed.

Her eyes widened in horror and because she was so

young, so inexperienced, she said the one thing she should not say in this situation.

The truth.

"You . . ." she whispered in shock. ". . . you're not Brinner. . . ."

The hands of the man—the *creature* she caressed struck her own hands away from his face.

The fragile bottle of *samsit* shattered in the violence of his action, and as if watching a slow-motion training simulation, Ezri saw in perfect, horrific detail how the laser-sharp shards of *samsit* crystal sliced into the thing's palm, spraying dark droplets of blood.

Dark droplets that shimmered into golden spheres of elemental changeling flesh before they reached the deck.

At last, Ezri screamed.

At last, half-falling, half-running, she pushed back from the monster she had kissed, screaming even louder as the changeling's arms snaked after her, writhing through the air like tentacles, sliding and slithering around her body like living water, to tighten around her neck and cover her face in a golden gelatinous mass that seeped up her nostrils, into her mouth and down her throat, strangling her from the outside, choking her from the inside, until her world turned black and all she saw was a spray of fiery sparks like those that encompassed Deep Space 9.

In those final moments, all she felt was the horrible, unending realization of how wasted her short life had been. The heart-wrenching loss of it seemed to last forever. . . .

Seconds, minutes, millennia later, a brilliant, blinding light exploded in Ezri's vision, drawing her forward as the voice of the Creator of All Things asked, "Are you all right? Ensign?! Answer me!"

For a moment, Ezri was bemused by the fact that her Starfleet rank had followed her into the afterlife. Then she opened her eyes and realized that the Creator of All Things bore a striking resemblance to Dr. Franklin Solon.

"Are you all right, Ensign?"

Ezri sat up from the diagnostic bed, coughing hoarsely.

"Do you know where you are?" another voice asked.

Ezri blinked to see a bald human doctor standing at the other side of her bed. It took her a moment to recognize him as the *Destiny*'s Emergency Medical Hologram.

The realization that an emergency existed was enough to clear her mind completely.

"Sickbay," she said. Her throat hurt but she went on. *"U.S.S. Destiny."* Captain Raymer was beside Dr. Solon so she felt that was the most likely location of this facility. "There was a changeling," she gasped.

"We know," Raymer said. She ran a hand through her short gray hair. Her eyes were tinged with dark circles. Her pale cheek was smudged with soot, as if she had been in a firefight. "A biotech heard your screams. We were able to get the security fields up in time. We got it."

Ezri sighed with relief, then shivered. "It looked just like Brinner."

Solon nodded. "That's what we concluded. But the security monitors were disabled throughout sickbay so we couldn't be sure." His dark eyes kept looking up at the diagnostic readouts behind Ezri, and she was suddenly aware she was wearing only a flimsy blue medical gown.

"Am I all right?"

"You'd better be," Solon said.

Ezri didn't like the sound of that. "Why?" she asked. She looked again at the EMH, then around at the other grim medical technicians surrounding her bed. "Where's Dr. T'pek?"

"That's how the changeling came aboard," Raymer said. She held up her hands in a gesture of helplessness. Ezri saw one of them was bandaged, a few spots of blood showing. "She was in *charge* of changeling detection. . . . If not for you. . . ."

Ezri noticed some of the techs were also wearing bandages. She could smell smoke in the air. "Has something happened?"

"The changeling had a communications device. When we cornered it, the ship was attacked by Jem'Hadar. You've been out a couple of hours."

Ezri's mind was spinning. She felt as if she had been given some kind of drug. But before she could ask anything more, she heard a life-support alarm sound from another room.

A nurse ran to Dr. Solon. "We're losing it, Doctor!"

Raymer suddenly took Ezri's hand. Ezri stared at her blankly.

"I've read your file," the captain said.

Ezri lurched as she was lifted on the bed's surface by two technicians with antigravs. Everyone walked at her side, following her toward the second room. Technicians shouted out medical orders.

"I know how you feel about symbionts," Raymer continued, her hand still gripping Ezri's.

Ezri peered ahead through her entourage. Saw two medical tables side by side in the operating theater. One was empty. The other was not.

"No . . ." she gasped, not willing to believe what was about to happen. "Where's Brinner?! Brinner wanted this! It's his dream!"

"We don't know," Solon told her. "The changeling probably killed him, just like it killed the real Dr. T'pek."

"Brinner," Ezri sobbed as the technicians locked her bed into place beside the table that held the symbiont.

"I'm sorry, Ensign, truly," Raymer said. "But as of now, you are the only Trill on the *Destiny*. The only one who can save Dax's life."

"Please . . ." Ezri whispered as the technicians pressed on her shoulders, compelling her to lie down. She felt a draft as her gown was pulled aside to expose her abdominal pocket.

The life-support alarm beeped incessantly. Ezri felt hot tears run down her cheeks. Raymer's hand was rigid in her own. Everything was happening too fast.

"Ensign, listen to me," the captain said. She leaned over Ezri so there was nothing else in Ezri's line of sight. "I've spoken with the Symbiosis Commission. With the damage we've taken, there's no way we can get you to new facilities within ninety-three hours. You know what that means."

Ezri did. "The joining . . . will be permanent. . . ." She felt her stomach contract as something cool was sprayed along the edge of her pouch. She wanted to vomit but whatever medication she had been given prevented anything from happening.

"That's right," Raymer said. "So the Commission is firm. No joining can be forced. Whatever happens next, it is your choice. Do you understand? *You* have to make the decision. The Dax symbiont has less than thirty minutes to live. You have your whole life. But whatever you decide, you have to decide *now,* one way or another."

Ezri turned her head, looked at all the people who surrounded her, staring, waiting, just as her mother had watched her in school plays and on sports days. The pressure. The waiting for failure. The need to be something different. The need to get away.

"What is your decision, Ensign?"

"I'm a Starfleet officer," Ezri said faintly, almost unable to speak. "You could order me." That would be the easy way out.

Raymer squeezed Ezri's hand so tightly Ezri flinched. "Because you *are* a Starfleet officer, I shouldn't have to order you. Now, Ensign, what is your decision?"

Ezri closed her eyes. The thoughts, the fears, the memories that came to her at that moment would take her years to sort through, to order, to comprehend. But somewhere, deep inside, one inarguable fact from her past could not be denied.

She *was* a Trill.

And one, inescapable realization from her present still burned in her consciousness with all the intensity of a dying thought.

Until now, her life had been wasted.

By all rights, Brinner should be here now.

By all rights, the changeling should have killed *her*, not him.

Somehow, she had been given a second chance.

How could she let that chance be wasted, too?

Ezri opened her eyes. "Do it," she said softly, regretting those words even as she knew she must say them.

The eyes of her captain burned into hers. "Are you sure?" she asked.

To her eternal amazement, for the first time in her life, Ezri Tigan was.

* * *

Beneath alien stars, in the cool of the Las Vegas desert, Ezri Dax withdrew her hand from beneath Vic Fontaine's sports coat to wipe a single tear from her face.

"Man oh man," Vic said quietly. "That was it?"

"Not quite," Ezri said. "It took about fifteen minutes to prep me. I had never done any of the stretching exercises, things like that. All I remember was poor Dr. Solon reciting everything he had read about joining over the past few days. I think he was more upset than I was."

"Fifteen minutes?" Vic said. "Instead of years of training? And then what, they just plug the slug into the pocket and . . . that's it?"

"No. That's just . . . just the beginning," Ezri explained. She retreated into silence as she remembered those first tendrils of connection, that first tentative contact with the mind—with *all* the minds of Dax. Slow it was, gentle, almost shy, until the pathways were in place, the nerve bundles fused, until, as if she were poised on the edge of an infinitely tall cliff, she had heard the first unforgettable, thrilling whisper of a thought not her own, welcoming her to an existence inexpressible to a single mind.

"Just the beginning," Vic repeated. Ezri could feel him slowly shake his head. "So then what happened?"

Ezri settled in more closely against Vic. She was reaching the point at which words could no longer express what had happened to her. That explosion of knowledge, of awareness, of experience . . . it was still overwhelming to her, more than a year later.

"What happened next," she said, "was . . . everything,

Vic. Eight lives and three hundred years of *everything,* all at once."

And as she saw Vic stare down wonderingly into her eyes, Ezri at last understood that, for now, her story had come to an end.

It was time to tell her stor*ies.* . . .

LELA

"What is a person if not the sum of her memories?"

—Lela Dax
"Facets"

Kristine Kathryn Rusch

Kristine Kathryn Rusch is an award-winning fiction writer who has won the Locus award, the John W. Campbell Award, the Hugo Award, the World Fantasy Award, and the Homer Award. Her short stories have been reprinted in six *Year's Best* collections. In 1999, she won three different readers' choice awards from three different magazines for three different stories.

Her novels have been published in seven languages, and have spent several weeks on the *USA Today* and *The Wall Street Journal* bestseller lists. She has written a number of *Star Trek* novels with her husband, Dean Wesley Smith, including one in the 1999 crossover series called *Double Helix: Vectors*.

Her most recent solo novel is the first volume in her Black Throne series, *The Black Queen*.

Jill Sherwin

Prior to compiling *Quotable Star Trek,* Jill Sherwin spent three seasons as an assistant to the producers on *Star Trek: Deep Space Nine*. Born and raised in Los Angeles, she currently writes freelance articles for numerous publications. Her next project for Pocket Books, *The Definitive Star Trek Trivia Book,* will be published in 2000.

First Steps

Kristine Kathryn Rusch

(based on a concept by Jill Sherwin)

UNTIL SHE WAS joined, Lela never dreamed of space. She dreamed of leading, of a life dedicated to the service of Trill. But she never dreamed of space.

How strange, then, that the Dax symbiont had never seen the stars, and yet it was the dream of stars that the symbiont had imparted to Lela.

Trill had pilots who flew into space, of course—they had warp capability after all—but only a few were authorized to venture outside of Trill's orbit. She would never be one of them. She'd been tested long ago, and lacked the dexterity, the eye-hand coordination, that a good pilot needed.

Her future was in politics. She had known that before she was joined. And she'd had great success: She was one of the first women elected to Trill's ruling council, and she was currently the *only* woman in that august body. The three that preceded her had retired long ago.

Yet she felt twinges, longings, that were all centered on the stars.

She never spoke of those longings, but sometimes, after particularly rough council sessions, she went to the observatory that was attached to the planetary spaceflight center. The center housed space traffic control, the controls for the planetary defense grid, and the finest observatory on Trill, one that was in constant use by the best scientists on the planet.

Usually the space center was quiet, a place for reflection. She often sat in the observatory and looked at the star charts, or the projections from the telescopes that showed up on the screens. Sometimes she spoke with center personnel, and sometimes she just watched.

It gave her perspective, perspective she sometimes needed when dealing with the other council members. She was still newly elected and they had yet to take her seriously. They had listened—and sneered—at her campaign slogans. She had said she spoke for those who lived only one lifetime— the unjoined, mostly—because she had only lived one so far, and she said she spoke for the newly joined, because she and her symbiont were both new to this. The other members of the council had been joined long before, and seemed to forget, she claimed, that the majority of Trill's population experienced but a single lifetime before their memories were lost forever.

Lela found it ironic that her biggest crisis, both legislative and personal, began at the space center.

She arrived one night to find the space center in chaos. Scientists filled the observatory—the large room was so full, she could barely squeeze inside. It was hot and stuffy and smelled faintly of sweat. It took a lot of bodies to make a room that large smell of sweat.

She was a small woman compared with most Trills and she had to push her way to the front of the group, excusing herself, apologizing, before she could see the screen to know what was going on.

A ship appeared before her. It was long and graceful, slender and glittery white. There seemed to be no portholes, no obvious engines, and no real place of entry. Just a long beautiful ship that reminded Lela of a feather.

"What is it?" she asked the scientist next to her.

He shook his head. "It went into orbit around Trill a few hours ago."

And no one had notified the council. She sighed. That was already a problem. But she couldn't seem to move either. She had never seen an alien ship, although she'd seen holos of the Vulcan craft that made first contact.

This was clearly *not* a Vulcan ship. A shiver ran down her spine at the thought. She had been just a girl during the Vulcan first contact crisis, but she remembered it vividly. Trill was horribly divided over the idea of any alien contact. After the Vulcans made their first landing and proposed an exchange of cultural information as a prelude to some kind of lasting friendship, the infighting in the council and among the people of Trill was almost frightening.

There was a fear among the Trill that any aliens posed a potential threat to the symbionts, who were fragile, defenseless creatures. Lela had heard, during her years of preparation for public service, that the contact with the Vulcans had led to a lot of changes in the government's policies concerning the symbionts. Even the access to the pools was guarded now.

There had been no other contact with aliens except the Vulcans. Trill continued to keep itself isolated, rebuffing any attempt at contact by aliens entering the system.

But no ship had actually assumed *orbit* of Trill since the Vulcans had come.

"Has anyone contacted the ship?" she asked the scientist beside her. He shrugged.

Then Sitlas saw her. He was a slender man with dark spots that ringed his face and made him look exotic. "Lela," he said.

She made her way toward him. He was an older, unjoined Trill, but he ran the space center with an efficiency that could not be matched.

"Sitlas," she said. "What's been happening?"

"We've activated the defense grid," he said. "And we've sent the message."

The message. It was a compromise that the council had made after the infighting that resulted from the Vulcans' first visit. The message stated simply that Trill did not want contact with outsiders, and that all alien ships were asked to bypass the planet.

"Any response?" Lela asked.

"Not yet," he said. "We don't even know if they can respond. We've sent the message in all known languages."

She looked back at the ship. She knew that the automated defense grid was monitoring it, as were dozens of large telescopes all over the planet. Yet the ship seemed remarkably unconcerned.

"You'd think if it got the message, it would leave," she said.

He nodded.

"Sitlas," someone said from the main control room. "We need you."

"Let's go," he said to her. He had to ask her to come, she realized. She was the only government representative in the building. She followed him into the main control room.

It was smaller than the observatory, except for the screen which covered one wall. The ship looked even lighter and more feathery here, the glitter of its white sides artificially bright. There were dozens of people at consoles, all of them looking down, none of them focusing on the ship at all.

"Sitlas," said a young man sitting behind one of the main consoles.

Sitlas went over to him. The young man looked at Lela as if she were a curiosity, then looked away. "We've gotten a response."

"We've never had a response before," Sitlas said. He pressed a spot on the corner of the console. An image filled with static and distortions replaced the ship on the screen. Lela could barely make out an alien covered in what appeared to be white fur, with long tufts rising out of its head. It did have eyes, though perfectly round and green, above what appeared to be a muzzle.

It spoke a language she didn't understand, but something—clearly from the alien ship, and not from inside the space center—attempted a translation.

"Come in need. Have [undecipherable]. *Will trade."*

Come in need. Lela frowned.

"Play them our message again," Sitlas said to the young man.

"Wait," Lela said. "Shouldn't we try to clarify their message?"

"They're talking about trade," Sitlas said. He waved a hand. The young man pressed an area on his console.

"It didn't sound that way to me," Lela said. "Maybe we should try to translate this ourselves."

"My orders are specific," he said. "We're to turn away all ships except those from Vulcan."

"But he said they came in need."

"His bad translation said that."

Lela stared at Sitlas. After a moment, he looked away from her. "All right," he said. "We'll see if we can find out what he really said."

She smiled. "Good."

"The second message has been sent," the young man said. "They aren't leaving orbit."

Lela sighed. "Maybe they're in trouble."

"Or maybe they're just trying to see how serious we are about wanting to be left alone," Sitlas said.

Lela stared at the ship up on the screen. "How serious are we?"

Sitlas said nothing, but she already knew the answer. The procedure was to send the message and then to ignore the encroaching ship. If the ship attacked, Trill's defense grid protected the planet. So far, that had never been necessary. All the other ships passing within close range of Trill heard the message and continued on.

"I think anyone who is just interested in trade would be leaving right now," Lela said.

"Perhaps," Sitlas said. "But they're aliens. Who knows what they'll do?"

The ship was still orbiting the following morning. Lela called a meeting of the council, the first time she had ever tried anything like that. Junior members were not supposed to call meetings, but she felt that delaying any longer would be a serious mistake. She had learned, in lower level jobs, that the longer the people in charge waited to make a decision, the greater the chance of making a mistake.

She was the first to arrive at the council chambers. The building was one of the oldest in the city. A long narrow two-story section housed offices and a majestic corridor that led to the council chambers proper. The chambers were in a huge, oval shaped room—supposedly the largest room on Trill—with an opaque dome that rose several stories above the floor. The effect was one of light and power, of age and beauty. Whenever Lela entered through the ceremonial double doors, she felt as if she had stepped back in time.

In some ways, she had. One of the council's many debates was on appropriating funds to build a new chamber, one more equipped to handle modern life. Lela knew that sometime in her lifetime—or more accurately, the Dax symbiont's lifetime—a new chamber would be built.

She would fight to keep the old one.

Lela loved this room. It was here, when she had visited as a schoolchild, that she decided she would make her future in politics. Fortunately the standardized tests showed that her abilities bore this dream out. She was well suited to a career here, a career she had known she would love.

That love had not changed, despite the difficulties of being a council member. As she sat in the back, where the youngest members were required to stay, she dreamed of moving down to the more important seats. The leader's podium stood at the very center of the room, rising out of the floor on antigravs and turning slowly whenever the leader spoke. The podium was made of acelon, a rare pearlescent material found deep within the ice caves. Before each member's seat was an oval-shaped acelon desk that mirrored the opaque dome, making it look as if the council members sat behind pieces of the sky.

"Lela Dax."

She turned. Darzen Odan stood in the doorway. He was an officious man who wore his hair long, hiding most of his spots as if he were somehow ashamed of them. He was as short as she was, and his dark eyes sparked with intelligence, an intelligence he often used to verbally assault anyone who opposed him.

"Perhaps you did not pay attention to your first year council training," he said. "It is your elders who call the meetings, those who have been in the council for more than one lifetime."

She straightened. Next to Odan, who had had at least seven hosts that she knew of, she felt like a child. She had felt that way around the joined when she had been unjoined, and now she felt that way with anyone whose symbiont had had other hosts.

Odan's dark eyes glistened, as if he knew how she felt and was exploiting it.

"And yet you're here," she said.

"Only to remind you that you do not have the authority to call this meeting."

She shook her head slightly, biting the inside of her cheek to control her temper. "Then I'll go back to the space center and deal with the crisis myself."

"Crisis?" That had gotten his attention.

"There's a ship orbiting Trill," she said. "It arrived last night. Surely you've heard by now."

Clearly he hadn't. And if Odan hadn't heard, none of the other members had heard either. She found this strange. They had so many sources within the political structure that they sometimes forgot there was a universe outside of it. Perhaps that was why Lela had the run of the space center; none of the other council members thought it mattered in the grand political scheme of things.

"If indeed there's a ship orbiting," he said, making it sound as if she were lying to him, "then it should be told to leave us in peace."

"It has been," she said. "The center sent its usual message, and the ship responded with one of its own. The center sent a message again, and the ship still has not left."

"A message of its own?"

Lela felt her cheeks flush. He was toying with her. If this became important information, he'd have it, and he'd take credit for it.

"Yes," she said. "That's what I wish to discuss in front of the entire council."

"Then I'll call them to order," he said. "None of them were going to come, not realizing, of course, that this is actually an important matter."

She bit back her response. Showing him how easy it

was to upset her wouldn't help her in the council at all. "You might want to tell them to hurry," she said. "This isn't something that's going to wait for the council's usual slowness."

He raised both eyebrows at her, as if surprised by her bluntness. Then he bowed slightly and went through the door into the corridor, leaving her alone in the chamber.

She let out a small breath. She hadn't been this angry in a long time. But Odan always found a way to get to her. He'd hated her campaign—"The disenfranchised unjoined?" he'd said. "As if what they want really matters. Long lasting change, as you shall see, Lela, is what counts. Continuity over several lifetimes"—and like so many others, he disliked the fact that a fourth woman had made it onto the council.

Trill tradition demanded that men rule the council— joined men—as they had done for generations. Men's roles and women's roles were dramatically different when the first council was formed. It was believed then that a symbiont would go from male host to female host and experience vast differences between the genders—that this was necessary to become a well-rounded Trill. But the joined Trills soon realized that while the genders had their biological differences, and those differences did make for a change in perspective, those perspectives merged over the course of time—and many hosts. By the time a Trill had the memories of several lifetimes, half as a man and half as a woman, understanding the other gender's perspective became relatively easy.

Despite the fact that Odan had been both male and female in his past lives, he honored tradition above all. He belonged to a more conservative party, one that believed rapid change—defined as any change that took place within two generations—was dangerous to Trill, and threatened the very life that he had sworn, as a councilman to protect.

Odan returned within a few moments, and walked past her down the stairs, taking his seat in the center of the chamber. For all his lives, he was himself a relatively new member to the council. Politics was something that had suited him only one other time in the past.

Lela remained by the door. She knew that Odan hadn't told the others that he agreed with her. She suspected that his announcement of the meeting had left her out entirely. So she greeted everyone who came in, whether she got along with them or not, thanking them for coming on such short notice. Part of her felt ridiculous, as if she were giving a party and had only invited people she disliked. Some of them nodded, most avoided her, and the rest greeted her with nervous smiles.

Odan ignored the whole thing, waiting at his desk for the meeting to start.

Finally all of the seats were filled but hers. Dax crossed the back row, and sat down behind her desk just as Lytus, head of the council, crossed the lower floor. He was a tall, lanky man with the thinness of a scholar. In two quick steps, he took his place behind the speaker's podium.

As soon as he touched it, the podium rose. It went high enough to be directly across from the center seats. Lela frowned. Lytus was stopping directly across from Odan. Lytus should have gone all the way to the top and stopped in front of Lela.

"I give the floor to Councillor Odan to explain the urgency of this meeting," Lytus said.

Lela stood as Odan did, but she spoke quicker, projecting so that her voice echoed throughout the chamber. "Forgive me, Mr. Speaker," she said, "but you should give the floor to me. I'm the one who called the meeting, although I did so improperly. Councillor Odan was kind enough to help me when it became clear that I had made a mistake in protocol."

Everyone in the chamber was looking at her, some with horror, some with barely repressed amusement. Her move was a risky one. If Odan contradicted her, he would show the other council members that she was unimportant. He would make this issue his own, and possibly corrupt it. He would also take away what little power she had.

It would be the first volley in a protracted political war, one fought with polite corrections and subtle interruptions and quiet outright lies. Lela knew she could win this battle—she hadn't told Odan everything and they both knew it—but she didn't have enough resources or experience to win the war.

Of course, if Odan did play along, it would look as if they had formed an alliance, something that would disturb his followers.

Odan stared at her a moment too long. She found that she was holding her breath. His eyes narrowed, and she thought he would renounce her. Then he bowed gracefully, and she let out the air she had been holding.

"I yield my time," he said in his most penetrating voice, "to our newest newly joined legislator, Lela Dax."

His barbed politeness made her flush. She had underestimated him yet again. While yielding the floor, he had reminded everyone not only of her youth and inexperience—in life as well as politics—but of the fact that he did not necessarily approve of her.

She made herself nod at him, though, and smile as if they were old friends. "I thank my colleague Darzen Odan for his unselfish assistance in this matter," she said, relegating him to the inferior position. "I had the good fortune to be at the space center last night when this crisis began. . . ."

Within the next few minutes, she explained the orbiting ship, and its strange response to Trill's leave-us-in-peace message. She concluded with:

"Esteemed members of the council, I am worried. The aliens' response to our initial message was translated by their own programs to be this— *'come in need. Have'*—and here what they said was something we haven't been able to translate. Then they ended the message with *'will trade.'* We are working on our own translation of their words, but have come up with nothing better yet. And we haven't figured out what the missing phrase is. I checked before the meeting."

The other councillors stared at her as if they couldn't believe what she was saying. Not because an orbiting ship made them incredulous, but because she had brought this before them in the first place. Odan, who was still standing— apparently he hadn't yielded all of his time—had a slight smirk on his face.

Lela gestured toward them all with her right hand. "I am concerned, as you should be, about the first part of their message. *Come in need.* We must find out if they're orbiting us because they're in trouble and they cannot go on."

"If that is the case," Lytus said, "then what does this *will trade* mean?"

"Perhaps it means they want some natural resource that they believe we'll give them, for the right price," Odan said. His comment was sly: Without saying anything he revived all the arguments against the alliance with the Vulcans. Lela saw the more conservative members of the council—the ones she knew disapproved of the Vulcans—nodding.

"We don't know what any of it means," Lela said. "We won't know that until we contact them again. I worry that, because of our silence, a ship full of beings might be in trouble. They could be ill or dying in our orbit. We shouldn't let our concerns for Trill outweigh our natural compassion."

"And what if we discover that they are simple business-people?" one of the councillors asked.

"Or worse," said another, "thieves."

"They wouldn't be thieves," Lela said, "not and contact us this way. And we'd discover if they have other motives while they're still in orbit. We will keep the defense grid on."

Lytus hadn't raised the podium to Lela's level, apparently in silent communion with Odan. "If I understand you correctly," Lytus said, "You would like us to send a new message to these aliens, asking them what they're about."

"Yes," Lela said.

"You realize that violates the resolutions passed two decades ago, forbidding contact with any new species."

"Except the Vulcans," Odan said in his kindest voice. Another jab, reminding her that she hadn't been a legislator then—that she had been little more than a child.

"Yes, I realize that," Lela said. "But a resolution is not a law, and it can be changed with a simple majority vote. That's why I brought this to the council. I think we have an obligation to make certain that these aliens are all right—"

"An obligation?" Lytus asked. "To whom?"

"To ourselves," Lela said. "We cannot isolate ourselves forever."

"Why not?" another councillor asked.

They all seemed to be staring at her, as if none of them could understand her concern.

"There are two reasons," she said. "The first is that we should help other beings in need."

"A fine sentiment," Lytus said, "but one that becomes infinitely more complicated when we start to consider lending our assistance to beings who are not from Trill."

She could get lost arguing that point forever. She would come back to it, but not yet. She wasn't going to let them derail her. "And, secondarily," she pressed on, "some day we'll have to come out of our box. Events won't let us remain isolated."

There was a murmur throughout the chamber. Her words were heresy.

"What sort of events?" someone asked.

"I don't know," she admitted. "But it became clear when the Vulcans arrived that we are part of an interstellar community. I think it's better that we know about our neighbors, know who these other species are and what they're about, rather than hiding behind our defense grid."

The murmuring eased. She had their attention now.

"We are taught from childhood that knowledge is the pinnacle of Trill society. That is one of the things the symbionts give us—a living knowledge of our own history, a respect and reverence for our past."

She nodded toward Odan as she said that. He was still standing, but he was silent, listening as if he hadn't expected her to be so eloquent.

"Yet," she continued, "we're closing ourselves off from knowledge that might become crucial some day. We need to know what lies beyond Trill, what possibilities exist in the stars."

Her words echoed for a moment. Her heart was pounding. No one spoke—no one moved—for what seemed like an eternity. Then Lytus said, "We have the capability of going to the stars. It was this capability that brought the Vulcans to us, and showed us we needed to protect ourselves from outsiders. Even the Vulcans offer no assurances that we live in a peaceful universe."

Lela felt the tension in her shoulders build.

"If we choose to find out about other species," Lytus said, "we can send our own ships out to explore. Or we can consult with the Vulcans. We do not need visitors on Trill."

There were murmurs again, but this time they were murmurs of agreement.

"I'm not asking them to tour the planet," Lela said with uncontrolled heat, and then caught herself. Sarcasm wasn't going to win this. "I just want to find out if they're injured or ill and in need of our help."

The councillors who were nodding had stopped. A few were frowning, but not in displeasure. In concentration. Her argument had some weight.

"And if they are?" Odan asked. She looked at him. He had a benign expression on his face. "What then?"

Was he trying to trip her up? She couldn't tell. He didn't really do things maliciously. He acted out of what he believed. Unfortunately, he believed in different things than she did.

"We see if we can help them," she said. It seemed so logical. Why were the councillors having trouble with that?

"And what if the only way to help them is to give the liquid from the symbiont pools?" Again, his voice held no animosity. Only the guidance a teacher might give a student.

Lela paused. There was the right answer, and then there

was the political answer. She tried to blend them. "If they needed the liquid, then we'd have to find out how much they need and how badly they need it, wouldn't we? If it's only a drop to a dying people, I don't know how we could begrudge that."

Her response was met with silence.

Finally, Lytus said, "If there is no more comment, we shall take the matter of contacting the alien ship to a vote."

Lela sat down, and as she did, she knew that she had lost.

She couldn't help herself. After the vote, she went to the space center. It was better than sitting around her apartment, browbeating herself. She had known the political answer to Odan's question. If the aliens had wanted liquid from the symbiont pools, no matter what the crisis, she should have said no, the aliens couldn't have it. The question was only hypothetical after all. And if the hypothetical proved to be what the aliens wanted, she should have fought with the council *then*.

Somehow she had expected more compassion from her fellow councillors.

The center was quieter today. The alien ship had, in the space of a few hours, become less of a curiosity, more of a nuisance. The scientists who had gathered the night before to see a glimpse of the ship's glittery whiteness were nowhere to be seen. The only difference between the observatory today and any other day was that there were more specialists sitting at various stations.

The ship remained on the screens. Lela stared at it for a long time, wondering what was happening inside it, wondering if the aliens had even understood Trill's message or if they had to ignore it for reasons of their own.

She sighed and went inside the control room. Sitlas was

there, looking tired and haggard. It was obvious that he hadn't been to bed. He hadn't changed clothing since the night before, and his spots stood out against his exceedingly pale skin.

When he saw her, he gave her a preoccupied smile.

"Any luck with the translation yet?" she asked.

He shook his head.

She had somehow expected that. "I need to send a coded message to Vulcan."

He nodded. The weariness slumped his shoulders. "Record your message. We'll send it encoded."

At least he hadn't questioned her about the council vote. Not that he had any real right to. She could always pull rank on him and make him do what she needed. She just hated using authority that way, even though it was some-times necessary.

She sat at the console he provided, downloaded a still image of the ship, and asked if the Vulcans were familiar with these aliens, and if so, what they knew. She also explained the situation, saying that Trill was not yet used to visitors from space.

From what she understood of the Vulcans, they would get the subtext of the message. They had known about Trill's isolationism. They had experienced it for years.

Then she called Sitlas over, and he sent the message, encoded and on a protected channel. She slumped in her chair. That was all she could do.

"Sitlas," one of the assistants said. "We're receiving a message from the alien ship."

"On screen," Sitlas said.

The message was as scrambled as the one before. The

static made the images blur, but the words were nearly the same. *"Please, need* [undecipherable]. *Urgent. Will trade."*

And then the screen went dark.

Lela turned to Sitlas. "How often has that message come in?"

"Every two hours," he said. She heard weariness and exasperation in his voice.

"Has there been any change?" Lela asked.

"Small things," Sitlas said. "It seems like a different alien has been speaking today. And the phrasing is somewhat different."

"Do you think they're in trouble?"

He shrugged. "I don't know. But we keep sending the go-away message. You'd think, if they weren't in some kind of trouble, they'd leave. I mean, that's logical."

"For us," she said.

He nodded. "And they're clearly not us." He looked at the ship, still glittering on the screen. "Maybe they'll go away soon."

"Maybe," Lela said. But she wasn't so sure. Maybe they couldn't leave. Maybe they'd stay until they got what they needed or until they died.

Finally she couldn't take it anymore. Common decency meant finding out as much as possible. The council's resolutions against contact were just that: resolutions. Not laws. She wouldn't be committing an illegal act if she contacted the aliens. She'd just be violating the consensus of the council.

"Open a channel to them," she said.

"Lela, you know—"

"Open a channel to them."

He stared at her. "The council said we can't do this."

"The council *suggested* that we not do it," she said. "Now open a channel."

"If I do, I could lose my job."

"Not if you blame it on me," she said. He didn't move. She crossed her arms. "Either you gamble on my word that I'll take the blame for this, or you lose your job now. You know I could fire you and direct these people myself."

His mouth thinned, and she wondered if she'd be as welcome in the space center in the future. Ah, well. The future was not something she'd worry about at the moment.

"Do it," he said to one of his assistants. The woman ducked her head, but pressed a finger against the console before her.

Lela leaned forward. "My name is Lela Dax. I am a citizen of Trill, but I contact you as a fellow being. I am not representing Trill in this matter. My planet wishes no contact with you. However, I have heard your messages and would like to know if you're all right."

For a moment, there was silence. And then static, as if the aliens were trying to respond, but couldn't.

"I am concerned that you are in failing health or in need of repairs. Are you in trouble?"

The ship winked off screen. The same alien appeared as before. *"Need* [undecipherable]. *Time is running out. Will trade."*

"Time is running out on what?" Lela asked.

"[undecipherable]. *Will buy. Whatever trade possible. Need* [undecipherable] *now."*

The two undecipherable words or phrases were very different. Obviously their languages weren't that compatible.

"Are you in physical danger?" she asked. "Is your crew healthy?"

"Need [undecipherable]. *Time nearly gone. Need now."*

And then the alien disappeared from the screen.

"Has the transmission been cut?" she asked Sitlas.

He shook his head.

She leaned forward, one last time. "I will talk with my people's leaders. I will get back to you as soon as I can."

But there was no response to that.

"Now the transmission's been cut," Sitlas said.

Lela nodded. These last few messages supported her theory that something serious was happening to these aliens. If she hurried, she might be able to help. But first, she needed to speak to another member of the council. Lytus had made his own position clear. She would get no help from him. But Odan prided himself on his open mind. Odan, at least, had listened to her earlier, even though he had embarrassed her before the council.

He also lived close to the space center.

"Keep working on the translation," Lela said to Sitlas. "I'll be back shortly."

He nodded.

She left the observatory and hurried through the technical buildings, where many of the scientists worked. Just beyond that were the industrial neighborhoods. This part of the city was the only place on Trill where acelon was refined. The process was more of a polishing than a recovery. Apparently acelon arrived in its raw state from the areas just outside the ice caves. It was stored in the large buildings behind the plants, and then its black outsides were polished away until the luminous material shone through. The process was expensive, which was one of the reasons the mineral was so rare. But the procedure didn't pollute or harm the environment, so it could be carried out safely inside the city rather than requiring a protected area.

Just beyond the industrial area were some of the city's best residential neighborhoods. On a slight hill, the houses were positioned so that the purple water of the ocean was just barely visible from the upper floors.

Odan was in his garden, as she had expected him to be. Gardening was a passion for him. He was bent over a row of multicolored flowers when she stopped outside his gate.

"Odan," she said. "Forgive me for bothering you at home, but I must speak to you."

He put one hand on his back, stood, and looked at her as if she were smaller than a bug. His wife came out onto the porch, a little girl clinging to her hand, but he waved her away.

Other neighbors, who had also been working in their yards, stopped. Apparently people didn't talk to each other on the streets in this neighborhood.

"I guess you'd better come inside the gate," he said pulling the door open. Lela stepped inside, careful to avoid the smaller blooms that twisted around the edges.

"I hope this is important," he said.

"And I hope you'll listen before you judge," she said, and bit the inside of her cheeks. The last thing she wanted to do was antagonize him, and that was the first thing she had done.

His dark eyes flashed. "I'll make the attempt," he said with undisguised sarcasm.

"Thank you." She took a deep breath and told him about her trip to the space center. She also told him about her decision to contact the aliens.

"You knew about the resolution," he said angrily. "This is not something you should have done on your own."

"I think they're in trouble," she said. "Their last message was 'Time is running out.' I ordered Sitlas to continue trying to translate what they want. I think if we know that, we might be able to act. They aren't going to leave, Odan."

He made a sound of disgust and turned his head away from her. Then he said, "You know this could get you censured, maybe even removed."

She was shaking. She hadn't realized it until now. "Yes, I know," she said. "But I couldn't face the thought of a dead ship orbiting Trill, not if its occupants could have survived if only we'd helped."

"We have no idea what's happening up there," Odan said. "Your scenario could be wrong."

"It could be," she said.

"And you'd risk your career for that?"

Her smile was small. "It seems I already have."

He nodded. He wouldn't meet her gaze. Perhaps she shouldn't have trusted him after all. She had just given him the tools with which to destroy her in the council—and on Trill—forever.

Suddenly there was a large explosion, and the ground rocked. Another explosion and another shattered the air around her. Her ears ached. She grabbed Odan and threw him to the ground, then looked up to see what was causing the problem.

Bright beams of red light were cutting through the sky, slamming into the ground below. Anything the light touched shattered. Dust clouds were rising, and several of the nearby houses were gone.

People were running, covered in dirt and dust. Lela thought they were screaming, but she couldn't be certain. Her ears were ringing: She couldn't hear anything else.

Odan struggled beneath her as another explosion rocked them. He stretched out his hand toward his house, and Lela's heart stopped. His family was inside. He wanted to get to them.

But for the moment, at least, the house was all right. He was in more danger on the street.

The explosions continued, and then she saw a blinding white light that covered the entire sky. The light focused down, disappearing on the streets around the industrial complex—or perhaps the space center. She couldn't tell.

Had she brought this wrath on them from the aliens? Was this their response to her message?

Had her impulsiveness hurt her people?

The ground continued to shake, only this shaking was continual, not like the explosions of moments ago. The white light grew dark, and then vanished altogether, leaving her seeing spots in front of her eyes.

Bits of rock rained down around them, and dust continued to fall like a light mist. People were still running, many of them bleeding, some heading toward the areas where the houses had been. Small fires burned and the air was filling with smoke.

Lela stood. So did Odan. Without a word, he ran into his house. Through the door, she saw him embrace his wife and daughter.

Lela's head ached, and her ears still ran. Something wet trickled down her jawline. She put a nervous finger to it, and looked at it, seeing blood.

The aliens had attacked, although she did not know why. How had they broken through the defense grid? What had they done?

What had *she* done?

She took a deep breath, put a hand over her belly, and noted that the symbiont felt fine. Then she walked toward the destruction, and began searching for survivors in the rubble.

It was night by the time Lela finally accepted medical help. Her hearing returned, slowly, the damage to her ears minimal despite the blood. The doctors said she would hear ringing for some time, maybe permanently, but she would be able to hear.

She supposed she should be grateful for that.

The doctors made her stay in the hospital overnight along with the others who were injured in the attacks. Because of her position on the council, her injuries were high profile: The doctors wanted to make certain she was fine before she left.

While she was there, she heard the statistics. Fifty-five dead, one hundred injured—many severely. Most of the damage occurred in Odan's neighborhood and in the industrial areas. Eighty homes were destroyed, and several businesses were wiped out. The acelon processing plant was in the center of the destruction and untouched, but all of the raw acelon was gone.

The ship had left Trill's orbit immediately after the attack. No Trill ships could be launched quickly enough to reach it, and no one was sure what they would have done if they had caught it. The alien ship's weapons were obviously far superior to Trill's. It had blasted through the defense grid as if it hadn't even been there.

Lela harbored a secret fear that it had been her message that had triggered the attack. After all, they were having language problems. Perhaps she had said something, led them to believe something, that made them feel as if they had to act now.

But she spoke of that fear to no one, at least not yet. She would wait to see what the translations brought. She didn't expect a vindication.

She no longer knew what to expect at all.

The next morning, when she left the hospital, she did not go home. Instead, she went directly to the space center. The screens showed stars as they had before. The lovely gauzelike ship, the bringer of such destruction, was really and truly gone.

Lela wasn't the only council member at the space center. Odan was there as well.

"How's your family?" she asked him.

"Shaken," he said. Then he frowned a little, as if he had realized he was being gruff. "But fine."

Lela nodded. There wasn't much she could say to him. There wasn't much she could say to anyone.

She found Sitlas. He was pouring over data on one of the consoles.

"Any translations yet?" she asked.

He shook his head. "We don't have common words, apparently, for some of these things." He pushed his chair back. "I do have a transmission from Vulcan, however, coded specifically for you. Would you like to take it privately?"

She sighed. Too little, too late. "If you don't mind."

He led her to his office, a large room off the observatory. The inside was decorated with plants and pictures of purple waves, crashing on famous beaches.

He directed her to his chair, punched the console, and then left her. The Vulcan IDIC symbol—a silver circle with a gold triangle overlapping its lower edge—blinked on the screen. She tapped it.

A young woman appeared. Her long face looked majestic to Lela, and she wore her dark hair piled high above her head. The hairstyle displayed, rather than hid, her pointed ears.

"The beings who orbit your planet are known to us as the L'Dira. They depend upon a substance you call acelon for much of their technology. They have exhausted the supplies of acelon on their homeworld and in the surrounding solar system."

The woman's speech was curiously accented, as if she were actually speaking Trill instead of letting a translation program make her words clear.

"The L'Dira will trade for any acelon they receive, but they are an impatient people. If they believe negotiations have taken too long, they will take what they need. Their weapons technology is quite advanced. We calculate an eighty-three-point-nine percent probability that they will overpower your defenses. The L'Dira are quite tenacious. They will not leave until they have what they came for. We suggest that, in order to avoid bloodshed, you negotiate with them, and come to a satisfactory arrangement before they decide to take matters into their own hands."

The woman then vanished from the viewscreen, to be replaced by the symbol.

Lela bit her lower lip. The message both relieved her and angered her. She hadn't caused the attack. The destruction would have happened anyway. But she *had* been wrong. She had thought the aliens in need, hurting. She had let her imagination rule her heart. There was no place for fancy in government. Perhaps if she had been looking more clearly, she would have focused on the word "trade" instead of the word "need."

The door opened. Sitlas stood there, Odan beside him. Lela stiffened.

"I heard there was a message from Vulcan," Odan said.

"It's for me," Lela said.

"I assume it's in response to your query. If that's the case, then it's for all of us." His voice was curiously gentle.

Lela got up and stood aside. Odan came into the room, but Sitlas remained outside, and closed the door.

Odan sat in the chair, and touched the screen, just as Lela had. The message played. The woman's voice had as much—or perhaps more—force on the repetition.

Lela did not watch Odan as the message played. She listened again, tried to see if there was any blame in it, but there appeared to be none. Only the logical and careful words of an ally. An ally who had been contacted too late.

When the message ended, Lela turned. Odan was rubbing his eyes with one hand. When he realized she was watching him, he made a weak attempt at a smile and stood.

"I thank you for sharing the message with me," he said. "I would like to play it for the council."

She nodded. Of course her role in all of this would have to be made clear. Odan would to see to it.

Losing her position on the council would hurt terribly—especially now. But she would take the punishment, if she had to, even though that meant she would leave the council in the hands of those who tried to keep outsiders away from Trill. Over fifty people had died because Trill didn't know the proper way to deal with the L'Dira. And if Lela had to sacrifice her career to prove that point, she would do it.

She wouldn't let anyone die on her watch again.

Odan presented everything to the council. Lela's actions, the response from Vulcan. Everything. He did so in a quiet voice, his head bowed, as if he couldn't look at his fellow councillors.

Lela sat in her chair in the back, unable to touch the acelon desk before her. All the processed acelon remained. Only the raw, newly harvested acelon had been taken. She could no longer look at the substance without thinking of the ground rumbling beneath her feet, the mist of dust, the bleeding people staggering through the remains of their neighborhood.

There wasn't much to say after Odan's presentation. No one even tried. Fifty deaths, the words of the Vulcan woman, the place that ignorance had brought them all was obvious even to the most isolationist council members.

The votes were swift and clear. Trill would no longer tell its alien visitors to avoid the planet. Each alien ship would be handled on a case-by-case basis. Protection for the Caves of Mak'ala would increase. Trill would do all it could to learn about its neighbors from the stars.

The first step, suggested by Odan, was to ask Vulcan to send a representative immediately, armed with information about all the species that Vulcan was familiar with. The representative would make a short verbal presentation to the council, as well as give Trill Vulcan's entire database on other life-forms.

Lela had a hunch Vulcan would welcome this request.

Then Odan relinquished the floor, and Lytus's podium rose. Lela watched in confusion as it rose to the highest level, the level of the beginners. Her level.

"We have one final matter," Lytus said. "and I believe it is as important as all the other matters we touched upon today."

He was looking at her. Lela's stomach tightened. She didn't know if he was going to praise her for her attempt at contacting the L'Dira or if he was going to chastise her in front of the council.

She wasn't sure she wanted to experience either one. She had been wrong about the L'Dira. She had taken the wrong actions for the right reasons, and in that, she felt as if she had failed.

"Lela Dax," Lytus said and Lela started, "has violated her oath as a council member. She has failed to follow protocol, failed to acknowledge our resolutions. When she contacted the L'Dira she took the business of governing Trill into her own hands. This is treason—"

"No!" Lela whispered, her voice cracking.

"—and shall be treated as such before the council. Lela Dax, you must stand."

She was shaking. She hadn't committed treason. She hadn't done anything criminal. She had only disregarded a resolution. She hadn't represented herself as the leader of Trill—in fact, she had been careful to avoid that.

But she said none of those things.

"You have been charged with treason. In closed session, the council will decide your future. Until then, you will not be allowed inside chambers, and all of your privileges as a council member are hereby revoked."

She had studied such things in Trill's history, but she thought treason charges happened only in the past, when Trill was a younger, less stable society. Her throat ached, and her eyes burned. She'd never expected this to happen to her. She didn't even know how to act.

Lytus was staring at her directly. "You must leave us now," he said, and his words weren't gentle.

She stood, nearly losing her balance, but she didn't put out her hand to catch herself. She wasn't going to fall, not now, not in front of everyone. She walked with slow deliberation, making the few steps to the door take forever.

Then she stepped into the corridor, and the double doors slammed behind her, maybe forever.

She put a hand on the wall and leaned against it heavily. Fifty-five people had died. The council needed a scapegoat and she was the obvious one. That, in some ways, was the political way to look at this.

But inside, she couldn't help wondering if, in her concern for the aliens—her *misplaced* concern, she hadn't actually done the things Lytus had charged her with.

She was shaking so badly she didn't know what to do. There wasn't anything she *could* do. Until the council finished its deliberations—apparently without her—she had no profession, no work. Nothing to do.

She couldn't even defend herself.

A hand touched her shoulder. She blinked twice, trying to compose herself before looking to see who was behind her. Probably someone they sent to kick her out of the building.

She took a deep breath, and turned.

Odan stood there. As soon as she faced him, he let his hand fall.

She braced herself. The last thing she wanted was another confrontation, but better to get it over with now when everything was going wrong.

He noted her new stance, and nodded slightly, as if in acknowledgment of their adversarial relationship. "It is customary in matters like this," he said, sounding even more formal than usual, "for the defendant to have an advocate in the council."

She had known that, but she hadn't remembered it until he mentioned it. All of the defendants in the treason trials—all five of them over the centuries—had had advocates to argue their case.

She opened her mouth to thank Odan for reminding her of this. He hadn't owed her anything, and yet he was willing to help her, at least this much.

But he spoke first. "If it's all right with you, I would like to be your advocate."

For a moment, she didn't think she had heard him correctly. Then she frowned. Another political trick? It couldn't be. Odan, for all his machinations, was too ethical for that.

"Thank you," Lela said. "But I don't really understand why you would want to, given our history."

For the first time, his gaze didn't meet hers. "Because you were right."

"No, I wasn't. I thought they were hurting—"

"You said we should learn as much about our neighbors as we can. You were right. If we had known about the L'Dira's behaviors, we wouldn't have made the mistakes we did. We wouldn't have lost all those lives."

"That's what you'll argue before the council?" she asked.

"That and other things." He raised his head. She had never seen his black eyes look so sad. "You've taught me much, Lela Dax. You've taught me that just because someone has lived several lifetimes doesn't mean he has an open mind."

The closed session was continuous, breaking only for meals and sleep. The councillors weren't allowed to speak to anyone and were, in fact, housed away from their families for the duration of the trial. Lela had thought the session would last a day, maybe two, but it seemed to drag on forever.

Perhaps more was at stake than her career. If Odan had made his argument about open minds, the entire chamber probably had erupted into anger.

On the morning of the third day, the Vulcan emissary arrived on Trill. The emissary wasn't allowed to speak to the council until the trial was done, and so was housed in a government apartment across the road from Lela's. Lela had hoped for an audience, but had been turned away by Trill security. For the moment, Lela was less than a citizen. She was no one at all.

Still, Lela heard rumors that the emissary was interested in the trial and its outcome, although she didn't know why. Lela herself had never met any Vulcans, and didn't know why they would be interested in the internal affairs of Trill.

On the other matters, however, Lela heard no rumors. She had no idea what the council would decide about her fate. She wasn't sure what she deserved.

Finally, on the fourth afternoon, she couldn't stand being confined in her rooms any longer. Desperate for some kind of clarity, she went to the only place left: the Caves of Mak'ala.

The Guardians let her in, of course. She wasn't sure they would. She wasn't sure of anything anymore.

The caves felt like home. She went deep inside, to the

pools. The grayish liquid looked inviting. Part of her missed the water, missed the interconnecting pools, and the warmth, and the sudden communication with the other symbionts. The faintly damp odor made her tingle, and she watched as a symbiont surfaced. Energy discharged across the water as the symbiont communicated with one of its unseen fellows. She felt as if she could almost, *almost* understand what was being said.

But almost understanding and truly understanding were two very different things.

She should have known that. She remembered what it was like to imagine being joined, and then experiencing the reality. They were nothing alike.

If she had remembered that, she might have known that she was making a mistake with the alien ship.

Maybe.

Odan was right. She was doubly young. And only beginning to learn.

She stayed in the caves for a very long time, watching the symbionts rise and play in the waters. What a carefree time that had been, and how she hadn't known it. The Dax part of her had wanted to see the rest of the world, the rest of the universe, and now it could.

At great cost.

Perhaps she wasn't worthy of her symbiont. Perhaps her ambitions were too small, her imagination too wild. Perhaps the Symbiosis Evaluation Board had made a mistake in choosing her.

But the choice had been made. To remove the symbiont was to kill Lela, and no matter what she had done, she wasn't ready to die.

Finally, she sighed and left the pools. Going back wasn't

the answer. Going forward, no matter what, was the only solution.

She turned away from the pools and took her first step.

When she returned to her apartment, she was startled to find three guards in front of the door. Two of them were Vulcan. The third was a man she recognized from the diplomatic corps.

"What's this?" she asked.

"The emissary from Vulcan made a request. I felt that we should honor it."

Lela frowned at him. "What request?"

"Please, just go inside."

She did. As she closed the door, a young and statuesque Vulcan woman turned away from the windows. She wore long robes and had her hands threaded together inside their sleeves. Her entire body had a majesty that Lela had never seen before.

Although she had seen the woman's face. It was the same woman who had responded to her message.

"I am T'Pau," the woman said. "We should talk."

It felt odd to have her here—to have anyone here—among Lela's meager possessions. Her furniture was provided. The bits of artwork on the walls had been done by a childhood friend. The sparseness of the apartment seemed to stand out painfully in the Vulcan's presence.

T'Pau seemed to sense Lela's discomfort. "You have great courage," she said.

Lela shook her head. "I am a great fool."

"I have seen nothing foolish about you." T'Pau glanced at the wooden chair beside her.

Lela blushed. "I'm sorry. Please, have a seat."

"I know it is not customary for your people to allow

others inside their private spaces," T'Pau said as she sat. "I should have gone through proper channels. But, it seemed, no one wanted us to speak. I thought this course the most prudent."

"It's fine," Lela said, wondering if what she had heard was actually an apology or if she had just imagined it. She sat in an upholstered chair she rarely used. It made her feel as if she were the guest in her own home.

T'Pau seemed focused on what she needed to say. "Your people are not used to first contacts. To meet another species is a difficult thing."

"I'm beginning to realize that," Lela said.

"We learn it every time we encounter one." T'Pau's speech patterns were oddly formal. She did not smile as she spoke.

Was this what made an alien—the subtle differences, the fact that even though they seemed the same, they were not? Or were the more obvious differences, like the ears, the most important ones? Lela couldn't tell.

"Our most recent encounter," T'Pau said, "was with a strange species. We did not expect them to have warp capabilities, but they did. They had suffered a devastating global war and were just recovering from it. A man in a remote area of their countryside built a warp ship as a beacon of hope. We saw it, and initiated contact."

Lela waited. Obviously T'Pau was trying to impart something important.

"They are a highly passionate people—so passionate that even their music stirs the emotions. My colleagues on the ship that made the first contact reported that much of their music was physically painful to listen to."

Lela frowned. She wasn't sure how this should matter to her.

"But they are a highly creative people, an intuitive people, who seem to use their intellect and their emotions in harmony to create new things. We believe that, given time, their potential will increase exponentially. Despite their recent troubles, and a long history of discord, we believe they are on the verge of becoming a powerful force for civilization."

"How do you know that?" Lela asked.

"Knowledge. Our experience observing other cultures has demonstrated that it is the species who strive, who try new things, who ultimately thrive among the stars. Those that hide their heads stagnate. They do not survive."

She understood that, and didn't like it. "I stuck my head out, but I made such a mistake. I believed the L'Dira harmless. I thought maybe they were in trouble."

"They were in trouble," T'Pau said, "in their own way of thinking. They rely on acelon. It is necessary for the way they live, and they will not learn any other way, even though they have used up all the acelon in their own system. It has driven them to become little more than pirates, even though they claim they will trade."

"I should have suspected something," Lela said.

T'Pau shook her head. "It is illogical to expect yourself to act differently in hindsight. However, you did not approach the L'Dira like L'Dira. You expected them to act like Trill. You must always trust a species to act in ways rational to its own culture. To do so requires you to understand that culture. It is not a task done lightly or quickly."

Lela nodded. That made sense to her. But it seemed so

logical, it made her wonder why she hadn't thought of it herself.

T'Pau was watching her, dark eyes unfathomable.

Lela folded her hands together. "Why would you want to talk with me? You know I'm in disgrace."

"I know your people have much to learn when it comes to other species. That includes understanding that your search for knowledge is Trill's only salvation."

Lela turned. She didn't know why she trusted this calm woman, but she did. Not with state secrets, only with her own. "I contacted the L'Dira after I sent a message to you. I asked them if they were in trouble. Did I do something that might have provoked their attack?"

"No," T'Pau said. "It is as I said in my message. They are an impatient people, even when negotiations are on-going."

Lela felt her shoulders relax. She didn't realize until that moment how much she feared that the attack was her fault.

"You have great courage," T'Pau repeated, "and vision as well. You do not fear to imagine what lies ahead. Do not allow others to extinguish that quality within you. You must always do what you believe to be right."

"Odan says I'm too young to know what's right."

T'Pau seemed to consider Lela for a moment. "In this universe we are all young, Lela Dax," she said at last. "That is the subtle truth that often eludes so many promising life-forms. Youth contains the potential for growth. Once an in-dividual—or a culture—forgets that, the growth stops.

"Your world needs people like you, Lela Dax. Never doubt that."

Before Lela could respond, T'Pau rose from her chair, apparently satisfied that she had accomplished what she had set out to do. She held up her right hand, paired fingers parted, thumb at rest.

"Live long," T'Pau said, "and prosper."

It seemed to have more meaning than a simple sentence. But Lela did not know how to respond.

"Th-thank you," she said.

Then T'Pau turned away, and let herself out of the apartment.

Lela watched her go. What Lela's people saw as a character flaw, T'Pau saw as a survival trait. And maybe they were both right.

For the first time since her indictment, Lela smiled.

A short time later, a runner knocked at her door. "The council has made a decision," he said. "You're to come with me."

She did.

Her meeting with T'Pau had left her calmer, ready to face whatever came at her, no matter what the cost.

The runner led Lela through a side corridor that went down, not up. He was taking her to the chamber floor. Her hands started to shake. She wouldn't be allowed to return to her desk.

They were going to throw her out of the council. Her political career would be over.

The runner opened a small door that led to a passageway under some of the desks. Then he swept his arm forward, indicating that she should go through.

At the door stood Lytus and Odan. She couldn't tell from the expression on their faces what the verdict was.

"Stand in the center of the floor, please," Lytus said.

She walked past him without a word, to the spot he had indicated. His podium was slightly to her left. He did not stand behind it. Instead, he waited on the periphery, like Odan. The other council members filled their seats. They looked tired, and the room had a faint scent of sweat and rotting food. They had spent a lot of hours here, debating her fate.

Her fate and, in its own way, that of Trill. Condemning her for trying to act when they would not would mean that, despite the resolutions they passed, they had no intention of learning about any other species.

"Lela Dax." The voice belonged to the sergeant at arms. "You have been tried on the charges of treason. The council has delivered its verdict. You shall stand and hear."

She stood straighter, but she couldn't turn to see the councillors behind her. The ones in front could not meet her gaze.

"Lela Dax," The sergeant at arms continued. "You have been tried on charges of treason, and found not guilty."

She let out a small breath.

"But because you have violated resolutions made by this august body, you must bear the consequences."

A shiver ran through her whole body. She wasn't guilty of treason. Odan had argued for her. And done well.

"Lela Dax. The council has issued a formal reprimand that will remain upon your record throughout all of the Dax symbiont's lifetimes. Should you ever act against council resolutions again, you shall face a harsher penalty. Do you understand your punishment?"

There was a small silence before she realized she had to respond. "Yes."

"Have you anything to say in your own defense?"

She stepped toward the podium. Odan's eyes widened and he shook his head slightly. Clearly, he didn't want her to speak.

Lela placed her hands on the podium, and felt it slowly rise, until it was in the center of the room. Then the podium spun, slowly. "I have nothing to say in my defense," she said. "But I do need to speak."

She surveyed the council. The members were watching her, their attention rapt. She thought she saw Odan stiffen, as if he was afraid she would undo all of his good work.

"I have learned much these last few days," she said. "I have learned, painfully, my own limitations. I have not yet realized how to look outside myself, and in failing that, I have not learned how to look outside my own culture. For that, I ask the council's forgiveness."

Several members were nodding. Odan blinked, looking faintly surprised.

"Thank you," she said, "for being lenient with me. I will do all I can to regain your trust."

Then she turned to Lytus. "And now you need to tell me how to get down."

Laughter rippled through the council chambers, and it sounded to Lela like relieved laughter. Lytus touched a small button near the base, and the podium came down on its own.

Lela left it. Lytus touched her arm. "You may take your seat again."

Lela smiled, but did not thank him. Then she walked back toward the door. She was still shaking, but she felt stronger than she had for a long time. Maybe stronger than she ever had.

She stopped in front of Odan. "I owe you my career," she said. "I don't know how to thank you."

He studied her for a moment. "I didn't do this for you," he said. "I did this for those who died. You weren't the only one who didn't know how to look outside our culture. The council—and perhaps Trill itself—had the same flaw. Only you tried. And if we had listened to you, lives would have been saved."

"Perhaps," Lela said. "A wise woman recently told me that it's not logical to expect yourself to act differently in hindsight."

"That's true," Odan said. "But it's important to examine your mistakes so that you won't make them again. I can't change what we did or how we handled the L'Dira. But I could change how we handled you."

She smiled slightly at the idea of having to be handled at all. "Still," she said. "I owe you thanks and more."

"Then do me one favor," Odan said.

"Anything."

"Don't let this incident cause you to lose your passion."

"I thought you disapproved of it."

His lips thinned, and it took her a moment to realize he was suppressing a smile. "I think I may have envied it, maybe even feared it. But I've grown to understand it. Your passion is your strength."

"And my weakness," Lela said.

He nodded slightly, then said, "In most things I probably won't be your ally."

"I didn't expect you to be."

"We're too different."

"I know."

"But you've taught me that differences can be a strength, too." He turned toward Lytus, who had watched the entire exchange. "We should send for the emissary from Vulcan now."

Lytus frowned. "This is happening too fast."

Odan glanced at Lela, and this time he did smile. "Some would say that this didn't happen fast enough."

Lela knew better than to get into the middle of that argument. Let the old-timers worry about the swiftness of change. She was glad that it was happening at all, that the doors were opening. She could scarcely wait to hear what T'Pau had to say about the stars, about the other species, about the minds who dwelled on distant worlds. Perhaps some day, in this lifetime or a different one, she would have a chance to see these exotic places for herself, to breathe their air, to speak with their people.

But for now, learning about them would be enough. Learning about them, and helping her world open its doors to the universe.

TOBIN

"Painfully shy, introverted, a certain lack of confidence . . . just the kind of person who would begin looking for ways to dazzle people with his 'magical' abilities."

—Julian Bashir
"Rejoined"

Jeffrey Lang

Jeffrey Lang and *Star Trek* came into the world at roughly the same time and have charted roughly parallel courses ever since: Peculiar childhood, awkward adolescence, unexpectedly pleasant adulthood. Thanks for the last have to be attributed largely to his lovely wife, Katie, who (unlike her husband) has never, ever been embarrassed about her geekhood. "Dead Man's Hand" is his first prose publication; most of his energies over the past ten years have been focused on writing comic books, including funny animal stories, a well-received science fiction miniseries called *Roadways,* the "Nanny Katie" stories, and *Grendel Tales: Devil's Apprentice.* Lang resides in Wynnewood, Pennsylvania, with his wife and their son, Andy.

Dead Man's Hand

Jeffrey Lang

A TINY, DARK craft fell through the void, tumbling and twisting wherever the solar wind carried it. No running lights burned, no thruster flared. It looked dead, but it was not. It was waiting, watching for ripples in space the way an angler watches the surface of a pond.

Within, two spoke softly, heads bent together. "Do you see?" one said, pointing at a scanner. "Here. And, again, here—nearer the star cluster."

"Yes. It is as the scientists said it would be." He tapped a key on his com panel and said, "Prepare the device." Without looking at his comrade, he said, "If we do not succeed, it would be better to plot a course into the heart of the nearest sun and hope that our families remember us with some honor."

"That would be faster," the other replied without humor, "than some of the alternatives."

His associate sighed, then said, "Faster. Yes, much faster." He tapped the scanner. "But not as fast as this. Look at it. Clumsy, badly armored, no doubt piloted by a coward and captained by an idiot, but look. Faster than light." He shook his head in wonder and disgust. "They could control the quadrant if they wished, but instead they squabble and argue among themselves, every voice raised, a cacophony of fools." He looked down at his hand and was surprised to see that he had clenched it into a fist. He uncurled it, then touched the scanner again. "But we will see, won't we? Even the fleetest can be tripped if you know where to place the snare."

Thrusters sparked for the first time in many days, nudging the craft onto a new heading. Something tumbled out of the ship's hold—something dark and spherical, less than a meter in diameter. The ship moved off, and waited.

The snare was set.

Tobin Dax extended the fan of pasteboard rectangles toward the only other person sitting at the table and made the traditional petition: "Pick a card, any card."

His dining companion, Skon of Vulcan, lowered his padd the two centimeters necessary to look Tobin in the eye without actually having to move his head. He was a picture of reserve, of calm acquiescence, but there was something in his tone that betokened a hint of impatience, perhaps even exasperation. "Why?" he asked.

Tobin, who was attempting to maintain the "cheerfully winning" expression recommended by *99 Great Card Tricks You Can Learn in Your Spare Time,* was momentarily taken aback. The grin slipped and his features drooped back into what appeared to be—judging by the well-worn spray of worry lines around his eyes and mouth—the expression that fit his face most comfortably: anxious confusion. "Well," he stammered, then faltered, Adam's apple bobbing. Rhythm broken, Tobin patted a pair of stray hairs back over his bald spot and knew he was blushing. "Well, uh, because—because if you don't then there won't be a trick."

"A 'trick?' " Skon asked. "You intend to 'trick' me?"

"No," Tobin said, feeling tiny drops of perspiration trickling down from under his armpits. "Not *trick* you, but, uh, *entertain* you. I'm *performing* a trick. It's an illusion, a sleight-of-hand." He was familiar with this sensation, though had only recently learned that the Terrans had a name for it (Terrans, amazingly, had a name for *every* uncomfortable, miserable, or otherwise unwanted emotional state); they called it "flopsweat." *You're flopping, Tobin,* said a tiny semirational voice inside his head. *And you're having an anxiety attack in front of a Vulcan. This is considered to be in bad taste.*

Tobin had been on board the *Heisenberg,* a ship owned by the Cochrane Institute of Alpha Centauri, for just longer than three weeks. His shared meals with Skon, who had boarded the ship a week after he had, were the closest thing he had to a personal relationship since leaving Trill. Most of the twenty-odd passengers and crew were, like Tobin and Skon, physicists or engineers who had been enlisted by the Institute to work on a project that would, they believed, revolutionize the exploration of the galaxy. Unlike Tobin and

Skon, however, all their shipmates were humans, mostly from Alpha Centauri, but a few from Earth and Mars, as well. Tobin had uncharacteristic confidence where the project was concerned, possibly because his own seminal work in the field was what had caught the Cochrane Institute's attention. But that didn't change the fact that living and working on a ship full of humans—generally considered the loudest of the known sentient species—while bouncing around the quadrant to pick up other members of the team on the way back to Alpha Centauri, was more than his overtaxed nerves could take.

Tobin liked the quiet, reserved Vulcan mathematician and greatly admired his work in quantum phase variance. So, typically, Tobin's way of demonstrating his respect and admiration was to annoy him with card tricks. No doubt, Tobin decided, Skon would subtly rearrange his schedule and take the rest of his meals in perfect, blissful solitude.

Tobin began to fold up the fan of cards (which had begun to grow sticky from his sweaty fingers), but before he could finish, Skon set his padd on the table, reached out, and took a card. "What should I do with it?"

"Uh, put it on the table," Tobin stammered, surprised. Skon did as he was told. The card was an eight of clubs. "Now take another," Tobin said. Skon took another card and set it down on the table. It was an ace of clubs.

"Is there some significance to the symbols?" Skon asked.

"I'm not sure," Tobin said. "When Captain Monsees gave me the deck and the book of tricks, she didn't give me any reference material about the history or sociology of the cards themselves. She just said, 'Here—something to keep your hands busy. You fidget too much.'"

" 'Fidget?' " Skon repeated.

Tobin shrugged. "Terran languages are full of words like that. It means I'm too, oh, ah . . ." He groped for a word that wasn't too unflattering. "Nervous," he settled on.

Skon picked up his padd and softly spoke a few words in his native tongue. Tobin knew that Skon was asking it to search the database for references and that he would check them later when he had a free moment. He placed the padd back on the table and asked, "Are we finished?"

"No," Tobin said. "Take another card." Skon did. It was the eight of spades. He placed it on the table next to the other two cards.

"I assume, then," Skon said, "that the next card will be the ace of spades."

"If I do it correctly," Tobin said.

"Do *what* correctly?" Skon asked.

"It's called a force. I'm *making* you choose particular cards."

Skon paused and pondered this for a moment. Then, he said, "When you tell me that you are trying to make me do something, do you not run the risk that I might attempt to resist whatever you want me to do?"

Tobin considered this, feeling his spots flush with embarassment. "Well, yes. So I have to account for that in my tactics—knowing that you know that. That's the trick then, isn't it?"

Skon, who had been reaching for another card, pulled his hand back, and stopped to study Tobin's determinedly blank—but "cheerfully winning"—expression. Then, he reached toward the fan, selected his fourth card, and set it on the table beside the other three.

Jack of hearts.

"Well," Tobin said, sounding disappointed, but not terribly surprised. "More practice."

"Indeed," Skon said, retrieving his padd. "Perhaps next time you should not inform your subject that he or she is being 'forced' to pick particular cards."

"Yes, yes, yes," Tobin said, slapping his forehead and pulling out the worn hardcopy of *99 Tricks*. "I forgot—I should have been running patter to distract you while you pick your cards. I'm supposed to tell you the story of 'Wild Bill Hickok and the Dead Man's Hand.' "

Skon's eyebrow raised a fraction of a millimeter. He lowered his padd again, interested despite himself. "Explain."

"It's an Earth legend," Tobin said, flipping to the correct page. "The tale of how one of their law enforcement officials was murdered. He was playing a game called poker—"

"I am familiar with the game," Skon said.

"—And was shot in the back by a criminal. After he died, Hickok's companions checked his cards and discovered he was holding two black aces and two black eights. Since then it's been called the Dead Man's Hand."

"Why would his companions check his cards?" Skon asked.

Tobin shrugged. "How should I know? They're humans. Who knows why they do anything?"

Skon's eyebrow climbed even higher, acknowledging the validity of Tobin's comment, then raised his padd again and resumed reading. Tobin smiled faintly, glad that he had amused Skon, or whatever passed for amusement among Vulcans. Tobin had known other Vulcans and found most of them brusque and haughty despite their espoused views about diversity. Perhaps Skon was different because, as Tobin had learned, his father had been a diplomat. Tobin suspected that having a diplomat for a father would make one pretty accepting of other people—even humans. From a point just to the left of the center of his being, an amused voice said, *Even pesty little Trills with too much time on their hands.*

Tobin's hands jerked and the cards he had been gathering fluttered wildly into the air. *Lela,* he thought, almost saying the name out loud. The doctors at the Symbiosis Institute assured him that the voice he sometimes heard was only his imagination, that the persona of Dax's only previous host had been completely integrated into his own, but it still made him jump every time he *imagined* he heard her. Tobin knew he could be annoying and he didn't need his subconscious—or whatever the voice was—reminding him. It was exactly the sort of thing that was starting to make him wonder what the Symbiosis Evaluation Board had been thinking when they chose him to host Dax. *What did they see that I can't?* he wondered as he gathered up the cards and stacked them into a deck.

He saw that Skon had already deposited his tray at the recycler and was standing at the door, looking back toward him to say, "I am returning to the lab. If you would care to accompany me, we can review the adjustments you made to the phase transition coils before we perform another test."

Tobin smiled gratefully and leapt up—too quickly as it turned out. He banged his knee on the lip of the table and points of light exploded behind his eyes. Even as he hopped around the room trying to get the pain under control while not careening into other tables or chairs, there came a low, ominous thud, then a shock and a shudder.

Tobin Dax's last coherent thought before everything went dark was: *Oh, great! Now what have I done?*

When the darkness began to recede, he was aware of only his aching head, his burning lungs, and something stabbing, stabbing, stabbing him in the eyes.

It was a sign, a sign from the Creator. A sign that he never should have left home, never should have let himself be lured away from Trill by these humans and their insane ideas. It was a sign that said, HULL BREACH.

Tobin was in a very cramped place. When his vision cleared, he recognized it as the ship's primary Jefferies tube, the one that ran almost the entire the length of the ship, from the computer core to engineering. He was wearing a rebreather, no doubt because there was smoke everywhere. Skon was there, too, his back against the opposite wall, calmly keying commands into his padd. A thin optical cable ran from the device into a dataport in the curved wall.

Tobin tried to sit up, but instead bumped his head against the low ceiling. Skon reached out and pressed him back against the wall. "The artificial gravity has failed or been deactivated," he said. "Do not exert yourself unnecessarily until you have become acclimated."

Tobin inhaled deeply, letting the rebreather do its job, and felt his stomach shift a bit on its moorings. He had experienced zero-g once or twice in his life and though he didn't like it, he wasn't cursed with the hopeless disorientation some people suffered. "What happened?" he asked. His voice echoed in his head, reverberated by the plastic cup over his mouth and nose.

"I am attempting to determine that now," Skon said, studying his padd. "The computer core has been damaged or gone off-line, though several of the peripheral servers are still functioning. The damage is . . . considerable. There are hull breaches on several decks, including the bridge. Most of the critical hull surfaces have buckled and one of the warp nacelles appears to have been shorn off. The *Heisenberg* is no longer spaceworthy."

"Did we collide with something?"

"Unlikely," Skon said. "Captain Monsees's crew is competent and the deflectors were functioning properly. The sensor logs show some sort of space/time rupture just before the ship dropped out of warp. Someone released an explosive near our flight path. Possibly a small amount of antimatter, but more likely a nuclear device."

"That would do it, wouldn't it?" Tobin said. "But who'd do such a thing?"

"External sensors are still functional—barely. But they detect the type of ionic energy associated with Romulan drive units."

"Romulans?" Tobin gasped, almost spitting into his rebreather. "But the captain said that the route we were taking to Alpha Centauri is one of the most secure in the sector! And their ships don't even have warp drive! The only way a Romulan ship could get this far away from their own space at sublight . . ."

". . . Would be if they had left their region many years ago," Skon confirmed. "But considering even what little we know about the Romulans, such a plan is not so surprising."

Tobin slowly nodded his head, working his way through the problem. He knew that the humans and Romulans had been engaged in a vicious border war for the better part of three years, ever since one of the Earth's exploratory ships had strayed into Romulan-claimed territory, the galactic equivalent of stepping into a hornet's nest. Very little was known about the fiercely xenophobic Romulans and the only thing everyone agreed on was that they were ruthless, implacable foes. It was a commonly held opinion among the local sentient species that the only thing that had saved Earth from being overrun was its FTL drive, and a cunning that Tobin, for one, found hard to reconcile with their offhand, sometimes foolish good humor. Ironically, as he and Skon had discussed on more than one occasion, the Terran-Romulan conflict could easily be interpreted as one of the reasons for the growing sense of political, scientific, and even military unity found among Earth's nearest neighbors.

"What could they possibly want from us?" Tobin asked. A thought struck him and he felt his heart skip a beat. "The prototype? You think they know what we have in the lab?"

Skon shook his head. "Unlikely. The device had not even reached the theoretical stage when they presumably left their space. No, if we are correct and have been attacked by Romulans, then I believe they are unaware of the purpose of our voyage." Light from his padd's display danced across Skon's angular features, cutting deep shadows around his mouth and eyes. "The lab has not opened to space," he reported. "I think we can assume that the prototype is intact."

"Well, that's something," Tobin said, relieved. "When the Romulans leave, we can dismantle it—take the data core and use the escape pods. . . ."

"That will not be possible," Skon reported. "All the escape pods are gone."

Tobin was stunned. "*Gone?* They left without us? Captain Monsees would never do that."

"I agree," Skon said. "So we must postulate another scenario that fits the facts: If the crew did not escape, then perhaps the Romulans jettisoned the pods to make escape impossible."

"But what could possibly be so important that they'd risk . . ." Then he understood. "Oh, no," he whispered.

"Yes," Skon said, closing his padd and slipping it into his belt. "It is the only logical conclusion." He pulled out a small worklight and shined a low beam down the length of the Jefferies tube. "This leads to engineering. We can confirm our theory there."

"And then what?" Tobin said, pushing himself off the wall, his stomach wobbling slightly.

"And then," Skon said, floating down the tube into the darkness, "we will do whatever logic dictates."

Moving through the Jefferies tube in zero-g turned out to be less arduous than Tobin had anticipated, rather like swimming with a mild current. It was one of the few times in his life that he could remember being *thankful* for his modest stature. The biggest problem, it turned out, was resisting the urge to push off the walls and zip along. But Skon, nearly half a meter taller and ten centimeters broader, was in the lead and kept their progress at a controlled rate. Closing in on engineering, they found an entrance to the air circulation system, unclipped the grate, and struggled into the considerably narrower space. Fortunately, Skon took the precaution of bracing himself against the duct walls when he stopped or he would have been shoved through the grillwork overlooking the engine room when Tobin bumped up against his feet.

Skon pushed himself up toward the top of the duct so Tobin could creep along beneath him until he could see through the grillwork.

He saw the Romulans at once.

There were two in plain view, clearly humanoid, though their armored EVA suits and the reflective visors on their helmets made it impossible to say anything more definite about them. That they hadn't removed their helmets suggested either that they didn't trust the *Heisenberg*'s atmosphere, or they had doubts about the ship's continued reliability as a container of said gases. Both soldiers held large energy weapons that Tobin presumed were the Romulans' notorious disruptors, named for their tendency to shake apart matter rather than, like the Terran lasers, bump up its energy state until it was vaporized.

The Romulans were herding prisoners toward the maintenance airlock on the starboard side, moving confidently in the zero-g. Tobin was relieved to see both Captain Monsees and First Mate Burgwin; the computer specialists Mira Laasa and Katie Lo; the Martian mathematician whose name he couldn't pronounce; Heyes the navigator and Chief Engineer Jarman; and two other engineers whose names escaped him. All were apparently injured. It looked like nine survivors, or half the ship's complement if he didn't include himself and Skon. Tobin pointed and whispered, "Over by the hatch. Do you see?"

Skon nodded, then spoke softly. "Personal thruster units. They came in through the airlock." That sounded right to Tobin. When the ship dropped out of warp, the Romulans must have had a boarding party ready to cross over. But why were they herding the prisoners toward the hatch? To transfer them to the Romulan ship? No, impossible—there was no way they could do that without EVA suits.

The Romulans arranged the prisoners in a loose semicircle around the hatch, then stepped back far enough that they could cover the entire group in a crossfire. When they were finished, a third armored figure floated out from behind the warp core, paused briefly to study the blue light that danced within the containment fields, then pushed off until he came to a stop in front of the airlock hatch. The Romulan commander—and Tobin had no doubt that was who this was—peered through the small round window, then tapped on it with the knuckle of his armored glove.

Tobin almost jumped back when a hand slapped the window from the the other side. It was replaced almost immediately by a face, a round, soft face—one of the project technicians—a woman named Williams. Tobin had been introduced to her when he had boarded, but they hadn't exchanged a word since because she worked the gamma shift and he tended to work during alpha hours. Her unprotected face was smashed flat up against the thick viewport as she screamed soundlessly at the Romulan. Tobin was surprised to see that she seemed more angry than frightened. In fact, though he was by no means proficient at lip-reading, Tobin was almost certain that Williams was cursing at the Romulan.

The Romulan leader moved his face closer to the window, apparently so he could study her expressions more carefully. It was disconcerting to Tobin to watch the woman go on and on, her breath fogging the glass. Everyone—including Williams—knew what was about to happen, but the tension of waiting for it to occur was almost more than Tobin could take.

Finally, Williams' cursing subsided and she only stared at the Romulan, her breaths coming short and fast. Then, almost offhandedly, the commander flicked a finger toward one of the guards who then jabbed at a switch on the airlock controls. Three telltales over the hatch turned red, one after the other, and the face in the window disappeared. Tobin thought he heard a sound of air being expelled, though he knew that this was impossible. Then, he heard it again and realized that the noise was coming from Skon, though whether it was a moan, a sigh, or a prayer, Tobin never knew for certain. All the scientists and crewmen seemed to sag into themselves. The telltales cycled through again and the lights shifted back to green.

The commander turned back to his prisoners, then walked the perimeter of the room and pointed to different pieces of machinery, control panels, diagnostic devices, until he finally returned to where the research team and crew now stood huddled together, some staring at the floor, others glowering at their captors. The commander prodded first one, then another team member toward various pieces of equipment, but each and every one sullenly refused to move. "The message is clear," Skon said. " 'Cooperate or die.' "

"But it doesn't look like any of them are going to do what he asks," Tobin whispered. "That's . . . that's . . . I'm not sure what that is. Incredibly stupid? Foolishly brave?"

"I have observed," Skon replied, in a manner that would have sounded admiring if he were anything but a Vulcan, "that humans are a very stubborn people."

The Romulan commander had clearly come to the same conclusion, and decided that another demonstration of the consequences of noncompliance would have little impact if the prisoners didn't have an opportunity to ponder the first one. He ordered the guards to move the humans down a short hall that, Tobin knew, led to a cargo hold. Even as the prisoners were herded off, a fourth Romulan emerged from the depths of the engine room and began to study control surfaces while the leader turned his attention to the reaction chamber.

Tobin and Skon eased back into a recessed area that was far enough away from the grill that they could speak in near normal tones without the risk of being overheard. "You were right," Tobin said. "They're after the warp technology," Tobin said.

"That," Skon replied, "would be a logical conclusion. It is suspected that the Romulan are years, perhaps decades, away from developing warp drive. However, if they had a model to study in detail . . ."

"Yes, yes. It won't take them long to figure it out. Fine," Tobin said, his voice rising sharply with impatience. "So, what are our options?"

"They are almost as limited as our resources," Skon said. "I would order our priorities thus: first, prevent the Romulans from taking possession of the *Heisenberg*. Second, if possible, free our comrades and escape."

"And, third," Tobin added, "save the prototype. Think of the combined years of work and research that have been sunk into it. We have to figure out some way to salvage the databases, if nothing else. I don't think any of the labs that have contributed work have copies of *all* the files, and there's work we've done on board that no one else has."

"I have not overlooked this," Skon replied. "But I think

we must consider it a distant third objective. Preserving knowledge is a high priority, but logic dictates that a higher one is preserving the lives of the device's creators, and preventing that knowledge from falling into the hands of those who might use it for evil purposes."

Tobin stared. "Skon, I'm . . ." he started to say. "Sorry, it's just that I don't think I've ever heard a Vulcan use the word 'evil.' "

"Do not misunderstand me, Tobin Dax," Skon said. "Evil—malice, malevolence—call it what you will, is not an abstract concept ascribable to some supernatural power. The desire to gain advantage over others either through deliberate action or inaction is one of the fundamental motivations in sentient beings. How could logic overlook such primal behavior?"

"I see your point, but it still doesn't address the question of what we're going to do!"

"Let us first rule out the things we *cannot* do," Skon said. "We cannot overpower the Romulans with force. I counted four armed soldiers and four thruster packs. I believe we can safely surmise there are no others, but the odds are still two to one against us, and we have no weapons. The element of surprise might aid us slightly, but not sufficiently. The *Heisenberg,* as we discussed previously, can no longer achieve warp speeds without substantial repair work. The Romulan vessel would enable us to escape, but we have no way to commandeer it, and our escape pods are no longer an option."

"I don't think I like where this is going," Tobin said.

Skon did not respond immediately and Tobin would have sworn that he could hear the sorted and resorted variables tumbling around in Skon's mind. Finally, he said, "Our options have dwindled to one, Tobin: We must destroy the *Heisenberg.* "

"What?" Tobin hissed. *"That's* the best 'logic' can come up with?"

Skon held out his hand in a soothing gesture. "Be calm, Tobin," he said. "Considering how carefully the Romulans planned the attack, it is remarkable that even that recourse is available to us."

"But to destroy the ship . . . the prototype . . . everyone aboard . . ."

"The Romulans are not known for taking captives," Skon said. "They will likely execute our shipmates anyway, whether they cooperate or not. The same is true for us. The ship is too small for us to avoid detection indefinitely."

"But still . . ." Tobin said, his mind racing. Tobin Dax would be the first to admit that he was not the cleverest Trill to ever grace the face of his planet—"Not the sharpest blade in the knife block," as his mother (a wonderful cook) used to say. His successes as an engineer were, he believed, more attributable to plodding perseverance rather than brilliance or insight. His only notable "talent"—if it could be called such a thing—was his ability to panic, or, more accurately, to think his way *through* panic. Rather than making his mind lock up, panic sent Tobin into cognitive overdrive. Perhaps it was this ability that made the Symbiosis Commission decide he would be a worthwhile host.

So when Tobin wrapped his mind around the idea that he might soon become a random and loose affiliation of atoms, his mind began leaping through possibilities until, without thinking, he blurted out, "What if . . . wha' if we blow up only *part* of the ship?"

Skon's eyes narrowed. "Explain."

"We could rig some kind of . . . wait. Give me your

padd." Skon handed the device to Tobin. "I don't know this interface. How do you call up schematics? Oh, wait." He fumbled with the keys. "There. All right—look here. The *Heisenberg* is designed like a lot of Terran warp-capable ships. Basically, it's just a big tube with warp nacelles slung underneath the back half. Engineering is separated from the habitat section by a safety junction with blast doors and heavy shielding on either end, the idea being to protect the rest of the ship in the event of a radiation mishap." As Tobin's thoughts grew clearer, he began to work the padd more confidently, his fingers flying over the controls. "Suppose we placed explosive charges here . . . and here inside the junction." Two points near the center of the ship schematic began to glow. "We could blow free of the engineering hull and push ourselves away with steering thrusters. Wait! Are the steering thrusters still available?" Tobin checked the diagnostic Skon had run earlier and nodded. "Yes. See? Here— we could fire them from an interface in the Jefferies tube."

"To what end?" Skon asked. "Even if we could, as you say, blow ourselves free from the engineering section, the Romulans would still have the warp engines, as well as enough fire power on their own ship to destroy the habitat section."

"Not if we blow up the engines first!"

Skon was silent for several seconds, forcing Tobin to reflect on what he had just said. *What am I thinking about? What's come over me? When did the solution to all my problems become blowing up something?*

Skon took the padd from Tobin and began to work the controls, probably, the Trill decided, to shut down the schematics on the display to conserve the padd's charge. When that didn't happen, he leaned forward to see what

Skon was working on and saw a surprisingly realistic slow-motion wireframe animation of the *Heisenberg,* breaking apart into sections. Then one of the sections—engineering—exploded in a flash. In the first three cycles, the habitat also exploded, but each time Skon pushed the simulation so that the two sections were farther and farther apart. Finally, the habitat survived—at which point he began to try to figure all the possible responses of the Romulan ship.

Five minutes later, Skon shut off the simulation and looked up at Tobin. His right eyebrow arched up. "It is an intriguing concept, Tobin Dax. How do you plan to destroy the warp core?"

Tobin tried to recall everything he had learned about the *Heisenberg's* warp engines since coming aboard. "Well," he began, "the intermix chamber is a fussy piece of machinery. Even if the whole system is on standby, we could probably touch off a core breach if we disrupt the coolant system. An explosion like that would blind the sensors on the Romulan ship. Maybe even disable it if it's close enough to dispatch a boarding party. But, wait—oh, damn! The cooling system isn't accessible through the ship's computer nodes so that they won't go off-line if the system crashes. We don't stand a chance of disabling the control systems with the Romulans in there."

Skon folded his padd and slipped it into his sash, then flicked on his small flashlight. His underlit features were grim and, Tobin thought, distressingly demonic, though his soft tone belied his expression. "Tobin," he said, "I do not believe you have considered all the possibilities."

"This," Tobin said, sometime after they'd made their way to the project lab, "is an extraordinarily *bad* idea."

"You may be correct, but it was, after all, *your* idea."

"It wasn't *my* idea to use the prototype."

"Not as such," Skon replied. "But it was your idea to try to set off a chain reaction in the warp core by blocking the coolant flow. As you pointed out, we cannot shut off the coolant system from inside engineering, so we must do the next best thing by placing something *inside* the coolant tank. I believe that lab table will have enough mass. We may be fortunate and the change in pressure will burst the tank. The Terran systems are, as you said, 'fussy.' "

"But even if that works and they don't notice the drain on the system *and* the whole power grid doesn't blow out," Tobin inhaled deeply, feeling himself to be on the verge of hyperventilation, *". . . I don't want to do this!"*

"Do you lack confidence in your own work?" Skon asked. "Have you not seen the test results? It should be extremely safe. Uncomfortable, perhaps, but safe."

"Couldn't we just . . . oh, I don't know . . ." Tobin paused, waiting for panic to produce an inspiration.

Nothing came. Either he wasn't panicked enough or his sense of personal danger was beginning to burn out from overuse. "All right," Tobin sighed. "Fine. I'll do it." He weakly waved Skon toward the ventilation shaft they had used to enter the laboratory. "Be careful. No sense in *both* of us getting killed."

Skon pushed off and floated toward the open vent, Tobin's sarcasm apparently lost on him. "Give me ten minutes to reach engineering and get into position."

"Fine, fine," Tobin said wearily. "It'll take me at least that long to power up the equipment and move the lab table into position."

"Of course," Skon said as he disappeared into the vent. "Do not forget that the table still has as much mass as it had when the gravity was functioning."

"Yes, yes," Tobin said, running his hands over the familiar controls. Lights glowed under the shielded chamber. The computers began to crunch gigaquads of data and check redundant systems. "Mass," he repeated. "No problem." The main console hummed to life. Tobin smiled a small, satisfied smile. Maybe . . . maybe this wouldn't be so bad after all. It was a machine, one that he understood inside and out, that he had helped design and construct. He trusted it—the theory behind it, anyway—in some ways more than he trusted himself. Perhaps that would be enough.

Less trustworthy were the two bombs and the makeshift retrieval device he and Skon had cobbled together. Not that he didn't trust Skon's workmanship on the retrieval device, but there hadn't been time for anything other than the most rudimentary testing. The bombs—well, a bomb was a bomb. Rigging together power cells to explode was no test of any capable engineer's abilities. The trick, really, was keeping them from going off prematurely.

The lab table, unfortunately, turned out to be a bigger problem than he had anticipated. Though Tobin was now getting used to pushing himself around in zero-g, he had no idea how to manipulate large, bulky objects. He was just about to give the table a tremendous shove toward the prototype when it occurred to him that he would then have to race around to the other side of the table and stop it before it smashed through the bulkhead. Dislodging the table and moving it carefully into place took much more time than he had allotted. Even as Tobin settled the table into place, his chronometer began to chime. Skon was in place, waiting for Tobin's signal.

He walked back to the control panel and checked the displays. Everything looked optimum, which was surprising, considering how badly the *Heisenberg* had been damaged. On the other hand, that was how they had designed it; the power supply could *not* be interrupted.

Tobin initiated the charge cycle and the generators hummed to life. Four large scanning units rose from their cradles on the perimeter of the chamber and locked into place with an intimidating *ka-chunk*. He rechecked the co-ordinates, slapped the COMMIT switch, and slid his hand to the row of control levers.

The telltale blinked green and Tobin listened carefully to the hum of the pattern buffers. When the tone hit the correct pitch, he gently shoved the row of levers slowly downward. The table began to glow faintly on the stage, then shimmered and shone with a silvery phosphorescence. By the time he had pushed the row of levers halfway down, Tobin could see through the table and its outline began to waiver. Then, checking all the scanners to make sure he was on target, he quickly reviewed all the readings and, finding there was no degradation in the signal, pushed the levers to the bottom of the row. The hum rose to a shrill crescendo, then quickly died away. The table was gone.

Or, more precisely—assuming the prototype matter transporter had performed as intended—the table was now reassembled in the warp engine coolant tank. With any luck, it had already become wedged in an intake valve, severely curtailing the flow of coolant to the intermix chamber. The temperature change would set off an alert to engineering stations on the bridge and the chief engineer's bug board. Since no one was manning either of those stations, failure to correct the problem within five minutes would set off the shipwide alarm. Skon had figured that would give them about eighteen minutes before the core went critical. Of course, the Romulans would know something was wrong and would probably begin tearing apart the engine room to find the source of the problem. They might even figure out that it had something to do with the coolant system, but not soon enough to do anything about it.

The transporter scanners dropped back into standby position and the generators began the recharge cycle in preparation for the next transport. It all seemed so noisy that Tobin began to worry about someone coming to investigate. Worrying about that unlikely possibility made it easier to not think about the other, more real terrors he was about to face.

Tobin tried to program in the next set of coordinates, but his hands shook so badly that he kept fumbling the settings. "You don't want to get this wrong," he said aloud, willing himself to be calm. After the third failed attempt, Tobin turned away from the console and patted his pockets in search of the deck of cards. Running through sleights sometimes had a soothing effect on him. *Sometimes.*

He slid the deck out of its box and restacked the cards to run Dead Man's Hand. Just as he finished, the warp core Klaxon sounded—much sooner than he had expected—and Tobin started back to the controls, banging his shin against the console. Knowing that Skon was waiting for him to act gave Tobin the focus he needed, so he ignored the pain, slid the cards into his pocket, and entered the settings correctly on the first try. Figuring out how long to give himself before the recall timer kicked in was difficult, but he finally settled on ten minutes. If he couldn't set up the bombs in that time, it wouldn't really matter.

After clipping the retrieval device—a thirty-centimeter tube containing an easily detectable isotope—to his belt, Tobin guided the two explosives into the transporter chamber. *The first humanoid ever to be transported is going to be carrying two very large bombs with him,* Tobin mused, shaking his head. *This really isn't what we had in mind.* He stepped into the transport chamber, inhaled once deeply and let the breath out slowly. The pattern buffers began to cycle and the sensors *ka-chunk*ed up out of their racks. For some reason, the noise made Tobin think about the amusement park rides his brothers had dared him to go on when he was a boy—the kind that would whir, clang, and groan before they began to subject him to sudden, sadistic changes in vector. Just before the rides would begin, everyone—*everyone*—would say the same thing. Tobin found himself saying it aloud as the hum of the generator reached its highest pitch. "Well . . . here we go."

Skon floated cross-legged by the grill overlooking the engineering section, his eyes half-closed in meditation, fingertips lightly touching the floor. He felt the *Heisenberg* shudder through his fingers. A Klaxon sounded—loud, shrill, and insistent. *These humans,* Skon thought. Studies had shown that a low-pitched, less *strident* sound was a more effective alarm, but, no, they insisted on *this*. His ears rang, but no more than he had anticipated.

The Romulans responded in an orderly fashion: Two were attempting to determine if their investigations had tripped the alarm, while the other pair darted around engineering looking for other signs of trouble. Unable to discover the cause of the Klaxon, the leader sent one of his men out of engineering on some errand while directing the others to continue their examination of the warp core. The leader himself moved out of sight to the other side of the core. In the scenarios Skon had been running through during his meditations, this outcome had been predicted seventy-three percent of the time.

Skon fingerwalked down the side of the vent to a grill he knew he could open without being seen. There was no need for greater stealth since the Klaxon effectively concealed any and all noise he could conceivably make. Slipping through the open grill, he pushed off the wall at an angle and floated toward the ceiling. Skon did not have a great deal of experience with zero-g, but these were simple calculations of force, drag, and inertia. Assuming his calculations were correct—and, naturally, they were—he would come to a stop approximately eight meters above the two guards. It was an easy matter then to push off from the ceiling and drop down silently behind the pair.

One thing troubled him as he fell. He'd had an excellent view of the engine room from the ceiling. The Romulan commander, it seemed, had disappeared.

One crisis at a time.

Skon had noted earlier a soft spot in the Romulans' armored EVA suits—where the helmet met the torso. No doubt it was meant to improve their mobility, but it was also a vulnerability Skon could exploit. He reached out with both hands as he descended, applying a nerve pinch to each man that rendered both of them instantly unconscious. He disarmed the pair, propelled them into the airlock, and then shoved the thruster packs in after them. Skon had no desire to cause any unnecessary loss of life, and if all went according to plan, he would be able to return in time to open the exterior hatch so that the Romulans could escape before the core went critical. Disabling the airlock controls so that the inner hatch could only be opened from Skon's side was only the work of a minute.

All was going well. The third soldier was still off on his errand. There was only the matter of the Romulan commander, the wild card in Skon's calculations, to contend with. *Wild card,* Skon thought. *When did that word enter my vocabulary?* He would have to query Tobin about the word's etymology if they ever saw each other again. In any case, if Skon could free his companions from the cargo hold and send them through to the habitat section within the next ten minutes, it was unlikely that the commander would be able to regain control of the situation.

Pushing off toward the short passage that led to the cargo hold, Skon looked right and left, then straight up, remembering his own attack on the guards. Nothing. Skon decided the most logical scenario was that the commander had followed the guard out of engineering, which meant that the odds of Tobin being found had to be recalculated. *But, no,* he thought, focusing on the task at hand. *Free the prisoners first. Improve the odds as much as possible.*

Skon released the lock, and the storage room door slid open, revealing the Romulan commander with a disruptor leveled only centimeters from Skon's chest.

There's something wrong with the transporter, Tobin decided. *Why is this taking so long?* He kept waiting to be *there,* to *be* there, but the silvery curtain lingered, shimmering, tingling, and finally burning. Tobin wanted to lift his arm and check his chronometer, but found he couldn't move. His eyes were dry and he desperately wanted to blink, but he couldn't do that either. *The pattern buffers,* he thought. *My molecular structure is too much for them. The transporter doesn't have enough memory to store the pattern of a sentient being—No, two sentient beings!* He began to wonder how long the transport beam could hold his pattern before it started to degrade. Six seconds? Seven? *And what happens if it tries to reassemble me without the portions that have degraded and been lost?* Tobin tried to imagine how the computer would decide which pieces would be left out. *A kidney? Part of my brain? The symbiont?*

And then someone shoved icicles into Tobin's eyes. Silver icicles. *Flaming* silver icicles. There came a shattering sense of dislocation, of his vital parts being turned inside out. He tried to scream, but his lungs were flapping like shredded balloons in a hot wind, his heart a dried up, shriveled husk. He heard a small voice in the back of his head say, *Stop being so dramatic.*

Lela! Tobin thought, *Save me!*

I'm dead. Save yourself.

And then he was floating in the center of the junction that separated the habitat from engineering. His ears were ringing. Tobin wanted to look at his chronometer, wanted to know how much time had passed, but he couldn't lift his arms. Everything felt simultaneously leaden and tingly, but then he realized that this could be accounted for by the fact that he was gripping the handles to the two makeshift bombs so tightly that his knuckles had turned white. Tobin released both and lifted his hands to his face. Encouraging sign—all fingers present and accounted for. And his ears still worked; they continued to be assaulted by the warp core alarm.

Tobin retrieved the bombs and went to work. The job was simple: Open the access panels, tap into the power feed, set the timers, and seal the panels up again. The converted power cells were so generic in appearance that few of the ship's crew, let alone Romulan invaders, would recognize them for what they'd become. Slamming shut the second hatch, Tobin began to feel some sense of relief. He checked his chronometer, saw that he still had a couple minutes before the transporter retrieved him, and decided that the best thing to do would be to find someplace to hide.

He never heard the hatch open behind him, never knew anyone was there until he felt the hand on his shoulder.

Without knowing exactly how it happened, Tobin's face was pressed into a bulkhead, the cold muzzle of a disruptor jammed into his cheek. He flailed, tried to fend off the attacker, but couldn't twist or turn, couldn't stop the hand that was patting him down, looking for weapons, identification, gold and precious gems, who knew what? All Tobin knew for sure was that he was a small and helpless Trill in a large and perilous universe.

Then the guard let him go.

When he turned around—slowly, so as not to provoke reprisal—Tobin saw several familiar items drifting lazily in midair: tools, his rebreather, the hardcopy of *99 Tricks*. The Romulan was holding the only two articles that held any interest for him: the retrieval device and Tobin's deck of cards. How much time had passed since he had last looked at his chronometer? If the transporter retrieved the Romulan, there could be all sorts of complications, not the least of which would be that Tobin would be left in the junction with two bombs primed to explode any moment. Panic welled up and Tobin did the only thing he could think of: He pushed off the wall and took a swipe at the retrieval device.

And missed.

The guard twisted to the side at the last second and, instead of the retrieval device he desperately desired, the confused Trill found himself holding the deck of cards. The Romulan's response was instantaneous and, Tobin thought, pretty reasonable: He raised his weapon and aimed it at Tobin's head.

"Cards! They're only cards!" Tobin shouted, holding the deck in front of him. Desperate to prove they were harmless, Tobin fanned the deck and extended it toward the Romulan and exclaimed, "Here! Pick a card! Any card!"

The Romulan hesitated. The weapon didn't waiver, nor did it fire. Tobin pointed at the cards and tugged at one to demonstrate. Cautiously, without moving his weapon, the Romulan put the retrieval device under his arm, then pulled out the card Tobin had indicated. Holding it close to his silvery visor, the Romulan appeared to study the symbols on the pasteboard. Stunned that he was still alive and wanting to prolong that condition for as long as possible, Tobin launched into his Wild Bill Hickok patter and extended the fan again. The Romulan took a second card, then a third. Tobin continued with his patter, but his mind was focused on other thoughts: *This should not be working. Why hasn't he killed me?* Then he seized upon the only answer that made sense: *He's an alien. He's never seen a deck of cards and he doesn't know my language. For all he knows, I could be offering him useful information, maybe even military secrets!*

And then, just as the Romulan was selecting his fourth card, Tobin heard the first notes of the now-familiar chiming.

Tiny silver pinpoints of light glimmered in the air around the retrieval device. Tobin wondered if the Romulan would be able to keep his wits about him long enough to fire off a couple shots before the dematerialization process was complete. He decided that the answer was yes, probably he would and once again lunged at the retrieval device.

He managed to grab the device in one hand this time, but the guard was quicker and managed to clamp down on it with his elbow, twisting to the side and throwing Tobin against the bulkhead. Tobin heard a crackling noise and felt the air above his left ear suddenly grow very hot. And, then, his head was gone.

The air was gone, too, and a silver curtain blocked his sight.

When the curtain dissipated, he was still disoriented, his vision occluded by a flurry of red, black, and white rectangles. His cards had slipped from his grasp when he rematerialized, and were now slowly floating across the room. Tobin reached out automatically and plucked the three of hearts, then the six of spades, and then the king of clubs, from midair. The queen of diamonds pirouetted gracefully before him until Tobin reached out and stilled her dance. This, as it turned out, was a bad idea. The queen had brought along an armed escort and one of them was aiming a disruptor at his head.

Skon waited for the flash, the shock, the heat of dissolution. But the Romulan didn't fire—did not, in fact, move at all for several seconds, during which Skon had noted the humans within the cargo hold, huddled together behind the metal grillwork of a storage cage. As ever, Skon did the most logical thing he could think of: He surrendered his procured weapons.

Suddenly the commander was on him, the metallic tips of his cold, unyielding gauntlets digging into Skon's throat, shoving him roughly against a bulkhead. He expected to die then, his larynx and windpipe crushed in the mailed fist.

But once again, he didn't.

Instead, the Romulan twisted Skon's head slowly from side to side, the helmet moving in close, seeming to examine every contour of his prisoner's face. Skon stared back at the Romulan's visor, trying to understand what was going on, but saw only his own distorted reflection. *Am I truly so alien to him,* Skon wondered, *or has he seen my kind before?*

The question would follow Skon to the end of his days. For at that moment, a low, eerie chiming sound began to build in the air, like raindrops dripping onto a crystal chandelier. Both turned toward the noise, and though Skon had a strong suspicion about its source, he found himself as transfixed by the spectacle as the Romulan.

It was Tobin, materializing out of thin air, a Romulan disruptor clenched in his shaking fist.

Unfortunately, he was floating upside down and facing in the wrong direction, but the Romulan leader was so stunned by the sight that Skon was able to relieve him of all three disruptors before he could react.

Tobin flailed around and righted himself. He took aim at the door of the storage cage. "Move back," he told the humans, and fired, shattering the lock. "We're almost out of time. Head for the habitat section. *Now!*"

Captain Monsees emerged from the cage and accepted

the disruptor that Skon handed to her. "What's going on?" she asked. "What's the plan?"

"We must abandon the engineering section as quickly as possible," Skon said. "There will be a warp core breach in less than seven minutes."

The captain's face fell, but before she could say a word, Skon explained Tobin's plan. After listening, Monsees closed her eyes and pinched the bridge of her nose with her thumb and index finger. "You couldn't come up with anything else?" she asked Tobin.

"Uh . . . not really, no," he replied uncomfortably. Finally, Monsees ordered her crew to help those less experienced with zero-g toward the exits. Then, when the last man was safely away, she turned to look at the Romulan commander. "What about him and his men?" she asked Skon.

"Two are trapped in the airlock. One is unaccounted for."

"No he isn't," Tobin said quietly.

Monsees looked at him, then at the disruptor in his hand, and nodded. "I assume you intend to let them go?"

"We are ill-equipped to handle prisoners, Captain," Skon reminded her, "I see no alternative."

"I do," Monsees said with barely contained rage as she glared at the Romulan. "After what they did to our people, to Williams—"

"Captain," Skon said gently. "You are not a Romulan."

Monsees continued staring at her warped reflection in the Romulan's faceplate. "No, I'm not," she said finally, and turned toward the exit. "Get them the hell off my ship."

Tobin's mouth tightened, then he gestured with his weapon, urging the Romulan toward the airlock. When they opened the inner hatch, they found the two other Romulans were conscious, both already wearing their EVA packs. Their commander floated into the chamber but almost as soon as the door slid shut, Tobin saw his helmet up against the viewport. Tobin could see from the way he was shaking his head that the commander was screaming into his helmet, possibly cursing them as Williams had cursed him. Then, his hand was pressed up against the window, two fingers raised. Tobin understood. *Only two!* he was saying. *Only two! Where is my third man?*

Tobin thought about Williams. Then he shrugged apologetically, waved goodbye, and hit the emergency release on the outer door. It blew open and the Romulans rode the wave of decompression out into space, dwindling to pinpoints within seconds as they fell away from the *Heisenberg.*

"We have four minutes, Tobin," Skon said. From somewhere deep in the engine room there came a dull thud and a blast of warm air. "Perhaps less."

Tobin's plan to separate the ship was successful. The power cells detonated on command, and the blast doors held as the ship broke apart. Skon fired the thrusters at full burn from the Jefferies tube, and the habitat section moved off, accelerating as it went.

The core explosion, when it came, was quite spectacular. The external sensors were knocked off-line by the blast, so the survival of the Romulan ship was never confirmed or refuted. The shockwave badly buffeted the remaining half of the *Heisenberg,* but it also helped push it away from the worst of the lingering radiation. Later, Captain Monsees confirmed that their distress beacon was functional. They would be found.

All hands had a great deal of work to do to restore gravity and secure the *Heisenberg* from any other mishaps, so it was several hours before Tobin and Skon had time to speak. Tobin found him sitting in the only lounge that had not been exposed to space, asking questions of an engineering officer and recording responses on his padd. Tobin glanced at the display and saw that they, once again, were schematics of the *Heisenberg*. "What are you working on?" he asked.

Skon tapped the SAVE key. "A paper I intend to deliver to the Cochrane Institute when we arrive at Alpha Centauri," Skon replied. "A proposal to create modular, detachable hulls for spacecraft. Our experience has convinced me such a feature would be most advantageous."

Tobin smiled wanly and said, "I want a co-author credit."

"Of course," Skon said. "And how are you, Tobin?"

Tobin pondered the question. "I'm . . ." he started. "I feel . . ." but found he could not easily complete the sentence, so he settled himself slowly into an empty chair. He reached into his pocket, pulled out his cards, and, running through sleights, told Skon everything that happened after they had separated. "When I rematerialized in the lab and saw that disruptor in front of me," he admitted, "I almost, well, I was *ready* to surrender."

"But you did not," Skon said.

Tobin shook his head, though whether in agreement or in denial he couldn't say. "No," he said. "I didn't. But only because it finally registered that the only thing in front of me was the hand and the disruptor. The rest of the guard was . . . he was beamed inside the bulkhead." He ran through another sleight, very skillfully burying the ace of hearts, then cutting the cards and pulling it out again.

The engineering officer smiled as he watched Tobin

work the deck. "I told the others that we have to build in more safeguards to make sure that never happens again," Tobin said quietly.

Skon only nodded.

The engineer, trying to lighten the mood, said, "But at least we have a deck of cards to pass the time until we get home."

Tobin fanned the deck, then flipped it so that he could look at the faces. "No," he said. "Not this deck. I'm four cards short: two aces and two eights. The Romulan was still holding them when he transported." Tobin folded the fan, and said, "I finally got the trick right." Then, he slipped the deck back into his pocket, knowing it would be a while before he took it out again.

EMONY

"She's got a worm in her belly? That's disgusting."

—Darlene Kursky
"Far Beyond the Stars"

Michael Jan Friedman

Michael Jan Friedman, *The New York Times* bestselling author, has written or co-written nearly forty science fiction, fantasy, and young adult novels, a great many of them in the *Star Trek* universe. More than five million of his books are in print in the United States alone.

Friedman became a freelance writer in 1985, following the publication of his first novel, *The Hammer and The Horn*. Since then, he has written for television, radio, magazines, and comic books. His television credits include "Resistance," a first-season episode of *Star Trek: Voyager*.

A native New Yorker, he lives with his wife and two sons on Long Island, where he spends his free time (what little there is of it) sailing, jogging, and playing rotisserie baseball.

Old Souls

Michael Jan Friedman

I'LL **NEVER FORGET** this summer, Leonard McCoy mused, as he lengthened his stride to keep up with his companion. *Not if I live to be a thousand.*

After all, McCoy was a small-town boy a few months shy of his eighteenth birthday. The venerable old campus of Ole Miss, with its magnolia-shaded walks and its ancient brick buildings, was like a dream to him. And some of the students who populated it . . . they were even more of a dream.

It wasn't as if McCoy had never heard of aliens, or never seen them on newsnets. They had maintained a continuous presence on Earth since the founding of the Federation nearly eighty-five years earlier.

However, they tended to stick to places like San Francisco and Paris, Tokyo and New York. As a result, McCoy had never met an alien face-to-face . . . much less imagined that he would someday share a dorm room with one.

"You know," he told his companion, "you *could* slow down. The competition's not supposed to start for another half hour."

Sinnit Arvid turned to peer at McCoy with red eyes that seemed to burn under the bronze ridge of his brow. Sinnit, a Tessma from Tessmata IV, was half a head taller than the human. With his chiseled musculature, he looked as if he had been carved from a generous hunk of rock.

"As I told you before," said Sinnit, his voice deep and resonant with resolve, "I must arrive early. I intend to emerge victorious in this gymnastics competition, just as I have emerged victorious in every other competition I have entered . . . just as I will emerge victorious in every *future* competition I enter."

McCoy chuckled at his roomate's typically Tessman lack of humility. "How could I forget? You've only told me the same thing twelve or thirteen times in the last two weeks."

"It is important," the Tessma insisted, his tone waxing grim. "Only by demonstrating mastery of every aspect of my education can I ensure myself an officer's berth on a Tessman cruiser."

It was the gymnastics meet that had initially attracted Sinnit to Ole Miss. However, his desire to become proficient at quantum mechanics and theoretical physics had led to his signing up for a summer course here.

McCoy was taking a summer course, too. But that, the

human mused, was where the resemblance between them ended.

As a member of a prominent Tessman family, Sinnit was expected to serve in his planet's defense forces from his twenty-second birthday on. Hence, the curved, razorsharp honor blade that hung on the wall over his bed, a token of his dedication and commitment to that career path.

Only Sinnit's rank and posting were still undetermined. They would be handed down in accordance with his academic performance—and to the Tessma, that included one's athletic accomplishments.

Sinnit desperately wanted to bring honor to his family by securing a high-ranking position. So when he said that it was important for him to win this competition, he was serious. *Dead* serious.

McCoy, by contrast, had no idea what he wanted to do with his life. His father was a doctor, but the elder McCoy's work had never held any real appeal for his son. The teenager imagined that he would find his calling someday, but he didn't expect it to happen anytime soon.

"Here we are," said Sinnit.

The Menlo T. Hodgkiss Memorial Gymnasium loomed ahead of them. It was a relatively new building with sand-colored walls and large, red-tinted windows that presided over an expansive green lawn—a fitting venue for an interplanetary athletic event.

Three other gymnasts, all of them humans, were approaching the building at the same time. McCoy could tell who they were by the skintight blue outfits they wore. As they caught sight of the Tessma, who had to be one of the favorites in the competition, they nodded to him.

But they didn't say anything—even though at least some of them must have competed against Sinnit before. It was as if they were too focused to utter pleasantries. McCoy glanced at his roommate's face and saw that he had taken on a more focused look as well.

Respecting it, the human was silent as he followed Sinnit into the cavernous, echoing gym, which had been specially outfitted for the competition. On one side of the room stood a set of titanium parallel bars. On the other side, there was a synthetic-leather vaulting horse. And in the middle of the place, a shiny set of rings dangled from cables embedded in the ceiling.

Some of the assembled gymnasts were already using the various apparatuses to warm up. One was a Vobilite, judging by his mottled red flesh and his protruding jaw tusks. Another was a bowlegged female whose zebralike stripes marked her as a Dedderac. There was also an Arkarian, a Mikulak and a huge, blueskinned Pandrilite.

McCoy couldn't help smiling. He had never seen so many aliens in one place. It was fascinating, to say the least.

"You see?" said Sinnit. "And you told me I did not need to hurry. You should attend more of these competitions, Leonard."

The human shrugged. "I stand corrected."

The Tessma scanned the gym calmly and methodically, no doubt taking stock of what he was up against. Suddenly, his crimson eyes went wide.

"Wikhov'na," he muttered, his mouth twisting disdainfully around the word. "Wikhov'na pan'tisha."

McCoy, who had never heard Sinnit use those terms before, looked at his friend. "I didn't catch that."

Sinnit used a long, bronze finger to point to the opposite end of the gym. "There," he said, with what sounded strangely like disgust. "At the judges' table. It's a *Trill.*"

At first, McCoy didn't know which of the judges his roommate was talking about. He recognized one of the males as a Vulcan and another as an Andorian, but the two women—a petite, lean-muscled blonde and a statuesque brunette—looked perfectly human as they stood with their backs to him.

Then they turned around.

Immediately, McCoy saw which one the Trill was. The spots that framed the sides of her face, inside her cascade of yellow curls, were a dead giveaway.

And it wasn't just any Trill, he realized with surprise and delight. It was the famous Emony Dax, three-time latinum medalist in the '24 Olympics on Aldebaran. McCoy hadn't even been born when she competed in those games, but his mother had been lucky enough to see them in person, and she still treasured the holos of Dax's upset victory over the favored Argelian athlete. Seeing her now, twenty-one years later, it was clear to McCoy that the holos hadn't done her justice. She was beautiful.

"Leonard?" somone said in a deep voice.

It took McCoy a moment to realize that Sinnit was speaking to him. "Hmm?" was all the response he could muster.

"What is the matter with you?" his friend asked, a note of impatience in his voice.

With an effort, McCoy tore his eyes away from Dax. "Nothing. Nothing at all," he managed.

Sinnit glowered at the Trill again. "Just my luck that she would be here—and as a judge, no less."

"You have a problem with her?" McCoy asked. If there

was something wrong with Dax, it sure wasn't obvious at a glance.

"Yes, I have a problem," his roommate snapped.

Sinnit was usually as even-tempered as they came. But clearly, Dax's presence here had thrown him for a loop.

"Want to tell me about it?" McCoy asked.

But the Tessma didn't seem inclined to say anything more. Instead, he moved off purposefully in the direction of the parallel bars.

McCoy gathered that Sinnit preferred to concentrate on his routine rather than whatever it was about the Trill that bothered him, which seemed like the sensible thing to the young human.

Left to his own devices, McCoy headed for the silvery metal bleachers that had been set up along one of the gym's long walls. They were only about half full of spectators—mostly humans, but a few Arkarians and a Dopterian as well. Not by accident, McCoy selected a seat near the judges' table.

He tried not to stare at Dax, but he couldn't help it. The Trill was far and away the most attractive and beautifully sculpted woman the human had ever seen—a work of art so fully and perfectly rendered that, to his teenaged eyes, she hardly seemed real.

He had barely completed that uncharacteristically poetic thought when the Trill surprised him. Suddenly, as if she had been aware of his scrutiny all along, she turned and looked directly at him.

McCoy felt like the proverbial deer caught in the headlights. Dax's eyes were frank and unswerving, transfixing him, paralyzing him.

Finally, he managed to look away—but the damage had

been done. The human cursed himself. He had been inexcusably rude. As if to underline his guilt in the matter, he felt his cheeks flush with embarassment.

McCoy counted to twenty before he allowed himself to look the Trill's way again. By then, he was sure, she would have turned away and—if there was any god at all in the universe—gone about her business.

But to his horror, he saw that she hadn't turned away. She was still gazing at him, still dissecting him. McCoy swallowed, not knowing what to do . . . but desperately eager to do *something*.

So he did the only thing he *could* do. He ventured a smile. With any luck at all, he told himself, Dax would recognize it as a heartfelt and embarassed apology and see fit to end his torment.

But she didn't do what he had hoped she would do. To his amazement, she did something infinitely better. She smiled *back* at him.

McCoy felt like a frog in a fairy tale, basking in the glow of something wildly undeserved. What's more, he wished he could bask in the glow of that smile forever.

But after a moment or two, Dax noticed the approach of one of the gymnasts and turned away after all—and in the process, left McCoy feeling hugely deflated. He expelled a breath, trying hard to remember when he had ever felt so thoroughly and completely enchanted.

Lord, he thought. *Sinnit's right. I've got to attend a few more of these gymnastics competitions.*

McCoy was about to look for his friend, to see how Sinnit was doing, when he noticed the spots on the neck of the gymnast approaching Dax. Another Trill, he realized. And judging by the young man's expression, he wasn't happy about something.

The human couldn't hear the conversation very well, since it was carried on in harsh whispers, but he heard enough to get the gist of it. Apparently, the male Trill didn't want to compete against "the Tessma"—an objection he seemed to have lodged at least once before.

"In that case, you're free to withdraw," Dax said in a husky soprano. "But in accordance with commission guidelines, you'll be barred from future competitions for a standard year."

Obviously, that wasn't what the other Trill had hoped to hear. Frowning, he shot a glance at each of the other three judges, inclined his head out of respect, and rejoined the other gymnasts.

McCoy wondered what had gotten under the male Trill's skin—and whether it had anything to do with Sinnit's references to Dax. Was there a hostility between the Tessma's people and Dax's that he wasn't aware of?

Before he could give the question much thought, the judges declared the competition officially open. The Vulcan judge reminded the gymnasts of some rules that seemed to vary from venue to venue. Then the human judge outlined the structure of the meet for the benefit of the crowd.

There would be three rounds, she said. The athletes with the four top point totals after the first two rounds would advance to the finals. The rest would be free to engage in a consolation round if they so chose.

When the judges were done speaking, the athletes retreated to chairs in a far corner of the gym, where they sat and waited their turns. A couple of them underwent last-minute medical scans at the hands of their personal physicians; the Trill was one of them.

Sinnit looked tense to McCoy, his brow furrowed as he watched a green-skinned Orion female lead off the rings event. But the human had seen that expression on his friend's face before. It only meant that Sinnit was focused on the task at hand.

At least, that's how it seemed to him.

Fifteen gymnasts had entered the competition. Sinnit was slated to go fifth, after a gray-maned Arkarian, a dark, leathery-skinned Mikulak, and a couple of humans.

Of the first four competitors, the Mikulak seemed the most skilled. But when the Tessma's turn came, he blew them all away. Sinnit's moves were powerful yet controlled, graceful yet economical. The only mistake he made was in the vaulting horse event, when he lost his balance a little in landing and had to hop half a step sideways.

The next two gymnasts, the Dedderac and a Rigelian, both scored high—but not as high as Sinnit. The Pandrilite displayed great strength, but he wasn't as smooth as his predecessors, and the human that followed made a major slip on the parallel bars.

With more than half the field accounted for, McCoy expected his roommate to be reasonably pleased. But he wasn't. Sinnit kept glaring at Dax, as if her very presence there offended him.

The next entry was a Dopterian, who turned in an error-free performance but didn't take any real chances. After him came another human and the Vobilite, neither of whom were very inspiring.

The Trill gymnast went thirteenth. He started out conservatively on the rings, but stepped up the drama on the parallel bars and then stepped it up again on the vaulting horse, ending with a perfect landing.

Impressive, McCoy thought. But to his mind, not as impressive as what Sinnit had accomplished.

The next two competitors, a female Bolian and a broad-shouldered Arbazan, were competent but not much more. It seemed certain that the Tessma had won the first round.

But when the judges' scores went up in green characters on the black screen behind them, Sinnit was in second place with a score of thirty-six—just ahead of the Rigelian, the Dedderac, and the Dopterian. The Trill gymnast, with a score of thirty eight, had placed first.

It didn't seem right to McCoy, though he conceded that his perceptions might have been colored by his loyalty to his friend. If Sinnit's expression was any indication, it didn't seem right to him either.

The Tessma went over and let the judges know it—for all the good it did. They recorded his protest, but refused to change his score.

McCoy had never seen his roommate so angry. As the second round began, Sinnit seemed unable to cool down. He stalked the sideline like a hungry predator, glowering at the judges—and Dax in particular.

The Arkarian went first again, but this time she was brilliant—as good as anyone else that day. If she had scored higher in the first round, she would have been certain to advance to the finals.

By contrast, the Mikulak and the two humans who followed him were lackluster, even more so than in their earlier performances. But McCoy didn't imagine Sinnit would be thinking about them as he walked up to the rings in the center of the gym. If the Tessma was concerned with any of his rivals, it would be the male Trill who stood ahead of him in the standings.

Come on, McCoy thought, cheering his roommate on. *You can do it.* He was so intent on Sinnit, he almost forgot all about Dax.

The Tessma didn't disappoint him, either. He pulled out all the stops on the rings, drawing gasps from the crowd. He was even better on the parallel bars. And on the vaulting horse, his flip was so high and so intricate that it seemed he might never come down.

But as before, there was a flaw in Sinnit's routine—and this time, it was a bigger one. In his effort to dazzle the judges and the crowd, he overrotated and lurched forward as he came down from his vault.

Even that might not have been such a tragedy in itself. However, the stumble seemed to rattle the Tessma, to anger him—to the point where he snarled a curse and gave up on his landing altogether.

Stalking off, he cast a baleful look at the judges again. Then he found a chair, sat down and threw a towel over his head.

McCoy heaved a sigh. He didn't know how Dax and the others would score Sinnit's omission, but he had a feeling that the Tessma's victory string wasn't going to remain un-broken.

As it turned out, he was right. When the second round was over and the scores were announced, the Trill was still in first place. The Rigelian had come in second, the Dopterian third and the Dedderac fourth.

Sinnit, in fifth, had failed to qualify for the finals.

The Tessma was furious, his bronze visage two shades darker than usual, his gaze as sharp as the honor blade on his wall. But he didn't go over to the judges' table to contest his score this time. He just flung his towel away and left the gym.

McCoy started to go after him, intending to console his friend as best he could. But before he could make his way across the gym, he found Dax standing in his way.

Mesmerized by her deep blue eyes, he wondered what he should say, wondered if he had it in him to say anything. Then the Trill saved him the trouble.

"I was just wondering what you found so interesting," she remarked—not in an accusatory way, but with a certain playfulness. "I think you spent more time looking at me than at the gymnasts."

McCoy couldn't deny it. But then, who *wouldn't* have spent every available moment looking at her?

"I . . . er . . . didn't mean to offend you," he replied at last.

Dax studied him for a moment, then shrugged. "It's all right. I've been offended by experts." She held out her hand. "Emony Dax."

McCoy smiled—a bit awkwardly, he feared. "Leonard McCoy."

The Trill smiled back at him—and it wasn't at all awkward. In fact, nothing about her was awkward. "Pleased to meet you, Leonard McCoy."

For a moment, there was silence between them—a silence as big as the gym itself. Feeling he should do something about it, McCoy asked, "So . . . have you had a chance to see much of Earth?"

Dax's expression turned suspicious. "Are you asking me out?" she said with a hint of incredulity.

McCoy felt the heat of embarassment crawl into his face again. He was about to assure the Trill that he wasn't asking her out at all, that he wouldn't have presumed to think someone like her would ever consider such a proposal . . . when Dax spoke up first.

"Because if you are," she continued, "you'd better get to the point." And this time, when she smiled at him, it was clear that she *wanted* him to ask her out. In fact, it seemed to McCoy, she had had that in mind from the moment she came over to him.

He spoke with a mouth that had gone terribly dry. "Er . . . dinner?"

"Dinner would be splendid," Dax assured him. "Time?"

"I'll be by to pick you up at seven," McCoy told her, his mind racing to think of a place where he could take her—a place she might actually like. "I mean, if that's all right."

"Sounds fine," the Trill replied.

"Well, I guess I'll see you then."

"I don't think so," said Dax.

McCoy's hopes fell. "What . . . ?"

"Unless you find out where I'm staying," she added.

He was washed with a wave of relief. "Oh, right. So . . . ?"

"The University Mews," Dax told him. "Number sixteen."

McCoy knew the place. "Great."

Dax smiled again, melting him at the knees. "You'll have to excuse me. I've got some results to report to the Gymnastics Commission."

"Of course," said McCoy.

And he watched her walk out of the gym.

When McCoy arrived in his dorm room, Sinnit was sitting on the edge of his bed, still wearing his blue gymnastics garb. The Tessma didn't look up as the human came in.

Hoo, boy, McCoy thought. But what he said was, "Come on. Things can't be all that bad."

Sinnit shot him a look. "Could they be worse? I didn't win the meet. I didn't even qualify for the finals." His hands clenched into white-knuckled fists. "That filthy Trill. How *dare* she sit in judgment of me?"

"Filthy?" McCoy echoed. "I guess that problem you have with her is a little bigger than I thought."

The Tessma sneered. "The Trill are a loathsome species. *Wikhov'na pan'tisha,* just as I said."

"What does that mean?" the human asked.

Sinnit's mouth twisted. "It means they're disgusting."

"In what way?" McCoy prodded.

"In every way," the Tessma snarled.

"You haven't told me anything," the human complained.

"I've told you enough," Sinnit snapped. "And if you're my friend, you'll take my word for it."

McCoy stared at him. "I may be your friend," he replied evenly, "but I'm not a bigot. And until now, I didn't know you were one either."

Leaving that accusation hanging in the air, he made his way out of the room.

Emony Dax heard the sound of chimes.

Crossing the tastefully decorated ground-floor apartment where the university had put her up, she opened the door. The gymnast had expected to find Leonard McCoy waiting for her outside on the stone steps. Instead, she found Kejjis Nar, her fellow Trill.

"I need to talk with you," he said, brushing aside an unruly lock of dark hair.

"This is a bad idea, Kejjis," Dax told him. "You're a gymnast, I'm a judge. It's improper for us to meet outside the gym while the competition is still going on."

Though Nar looked younger than she did, he had lived more lifetimes. He should have known better.

"I don't care," he insisted. "What I have to say is important."

She folded her arms across her chest. "All right, then. Say it."

"It's useless to try to build relationships with Sinnit's people. They'll never change, no matter how many competitions we attend."

"I disagree," Dax said.

Nar was incredulous. "Didn't you see the way Sinnit glared at you after the scores were announced? Didn't you hear the words he used? To him, Trills will never be anything but *wikhov'na pan'tisha.*"

"I'm a bit more optimistic," she maintained. "I think we can still make headway. It'll just take a bit more work than we—"

Suddenly, the Trill heard someone clear his throat. Whirling, she saw McCoy standing there at the foot of the steps.

"Sorry," he said. "I didn't mean to interrupt anything."

But clearly, that wasn't true. The human *had* meant to

interrupt. He had sensed that she was having a conversation she didn't want to have and he had politely done what he could to end it.

It was a chivalrous notion—one that made Dax smile. She had been right about Leonard McCoy, it seemed.

"I ought to be going," said Nar, looking a little self-conscious.

Dax nodded. "See you tomorrow."

Nar jammed his hands into his pockets and walked away, leaving McCoy standing there. The human turned to the Trill. "Is everything okay?" he asked.

Dax sighed, reluctant to get McCoy mixed up in Nar's contentions. "I suppose that depends on whom you ask," she replied cryptically.

He shrugged helplessly. "Am I supposed to understand what that means?"

Dax couldn't help chuckling a bit. "No," she assured him. "It means I can't wait to have a nice, quiet evening with you."

McCoy looked relieved. "Same here."

Charmed by his innocent good looks, Dax let the door slide shut behind her and descended the stone steps. Then she took the young man's arm and allowed him to see her to his vehicle.

McCoy had been nervous about choosing a restaurant, since he didn't know what kind of food Trills liked or didn't like. In the end, he had decided on a little French bistro—the only French restaurant in all of Oxford, Mississippi.

It turned out to be a terrific choice. Dax ordered the escargot appetizer and sautéed sweatbreads for a main course and loved them both. McCoy himself was a little less adventurous, opting for vichyssoise and veal in a buttery herb sauce, but he was happy too.

The wine was a Chateau Picard '28—a good year, according to their waiter. Dax had high praise for that as well. McCoy just knew that the stuff made him light-headed.

After dinner, he programmed his car to take them to a secluded spot in the hills that overlooked the town. The vehicle stopped in the lee of a two hundred-year-old magnolia tree and McCoy came around to open Dax's door.

"You're quite a gentleman," she observed.

"I'm from the South," he replied. "We're all gentlemen."

"All?" the Trill asked.

"Well," he told her, "we were all *taught* to be gentlemen. I guess a few of us forget from time to time."

"What else were you taught?" Dax wondered aloud.

McCoy felt a warm breeze caress him. It smelled of tupelo sap. "In my case, to value learning. My father's a doctor, you know."

His companion looked into his eyes. "And you?"

He shrugged, remembering a conversation he had had with his parents not so long ago. "Still a student. I don't know what I want to be. That bothers my folks a little—Dad especially."

The Trill nodded. "My parents wanted me to be something else, too. But when I won those medals at Aldebaran, they began to come around to my way of thinking."

"I'm not surprised," said McCoy.

Suddenly, he felt Dax's hand slip into his. It felt cold—colder than any hand he had ever felt.

"Are you chilled?" he asked, concerned.

"No," she said, obviously having heard the question before. "Our hands are just colder than those of most other species."

The reference to other species reminded McCoy that he hadn't been quite honest with her. He decided to rectify that problem immediately.

"Um . . . I think should tell you something," he said.

"What's that?" she asked.

"Sinnit?" McCoy said. "The Tessma?"

"Yes?" she responded.

"He's . . . well, he's my roommate."

Dax looked at him. "You're kidding."

He sighed. "I know. I probably should have said something earlier."

The Trill thought about it for a moment. Then she shrugged. "It doesn't matter. You wouldn't be here if you thought the way he does."

"To tell you the truth," McCoy said, "I don't understand the friction between you and him."

Dax shook her head. "It's not just Sinnit and me. It's our respective species. They don't seem to get along very well. In fact, a lot of species don't get along. That's one of the reasons we set up these competitions—to help people understand each other. To help them find some common ground that they can build on." She smiled ruefully. "Unfortunately, we're finding that there's a gap between theory and practice."

McCoy was fascinated by interspecies relations. He said so.

"I'd find it fascinating too," the Trill told him wistfully, "if I didn't have to listen to Tessma insults quite so often."

He recalled the words Sinnit had used to describe her. "What does *wikhov'na pan'tisha* mean?" he asked.

Dax's face took on a stern demeanor. "It's a slur," she explained. "It means 'vermin lover.' "

McCoy frowned. "Why that?"

"It's a reference to something that happened about ten years ago, when relations between the Trill and the Tessma were more promising. Some Tessman ambassadors were out hiking in our Mak'ala wilderness when the ground gave way under them and they fell into a previously unknown subterranean cavern. The Tessma were unhurt, but they found their way into a network of underground pools that are off-limits to non-Trills."

"Off-limits?" he echoed.

Dax nodded. "They're home to a life-form that's very important to my people—so important that the Tessma caused a diplomatic incident just by being there. Harsh words were exchanged by both sides. And because we Trill were so protective of a life-form that looked like a worm to the Tessma, some of them began to refer to us as vermin lovers."

McCoy frowned in sympathy. "I thought I knew Sinnit. I guess I didn't know him at all."

"Not your fault," Dax told him.

He wasn't sure he agreed.

She must have sensed his discomfort, because she changed the subject. "The stars are coming out," she said.

McCoy looked at the sky. Sure enough, it was getting dark enough to see some of the constellations. He pointed to one of them.

"See that group of stars?" he asked the Trill. "It's made

up of the seven principal stars in Ursa Major. People call it the Big Dipper."

Dax considered it. "I can see why."

"It's my favorite of all the constellations," he confessed.

"Why's that?" she asked.

"Some time ago," McCoy explained, "before my people came to their senses, there were slaves in this part of the world. When they escaped, they would sometimes follow this constellation to freedom."

"Is that your field of expertise?" Dax asked. "Astronomy? Or history?"

He shook his head. "I don't really have a field of expertise. I guess I know a little about a lot of things, but not a whole lot about anything in particular. I've got no . . . calling, I guess you'd say."

The Trill's hair lifted in the breeze. "My people tend to take career issues rather seriously. But sometimes the only way to find what you're looking for is to stop looking."

McCoy felt closer to Dax than ever. "I can't," he said.

"Can't what?" she asked.

"Stop looking," he told her, gazing into her eyes with a longing he couldn't contain anymore.

Dax's eyes crinkled at the corners. "Me either," she admitted.

Suddenly, he kissed her.

It was a deep kiss. A passionate kiss. And she returned it with the same kind of passion. Slowly, she pulled him down to the ground and drew him to her. And there, under the velvety Mississippi sky, Leonard McCoy and the woman from the stars made love.

* * *

Dax brushed the matted hair off McCoy's forehead with her fingertips and kissed him gently on the lips. "That was wonderful."

He smiled up at her. "It was, wasn't it?"

"You know," she said jestingly, "I think you should become a doctor like your father."

McCoy didn't understand. "Why do you say that?"

Dax grinned. "Because you have the hands of a surgeon."

McCoy laughed. It pleased him to hear her say so. "Thanks."

"Don't mention it," she told him.

They gazed at each other a little while longer. Then McCoy said, "Tell me something."

"All right," the Trill agreed.

"Why did you want to go out with me? I mean, someone as beautiful as you are . . . you could have your choice of anybody."

Dax laughed softly. "You don't give yourself enough credit, Leonard. You're a very attractive young man."

He blushed at the remark.

"More importantly," she added, "you're honest. I noticed it in your eyes the first time I saw you. That's why you had to tell me about Sinnit—because you can't stand the idea of deceiving anybody. And a lot of the people I meet . . . let's just say they're not as open as you are."

McCoy grunted. "I like you for the same reason. You don't hide anything. You don't play games with people."

Dax felt guilty. After all, she *had* kept something from him. She was living by rules that demanded she keep silent about her people's relationship to the symbionts.

But McCoy was a different story, she mused. She felt she could trust him with anything—even the secret of what she held inside her.

"Actually," Dax said, "there *is* something I haven't mentioned to you yet."

"Oh?" he responded, obviously curious.

She nodded. "Remember those life-forms I told you about? The ones who lived in those underground pools?"

"Sure," said McCoy. "But—"

Dax put her finger over his lips. "There's a reason those life-forms are so important to us."

And she told him. She shared with him the secret that very few non-Trills had been trusted with—that those wormlike life-forms were very long-lived, and sentient. That some Trills were able to take those life-forms into their bodies and become joined beings.

McCoy looked intrigued. "Wow. Have you ever spoken to one—a Trill who's been joined, I mean?"

Dax smiled. " Leonard, I *am* one."

His brow puckered as his eyes were drawn to her flat, muscular belly. "You have a . . . another life form inside you?"

"Technically," said the Trill, "it's the symbiont whose name is Dax. My birth name was Emony Odaren."

McCoy blanched. "That's amazing," he muttered. "But if the symbiont lives for centuries . . . does that you mean *you* do too?"

She shook her head. "I live a lifespan comparable to a human's. When I die, the symbiont takes another host."

"So are you its first host?" he asked, grappling with the concept. "Or were there others before you?"

"There were two," Dax told him. "One was Lela Dax. She was a great lady, a member of the Trill governing council. The second was Tobin Dax." She smiled to herself, remembering. "Tobin was great too. He was a scientist, a—"

Suddenly, McCoy sat up, his eyes as wide as the rising moon. *"He?"* he sputtered. "You were a—"

"A man?" she said, finishing the question for him. "I guess you could say that. I mean, Dax spent a lifetime in Tobin, and now Dax is in me."

If the human had turned pale before, now he was positively white. "I . . . I've got to get back," he told her.

"Back?" she replied wonderingly. "But—"

"Now," he insisted. And before she could answer, he began pulling his clothes back on.

The Trill's heart sank. Obviously, she had made a terrible mistake.

When McCoy woke up in the morning, he couldn't believe what a solid gold ass he had been.

The most beautiful woman he had ever seen had offered him something precious—her trust. And what did he do with it? He made her feel as if she had committed a crime just by being who she was.

I'm no better than Sinnit, McCoy told himself. *I'm every bit the bigot he is. I'm incapable of accepting anything unfamiliar to me.*

What difference did it make that one of Dax's previous hosts had been a man? The symbiont was inside Emony now—and if she wasn't a woman, no one was.

He shook his head, trying to imagine what she thought of him after he had taken her home and refused to even walk her to the door. *I'm just a kid,* McCoy reflected, *a kid who doesn't deserve someone like Dax. If she didn't know that before, she knows it now.*

He groaned out loud, glad that Sinnit had left their room before McCoy woke up. *I have to apologize,* he told himself. *She may not think any more of me for it, but I have to try.*

Pulling off his covers, he got dressed. Then he headed across campus to Hodgkiss Gym, where Dax would be judging the gymnastics finals all that morning.

All the way there, McCoy tried to frame an apology to the Trill. But nothing he could think of seemed to work. When he reached his destination, he still had no idea what words he was going to use—only that he would unconditionally throw himself on her mercy.

Entering the gym, he saw that the crowd hadn't diminished appreciably from its numbers the day before. Making his way across the floor, he took the same seat and looked to the judges' table.

Dax was discussing something with the Vulcan judge. She looked up now and then to glance at the four finalists, but she didn't seem to realize that McCoy was in the building.

He didn't mind in the least. What he had to say would best be said after the competition was over.

Just as McCoy thought that, he heard a commotion at the far end of the bleachers, closer to the door. People began leaving their seats, startled looks on their faces.

At first, he couldn't see what was driving them. Then he got an unobstructed view and he understood. It was Sinnit—and he had something in his hand. It took McCoy half a heartbeat to realize what it was.

The Tessma honor blade. The one that had hung on their wall.

It didn't make sense, he told himself. What was Sinnit trying to do with the ritual weapon anyway? Disrupt the rest of the competition? Show everyone just how angry he was?

Then McCoy saw the twisted expression on his roommate's face and he began to understand the Tessma's true intent. Sinnit wasn't just trying to scare them. He really meant to use the razor-sharp weapon on someone.

And judging from the angle of his path through the crowd, the one he meant to use it on was Dax!

But the Trill's view of Sinnit was blocked by the surging throng. Everything was happening so fast, she had no idea what was causing the disturbance, much less that she was in danger.

I've got to do something, McCoy thought. *I've got to stop Sinnit.* He was moving even before he completed the thought, slicing sideways through the mass of spectators, heading for Dax in the hope that he could reach her before his roommate did.

But before McCoy could get even halfway there, he saw that he would be too late. Sinnit was making better progress than he was, thanks to the eagerness of people to get out of his way.

"Emony!" McCoy shouted at the top of his lungs, his heart banging with fear for the Trill. "Emony, watch out!"

She turned at the sound of her name, her expression one of surprise and trepidation. But it seemed she was still unaware of Sinnit and the danger he represented.

"Behind you!" McCoy bellowed in desperation.

As he got closer to the Trill, Sinnit raised the honor blade above his head. At the last moment, Dax seemed to understand what McCoy was saying. She began to turn to face her attacker. . . .

But by then, it was too late. The Tessma was big, strong, every bit as quick and agile as Dax was. There was no way she could stop him.

Sinnit's blade came down in a short, devastating chop. McCoy watched in horror, expecting the weapon to embed itself in the flesh of Dax's chest. But to his surprise, a blue-clad body flashed in front of her and took the brunt of the Tessma's attack.

Everything seemed to stop for a moment, as if time had frozen solid. And in that strange, static moment, McCoy saw that it was Nar who had absorbed the force of Sinnit's blow.

Suddenly, everyone began to move again. The Vulcan judge leaped over the table in front of him and wrestled the Tessma to the floor, his powerful fingers closing on the hand that still held the honor blade. At the same time, Dax grabbed Nar and lowered him to the floor, gently placing his head in her lap.

There were screams of terror and deep-throated accusations as McCoy made his way to Dax's side, feeling numb and disbelieving. He could see even before he got there that Nar had been wounded badly. His midsection was dark and wet with blood, and the stain was spreading before the human's eyes.

McCoy had seen his father treat wounds, though none of them had ever been as bad as this one, and he didn't have any medical training of his own.

Dax glanced at him. "Help me," she said, her eyes imploring him, her voice barely audible above the shouts of the crowd. And she looked down at her hand, Nar's blood seeping between her fingers.

Abruptly, McCoy realized there might be more than one life at stake—there might be *two*. And if that was true, it was still a secret the Trills wanted kept to themselves.

McCoy turned to the crowd and shouted, "Stand back!" with a tone of authority he didn't know he had.

Staring at him, the crowd did as he asked. But one of them, at least, would have to do more than that.

McCoy pointed to a middle-aged man, the father of one of the human gymnasts. "You!" he snapped. "Get the Trill doctor! No one else!"

The man nodded, then turned and scanned the crowd.

Satisfied that help was on the way, McCoy knelt beside Dax again. But as he caught another glimpse of Nar's face, which had already gone deathly pale, the human began to wonder if that help would be in time.

"Never a physician around when you need one," Dax rasped. "Stay with me, Kejjis. We'll get you through this, I promise."

The muscles in her jaw rippling, she pulled up Nar's tunic to reveal his wound. All McCoy could see was a mess of dark blood that made his stomach churn. If Dax was put off by the sight, she didn't show it. In fact, she inserted her fingers into the wound and felt around inside.

Nar writhed and bleated in gut-wrenching agony, but he didn't have the strength to stop her. All he could do was clutch ineffectually at Dax's wrists as she continued her ministrations.

Finally, Dax looked up at McCoy. "The blade cut an artery," she said. "I need you to hold it."

The human felt the blood rush out of his face. "But I—"

Before he could complete his protest, Dax guided his fingers into the wound and pressed them closed around something soft and slippery. Clenching his jaw, he forced himself to maintain the pressure.

Then, just when McCoy thought he could cope with what he was being asked to do, he felt *something* slither around his knuckles. Not just once, but over and over again.

It seemed to McCoy that he held Nar's artery in his fingers for an impossibly long time. Then, to his relief, he saw the crowd of onlookers make way for the Trill doctor, who knelt beside Dax and pulled out a Trill version of a medical tricorder.

The physician had an angry cut across his forehead. Apparently, he had been injured in the rush of the crowd.

"Bad," he said of his patient. "But not fatal, if we take care of it quickly."

McCoy wondered if the doctor was talking about Kejjis or the symbiont. *Both,* he hoped fervently.

Working quickly, the physician removed several other instruments from his shoulder bag. The human had seen his father use some of them, but others seemed to be strictly designed for Trill anatomy. One of them must have contained anesthesia, because Nar began to relax, his cries of pain turning into plaintive whimpers.

Before long, the doctor was just as bloody as Dax and McCoy. But it didn't seem to bother him. He remained focused on his work, his eyes hard and intent. Finally, after several tense minutes, he leaned back on his haunches and exhaled with heartfelt relief.

"You're going to be all right," he told Nar.

The wounded gymnast was still deathly pale, but he managed a smile. "Thank you," he said softly.

McCoy knew that Nar wasn't speaking only for himself.

"You're welcome," the doctor told him.

Something about the exchange moved McCoy in a way that he had never been moved before. The ability to help, to heal . . . he had never appreciated the magnitude of it. But he did now.

"*Wikhov'na!*" came a snarl.

McCoy turned and saw Sinnit standing there, his muscular arms still in the grip of the Vulcan judge. The Tessma's face was dark with anger, his ruby-red eyes smoldering with hate.

"*Wikhov'na pan'tisha!*" Sinnit barked.

"No!" McCoy heard someone yell.

It took him a moment to realize that the someone had been *him*.

Swept up by his fury like a piece of flotsam on a crashing wave, McCoy felt an urge to plant his fist in his roommate's face. He even took a couple of steps toward Sinnit with that in mind. But in the end, he convinced himself that there had been enough violence there that day.

"Are you proud of yourself?" McCoy spat at the Tessma. He held up his bloody hands. "Are you proud of *this?*"

Sinnit's eyes blazed, but he didn't answer his friend's questions. He just turned away.

"I hope you are," McCoy said in a more subdued voice, overcome by a sudden and unexpected sadness. "Because it's probably the last thing you'll ever do on this Earth."

The Tessma didn't answer. He didn't say anything even when security finally came and took him away.

The dormitory hallway was a mellow orange, illuminated by the golden light of late afternoon. Dax walked the length of it until she found what appeared to be the right door.

It was ajar, but she knocked on it anyway. After a moment, the door swung open the rest of the way, revealing a surprised McCoy.

"Hi," he managed.

"Hi yourself," she said.

Clearly, McCoy was at a loss as to what to say next.

The Trill helped him out. "Mind if I come in?"

"Of course not," he told her. He stepped aside and gestured to the room beyond. "Make yourself at home."

Sinnit wasn't there, of course. He was in the custody of the Oxford authorities. Finding a chair, Dax sat down and regarded her human host.

"I just wanted to see if you were all right," she told him.

McCoy nodded. "I think so," he said, but it was evident that he was still struggling with the events of the last twenty-four hours. "So I guess the competition's pretty much down the tubes."

"Pretty much," Dax agreed. "And that's too bad. But in a funny way, it served its purpose."

McCoy looked at her. "What do you mean?"

"What Sinnit did in the gym . . . somehow it ended up doing more to bring everyone together than a month's worth of competitions. Everyone—humans, Trills, Vulcans, Rigelians, Tessma—they're all reaffirming their commitment to the goal of mutual understanding. Even Kejjis is amazed at the dialogues that have started."

McCoy smiled disbelievingly. "You're kidding."

Dax shook her head. "I'm not."

The human's smile faded. "You know," he said solemnly, "I have to apologize. For what happened last night, I mean. I was just—"

She held up a hand, stopping him. "You don't have to explain. I've had two lifetimes to get used to other life-forms. I sometimes forget that others haven't had the benefit of all that experience."

He looked grateful. "I meant to say something earlier. That's why I came to the gym. But with all the confusion . . . and then you disappeared. . . ."

"I had to file a complaint," the Trill explained.

McCoy nodded. "I figured it was something like that." He paused. "But I didn't think you'd let me off the hook so easily. You're one surprise after another."

"The universe is *full* of surprises," Dax told him. "As you go on with your life, you may find that running toward them is more fun than running away."

She had expected him to blush at the remark, but he didn't. "I'm starting to understand that," he said.

Silence reigned between them. But it wasn't an uncomfortable silence. It was unhurried, companionable, the silence of two old friends.

Suddenly, McCoy did something she didn't expect. He came forward and took her hand.

"You know," he said earnestly, "I don't care what you used to be. I mean, it's the future that matters, right? And—" He took a deep breath, then let it out. "I was hoping we could spend some of it together."

The offer caught Dax off guard. *How about that?* she reflected as she gazed into McCoy's wishful young eyes. *Even after a couple of lifetimes, I can still be surprised.*

She put her hand over his, feeling its alien warmth. "Much as I know I'd enjoy spending more time with you, Leonard, I think our destinies lie in different directions. Besides," she added, "you already have an old soul. You don't need another one."

McCoy was disappointed. That much was clear from the way he looked at her. Nonetheless, he managed to take Dax's decision in stride.

"Will I ever see you again?" he asked softly, poignantly.

The Trill smiled at him. "I can't say for sure, of course. But something tells me that our paths will cross someday."

The human swallowed. "I'll never forget you, y'know."

"And I'll never forget *you*," Dax responded, shooting him a sly look to lighten up the moment.

Then she kissed him on the cheek and departed.

But she hadn't lied, she realized, as she emerged into the bright golden light of the Mississippi afternoon. She really *wouldn't* forget the boy named McCoy, even if she lived to be a thousand.

AUDRID

"When one of my kind stumbles, Benjamin . . . it's a mistake that's there forever."

—Jadzia Dax
"Dax"

S. D. Perry

S. D. (Stephani Danelle) Perry writes multimedia novelizations in the fantasy/science fiction/horror realm for love and money, including several *Aliens* novels, the novelization of *Timecop, Virus,* and a series of novels based on the videogame *Resident Evil*. Under the name Stella Howard, she's written an original novel based upon the television series *Xena, Warrior Princess*. "Sins of the Mother" is her first work of *Star Trek* fiction. She lives in Portland, Oregon, with her husband and a multitude of pets.

Sins of the Mother

S. D. Perry

My Dearest Neema:

In past weeks, I've gone over a thousand different openings to the letter you now hold in your hand, searching for a phrase or sentiment that would inspire you to read past the first words. Now, as I write, I know that there is no way for me to do this thing. When you were a child, no bribe or threat would make you do what you did not choose to do. It was a dominant trait of my daughter from the very day she was born, and I would be surprised to learn that you've lost your willful streak. Perhaps it's this stubbornness I should appeal to, or call upon any lingering sentiment and demand your attention this final time; in truth, I don't know. Eight years have passed since we last spoke, and any presumptions on my part would surely be false. You are Neema Cyl now, and all I can offer is that this letter is an important one, and I hope that you will read it.

So. Having implored your attention, I'm now at a loss for where to begin. Please bear with me as you read, as I write; there's a story to be told, and it's been locked inside of me for so long that I'm unsure of how to tell it. At one time, I swore to myself that I never would. I chose ink and paper so that I might find my way through my own carefully layered defenses, that I might create each letter, each symbol, and etch the emotion into reality. It sounds fool-

*ish, perhaps, but I feel almost as though it will erase time and dis-
tance between us—words from my heart to yours, your fingers touching what I have touched.*

*Eight years, and I speak now to a joined Neema. It's not
much time for a Trill, I know, but I've felt every day of our separa-
tion. I've heard that you're a gifted teacher of sciences. Tobin Dax
once heard Deilas Cyl speak at that botanical conference on Halii,
the presentation on light alternatives, and remembers a pleasant, soft-
spoken man of thoughtfulness and gentle wit. How wonderful for
you, Neema Cyl. Perhaps we can someday—*

*I get ahead of myself. I find ways to avoid writing, even in the
process. No more delays.*

*Neema. Your father, my beloved husband, Jayvin Vod, died
when you were fourteen, and the true circumstances surrounding his
death are what I mean to address. You already know some of it: Fifteen years ago, your father and I were involved in a confidential deep
space mission. He was badly injured. The symbiosis between Jayvin
and Vod dissolved, and Jayvin died.*

*I remember telling you. I remember waking you, sitting on
your rumpled blankets in the early light, remember your pale young
face turned up to mine. The tears that spilled from your dark eyes—
your father's eyes. I told you then, and let me tell you once more,
how much he loved you and Gran both. You were the suns in his
sky, the beat of his heart . . .*

*I'm struck suddenly by a memory, of your father holding both
of you in his arms, in the house we lived in just after Gran was
born. You were all of three when we brought Gran home, and I remember that Jayvin called you into our room to meet him. We sat on
the floor, in a shaft of sun that came in through the window, and
Jayvin encouraged you to introduce yourself to Gran. You were shy at
first, although grinning as your father pulled you into his lap and*

held up the newborn for you to see. I felt whole then in a way I had never felt before, perhaps even in memory. Jayvin smiled up at me, his dark hair tousled, his face lined with sleeplessness, and told me that he too, was complete. "I've never been this happy," he said, and he wept. I weep now, remembering.

I misled you about what happened to your father. I was deliberately vague with you about the nature of his injuries, and when you pressed for information, I told you that the Vod symbiont had gone to a new host. It's my shame that I manipulated you, that when you became persistent with your questions, I cloaked myself in sadness so that you would stop asking. I used my pain to frighten you away from the answers; although I never told you outright, I made it clear how very terrible it was for me to relive the event that caused Jayvin's death. It was, is true, but only a fraction of truth, a grain in a sea of grain. Even when you were accepted as a host initiate, when your questions had become pleas, I found a way to elude. To hide. It's no solace, I'm sure, for you to know how many nights I spent awake and alone, so choked with guilt and self-hatred that I could not sleep—but I don't mean to try and arouse your sympathies. This letter is for you.

I should have known that your curiosity would lead you to do what you did. Your stubborn spirit, inherited from both of your parents—I allowed myself the luxury of delusion, of believing that my daughter would know better than to seek Vod's new host. I had been head of the Trill Symbiosis Commission for over seven years when you were accepted; you had heard so many stories of reassociation disasters, of lives destroyed by past-host folly, that I told myself you would never break with Trill custom. Idiocy. I knew your heart, and pretended that I did not.

So when, seven years after Jayvin's death, you used my private access code to look into the TSC files, and discovered the truth—I

can hardly claim I was shocked. What you found out must have—
better just to say it, to tell it the way I believe you saw it. Vod died
with Jayvin on the table, even though the symbiont was physically
uninjured. No action was taken to save its life—so far as I know, an
unprecedented act—and I was instrumental in that decision. Your
own mother, guilty of allowing your father's symbiont to die. Even as
head of the commission, it took more than just my word—but it was
after my rushed testimony that the few attending doctors and commission members left Vod inside of Jayvin, left it trapped in his dying
body. The case was sealed, the specifics unrecorded, and I lied to you,
I told you that Vod lived.

I told myself that as head of the TSC, it was my ethical responsibility not to speak of it. I told myself that you had already
suffered enough, that we both had. I knew it would give you comfort
to believe that your father's memories, that his love for us, still existed as an empirical reality. Perhaps most persuasive of all, I told myself that Jayvin would have wanted you to believe he'd died
peacefully.

These aren't excuses, nor do I expect you to forgive me my
reasoning—I want only for you to understand why I let you believe
what you've believed for so long. When you confronted me with what
little you'd learned—I'm ashamed to tell you that I was relieved.
You didn't know everything, you didn't know _why_. I told myself
that it was for the best; that it was better for you to despise me than
to know the truth. I've restated and rationalized that for the last
eight years, and I was wrong.

The truth isn't all that came between us. When you confronted
me, the initial terror I felt turned my anger into something like hys-
teria. I told you—screamed at you—that I couldn't believe my
daughter was a thief, and I recall so vividly the fire in your gaze, the
heat there that belied the chill of your voice.

"And I can't believe my mother is a murderer," you said. "A murderer and a liar."

You walked out—and although we had a few strained and dismal exchanges afterward, I believe that was the last time an emotion passed between us. If you accept nothing else from all of this, accept that I am deeply ashamed of how I acted that day.

Neema, this is so hard! Not for me to confess my mistakes, although that isn't such an easy thing, either—but simply to tell you, even admitting that I've been wrong to keep it from you. I write now because . . . there are too many reasons to list, and perhaps you'll understand by the end of this growing document. The reasons aren't even important; what's important is that you only know part of the truth, and when I've finished, you'll know it all.

In the cool autumn of Stardate 1229, I was forty-one years old and had been head of the Symbiosis Commission for less than a year. Jayvin and I were close, perhaps closer than we'd ever been, in career and in marriage; he'd been appointed head of the xenobiology department at the Kem'alta Institute, and was consulted on all sorts of matters relating to our exploration missions. I was enjoying my own appointment, putting to work the political acumen I'd learned as Lela Dax. I was too busy to continue pursuing my science, but Jayvin kept me updated on medical advancements in Trill biology, a subject we shared a passion for; we had written and published several papers together on symbiont chemical anomalies, back when I was still teaching. You and Gran, our brilliant and beautiful children, were growing so fast. . . .

We were happy then, Jayvin and I, blissfully unaware that things could change, that they aren't always as they seem. You'd think that between our ten lifetimes of experience, we would have known better—although as I'm sure you know, some lessons are *harder to learn than others. And some must be learned again and again.*

As now, there was much debate over the simultaneous evolution of host and symbiont on Trill—there always is, and I've come to believe that there always will be; no culture is so small as to accept a single possibility, regardless of evidence, regardless of faith. But I also believe that no intelligent species will ever stop looking for answers, and the call that came to our government, only eight months after I accepted the TSC position, was one that no Trill could ignore.

The message we received was from Starfleet, and was a source of great excitement within the governing council as well as the TSC. There was a newly discovered comet just outside the Trill system, headed, in fact, toward Trill. In some thirty years it would pass us, there was no apparent danger—but upon a routine survey, a Starfleet probe had brought back information that was of profound interest to us. The probe had detected a unique bioelectric signature emanating from inside the comet, one that Starfleet scientists found comparable to that of a tiny percentage of Trills. They didn't know that the Trill are a joined species, of course, didn't understand what they'd found, but we knew immediately—Starfleet had detected the biosignature of a symbiont.

I'm sure you can imagine the stir this caused—what it could mean for us, what we might learn about ourselves. There was a closed door discussion within the governing council over our continued interest in keeping our symbiotic nature to ourselves, even some concern that whatever the comet contained might give us away—but really, there was never any question that we would send a team. It helped that Starfleet didn't seem nearly as interested in the biology of what they'd found as they were intrigued by the comet itself, in its unusual proportions of mass and density. Further, their science officers insisted its composition didn't match that of the cometary halo surrounding the Trill system; it had come from somewhere else.

And for our part, all <u>we</u> cared about was the symbiont reading. I've spent countless hours regretting that disregard, thinking that if we had only investigated more closely, waited before making a decision . . .

If only.

Apart from a few councillors within the government, there were only a handful of commission members and scientists who knew of Starfleet's invitation to join its landing party. It was agreed that the matter should be kept quiet until more was learned. This meant that our team would have to be selected from among our own small circle. As head of the TSC and with no small knowledge of symbiont biochemistry, I was eager to go, and Jayvin was my logical companion.

Things fell into place quickly. We were to join the Starfleet team aboard the <u>Tereshkova</u>, a small scientific survey vessel that would come to Trill and take us to the comet. Jayvin and I hardly had time to gather the proper equipment before it was time to leave. We were so excited, digging through the TSC's labs for fluid test kits and specimen peels, both of us trying not to get our hopes too high, but hoping anyway, that whatever was on the comet would be the beginning of a new understanding of and for Trill. Neither of us voiced our truest wish, although I could see it in Jayvin's eyes, as I suspected he could see it in mine—that we would return to Trill with a symbiont, one not born on our world.

You may recall the day we left, the state of near jubilation that we were in. I remember telling you and Gran that we'd be gone for a day or two on TSC business, and then working all afternoon with your father, packing and repacking our equipment, trying to organize. We left just after sunset, tired but enthused and before we left, we looked in on you both, together, watched you sleep for a moment, both of us silent and proud in the early morning light. Both of us hopeful for the future.

The <u>Tereshkova</u> *beamed us aboard on schedule. We were greeted in the transporter room by the captain and first officer of the ship, who, after showing us where we could store our equipment, led us directly to the briefing for the expedition. It was there that we met the Starfleet officers who would be with us, four human men. There were two scientists, Doctors Jaurez and Milton, a xenobiologist and an astrophysicist respectively; a security officer named Jon Chin; and a fleet captain, Christopher Pike, of Starbase 11. It seemed unusual that such an esteemed member of Starfleet would be leading a relatively minor scientific expedition, but it turned out that the comet had been discovered under Captain Pike's command, during some kind of cadet training voyage.*

Of all of them, Christopher Pike stands out most clearly in my memory. There was something about him . . . He had the look of authority, silvering hair, rather piercing blue eyes, the shoulders-back carriage of a man used to command. But it was more than that; a kind of casual brilliance, I suppose, a flexibility of thought that only rarely exists in men of his age and position. I had been concerned that we would be led by some stiff and unimaginative military type, someone who wouldn't allow us to do the kind of work we had planned. But after just a few moments of informal conversation, I decided that I was most pleased that he would be with us. If something were to go wrong, Womb forbid, Captain Pike would hold together.

The mission briefing was short and simple: Get in, collect data, get back out again. The probe had detected traces of kelbonite, a transporter inhibitor, so we'd be going down by shuttlecraft. There were a few questions from Doctor Jaurez about the bioreading, which

Jayvin managed to answer without answering; the two hit it off, actually, spending several hours after the short meeting exchanging thoughts on various developments in multispecies pharmacology. Looking back, I'm glad that Jayvin's last day was spent with a colleague, learning and sharing. It was what he loved.

I spent some time with our mission leader while Jayvin talked science with the others. Pike and I had an engaging conversation about the responsibilities of leadership, and he told me several interesting stories from his days as a starship commander. When I asked why a fleet captain had chosen to head the expedition, he said that it kept him young—not field work, but remembering that he was never too old to learn. At times, I had to remind myself that I wasn't talking to a joined Trill; a very thoughtful man, for so short an experience.

When we reached the comet, it was the middle of the night for your father and me, but we pressed to begin the investigation immediately. There were no objections; all six of us were excited for the unlikely adventure. As we suited up and loaded the shuttle with our various tools, the exhilaration was a palpable thing. Even Mr. Chin, who would almost certainly have nothing to do outside of piloting the shuttle, was eager, joking about ice monsters in the dark mass. We all laughed.

We got our first good look at the comet from the shuttle, or at least I did; I'd been too busy gathering equipment aboard the Tereshkova *to bother with a visual survey, and although I had read the stats, I was surprised by the barren immensity of it. Fifty-four kilometers in diameter, its gaseous tail stretching out over a hundred thousand kilometers behind it, ice and grit repelled by the system's sun, a hazy path in the solar winds. Dr. Milton was intent on the computer reads as Chin took us down to the surface, the scientist frowning at what he called an "unknown agent" amid* the hydroxyl radicals. At the time, it was just another anomaly to be catalogued.

Starfleet had been unable to pin the source of the life reading, but we quickly assessed that it was coming from somewhere deep inside; the comet was riddled with labyrinthine caves, the ice sculpted into yawning tunnels that twisted randomly throughout the massive body. We had expected as much; what we _hadn't_ expected was the faint, phosphorescent glow that appeared to emanate from the fissures in the comet's surface, not visible until we were within a few kilometers of setting down.

Milton mumbled something about clouded ice formations, but it was obvious that he was as unnerved as the rest of us. There was nothing beautiful about the erratic glowing lines that scarred the comet, that crept into the darkness of the gaping caverns; it was a sickly light, the yellow-green of bruised flesh, the luminosity like that of some deep-sea creature that lives and dies in darkness. Jayvin and Doctor Jaurez checked readings, directing our pilot to where the biosignature was strongest, somewhere beyond the mouth of one of the larger caves.

We set down just outside of the cavern, the initial excitement of our party considerably muted by the sight of those unhealthily shining lines. It appeared that the probable life-form was only three or four kilometers past the opening, and Pike suggested that we could examine the strangely lit cracks on our way to the source. We loaded up, activated the Starfleet-issue environmental suits and gravity boots, and left the relative warmth of the shuttle for the sub-zero dark.

The nearest light-line was twenty meters or so from the shuttle, running up one side of the cavern's opening. Each of us carrying our equipment and the Starfleet party armed with handheld phasers, we moved to the line and gathered around, leaning in for a closer look. It was perhaps half a meter wide, and according to Dr. Milton's tricorder, not much deeper—and as he adjusted his sensors for composition, Jayvin got a flash of signal on our plisagraph. An electrical impulse, invisible, had traveled through the glowing matter. Jayvin handed the 'graph to me, keeping his face carefully neutral as Milton told us what we already knew; the opaque, luminescent stuff was liquid. Viscous, the consistency of dense mud and covered with a layer of ice, it was capable of conducting the electrical language of a symbiontlike being. Their tricorder hadn't caught the split second of mild current, but we knew. We knew that somewhere inside of the comet, some as yet unknown relative of Dax or Vod, of Cyl—someone was there.

Unable to break down the composition, Milton took a scraping of the frozen top layer and we moved deeper into the cave, both Jayvin and I exchanging looks of renewed zeal. We had already discussed how to handle the possibility of actually finding a symbiont in front of the humans. Our explanation would be a half-truth, that the symbiont was a primitive life-form, one with a complex arrangement of RDNAL strands that some Trills had inherited. Our plisagraphs, designed specifically for the study of symbiont life, would give us precise readings; their tricorders wouldn't, or so we hoped. That Milton hadn't been able to pick up the faint pulse in the glowing liquid seemed a good indicator.

I know that you understand our excitement, the multitude of questions and hopes and theories that swept through us when we realized what we were facing. Was some ancient traveler from another world responsible for the beginning of life on Trill? Were the symbionts even indigenous to the homeworld? What if there was another homeworld, one that preceded Trill by hundreds, even thousands of centuries? I remember the bright intensity of Jayvin's gaze behind his visor, the smile that he couldn't seem to wipe away. I remember *wondering at the implications for Trill . . . and thinking that we shouldn't assume anything, even as I assumed that we would find a race of beings like our own, a connection between ourselves and the universe that would bring us into a new era of self-awareness.*

The cavern twisted and turned, always sloping down, randomly branching into intersections and tunnels that wound through the icy rock. If not for our various sensory devices, we would have been hopelessly lost. Pike led the way, Milton and Jaurez giving direction, Jon Chin bringing up the rear, and we passed many more of the communication lines, shining like dying fires and casting much of the rough cavern into deep shadow.

We walked for what seemed like days, each moment dragging. I was so eager to find the origin of the life sign, to communicate with it, that I could hardly keep from running. Several times we had to backtrack, led astray by curves and twists, which only made my anticipation greater. Jayvin felt the same; I could hear it in his tone, as he relayed distance and signal strength, as he and Jaurez made small talk about human ancestry. We were impatient and impassioned, those feelings blocking out anything else we might have intuited about the situation.

Finally, Pike had us stop just outside of a rather large chamber lit with the slimy glow of the liquid conductor. We had reached our destination. A haze of sallow light spilled out into the passage, and as Pike and Mr. Chin drew their phasers—Pike setting his on stun and ordering Chin to set his for a higher intensity—Jayvin and I waited anxiously. I thought we had been discreet, but as Chin stepped ahead of us into the greenish light, Pike held back, fixing us with a searching gaze as he touched the communication control just below his helmet. The other two scientists followed Chin into the chamber, and I saw, with no real surprise, that Pike had cut his men out of the com-circuit; he meant to speak to us privately.

"You know what's in there, don't you?" he asked softly, but it wasn't really a question. "You don't have to explain, not now . . . but you know. All I need to know is whether or not it's dangerous."

Jayvin looked to me to answer, and although I had our lie on my lips, I found that I couldn't tell it. I doubt very much that he would have believed it, anyway, but I did the best I could—I told him that we knew nothing certain, but that we had hopes, and that we couldn't speak any further on it until we had a chance to see for ourselves.

"And no," Jayvin added, smiling a little, "it's not dangerous."

Pike studied both of us a moment longer, then nodded slowly, letting the matter drop. I found out later that he blamed himself in part for the events that followed, because he hadn't pursued it any further. It's almost funny, how we all rush to take responsibility when something goes wrong, when we feel that we should have acted differently. I've spent a lot of time thinking about that, trying to assign blame to whomever deserved it most—only to come to the painful realization that sometimes, things happen that no one can foresee. Things happen because they do.

Together, we went to join the three men who had already found the source of the biosignature, Jayvin and I fumbling with our plisagraphs and test kits and cursing our bulky gloves. I suppose I had expected something like the Mak'ala cave pools, even in the sub-zero temperature—but other than the fact we were in a cave, nothing was the same.

The reading came from a raised basin at the far side of the chamber, filled with the same luminescent sludge that ran through the comet like lifeblood. Jagged shards of murky ice crusted the sides and top of the raised vessel, which was only a meter across and hewn from the same composite rock as the rest of the chamber. Great trails of the sludge liquid crisscrossed the walls all around, making strange light patterns across the faces of the men standing in front of the chest-high basin, throwing shadows against the piles of broken rock on the uneven floor.

Jayvin aimed his 'graph at the pool and grinned, holding it up for me to see even as Jaurez began to report.

"There's a life-form of some kind in there . . . complex arrangement, carbon-based, it should be frozen, but . . . I can't get an exact size, it seems to be shifting—" The Starfleet xenobiologist shook his head. "Between eight and twelve centimeters long . . . and according to this, it's at least four thousand years old."

Our readings were more definite—and it was closer to six thousand. The machine registered complex neural activity, and picked up more of the soft electrical pulses that we'd noted earlier in the glimmering organic fluid. It was not a symbiont, it was smaller and the shape was different, but it was so close at a genetic level that there was no doubt they were related. No doubt in my mind.

Jayvin was still grinning as he pointed to the gentle flux of numbers on the 'graph's monitor; he didn't need to speak. It was trying to communicate with us, we knew it, and I knew that nothing would ever be the same, that I could no longer think of our people as isolated, as alone. Tragically, I was right.

The Starfleet men put away their weapons and all of us moved closer to the basin, my heart pounding, my thoughts rac-ing—when I felt a sudden, sharp pain in my head. It was like the onset of one of Emony's headaches, but much more intense—the sensation of a raw knife sliding into soft tissue, horrible, killing pain—and then it was gone, just as suddenly. I faltered, putting my hand on Jayvin's shoulder, speaking his name—but he shrugged it off and kept walking. I was surprised at Jayvin; it was unlike him to ignore me.

"Jayvin," I called, and again, he didn't respond. I think that's when I first knew something was wrong.

Everything happened quickly after that.

The Starfleet scientists were studying their tricorders. Mr. Chin was looking down into the pool, perhaps trying to catch a glimpse of the creature beneath the sheet of gleaming ice. Pike took a step toward me, frowning, perhaps about to ask me if I was all right, but I was watching Jayvin, suddenly worried. Suddenly afraid.

At once, all of the alarms on his suit began to go off. A series of shrill bleats poured into my helmet, spurring my fear to panic. His heart rate, temperature, and blood pressure had all spiked dangerously high, and they continued to rise as he stepped toward the basin, as he dropped his equipment and bent down over it.

All of the men were talking at once, confused, Pike shouting for Jayvin to move away. I took a single step forward, my own suit's distress alarm sounding, memories of fear joining my own—

—When something shot out of the pool, something small and dark, splinters of ice shattering—

—And Jayvin staggered back silently. His hands flew to his head and he stumbled, ice crystals falling around him like mist, the terrible, rotting light surrounding him like a wash of poison.

Mr. Chin was closest. He reached out and Jayvin clutched at him, pulling him off balance. I didn't understand what was happening until Jayvin shoved Chin away, still silent, one hand still pressed to his faceplate—and Chin's phaser in his other hand.

There was a blast of light and the security officer screamed, but only once. Jayvin spun, pointing the weapon at the two scientists as Chin collapsed to the floor, the rush of air from what was left of his suit expelling in a _whoosh_—

—And then Pike fired, hitting Jayvin in the chest—but to no effect. Jayvin was still standing, seemingly unaffected, and before

Pike could change the setting on his phaser, Jayvin was firing at us. Pike jerked me away, pushing me back to the tunnel as rock exploded silently in flashes of blue-white. I struggled, screaming for Jayvin to stop as Pike fought to get me out of the chamber. If he hadn't, I would have been as dead as Chin, as Jaurez and Milton. They didn't even have time to drop their tricorders before the brilliant strobe of the deadly Starfleet weapon filled the vacuum, twice more.

I heard Jayvin shout, a single cry of what might have been terror—and Pike pushed me behind an outcropping of ice, slapping at the controls on both of our suits to turn off the blaring alarms. The chamber was clouded with frozen air, a billion reflectors for the diseased light of the yellow-green ooze.

Jayvin wasn't Jayvin. It was the creature, the thing we had thought was a symbiont.

I started talking, fast, unable to keep the desperation from my voice. I begged and commanded, I swore and reasoned, telling Jayvin not to let it take hold, not to let it win. I pleaded for Vod to stop it. I said a lot of things, the words blurring together as Pike continued to dart glances back into the chamber, trying to shield me as he stabbed at the emergency call on his suit.

Jayvin didn't answer; he said nothing at all, and when I risked a look back into the gangrenous light of the alien's womb chamber, I saw him standing and shuddering, a smear of clouded ice across the bottom of his helmet. He still held the phaser, but seemed unaware of our presence.

Pike saw our chance, and took it. He motioned silently for me to stay put and stepped away from the wall. As quickly as he could, he crept back into the chamber, holding his phaser ready, obviously meaning to stop Jayvin without killing him. I kept talking, not knowing what else to do, but I don't believe that Jayvin heard me. Already, he was past that.

Pike had almost reached him when the thing took hold again. I caught a glimpse of Jayvin's eyes, all that was visible above the crackle of jaundiced ice that had resealed his helmet in the wake of the creature's violent passage. His eyes were blank and unseeing, the slack gaze of a corpse—but it saw us. It snapped the phaser up, faster than should have been possible, and pointed it at Pike.

I remember screaming, and Pike kicked off of the ground, hurtling himself at the creature that wore Jayvin's body. Pike crashed into him, losing his own phaser as the creature fired, the phaser's beam turning another chunk of wall into powder—and then they were battling for control of the weapon, Pike gasping, Jayvin not seeming to breathe at all.

I watched in horror as the phaser went off again—and another rush of air blew into the chamber, new ice crystals forming and floating and bathing the two men in shining fog. Pike fell away, clutching at the massive tear in his suit, shouting for me to run as he worked desperately to hold together the scorched fabric across his side.

I knew that Pike could not defend himself against further attack, but I don't pretend that I meant to lure the creature away from him. I ran because I was terrified, because I was in shock, because I was in danger. Because in some panicked recess of my mind, I connected the creature's chamber with all that had happened, and wanted nothing more than to get away from that terrible place. I turned and stumbled into the tunnel, struggling with the grav boots, not knowing where to go except away.

The next moments were a blur of luminous shadows and panic. The environmental suit had a communicator, but I wasn't thinking clearly enough to do anything with it—even if I had been, it wouldn't have mattered. Pike had already transmitted a distress signal, but any rescue party would be a long time coming, the _Tereshkova_'s transporters useless. I had faint memories of control, of *gathering myself and thinking calmly in crisis, but all I could see was the way Jayvin's eyes had looked behind the faceshield. I was alone, Pike surely as dead as the others.*

I might have continued in that half-aware state for a while longer, hurrying blindly through the freezing tunnels, looking to escape the fear that had taken me over as surely as the creature had taken Jayvin—but the sound of Jayvin's voice brought me back to myself.

Before I tell you what he said, what happened, I want to make sure you understand—it wasn't Jayvin Vod. It was his voice, his body, even some of his memories . . . but I don't believe the man who was my husband, your father, was aware at any point past the initial attack. It's small consolation, perhaps, but I cling to it now as I have for the last fifteen years, and I believe it to be true. Jayvin Vod was already dead.

The shouts that rang in my helmet were incoherent at first. Unintelligible nonsense, words that weren't words, punctuated by wild fits of emotion—laughing, crying, howls of rage, and of joy. I became aware of myself again, running, listening, lost in the passages of the comet but slowly regaining self-control. I didn't know what I was going to do, but I slowed down and began to choose my direction, searching for ascending tunnels.

The creature continued to babble in Jayvin's voice, running through his emotions as carelessly as one might go through a box of tools. By the time I had come up with a course of action—get to the surface, call for help from the <u>Tereshkova</u>, reach the shuttlecraft—it had started using words and sentences pulled from Vod's memories.

It was coming after me, I knew, it kept saying, "where," again and again—and as it became more coherent, I realized that it had immersed itself in Vod in a way that was more terrifying to me—to any joined Trill—than the threat of pain or death. Neema, it was like some nightmare parody of <u>zhian'tara</u>, only instead of past hosts emerging to share and teach, the creature had separated Vod <u>within</u> Jayvin. The alien twisted through five lifetimes, dredging up memories of anger, working to express itself using the thoughts of Vod's constituent personalities.

I heard Jayvin among the others—Timus, Kelin, Calila, Baret, and Devinel all spoke, but the phrases they used were chosen by the creature, all of the sentiments bitterly angry. I tried to speak with it at first, but it wouldn't respond; although it was obviously trying to communicate, it seemed uninterested in what I had to say—and as I continued to wind through the barren tunnels, exhausted and afraid, it finally found its own voice. Much of what it had to say was as incomprehensible as its earlier outbursts, the violent emotions it spewed taking the form of wordless, raging screams. In the hours that I wandered the frozen underground, it told me enough for me to be grateful that Jayvin was no more.

Its grasp of language was still new, so I don't know if its thoughts were translated with any precision. It talked until Jayvin was hoarse, drifting off into strange loops in which it repeated itself for moments at a time, but the thrust of its message was so deeply unsettling that I didn't want to credit it as any more than delusional ramblings. It was an aberrant creature, a thing that referred to itself once as "the taker of gist." I listened, and gradually I found out why it had attacked—and what it meant to do.

It wasn't a symbiont at all. It was a <u>parasite</u>, a thing that dominated its hosts, feeding from them, and it said that it was "the first of many." It said that its ship, controlled by "the veins," was taking it to find "the weak ones." Now that it had a host again, nothing would stop it from paving the way for those who would follow; it bragged that nothing <u>could</u> stop it. And as it poured its diseased feelings out, it expressed a depth of hatred and contempt for the Trill that seemed boundless. That it knew about us before we'd come to its ship, there was no question; how, I never found out.

I kept climbing, aware that my air wouldn't last forever, knowing that I had to warn others about the creature before I was allowed the luxury of grief. In spite of my resolve, I cried steadily; hearing the parasite speak in your father's voice was torture, and more than once, I didn't think I could go on. What kept me moving, beyond the awareness that it would kill me if it found me, was the thought of my children. In the tumult of my feelings, I found a kind of relief that you were at home, safe, untouched by the horror that I was enduring.

It seemed that I had been running, walking, sobbing for a lifetime, the parasite's words and feelings creating a shroud of ugliness around me. Perhaps that's why, when I stumbled upon a dead end, I didn't immediately turn around. Just a moment's rest, I thought, sagging against the icy rock, so tired that I felt I might die from it. When the parasite started to laugh, I knew it had found me.

I turned to face it, knowing what I would see and yet still surprised by it—Jayvin Vod, my lover, my friend, the father of my children, walking toward me with a look of pure malice. Although I couldn't see his, <u>its</u> mouth, I knew it was smiling. The parasite, the taker of gist, had won. I had no weapon, no strength, and only the vaguest desire to survive, so overwhelmed by the horror of the endless night that I simply waited. Waited for the thing to put an end to my torment.

I hardly knew I had spoken until it answered my whispered question, the thought that had been with me for much of that eternal chase.

"Why him, why not me?"

The Jayvin-thing tilted its head to one side, and took a step toward me, raising the phaser.

"Because he was closer," it said.

I thought of you, of Gran, closed my eyes—and opened them again as the parasite crumpled, a grunt of shock emerging from its last second of consciousness, a huge dent in the back of its helmet.

Christopher Pike stood behind it, holding a slab of frozen rock in one shaking hand. The side of his suit was covered with ice, hastily applied handfuls of the same viscous fluid that had served as the parasite's habitat—that had resealed Jayvin's visor. He—_we_—had survived; it was over.

Although not wounded, Pike was freezing, almost out of air, and I was physically and emotionally wrung out—but somehow, we managed to get back to the shuttlecraft, carrying Jayvin's body between us. I remember wondering how I could possibly go on, each step an exercise in force of will—but we did it. Pike piloted the shuttle back to the _Tereshkova_ and ordered the captain to get us to Trill, maximum speed. You've probably deduced the rest of the story, but I want, I need to tell you. There are facts . . . and then, there is truth.

I spent the journey home in sickbay, doing what little I could for Jayvin. We pried the helmet off, and a scan showed that the parasite had attached itself to Jayvin's brain stem just inside the base of the skull, the only visible sign of its domination a tiny barb protruding from the back of his neck. The technology to detach the creature without killing Jayvin didn't—doesn't—exist. There was nothing we could do.

While the medical officer was tending to Pike, I scanned Vod, but the Starfleet equipment wasn't able to tell me anything. For the trip home, we kept Jayvin sedated. I thought that at least we could keep him from suffering anymore.

The best transplant surgeons were standing by when we beamed down to Trill, a host prepped, and a hastily convened session of the governing council waiting for me to tell them what had happened. I stayed with my husband instead, waiting for the doctors to examine him—though what they told me was as I'd expected. The symbiosis had dissolved, both Jayvin and Vod were dying. Still, I prayed for the symbiont, that we could transplant Vod and save Jayvin's memories—but remembering the monster that had hunted me through the cold dark, a worse dread took hold of me. I ordered a scan of the symbiont's neural patterns, and my fears were confirmed yet again—the parasite's consciousness had joined with Vod's, the union permanent and complete.

It was then that I met with the council members, and made my recommendation.

To transfer Vod to another host was unthinkable. There was no choice, none, except to let him die, and with him six lifetimes of knowledge, memories, and experiences—including Jayvin's.

I stayed with them until it was over, and then I went home.

Christopher Pike was waiting there, sitting outside in the light of early dawn, looking as tired as I felt. He'd come to tell me what had happened with the comet, to reassure me that the immediate threat had passed—although to be honest, my thoughts were elsewhere. Selfish, perhaps, but I was still trying to understand that Jayvin was gone. When Pike asked after him, I couldn't speak—I only shook my head, and struggled not to cry when I saw the sympathy in his eyes, as he told me how sorry he was.

I sat down next to him on the front step of our home, knowing that we had to talk, knowing that I had to bear my responsibilities as a leader—but all I wanted to do was collapse. Pike seemed to understand, keeping his speech brief and his tone gentle.

He told me that he'd spoken to Starfleet, and that they were most displeased; less than an hour before, three Trill ships had converged on the comet and blown it to so much vapor. I'd had nothing to do with the decision, although it didn't surprise me overmuch; we still had our secret, you see. What we could have learned about the creature from studying the comet—it was apparently not as important as keeping our symbiotic nature to ourselves, or at least not to the councillors who'd called for the alien ship's destruction.

Pike knew, of course. He'd heard the parasite's ravings, all of it, and had deduced what was not obvious. He told me that he understood why our government had felt compelled to destroy the comet, and assured me that he would keep the entire incident classified on his end—our symbiotic nature would remain on a strictly need-to-know basis in Starfleet, until we decided otherwise. He told me that if Starfleet learned anything at all about the parasites, he would contact me—but made it clear that he felt the action of the Trill had been ill-advised.

I nodded, grateful that he was willing to keep our confidence, knowing he was right to reproach us, however gently he phrased it. I had no doubt that our own files would be sealed, but told him that I would also share whatever information we found from examining the remains of the parasite. I believed then that seeking out the deviant breed would become a priority for the Trill; I was naive, to say the least. It hadn't occurred to me yet that the knowledge of a malevolent species so close to the symbionts would be unwelcome within our society; that no one would want to pursue a truth that carried implications of a connection between our precious symbionts and the thing that took Jayvin away.

I didn't know, then, and I suppose Pike didn't, either. I thanked him and he started to go—but stopped, turning back to ask a final question.

"Your people's secret, Dr. Dax," he said softly. "Is it that important? Was it worth all of those lives?"

I thought I was too tired to cry anymore, but I was wrong. He waited until I could compose myself, waited for my answer, and I knew that he wanted to hear me tell him that it was—it was what we both wanted to believe.

"I don't know," I said finally, and it wasn't much of an answer, but there wasn't any other.

He left me then to my final task, one that I hardly had the strength to complete—telling you and Gran that your father was dead.

It sounds like some childish attempt to avoid responsibility, but I didn't mean to lie to you. I was adrift in my own pain, and wanted only to ease yours. I told you what I thought would save you from the intensity of loss that I felt, and by the time I understood the magnitude of what I'd done, I didn't know how to take it back. And by then, I had constructed the foundation of denial that has been with me ever since.

Seven years later, you found out, and our estrangement began. As I said before, I found ways to rationalize, my position, my work—but politically, at least, nothing had changed. The powers that be had moved on to other matters, and I'd all but given up trying to convince the few council members who knew of the incident to take any kind of action. There is no official record of the parasite's existence anywhere on Trill, no autopsy report, nothing. The council saw to that. I imagine that the records were destroyed along with the creature's body, or all of the evidence was filed away somewhere, a dusty box in a dusty room, purposely forgotten.

And it seemed that Starfleet, too, had decided to treat the disastrous mission as an isolated event. I tried to contact Pike, more than once, but I couldn't track him down; only a year after we met, he was badly wounded in some kind of radiation accident, and disappeared soon after. No one could even tell me if he was still alive.

As far as I know, the parasites have never resurfaced, but every day for the last fifteen years, I've watched and listened, doing what little one being can hope to do. I tried communicating with the symbionts, to ask them about the creature, but the younger ones knew nothing. And the oldest among them seemed not to hear my questions.

I am alone in my vigil, I believe, and am always praying that the thing was lying. That it was one of a kind. But surely I tell myself lies, too. You decide.

Four days ago, on my fifty-sixth birthday, I stepped down as head of the Trill Symbiosis Commission. For weeks, I've known that I would write this letter to you, that I couldn't continue to use my position as a shield. That I wouldn't. I've let too much time slip away already, my Neema, too much time regretting my mistakes and not letting myself understand that I was making a much worse one. When Gran died five years ago, never knowing any of this, I thought I would tell you then—that we would find comfort in each other, and the truth would have to come out—but somehow, we managed to avoid each other. To hold on to our own private sorrows, sharing nothing. Time now for me to end this loneliness, or at least to try.

I've accepted your anger as some kind of penance, as though I deserved to be hated by you for surviving. For coming home, when your father did not. I've been selfish and stupid, and in denying myself a loving relationship with my only surviving child, I've denied you.

I don't expect for you to forgive me. Writing these thoughts, understanding that you've been alone with your pain and anger for eight years now . . . I do understand, at least in part, and I'm not asking for you to throw aside your rightful feelings and embrace my apology. I'm not sure what I expect, or what I can even hope for, for *myself. But for you—my daughter, for you, I hope for peace. I hope that you will accept that I love you, that no hour passes for me without you. Whether or not you choose to have me in your life, you are always in mine.*

Forever,
Audrid Dax

NEEMA CYL TURNED the last page over, sighing, absently smoothing out the wrinkles and lines in the soft paper. No tears this time, although there was a heaviness in her throat that wouldn't go away, and that was all right. In the weeks since she'd first read the letter, she'd felt the bitterness seeping away from her feelings of sorrow, and sorrow alone wasn't such a terrible thing.

She checked the time and sighed again; it was getting late. Gingerly, she folded the rumpled pages and stood up from her desk, slipping the letter into the top drawer. The house was silent and still, the darkness outside making her feel that her small home was a sanctuary, a haven against the night, against the unknown. Since receiving Audrid's letter, she couldn't help but feel that the world—that the universe—was no longer safe. Knowing the truth had changed things, had created a sense of wariness in her that had never existed before . . . but that wasn't such a terrible thing, either. There was much to be done, and learning to be watchful was the first step.

She took a deep breath, letting it out slowly. There would be time for that later. Tonight, she had other business, and it was already late. Maybe too late. Neema looked at the clock again—

—And the door chimed softly at her, and she couldn't

get there fast enough. Another deep breath, a rush of belated fear that too much had been lost, and the door slid open.

The heaviness in her broke apart, the tears spilling out as Audrid, older, stronger, gazed lovingly into her eyes.

Eyes like my father's, Neema thought, and stepped forward, both of them reaching out, both of them crying.

"Mother," Neema whispered, and they stood in the open doorway for a long time, each unwilling to let the other go.

TORIAS

"Life's too short to deprive yourself of the simple pleasures."

—Torias Dax
"Facets"

Susan Wright

Susan Wright is the author of several *Star Trek* novels, including *The Best and the Brightest; Star Trek: Voyager—Violations; Star Trek: The Next Generation—Sins of Commission; Star Trek: Deep Space Nine—The Tempest;* the two-volume series, *The Badlands,* featuring all the *Star Trek* crews; and the upcoming two-volume mirror universe saga, *Dark Passions.*

Wright received her masters in art history from New York University in 1989 and has been a full-time writer in New York City since 1991. She's written a number of non-fiction books on art and popular culture, such as *Destination Mars: In Art, Myth, and Science* (Viking); *UFO Headquarters* (St. Martin's Press); and *New York City in Photographs: 1850–1945* (Barnes & Noble).

Wright's work has appeared in magazines such as *Cosmopolitan* and *Redbook.* She has also written comic books, including several for *Magic: The Gathering,* and the *Timewalker* series. She was contributing writer and editor on the CD-ROM action/strategy game *Magic: The Gathering—BattleMage.*

Infinity

Susan Wright

TORIAS DAX VERIFIED the heading of the shuttlecraft. All systems were go.

"I'm at full impulse power," he reported to control. "Engaging transwarp engines."

The starfield turned into broad streaks radiating from the middle of the viewscreen as the shuttle began the transition from one-quarter light-speed to warp 10, bypassing conventional warp speed entirely. Torias was pressed back into the pilot's seat. He reached out to adjust the warp frequency as it began to fluctuate within the dilithium crystals.

The velocity indicator went off the scale. The pressure against his body grew stronger.

"Engines at maximum output," he reported steadily.

When the shuttle crossed the warp 10 threshold, the strain suddenly released, letting him breathe again. A burst of light flooded the cockpit.

"I'm at warp 10!" Torias announced.

His adrenaline was pumping from the successful flight. He had done it dozens of times before, but he still savored the moment of victory.

The illusion was rudely broken when Captain Styles cracked the seal on the simulator room. Torias was back in the shuttle simulator on the Starfleet Spacedock station in orbit of Earth. But for a moment, the transwarp flight had seemed real.

"Well done." Styles strolled into the simulator, his swagger stick tucked under his arm. "You handled her nicely, Captain Dax."

"Thank you, Captain Styles," Torias replied courteously.

"It'll be some show when the *Excelsior* crosses the warp 10 barrier," Styles added, glancing around the simulator with great satisfaction. "I'll have the engineers refit this unit with the *Excelsior*'s bridge. We can begin the simulator runs immediately."

Torias kept his smile firmly in place. "After tomorrow, you won't need a shuttle simulator anymore. You'll have a real shuttle that can travel at transwarp speed."

"Yes, that's the plan." Styles paced around the simulator, undoubtedly with an eye to ripping out the fittings.

Torias tolerated Captain Styles as a means to an end. Styles was scheduled to take official command of the Federation starship *Excelsior* at the commissioning ceremonies in two days. But first Torias would get his chance. The transwarp team had received permission from Starfleet Command to flight test the transwarp shuttle tomorrow. Getting Styles's permission to proceed was a mere formality, but Torias knew that Styles could delay the test if he decided it was in his best interest.

"The Great Experiment," Captain Styles said, as if the words themselves were satisfying. Torias wasn't sure if he meant the transwarp project or the *Excelsior*. Probably both. Styles already seemed to consider them the same.

"Excuse me, sir," someone said as she entered the simulator. She wore a red jumpsuit uniform with the bright red collar and placard indicating she was still a cadet. Her dark hair was twisted up in a knot high on the back of her head, revealing pointed ears.

"Yes, Mr. Saavik?" Styles said absently.

"Sir, the fluctuations in the warp frequency continue to create a velocity differential." Saavik glanced at Torias, knowing he would be concerned. They had worked together for the past several weeks, ironing out the last snags in the transwarp drive.

Torias went directly to the control room adjacent to the simulator. The readouts were being discussed by the three quantum warp scientists who had developed the transwarp project from its inception at the new Daystrom Institute. Lieutenant Lahra and Professor Pokano were Starfleet officers, while Nilani Kahn was a fellow Trill. She was also Torias's wife.

"The unexplained anomalies in the warp frequency continue to cause fluctuations," Nilani told Torias, pointing to the spikes in the readout.

"It could be a phantom echo resulting from the lack of sensor data at warp 10," Torias reminded her.

"But it appears in the mathematical readout as well,"

Nilani said thoughtfully. "That's counterindicative of phantom echoes."

Captain Styles joined them, his chin lifted high with satisfaction. "We can't theorize about conditions on the other side of the threshold. Warp 10 itself is a theoretical impossibility."

"Not any longer, sir," Nilani pointed out respectfully. The alluring Trill scientist could silence Styles like no one else could.

Torias grinned at his wife behind the captain's back. He had taken to imitating Captain Styles when he and Nilani were alone in their quarters, usually by swinging around an old servo wrench in the same way Styles punctuated his conversations using his swagger stick. Nilani would curl up in laughter, saying his imitation was "too good."

Torias understood what she meant. He had been called arrogant himself by a few Starfleet officers since they had transferred the transwarp project to the Earth docking station. But no one knew that he was the fifth host of the Dax symbiont. Torias himself was young, having left the Symbiosis Institute only half a year ago after struggling for weeks through the confusion of his new memories. But his strongest memories were naturally of Dax's last host, the venerable Audrid, former head of the Trill Symbiosis Commission. Because of her many outstanding achievements, he felt a certain pressure to make his life remarkable, to live up to his symbiont and its former hosts.

Nilani said she had felt the same way at first, but having had her symbiont for nearly a year, she assured him that the fierce driving memories would surely ease. Nilani had always comforted him, as he had supported her during the years they had trained together as initiates at the Symbiosis Institute. It had created a deep bond between them, stronger than the trust usually shared by lovers. They had married the day after Torias left the institute, and they joined the transwarp developmental project soon after that.

Captain Styles smiled at Nilani. "I've asked Cadet Saavik to do the next simulator run. If you're ready to proceed?"

"Please give us a moment to clear the last test results, Captain." Nilani concentrated on her console. Lt. Lahra and Professor Pokano stayed at their posts, prepared to monitor the telemetry from the next simulator flight.

Torias was forced to step to the rear of the control room, watching through the one-way window as Saavik settled into the pilot's seat of the simulator.

"Proceed," Captain Styles ordered. He paced back and forth behind the scientists' shoulders, watching the readouts as the simulation ran. The silver end of the swagger stick protruded from under his left arm.

Saavik handled the simulator controls with competence. She had a girl's face, with full lips and cheeks, yet the stoic demeanor common among her people made her seem older than she was. Saavik had been assigned to assist with the flight simulations because of her exceptional expertise in warp navigation, despite being a cadet.

Watching her go through the simulation, Torias knew it wouldn't be much longer before he was officially thanked and shown to the door. After the *Excelsior* was commissioned and Captain Styles took command of the project, there would be dozens of experienced Starfleet pilots lining up to cross the transwarp threshold. A Trill volunteer wouldn't have a chance.

"Nearing critical velocity," Saavik reported.

Torias's reflection in the glass of the simulator looked

grim; a tall, slender, dark-haired man. Captain Styles was much closer to the window, with his thinning hair and trim mustache catching the light. Torias wished that Styles wouldn't lean so close to Nilani's upswept hair. He was practically breathing down her neck, making her auburn curls shift against her collar. But Nilani was concentrating on the simulation and she didn't notice anything else around her.

"The warp 10 threshold has been crossed," Saavik announced.

Torias was disturbed by Saavik's calm, assured tone. Not that he had anything against Saavik. She was a good kid—a genuine sentiment, though one undoubtedly amplified by the warm memories he'd inherited of Vulcans known to Dax's previous hosts.

But Saavik and the other Starfleet pilots represented an end to his dreams. Torias had worked too hard for this project to lose his chance now. The transwarp shuttle, the *Infinity*, was ready to fly. So was he.

"I'm reading minimal fluctuations in the warp frequency," Nilani reported. "They're within an acceptable margin of error."

"Well *done!*" Captain Styles was as pleased as if he had piloted the simulation himself.

Saavik left the simulator room as Lt. Lahra congratulated the cadet. "That was the best run we've had so far, Saavik."

Saavik shrugged off the compliment. "I compensated by recalibrating the field symmetry of the dilithium crystals. However I believe the fluctuations indicate there is a malfunction in the triangulation of the navigational system."

"I've been worried about the differential velocity, too,"

Nilani agreed. "The numbers work, but what if there's an unknown factor that is uncounted for by the simulation?"

Captain Styles let out a disbelieving snort of laughter. "Then why was Saavik's run clean?"

"The fluctuations appear to be random," Nilani said slowly.

"Perhaps additional theoretical work is needed before a test flight takes place," Saavik suggested.

Lt. Lahra and Professor Pokano joined in the discussion, considering the possibilities. Since warp 10 was theoretically infinite velocity, it should be possible to occupy every point in the universe simultaneously. But they didn't know if the navigational array would work in transwarp.

Torias patiently waited until the scientists were brought back to the same point. They couldn't answer their own questions because they were dealing with the unknown.

That's when he stepped forward. "We've done everything we can do in simulations. We won't know for sure until I test the transwarp shuttle at full impulse power."

"Quite right," Captain Styles agreed. "The only way to find out is to forge ahead."

Lt. Lahra and Professor Pokano agreed. Even Saavik nodded. Only Nilani was frowning slightly in concern. Torias resolutely avoided her eyes.

Styles saluted them with his stick. "Congratulations everyone. The test will proceed at oh-nine-hundred tomorrow morning. It will be a momentous event, a fitting kickoff for the commissioning ceremonies of the *Excelsior*."

Torias spent some time with Saavik going over the recalibrations of the field symmetry she had used to compensate for the warp frequency fluctuation in the dilithium crystals. Then he filed his report on the daily simulator run. He was pleased when he received his flight orders for the test the next day.

After that, he transported back to the *Excelsior*. The starship was enormous, the first in its class. A skeleton crew was already on board installing the transwarp core and running induction diagnostics on the systems. The *Excelsior* even had that new-ship smell; a hint of fresh coolant fluid, synthetic fibers, and recently scrubbed tritanium. Torias thought it was invigorating, but then again, he lived to fly new starships.

Torias and Nilani had been assigned quarters on board the *Excelsior* when the *Infinity* was transferred from the Daystrom Institute. Their rooms were clearly guest quarters rather than standard crew accommodations.

Though Torias knew that Nilani would be waiting for him, he stopped by the hangar deck to take one more look at the *Infinity*.

A security guard challenged Torias before recognizing him as part of the development team. Captain Styles had heightened security several weeks ago when the team informed him they were close to a breakthrough.

Torias paced around the *Infinity,* as familiar as an old friend. He had helped develop the structure of the shuttle and its appealing ergonomic style. The bow came to a low point, and the hull swept back at a sharp angle. The nacelles were tucked underneath the body of the shuttle.

Torias wished the commissioning of the *Excelsior* had been delayed a week or two, allowing them to complete the flight test in a quiet, professional manner. But Captain Styles liked to make an impact, and he was using the transwarp project for every bit of notoriety it could bring him.

Dignitaries were already arriving to view the flight test. The chief of Starfleet Command himself, Admiral Morrow, had transported up from Starfleet Headquarters and was staying in his quarters aboard Spacedock. Nilani had mentioned that another noteworthy member of Star-feet brass, Admiral Kirk, was coming in tonight from the Academy.

Torias still half-expected a hand to fall on his shoulder, informing him that he had been replaced with a Starfleet pilot for the flight test. It would surely complicate diplomatic relations with Trill if he was replaced at this late date, but they were dealing with a great deal of power in this project. Transwarp technology could transform interstellar travel and change the way everyone lived.

Torias ran his hand along the port hull of the *Infinity.* There was a lot of activity on the hangar deck with techni-cians noisily adjusting a bent pylon on another shuttle near-by. But Torias had eyes only for *his* ship. Together they would make history.

His fingers brushed over the name. The waiting was over. Tomorrow he would reach for infinity.

When Torias returned to their quarters, he found Ni-lani hunched over her tricorder. Her brow was furrowed and one foot rapidly tapped the table in front of the couch. A sure sign she was distressed.

"What have you got there?" Torias leaned over and kissed the top of her head. He breathed in deeply the fresh scent of her hair.

"The readouts from your simulator run," Nilani said without looking up.

"Aren't you going to give me a kiss?" Torias asked plaintively. "I've had a hard day busting the warp 10 barrier, you know."

Nilani raised her head to return his kiss.

"Mmm . . ." Torias murmured. "That's a better way to greet your loving mate." He went toward the food slot. "What do you want to eat tonight?"

"It doesn't matter to me." Nilani returned to the readouts on her tricorder.

Torias could see it wasn't going to be easy to distract her, so he didn't bother. While she worked on the mathematical calculations of the transwarp drive, he dialed up their dinner. He asked for samples of a dozen of their favorite foods, many of them discovered while they were working at the Daystrom Institute.

He ordered the computer to play some Trill bell music for background ambiance, while he set out one glass of a bubbly celebratory wine that was popular on Earth. None for him tonight. He had to be sharp tomorrow for the flight test. Tomorrow night he would share a whole bottle with his wife.

"Dinner's served," Torias announced.

Nilani looked confused, as if she hadn't realized what he was doing.

"Put that away," he told her. "Let's spend some time together."

Nilani sat down across from him, her sweet face unusually serious. "I'm worried about the flight test tomorrow. I don't think the shuttle is ready."

"It's ready." Torias scooped up some of the crispy shellfish she liked. He fed her one and her lips automatically closed around it. "Even if it does blow up, I'll be wearing the emergency transporter suit, so I'll be fine."

"Don't say that," Nilani protested with a shudder.

"You should be glad." Torias leaned closer. "We've done it! We've worked nonstop for months to develop transwarp, and we've done it."

"But there are so many unknowns in multispectral subspace mechanics—"

"And tomorrow, we'll know more," he interrupted. "I fully expect there'll be a few kinks to work out. That's what flight testing is all about, to work out the last details."

"But it's so dangerous . . ." Nilani murmured, bending her head.

"It's my job," Torias reminded her. "You knew that when you married me. I've been training for this for months, wearing that infernal ETS."

Nilani actually smiled at the thought of the days he had spent in the emergency transporter suit; flying the shuttle, walking through the corridors of *Excelsior,* even while he was eating dinner. But it had conditioned his reaction time to the bulky, mesh-line jumpsuit and helmet. In effect, the ETS was a modern analog to the ejection seats of some primitive aircraft. The suit was a pattern enhancer designed to relay homing telemetry to a transporter on board the *Excelsior* that was on constant standby.

"It's not as dangerous as you're imagining," Torias said lightly. "I think you worry too much because you don't know what you'd do without me—"

Nilani shook her head and raised her hand to his lips to stop him.

"Then come here and kiss me." Torias insisted on pulling her closer to sit on his knees.

She laughed and cuddled into his lap, returning his kisses. The bell music played on.

After that, it was all right. They talked about everything but the flight test as they sampled the delicious food. Nilani told him that Lt. Lahra was going to recommend her for a permanent post on the *Excelsior* to assist in training the Starfleet engineers in transwarp theory. Torias was agreeable to staying on with Starfleet, but Nilani thought it would be difficult working with Captain Styles.

So they talked about returning to Trill where they could create their own transwarp design facility. Nilani seemed to prefer that idea. Torias didn't care where they went, as long as they were together. No long separations for them. If they had to, they would take turns helping each other further their careers. That's why a Trill transwarp facility appealed to both of them. Torias could train the pilots while Nilani headed up the developmental design team.

Torias stood up with Nilani in his arms, spinning her around the room. Their sleek Starfleet quarters suddenly felt very alien. "Then let's plan on going home, what do you say?" Torias asked.

Nilani's arms tightened around his neck. "Yes! As soon as I get clearance to copy the data on our research."

"That should be no trouble; it's part of our technological exchange agreement," Torias said.

"But there's the commissioning ceremonies for the *Excelsior* day after tomorrow," Nilani said doubtfully.

"I know you want to meet this Admiral Kirk everyone's talking about," Torias teased, rubbing his nose against hers. "I don't mean that soon."

"It's not just Kirk," Nilani protested. "It'll be exciting to see the *Excelsior* launched. And I'd like to incorporate the results from the flight test tomorrow. . . ."

Torias silenced her with kisses before she could get worried again about the test. He carried her into their bedroom. It didn't matter when they left or how long they stayed. They had their whole lives ahead of them.

Torias was finally able to let the preflight euphoria wash over him . . . knowing that anything was possible. He always felt this way before a test flight. It was even better than going into battle. The transwarp flight would give him the chance to do something remarkable, something that would change people's lives.

The anticipation made him heady as he caressed Nilani, wanting to touch every part of her. Standing on the threshold of infinite speed was a powerful stimulant, and making love to Nilani took him right over the edge of his senses.

Torias woke early the next morning, feeling fresh and wide awake the moment his eyes opened. He carefully slid out of bed without disturbing Nilani. Her beautiful curves were tempting under the flimsy sheet, but he restrained himself from waking her.

In the fresher, his flight suit was waiting. Torias quickly washed up and dressed. His spots were dark, like his hair, and were stark against his pale skin. Pausing for a moment, he stared at his black eyes. "Too intense" one young woman had called him, just before he had entered the Symbiosis Institute. Well, that intensity had gotten him everything he wanted, including Nilani and the transwarp flight test.

Torias walked softly through the bedroom. He knew the comm would go off in a few minutes to wake Nilani, but he wanted to slip away before that. He wanted to remember her like she was last night, warm and loving, not nervous and analytical like she would be this morning.

At the doorway, he looked back. Her hair spread against the pillow, the fiery strands glowing in the dim light of the bedroom. One hand was palm-up on the bed, and he wanted to kiss it. Instead he whispered softly, "I love you."

He knew she would have too much to do in the science lab before and during the test to worry. By the time he got back, she would no longer be angry at him for running off without a proper good-bye.

Before Torias left their quarters, he found her tricorder where she had dropped it last night. He propped it up on the table next to the door where she would see it. She was always misplacing her tricorder—his sweet absent-minded professor.

During the prelaunch preparations, Torias went over the entire shuttle with a hand-scanner. He was looking for micro-fractures that could react adversely to the slightest velocity differential in the hull. But the *Infinity* had been reinforced and was sealed tight. Even if there was unusual stress on the hull, the extra fusion generator would compensate by increasing the structural integrity field.

Torias slid out from under the starboard nacelle and was brushing off his hands when Captain Styles rounded the shuttlecraft. A group of a dozen or more Starfleet officers were following him.

"There you are, my boy," Styles said heartily. "Ready for the big flight?"

"Aye, aye, Captain," Torias said evenly.

As they came closer, Captain Styles gestured to a tall dark gentleman wearing an admiral's placard and collar. "Torias Dax, this is Admiral Morrow, Chief of Starfleet Command. Admiral, this is the young man I've been telling you about."

"Pleased to meet you." Admiral Morrow shook Torias's hand in the human ritual greeting. His thick black mustache almost hid his smile, and a dusting of gray lightened his short curling black hair. "Starfleet is glad to have this opportunity to work so closely with Trill in this bold undertaking."

"Thank you." Torias relied on past-host memories of diplomatic protocol. "Trill is proud to be a part of this historic event with the Federation."

Frown lines appeared between the Admiral's eyes. "As long as the shuttle is ready."

"The *Infinity* is ready," Torias confirmed.

But he tensed when the admiral waved a young woman out of the knot of Starfleet assistants who were politely standing back. "Cadet Saavik has a suggestion. Cadet?"

Saavik came forward to give her report. "I believe I have discovered a way to prevent the fluctuations you experienced in the warp frequency. It would require an alteration in the computer software program to synchronize the navigational constant with the transwarp field of the *Infinity.*"

Captain Styles seemed irritated. "It would take days to reprogram the navigational computer, Cadet. Then another week of simulator runs before flight testing could take place."

"But if it would be better to wait," Morrow cautioned,

"then let's take our time. This is an important experiment, and I wouldn't like anything to go wrong."

Admiral Morrow glanced at the wall of windows lining the upper hangar deck. Torias followed his gaze and for the first time realized the observation lounge was filled with people. Many of them were wearing the formal gold-braided Starfleet uniform. This was turning into quite the event.

Torias had already noticed the group of Starfleet pilots gathered to one side of the bay, restricted from getting any closer to the test shuttle. But their envious expressions spoke clearly—they all wanted a crack at the *Infinity*. Perhaps Morrow was also seeing the advantages to having a Starfleet pilot be the first to cross the transwarp threshold.

Torias firmly stilled his panic. He wasn't going to let the test flight slip away from him now. He asked Saavik, "Did you show the scientists your calculations?"

"Yes, they agreed the alterations may correct the problem."

"They didn't have much time to examine your theory, did they?" When she shook her head, he said thoughtfully, "Then it must be an extension of the work they were doing, rather than a new approach."

She raised one brow slightly. "That is correct."

Torias turned to Admiral Morrow. "Cadet Saavik has merely suggested a refinement in our current navigational procedure. However, the project scientists have already agreed that the fluctuations are within an acceptable margin of error. I'm sure we'll discover additional areas of refinement during this flight test."

"Quite right!" Captain Styles agreed. "The transwarp

design will undoubtedly be improved as we put the *Infinity* through her paces."

"What's the level of risk in testing the shuttle with its current navigational program?" Morrow asked Torias.

"Minimal," Torias replied. "With the use of the ETS, I would say the risk is closer to nonexistent."

"Ah, yes," Captain Styles said. "The emergency transporter suit. An incredible machine. Would you like to see it, Admiral?"

Captain Styles led Admiral Morrow toward the suit where it hung on the rack, prepared for Torias to put on prior to departure. Torias had made several tests of the emergency transporter suit, and each time he had been examined and cleared by Dr. Dareel, the Trill doctor in residence at the Trill Embassy on Earth. Torias had also been examined by Dr. Christine Chapel of Starfleet Medical, but the Federation doctors had been unable to differentiate the symbiont from his Trill anatomy. Trill continued to be committed to a controversial policy of nondisclosure when it came to the symbionts, but Torias and Nilani had dutifully complied.

While the rest of the crowd of Starfleet observers joined Admiral Morrow around the suit, Saavik stayed behind. "As I indicated," she told Torias, "I do not believe you understand the implications of my research. The subspace torque from the differential velocity could destroy the shuttle."

"She's a strong ship." Torias patted the tritanium hull of *Infinity*. He didn't blame Saavik for her insistence. She was just an eager kid trying to impress her superiors.

"I do not understand your desire to continue with the flight test," Saavik said.

"You're a navigator, not a test pilot," Torias reminded her. "Most people would delay forever rather than take a chance with the unknown."

Saavik shook her head slightly, looking perplexed.

"Come Saavik!" Captain Styles ordered from across the hangar deck. "You can discuss your theories later. Captain Dax has a flight test to complete."

Saavik glanced down, absorbing the public rebuff without a murmur. Then she told Torias, "I wish you well."

"Thank you, Saavik." Torias winked at her. "You'll see that I'm right."

Getting into the emergency transporter suit took some time, but finally Torias was ready in the pilot's seat of the *Infinity*. His fingers were left free of the mesh suit, and he acknowledged the final cross-checks with a few taps on the panels.

Then he activated the viewscreen, clearing the pale blue Federation symbol of a starfield supported by laurels. He opened a channel to the transwarp science lab on board the *Excelsior*.

Nilani answered, looking up at the screen. "You're ready, my love?" she asked.

"I'm waiting for the go-ahead." He thought it was just like her not to mention the way he had left this morning. "I'll be back soon."

Nilani glanced over her shoulder to make sure no one was listening. "Warp 10 might be just fast enough."

Torias smiled into her eyes, remembering last night. They both laughed as they signed off. He couldn't wait to celebrate with her.

He switched to the command channel. "Shuttlecraft *Infinity* prepared for launch."

The hangar deck had been cleared except for the people filling the observation lounge along the upper level.

"Depressurizing hangar deck," Captain Styles replied. He was standing at the command console in the launching control room. "Infinity, *you are cleared for launch."*

The lights flashed red in the bay to warn any lingerers that the atmosphere was being removed. Torias settled his helmet one last time as the tractor beam conveyed him out of the *Excelsior's* hangar deck. He could see arms waving in the observation lounge.

Engaging thrusters, he took over control of the *Infinity*. He maneuvered through the inside of the enormous Spacedock station, a curved enclosure containing a number of Starfleet vessels.

As the *Infinity* moved away from the starships, Torias could see the interior walls of the station lined by observation windows. Some were several levels high, and they also were filled with people waving at him.

The great square docking doors were opening, revealing space beyond. The shuttle passed through, then lifted over the spindle-shaped station, clearing the series of graceful domes and spires that capped the top.

As the *Infinity* pulled away from the station, the brilliant blue and white Earth dominated the viewscreen. At a distance of ten-thousand meters, the station looked small against the planet below.

"Infinity is clear of the docking station," Torias reported.

"Bon voyage, Infinity," Captain Styles said over the comm.

Torias engaged impulse engines and the *Infinity* shot away at one-quarter impulse.

For a moment Torias felt as if he were back in the simulator. The two cockpits were identical. But the subtle movements of the genuine shuttle couldn't be imitated. His breath came shorter as his body reacted to the experience of hurtling through space. Some people couldn't tolerate space, but Torias had loved it from his first interplanetary voyage when he was a boy.

"Increasing speed to one-half impulse," Torias reported, trying not to think of all the people listening back at the station.

The velocity indicator climbed to three-quarters, then reached full impulse speed.

"Infinity, *you are cleared for transwarp velocity,*" Captain Styles informed him.

"Engaging transwarp engines," Torias confirmed.

The shuttle began to shake and the interior lights dimmed. The glow from the screen brightened as the stars blurred into streaks. Torias was pushed back into his seat as the transwarp drive leapt beyond warp speeds.

"Vector's drifting!" he called, noticing the navigational shift. "I'm stabilizing the field symmetry."

The vector wavered then held steady. He kept a close watch on the warp frequency, but it, too, held steady. Everything was go.

"Velocity is off the scale. I'm approaching the threshold."

Torias could feel it . . . as if he was stretching out and slowing down. His hand moved slower as he adjusted the flow regulator to the dilithium crystals. The warp frequency fluctuated—

* * *

Suddenly the universe was still. And for an instant, Torias was everywhere.

He was not only in the pilot's seat of the Infinity, he was also on the bridge of the Excelsior, and on the observation deck with all the dignitaries. He could see Saavik bite her lip in an uncharacteristic show of concern. He could see the blood vessels quivering on the surface of her eye. . . .

But somehow Torias was also back on Trill, in the farthest depths of the symbiont pools. He was flying over the wind-blown icy cliffs of Tenara, and standing in the purple waters of the southern ocean with the sun beating down on his head. . . .

He was in places too numerous to count, with experiences flashing through him; from a deep space freighter near a supernova to a slow-moving microbe on an inductor chip. He could hear the voices and cries of trillions of beings merging into one vast booming, living mass. He could see everything at once. He knew everything. He realized he could be anywhere he wanted to be.

At the same time he was standing next to Nilani in the science lab where it was perfectly silent. She was radiant, her hair and skin aglow. He felt himself reach out to touch her face, feeling his fingers brush aside individual atoms as they parted the air, feeling everything. . . .

Nilani's eyes were fixed on the viewscreen as the Infinity exploded. She tried to tell herself the flare was simply a result of crossing the warp 10 threshold. She couldn't believe her eyes.

But everyone's reaction was unmistakable. Lt. Lahra cried out and covered her mouth with both hands.

"Transporter room?" Captain Styles called through the open channel from the hangar deck. The hush seemed too heavy to bear.

"We have a medical emergency!" the transporter room responded. *"Something's wrong. He's having trouble breathing—"*

The communication was cut, maybe by someone who didn't want the news going over an open channel. But Nilani was already running to the turbolift.

She could hear people talking to her but she didn't know what they were saying. It didn't matter. Nothing mattered but finding Torias.

The transporter room was crowded but the others parted to let her through. Dr. Chapel was scanning Torias, and she glanced up at Nilani, her expression stark. "The shuttle was breaking apart when he transported. He's suffered massive internal injuries. I'll have to operate."

Nilani knelt down next to Torias, her heart clenching at the way his body was contorted. He looked bad, very bad. She might have stared at him forever, but her years of training spoke for her. "Stasis," she managed to say. "He must be put in stasis until our doctors can get to him."

Dr. Chapel hesitated, but medical protocols involving Trills were strict. "I'll transport him directly into a stasis chamber," she agreed.

As Torias dematerialized, Nilani reached out to touch him. She couldn't bear the agony on his face. Then he was gone.

"The *Infinity* didn't pass the warp 10 threshold," someone said regretfully.

It was Saavik. The cadet helped her to stand up. Nilani wasn't sure how Saavik had gotten there, but she was grateful to be able to cling to someone familiar.

"I am sorry," Saavik said. "I attempted to warn Captain Dax that a hazardous subspace torque could occur."

"He convinced us it would work," Nilani said, dazed.

She saw faces everywhere, watching her, their eyes sympathetic. It was too much.

"Perhaps I failed to communicate my concerns properly," Saavik said.

Nilani realized that Saavik was upset, as upset as Vulcans ever got. She also realized there would be terrible consequences for everyone involved. But right now, she couldn't think.

"Please take me to the sickbay," Nilani told her. "I want to be with Torias."

Nilani reached the stasis chamber not long before Dr. Dareel transported up from the Trill Embassy in Nagano. While the doctor examined Torias through the stasis field, Nilani stayed nearby. She couldn't touch Torias while he was in stasis, and that bothered her.

She didn't want to believe it, but she could read the soft pings on the monitors as well as the medical technicians. There was nothing they could do to save Torias. His body lived while he was in stasis, but there was no brain activity.

Soon the Trill diplomatic ferry arrived with its appropriately equipped medical lab, where Dr. Dareel could perform the delicate operation to remove the still-living symbiont from its host. That was the important thing, to save the symbiont with its precious memories. Everyone on board was congratulating Nilani for her quick thinking. Stasis had saved Dax.

Once the symbiont was removed, Nilani was allowed to be with Torias in the operating room as his lifesigns faded. No one watched her cry because no one was interested in the empty host . . . the flesh she yearned for.

She couldn't stop touching him to feel his fading warmth, to smell his skin. She couldn't face the long years ahead, knowing how deeply she loved him, knowing how much he loved her. She couldn't imagine what life would be like alone, with everything they had planned and dreamed impossible now. Gone in a heartbeat.

As the doctor carried away the symbiont, Nilani was alone with Torias at last. She pressed his hand against her cheek, touching it against the spot that still tingled ever since that final, terrible moment in the science lab . . . and she knew that moment would define the rest of her lives.

JORAN

"I've been ignored far too long."

—Joran Dax
"Field of Fire"

S. D. Perry

"Allegro Ouroboros in D Minor" is S. D. Perry's second contribution to *The Lives of Dax*, following "Sins of the Mother." She plans to return to the *Star Trek* universe soon.

Robert Simpson

Robert Simpson made his first professional sale at age sixteen and in the last eighteen years has been an agent, a writer, and an editor who has worked with hundreds of authors including the "ABC" of science fiction—Isaac Asimov, Ray Bradbury, and Arthur C. Clarke. A former editor for *Twilight Zone* magazine, he has also written and edited novels, websites, CD-ROMs, comics, magazines, and other projects for Lucasfilm, Paramount Pictures, HarperCollins, Topps Publishing, DC Comics, Nickelodeon, Bantam Books, Pocket Books, Golden Books, Scott Rudin Prods., Marvel Comics, The United Nations/World Health Organization, and the New York chapter of The National Epilepsy Foundation. A fan of true crime stories, he also served for a brief time as the reprint editor on the classic book of murder and obsession *Helter Skelter.* He lives in New York.

Allegro Ouroboros in D Minor

S. D. Perry and Robert Simpson

THE FIRST NOTES spilled out into the darkened room like rain, soft but not gentle, conjuring memories of twilight summer storms from childhoods past—of suddenness, of unexpected drama, of something new in the face of the existing. It was a strong beginning, and as Joran's fingers found the keys, stroking the composition to life, he felt its power wash over and through him with the violence of a tempest. Thought fell away, replaced by feelings of connection and movement that harmonized perfectly with the smooth sounds rising up from the *syn lara*. With the pale,

dancing light and deep undertone of his most recent con-
quest playing alongside his last, both images in their proper
places above and behind the stringed instrument, he could
feel the piece coming together like never before.

In his space of concentration, he was reborn into the
music, becoming the body within the storm. He rediscovered
the melody of dissonance that was its heart, and felt the beat
in his own veins. From the shifting light that bathed the
room in motion, he created thunder, becoming its wrath
even as he sought shelter within the circle that was forming,
shining into life and fading to ash, the end as the beginning—

A single note hesitated, stretching an instant too
long . . . and it was over, that simply. The music was lost, and
he was only Joran Dax again, hunched over the grand *syn
lara* in the near dark of his private parlor.

"Lights," he snapped, his voice sharp with frustration.
The sudden glow from the wall panels faded the dual projections into ghosts, illuminating the soundproofed chamber and
transforming it from a place of dreams to a banal reality—and
illuminating the problem, which he'd already guessed at. A
slender crust of dried blood had wedged between two of the
keys, changing the delicate quaver of the middle C to a
crotchet.

His impatience had cost him this night's practice. He'd
been overly eager, rushing to see what would be added to the
piece before cleaning up properly; it wasn't the first time.
Joran sighed, suddenly too exhausted to be angry with himself.

He stood up and moved toward the door, really seeing
himself for the first time in hours as he stepped out of the

hidden studio and into his small, but elegant, living room. The subtle lighting that played off the richly adorned walls was somehow more revealing than the utilitarian brightness of his composition room. There were rips in his smudged clothes that he hadn't noticed before, and his hands were filthy, rimes of dark matter beneath his nails. Really, he had to learn to control his enthusiasm; the *syn lara* was an instrument capable of great emotional power, but it was delicately structured—

It had been a long day; he'd see to the *syn lara* tomorrow before he started editing the new program. For now, a shower, a hot meal, and a good night's sleep were what he needed most.

"That and an alibi or two," he said softly, and grinned, pleased with his newfound ability to laugh at himself. Belar's sense of humor had tended toward nonexistent.

But with Dax . . . everything is different now. Everything is the way it should be. The way it was meant to be.

Three more notes; after that, Joran Dax wouldn't need an alibi. After that, those who surely sought to destroy him would be forced to acknowledge his contribution to infinity, whether they appreciated its complexities or not. Whatever happened to him, the composition would inspire beings the universe over to a new understanding of life.

His grin widened as he walked toward the bathroom, shaking his head. Three more, and the quinary would be complete. Assuming he could work unmolested for another week, two at most, Joran Dax would redefine the meaning of inspiration; the time was at hand for him to show them all.

*   *   *

The park wasn't anything special, but it was close to home, quiet, and reasonably flat. Verjyl Gard had always liked to jog, but he'd left steep hills and rugged terrain behind along with his thirties. Real running was for athletes, for people interested in physical fitness; for him, mornings in the park were about sanity and fresh air, about not having to think for a little while unless it was to decide on what to have for breakfast.

He'd been imagining something deep-fried until he saw Kov jogging toward him, the younger man's carefully blank expression killing Gard's appetite. *No breakfast today.* Gard continued his shagging pace, ignoring the sudden vague urge to turn and run the other way. It wouldn't change anything. He could only pray that it was a standard consultation.

Kov fell into step beside him, breathing easily. Together, they jogged through the sun-dappled trees for a full minute without speaking, the silence broken only by the soft pelt of shoe against path, by distant bird song, and the rush of blood in his ears. Gard ran through what he remembered from the morning newscasts, knowing that Kov would wait until he was ready; he always did.

"Is it the girl?" Gard asked finally. "The student?"

Kov nodded. "Yeah. We think she's the second . . . the first was two weeks ago, at the Devritane Museum—"

"—the shuttle pilot, I remember," Gard said, sighing inwardly. He couldn't help remembering. It was what he did best.

"We also think . . . we have multiple lines here, Gard."

Gard felt something tighten inside, but only nodded warily. So much for praying.

They reached a fork in the path and Gard steered them to the right, knowing they'd be less likely to run into anyone along the more heavily wooded route. Talking about murder was bad enough; it was talking about the murderer—apparently, *this* murderer—that they needed privacy for.

In all the centuries of Gard's life, there had only been a handful who'd known what the symbiont's forte was. Even after the impressively complicated screening process he'd gone through prior to being joined, Verjyl Slest had been surprised—although very little surprised him anymore.

Murder was rare on Trill, and only the unjoined killed; that was what he'd believed before he was joined, what the world still believed. Candidates for joining were balanced, well-adjusted people; the mentally or emotionally infirm were weeded out before they even got close to the first interview, and for a joined Trill to commit murder . . . impossible. Unthinkable. Law-enforcement agencies had never had to deal with such a case.

And they never will, Verjyl had quickly realized. *Not as long as there's Gard. . . .*

Each joining created uniqueness, the fruition of the host's potential combined with the symbiont's. According to the Symbiosis Commission, an unsuitable host would reject his or her symbiont in a matter of days; it happened, but rarely. But even more uncommon was the symbiosis that birthed a monster; a darkness within the host brought into the foreground, a creature that was the direct consequence of joining.

Gard understood anomalies; the Gard symbiont was one of a kind, old enough to have forgotten how it came to be what it was.

But not to forget what I'm here to do. Never.

Gard's hosts had all trained extensively to prepare for

such instances—and there had been only four. Four monsters; combined, they'd killed thirty-seven people and destroyed the lives of countless more. Two of the four had committed suicide, perhaps the symbiont exerting its last shred of control; one had been killed trying to escape the authorities, back when the authorities still enforced the law with sticks and stones—and the fourth had been executed by the soldier Kirista Gard, some 90 years past. . . .

. . . *its gaze, as bleak and cold and desolate as deepest, blackest winter, its lips curled with hatred, the slick intelligence behind its mask of flesh* . . .

Gard slowed to a walk, breathing raggedly, a little shaken by the sudden intensity of Kirista's memory. Kov stopped and watched him, and Gard was surprised to note that the young op seemed worn out, his face flushed. In the eight years that Kov had been his go-between to the Symbiosis Commission, Gard had never known him to work up much of a sweat over anything.

We're all getting old. Old and tired.

"Let's walk for a while," Gard said, smiling a little at the obvious relief that flitted across Kov's face. "In fact, why don't you fill me in on the way back to your transport?"

They both smiled, and Gard did his best to enjoy it; odds were, the days to come would bring very little to be happy about.

The outdoor cafe *St'asla* sat at the edge of the campus common, fitted with all the pretensions and posturing that only a student-run cafe could manage. Today it was more crowded than usual, the Tenaran Music Academy's best and brightest indulged in a frenzy of table-hopping, the late afternoon air filled with their mindless buzzing. The discovery of Mehta Bren's body was undoubtedly the most exciting thing to have happened in quite some time.

An impromptu concert had broken out on the carefully manicured lawn across from where Joran sat, a memorial for the slain flautist. The musicians—two young women laboring over the strings of an Astian *bi-tanle* and a joined professor, a not-so-accomplished dulcimer player—had chosen an overused mourning piece, the unapologetically maudlin *Dal's Requiem Trio,* and had drawn a rather large group of listeners.

Joran watched the crowd, wondering at the tear-streaked faces and slumped shoulders as he sipped at his wine. Mehta's talents had been unremarkable, to say the least, and he knew for a fact that she'd had few friends; the false sentiment was distasteful to him. What was it about death that brought out such hypocrisy? People who'd never met her were suddenly overwhelmed with emotion, remembering the girl's genius, fondly spinning tales of her great wit and beauty, imagining that they knew her. The truth was, he was closer to her than any of them. Unlike the assembled faithless, her death actually meant something to him; musically, the first-year student would accomplish far more by her passing than she ever could have managed had she continued to practice—

Joran's thoughts were cut short as the musicians began a new piece, the soft opening strains of T'saln's *Cicadian Suite No. 9* floating across the lawn like a haunted breeze. Joran closed his eyes, frowning, soothed and troubled at once; it had been one of his favorite compositions when he'd still been Joran Belar, written by a Vulcan woman well before Dax's first implantation. The simple repeating melody of the piece was built upon by graceful, willowy harmonies that grew more complex with each repetition, the notes flowing into one another, becoming, reaching . . .

Belar's first year at the Academy, so arrogant, so sure of himself—young, bright, a full scholarship handed to him when his older brother had been forced to seek patronage from the Arts Board. Called to play his best work by the instructor of Advanced Interpretation, the first class of his first day, and choosing No. 9. Executing it flawlessly in front of his "peers," knowing how good it was, turning to accept their envy and admiration as the last notes spiraled away into silence—

Dr. Silvet nodding, smiling, her tone gentle, her words brutal, impossible to forget. "An ambitious choice, Mr. Belar, and technically perfect . . . but did you feel anything?"

She addressed the class, turning his shame into a lesson for all. "Notes can be mastered by anyone; that is the craft of music. But the art . . . you must learn to find the immortal that exists in each piece, the continuity of the eternal that elevates a series of notes into something more—and to recognize it, you must feel it. If you can't find your place within the living cycle that is music, if you can't learn humility in the face of the eternal, than you can never hope for better than technical mastery."

The living cycle. The face of the eternal. The birth and rebirth, the joining, the perfect circle, the five—

—applause, and Joran blinked, startled from his thoughts. The trio of musicians were bowing humbly, accepting praise for their amateur efforts from the gathered listeners, even those seated at the cafe. Joran closed his eyes again, irritated with the obvious sincerity of the crowd; hadn't they heard the fumbled notes? Was he the only one who'd perceived the mawkish execution of the secondary interlude, *largo* that had been written as *andante?* Pathetic, just as Mehta had been in the end, absolutely—

"Tragic, isn't it?"

Joran looked up to see a young woman standing by his table, her dark gaze fixed on the musicians as they put away their instruments. He wasn't particularly interested in gossiping about the deceased, but it wouldn't do to seem *too* uninterested. As it was, he was taking a risk; he had a recital in a few days, and hadn't planned to be seen on campus before then. He applied a sorrowful expression, aware that his whim could cost him if he wasn't careful.

"Yes. I heard she had great potential . . . such a waste."

The woman arched an eyebrow. "Actually, I meant the performance," she said lightly, still watching the players. "I think we were the only ones not clapping. . . ."

She looked down at him when he didn't respond immediately, smiling nervously. "I'm sorry, you're right, of course—I just thought they weren't very good, but I didn't mean—"

Joran smiled back at her, unable to resist. "Don't be sorry. I agree, they weren't up to it. . . . Although not many are."

She lifted her chin, and somehow then spoke without a trace of conceit. "I am."

He felt a flutter of amazement at her brashness, and though he knew he should let the conversation drop, that he shouldn't be seen talking to anyone here about anything, he suddenly realized that he would deeply regret not learning more about her.

He motioned at the chair beside his, letting the charm into his smile. "I'm Joran Dax, I used to be a student here. Please . . ."

"Temzia Nirenn," she said as she sat down, "and I'm still a student here, but I'm starting to wonder if it's worth the effort. I mean, are they going to teach me anything new, or is it going to be the same old tune about examining my feelings and becoming the instrument of true art?"

Joran laughed out loud, enchanted—and as they slipped easily into a conversation that delighted them both as afternoon deepened toward dusk, Joran found himself feeling more than amazement at the intensity and passion of the young woman.

It wasn't until much later that he realized it was fear.

Mehta Bren could have been sleeping, curled beneath the bright lights of the lab in the sterile cold, her delicate features unmarred by the violence that had taken her life. With the table's stasis field deactivated, the illusion was quickly lost; the slender hole in her abdomen began to seep, and even as Gard gazed down at her, he imagined that he could see the last blush of life drain away, the lines of her face settling into permanence.

Sorrow, anger, despair. Gard watched her until he felt nothing but curiosity and the small measure of guilt that came with the shift of emotion. As with the pilot from two weeks before, the murder weapon had been a *sh'uk,* an antique; it had been nearly three centuries since Trill authorities had used the needle-shaped tool for executions, a quick and relatively painless death in a time when death had still been crime's answer.

Neither quick nor painless for her, for either of them . . .

There was no evidence of torture, but in both cases, selected vertebrae had been broken, effectively paralyzing the

victims prior to their deaths—the forensics teams had esti-
mated twenty minutes to an hour on both victims, long
enough for the killer to . . . to do *something,* something he
wanted his victims to witness or experience.

The pilot, one Jelim Niecta, had already been immolated
in keeping with his family's wishes, but the body's condition
had been extensively documented; Gard had studied the files
in the flyer on their way over the Ganses Peninsula, returning
again and again to what little the Devritane Museum' s sur-
veillance camera had gathered from the night of the murder. A
dark shape in a darker hallway, nothing established except that
the killer was humanoid. Still, Gard had watched obsessively,
memorizing the smudge of blackness. If Kov had been bored
by the repetition, he'd had the tact not to say so.

Two murders with a *sh'uk,* no witnesses, no apparent
motive or connection between the victims except that neither had been joined. Gard knew that was important, but
that he wouldn't know why until he had a chance to investigate further—and that the killer would give them very little
to investigate. In his experience, joined murderers were ex-
ceptionally careful about what they decided to reveal.

Multiple lines . . . the suggestion of past-host influence
that had flagged the crimes was unmistakable, and it was the
best chance they'd have to catch the killer. No matter how
clever the current host, there were some things that he or she
wouldn't recognize as intimations of self, wouldn't know to
avoid. Gard had been called in to analyze the traces, to build
a history for the monster, and he could only hope to finish
and apply his work before it killed again.

Mehta Bren. What a pretty name. A pretty girl. To see life
ripped away from one so young. . . . There was something

inside of him that ran deeper than emotion, that accepted the reality of her death and used it to create a kind of need—for justice, for a return of balance to his own life and the lives of his kind. It was self-manipulation perhaps, a trick—

—*but I won't rest until I find who did this to you,* he thought, staring into the face of a girl who could no longer care on her own behalf. *Mehta . . .*

"Forensics has a reconstruction on her," Kov said softly, and Gard finally looked up from the near-sleeping child. The op stood by the door, arms folded, his expression as impenetrable as usual. Gard liked Kov; what others perceived as unfeeling in the young agent, Gard knew to be professional detachment. He'd been around long enough to recognize the pain that Kov buried, the tightness around the eyes and mouth that spoke of learning how to avoid certain thoughts on nights when sleep wouldn't come.

It took one to know one, or so he'd heard. He nodded, motioning for the lab attendant to take care of Mehta before joining Kov. Together, the two men walked down the well-scrubbed corridor of the TSC's regional science facility, Gard reflecting absently on the progress of technology. The first time he'd tracked a joined Trill, there had been no such thing as harnessed electricity. But then, there'd been no such thing as criminal psychology, either; Trill had believed that the Butcher of Balin had been possessed by evil spirits. Considering his crimes, perhaps they hadn't been so far off the mark.

"You ever seen one of these?" Kov asked, as they stepped into yet another of the laboratories that made up the facility, a dimly lit room dominated by a holotank in the center. Gard shook his head, taking in their new surroundings. The walls were lined with banks of softly blinking lights and various key-panels, monitored by a rather nervous-looking male tech. He knew of them, of course; using all of the information that the forensics teams could gather, the reconstruction program would show the most likely sequence of events leading up to Mehta's death; Gard doubted it would be much, but it was worth a look.

"Run it," Kov said simply, and the tech started pressing buttons. Gard fixed his attention on the tank, watching as a small set of rooms flickered into view—a student's apartment, decorated neatly but cheaply. The sight of the inexpensive wall-hangings and fresh flowers wilting in a chipped water glass by the front door made Gard clench his jaw. Her first apartment.

A featureless humanoid appeared in the living room, and seemed to be pacing aimlessly, walking in circles. Although there was a slight possibility that the killer was a tall female, Gard allowed his intuition to decide for him: a man. The unknown male carried a *sh'uk* and wore a dark gray tunic; after a moment of restless agitation, he moved across the room to stand behind the girl's desk.

Want to be in the shadows, hiding, waiting. What's on the desk? Pacing . . . nerves? Excitement? When will she come home?

A part of Gard's mind was formulating lists as he watched—males implanted in the last year, Academy students, museum patrons, collectors of weaponry . . . friends of Mehta's? A lover? The lock hadn't been forced, although someone could have stolen the override entry code easily enough. . . .

The door opened again and Mehta Bren entered, a shopping bag balanced on one hip. She dropped her key card next to the makeshift vase, calling for lights as the door closed behind her—

—and the killer sprang, across the room in a flash. Mehta dropped the bag, various purchases flying, a container of soup splashing everywhere as she fumbled for the door—

—and it was too late. Gard watched the ensuing struggle, determined not to feel what was welling up inside as Mehta fought her attacker, as she fought for her life. The forensic interpretation was graphic if not bloody, the expression of terror on the girl's face painful to see—but as he watched, his experience pointed out a flaw that nullified the program's effect.

That's not right. He wouldn't have—wrong, they have it all wrong.

Gard let it play to its inevitable conclusion before thanking the tech and with Kov, retreating to the hallway; he saw no reason to be rude, and the program might be valuable in other circumstances.

"Worthless," he said, and was pleased that Kov didn't seem surprised. "The time that he took to disable her, his actions before and after the crime—it was carefully planned, not some bloody rampage. Just like the pilot."

"So what next?" Kov asked.

"We go to Mehta's apartment, and see if we can figure out what really happened."

They'd played for hours, their spontaneous harmonies forming a sensual tension between them that only grew as their music progressed. Temzia did not have a piano or *syn lara,* but Joran had some skill with the instruments she did keep—the Vulcan lute, a *li'dswed,* a Tellarite hollow bell line.

He tried all three while Temzia played a cello, an Earth string instrument that produced deep, rich sounds. It made him think of polished stone and age, of wealth and oceans; it was almost as beautiful as she.

For long periods, he thought of nothing at all, simply reveling in the sounds they created, lost in the joy that filled her rooms. With each pause, however, he felt the fear return. It simply wasn't possible—that this incredible, passionate, talented musician, as sure of her brilliance as he was of his own—that she was alone. Unjoined.

The music ended, finally, and they talked into the early morning hours, curled together on the thick carpet of her living room. There was no question that the attraction was mutual, but Joran found himself resisting, dodging Temzia's attempts to touch him. At last she sighed, leaning back against her couch and studying him, a playful scowl dancing across her lips.

"What is it?" She asked. "You *are* interested. . . ."

It wasn't a question; already she could read him, and it added to his fear. The circle, the eternal—becoming joined to Dax had been the key, unlocking his true understanding to music, to himself as an artist and as a being. Without Dax, there had been no focus. How could this girl—this child— have achieved such clarity of purpose without a symbiont?

She was waiting. "I'm—my last serious relationship ended badly," he said. Not really a lie, considering his last relationship had been as Torias Dax, who'd left his wife a widow. He clamped down on the thought, not letting it go any further; he didn't like remembering the others. Not any of them.

Temzia smiled. "That's your past. I'm your present."

No hesitation, no question. He stared at her, the fear making him uncertain. "It's all connected. . . ."

She shrugged, throwing away his beliefs in that single, uncomplicated motion. "I know the joined believe that, but I don't agree. How can you deny yourself what is here, now? What does this moment mean if you spend it remembering another, or planning the next?"

For a beat, Joran had no answer. "You're saying we shouldn't deny our true natures . . . ?"

Temzia nodded slowly, and in that moment, she was the teacher, a truth greater than the circle, the connection between the infinite and the need—it wasn't enough to understand the concept, he wanted to *feel* it, to touch her and know more.

They kissed, and for a little while there was silence, and it was sweeter than any music he'd ever known.

They stood in the wreck that had been Mehta's apartment, the same as the final image from the holographic recreation. What the program had been unable to include were the smells of dead flowers and spilled soup, the quality of sluggish shadow, the flush of violence that still tinged the air like some half-remembered dream—in effect, the reality of murder. There was nothing else like it.

While Kov tampered with the police holoprojector mounted in the northeast corner of the room, Gard checked out the student's desk. He stood in the same place the killer had waited, breathing deeply, letting himself know what the killer had known.

It was dark, and she would be home soon . . . anticipation building, the sh'uk *warm, watching the door open and . . .*

Gard frowned. Why here? It was the murderer's luck that she hadn't escaped while he'd been dashing across the room. He looked down at the desk, at the blank screen of her personal computer, at the scattered mass of Academy disks—music, history, composition—at a framed holo of a younger Mehta proudly holding what appeared to be an alien flute, the front cracked, distorting her smile into a toothy scream.

Gard felt they were looking at three distinct sets of memories so far, although he suspected more. At the museum: planned for privacy, timed to avoid security, and a careful adjustment to the lighting prior to the attack, but the recklessness of allowing himself to be caught on camera. At both sites, the humidity filters had been reset, possibly in consideration to the indoor plant life—in Mehta's bathroom, a dying fern had been lovingly trimmed and watered after her death. The killer had chosen an antiquated weapon for both murders, unused for centuries, yet in both cases had taken great care not to use the weapon as intended, paralyzing his victims first—

—*a perfectionist, consumed by details, suggesting a background in mathematics or engineering, perhaps some kind of artistic connection. An interest in botany. A historian, or someone with an interest in capital punishment. So many possibilities—*

A flicker of light diverted his attention; Kov had the projector working. The image of Mehta's body as she had been found appeared on the floor, halfway between the desk and the front door. Her face was turned toward Gard, and like the shuttle pilot, her limbs had been arranged to denote rest, her eyes closed and head tilted as if she were listening to something. . . .

"Was there music playing?" Gard asked.

Kov shook his head. "Nothing was loaded—unless you count a misfed data ring. The reads taken indicated that her computer was on at the time of death, but it was a glitch."

"How can you be sure?"

Kov pulled a notepad from inside his coat and tapped a few keys. "According to the memory log, a single tone was produced by the sound card for something like an hour—didn't change in pitch or volume, and there was no evidence that the attacker tried to access anything. Malfunction."

Gard frowned. "And it was still playing when they found her?"

"Actually, no . . ." Now Kov was frowning. He walked across the room, Gard noting that he stepped carefully around the image of the body almost without thinking about it. Kov leaned over the computer and started punching in commands.

After a moment, a low sound spilled out into the silence from the dead girl's computer, a single unvarying note, flat and tuneless. Gard closed his eyes, listening, but it reminded him of nothing.

"Malfunction," Kov said again.

"I doubt it." Gard saw Kov move to turn it off, and shook his head. "Let it play. Anything like this at the museum?"

"I don't . . . They checked for tampering with files, but nothing else. It's possible. I'll find out as soon as we get back to the facility."

As Kov spoke, Gard moved to the still image on the floor, letting his thoughts carry him. He crouched next to the body, then lay down in the projection of light, merging with her, assuming the same position. He closed his eyes again, letting the monotonous note fill his mind, hearing what Mehta heard as she died. What the killer heard as he took her life.

A single note, he wanted her to hear it . . . or wanted it to be playing so that he could hear it, so that he could connect the sound with the memory of her death. . . .

Gard opened his eyes and without moving, studied as much of the room as he could see, paying close attention to the wall behind the desk. Once he knew what he was looking for, he found it in a matter of seconds: three tiny holes set in a triangular pattern, high in the room's southwest corner. If he were to remove the police holo projector's mount, he would find the same pattern.

Gard sat up and ran his hands through his hair, his sudden certainty making him feel very tired. There was no question in his mind that one of the museum's computers had also suffered an aural "glitch," or that whoever checked the scene would find an identical trio of holes somewhere in the room.

"He's recording them," Gard said softly. He had to repeat himself to be heard over the unchanging note, the sound clogging his senses with echoes of a madness he was only beginning to understand.

Things weren't happening the way he'd planned. The quinary circle wasn't half finished, the perfection incomplete—and since meeting Temzia, the need to conclude had ceased to dominate his every waking thought. He knew he had to finish, knew that someone would be coming. . . .

. . . stop. Breathe. Now is not the time.

". . . without further ado, I present our friend and colleague, Joran Dax. Mr. Dax will be playing an original composition for us, a symphonic ode, *Untitled, To a Truth.*"

Joran stood up, smiling and nodding to the assembled group of teachers and graduate students as he walked to the raised platform, trying to clear his mind of everything but the music. The quarterly recitals were tiresome but necessary if he meant to maintain his status as one of the Academy's finest; he'd seriously considered skipping this one. Temzia had almost coaxed him to spend the day with her—but now was not the time to draw attention to himself.

And why not? Why not, when your grand composition lays untouched, when you allow doubt to cloud your brilliance, to keep you from action? Why not quit now, retire into obscurity with an unjoined as your playmate, leave the important work to those with the strength to follow through—

Enough!

Joran humbly thanked the woman who'd introduced him, an aging spinster of little talent, and moved to the piano, an antique Steinway imported from Earth. It was time to play, the one thing that could still soothe away his troubles.

He sat at the bench, closing his eyes to fix the piece in his mind's eye. It was one of Belar's, simple but dulcet, not his best work but easily better than the insipid noise his audience was accustomed to hearing. He could worry about the circle later.

Joran began to play, the gentle lines of the ode working their magic. From the first stanza, he ceased to exist, becoming the spaces between the notes, becoming each delicate, ringing sound, the eternal inside of him finding a place to rest. The melody was uncluttered by fear or indecision, there was no morality to be concerned with; it was what it was, and it was good.

There was some movement in the audience as he played, but he recognized it as if from a great distance, entranced by the miracle that was music, that he was blessed to share in. Still, a part of him wondered how anyone could be so rude, to detract from the others' experience. At the calando bridge, he glanced across the small assembly—

—and lost his place, the timing horribly jumbled, three notes in a row buried. Dr. Hajan, here, now! There was no mistaking the stern countenance, the faded spots of his hateful, white head—the disapproving gaze of the man who'd recommended that Joran Belar be expelled from the initiate program.

After his joining, he'd been told that it wasn't uncommon for evaluating staff to visit, unannounced, those they'd recommended be dropped—it was even encouraged by the Commission, the idea being for the doctor or field docent to witness the success of the joining they'd discouraged, to lay to rest any lingering doubts.

Dr. Hajan's timing couldn't have been worse. *Not now, not with so many unanswered questions, so many doubts of my own!*

Except . . . poor timing was a matter of perspective, wasn't it?

All of this flashed through his mind in a split second, before his shock was replaced with a renewed sense of purpose. He had been weak, he had almost lost his connection to the circle, but in that instant of awareness, he saw what had to happen next—and it filled him with pleasure, almost physical in its intensity.

Joran regained his composure and finished the piece without another flaw.

* * *

The call came just after dark—a third murder, this one committed within the very walls of the Symbiosis Commission, not an hour's flight from where Gard was staying. The details were few, but gave Gard his first real hope that the hunt might soon be over; the killer had been interrupted at his work by security, fleeing the victim's office before he'd had a chance to complete his ritual. The guards had lost him outside, but Gard's hope was undiminished; he could feel how close they were to understanding him—and understanding inevitably led to capture.

Kov picked him up and they rode in near silence to the Institute, a steady drizzle raining down on them from the gathering night that did little to dampen their guilty optimism. Earlier, they'd received confirmation on the museum slaying connections, the holoprojector marks and the single tone—a different pitch, but doubtlessly for the same as-yet unknown purpose—and now a third murder, less than two hours old, the site secured and waiting for them. The victim was one Dr. Foris Hajan, a senior member of the Institute's evaluation team, and a TSC tech was already compiling a list of his recent recommendations, as well as an itinerary for the past few months. Gard had little doubt that the killer's name would surface—but Gard had no doubts either that the murderer had accelerated his spree, and that they needed to find him as quickly as possible.

Dr. Hajan's office was in the Institute's west wing. Kov and Gard hurried through the dimly lit hallways, past ashen-faced guards and the few staff members who'd still been working, who lingered now in aimless confusion. As they neared Hajan's office, Gard heard the sound he'd been searching for—the flat, featureless tone that they now knew as the killer's signature. Apparently, he hadn't had time to silence his strange obsession.

Kov stopped at the door to talk to one of the techs while Gard stepped into the nightmarish scene that had been Hajan's last. Chairs and bookcases had been overturned, various ceramic pieces shattered, the debris cast randomly about—and in the middle of the room, eyes open and staring, lay Dr. Hajan himself, a single stab wound through his throat. Above it all, the relentless drone from the undamaged computer played like some endless mechanical shriek, somehow all the more terrible for its utter lack of emotion.

Gard knelt next to the body, assessing the attack. Hajan had been surprised, surely, the entrance to the wound at the back of his neck, a change in pattern that suggested a different relationship. The killer hadn't wanted for Hajan to see him, had perhaps wanted to avoid the condemnation in his eyes—

—couldn't bear to be seen, but wanted Hajan dead so badly that he didn't care whether or not the doctor's death could be connected to him. Whatever he's trying to do, he means to finish it soon. . . .

"Here it is."

Gard stood up and saw that Kov had joined him, and was pointing at a triad of marks on the far wall. Even rushed, the murderer had been determined to take his trophy, to have his prize. Gard nodded thoughtfully as he moved to the still-crying computer, his trained mind working at the details, fitting them and refitting them; the ancient weapon, the recordings, the seemingly random destruction, the obviously obsessive nature—there were contradictions everywhere, but only because he didn't fully understand.

"It's not the same note," Kov said. "It's—higher, I think, than either of the other ones. We'll have to feed them into the computer when we get back, see if we can find the connection."

Gard shook his head. He could feel time slipping away, and the need to *know* was like a fire in his mind. "Do it now, here. Do you have the specs?"

Kov barely hesitated before nodding. He produced his notepad and picked up an overturned chair, sitting in front of the computer as Gard walked back across the ravaged office, talking almost to himself.

"No one uses the *sh'uk,* no one. Executions, goal-oriented, not process, but he records the process, he breaks everything in sight but it's not real, it's like he's deliberately . . ."

Gard froze.

Lying. Creating a false biography.

It all fell into place, and Gard ran through the lies one at a time, discovering the reality at the base of each.

The murder weapon, so appealing because it's so rare, so emotionless . . . a blind alley, and a disguise for his true rage. The special care given to the plants . . . a detail he wanted us to notice, because he's not a noted botanist. The murder sites, seemingly the work of a clumsy, rampaging beast . . . a dancer instead, or an athlete, someone capable of precise movement.

And why, why invent a false background of hosts to mislead . . . unless you knew that someone would be investigating a joined murderer, which you could not know—

—unless you served on the Commission at some point.

As if to punctuate the enormity of his realization, the room fell silent, the note snapping off. Kov stared at the screen, seemingly awestruck.

Gard hurried over, already knowing the nature of what he would see if not the specifics.

Connection, completion. It's about completion, somehow. . . .

"They're notes," Kov said softly. "The first three of a pentatonic scale, five tones in all."

There, on the screen—five dots, three of them highlighted. The computer had arranged them in a circle.

"Ouroboros," Gard breathed. Kov looked up at him, frowning. Gard elaborated, feeling his heart pound with the truth of it.

"A human myth. The serpent that devours its own tail. It symbolizes the cycle of change and continuance, of past and future, united. Think of it—a joined killer, experiencing himself as the rebirth of his symbiont, creating death as he is born."

Gard grinned, and not a trace of humor lived in his smile.

They had him.

It was almost midnight when Temzia let herself into Joran's apartment, excited by the feeling of daring that flushed through her as she punched his entry code into the door panel. He hadn't exactly tried to keep it to himself, had he? Besides, she had waited over a cooling meal for hours; he'd promised to meet her after his recital, and she was unaccustomed to being denied. If she interrupted him in the middle of something private, well, it was his own fault, wasn't it?

The rooms were dark, the only sound that of the pattering rain at the windows. Enjoying the thrill of her intrusion, she let the lights stay off, moving as quietly as a thief.

There was a little light coming from the wide, unshuttered window in his living room, the thin and watery moonlight adding to her sense of stealthy purpose.

She circled through his bedroom, bathroom, and kitchen, returning to the tastefully decorated living room when she realized that he wasn't home. *Disappointing, to say the least. Stay or go?* She decided to stay, at least until she got bored. Joran was worth it.

The environment was elegant, if a trifle cold; Temzia wandered through the room, studying his collection of instruments, peering at his wall of antique instruments and lightly touching the paintings and prints that he'd collected, probably as Joran Belar. It was strange, being with a joined man; no one in her immediate family had been implanted, and most of her friends were musicians, far from the math-science types who usually sought candidacy. She liked it; she liked *him,* and as she ran a nimble finger across a row of hard-copy texts, she found herself wondering what it would be like to be in love with Mr. Joran Dax—

"Oh!" The sound was startled out of her as the line of the shelf jumped into her hand with a soft *click.* She grinned, at her own surprise as much as at what she'd found.

"Secrets," she whispered, still grinning. A secret room. Maybe he kept his mistresses there, hidden away from prying eyes. Joran would laugh at that when she told him. . . .

Temzia slipped into the room, her gaze adjusted enough to the dark to see the *syn lara* that dominated the otherwise empty chamber. A work room, obviously—no decorations, nothing to distract a composing musician. She loved that he was so dedicated to his music; she'd never met anyone as impassioned as Joran, or as talented.

He probably wouldn't like me nosing around in here. . . .

Her grin returned. He probably shouldn't stand her up, then.

She walked to the *syn lara* and perched on one corner of the bench, her gaze running over the use-polished keys. She saw the control box for a holo projector sitting on the raised lip of the instrument and, still smiling, turned it on. Probably scenes of nature, or some such, one of her profs had recommended using visuals for inspiration, and—

—and her smile faded as part of a chord filtered from the projector's speakers, and two images sprang to life, both dramatically bright in the darkness. Two rooms, other than these; two strangers, a man in an empty hall, a girl holding a bag, both turning toward her, twin expressions of shock on their faces. Both of them screaming wordlessly, the haunting notes erupting from their opened mouths as Joran stepped into their rooms, Joran holding something shining and sharp—

Temzia sucked in a breath and scrambled backward, falling off of the bench, unable to look away from the horror unfolding in front of her. *Oh, oh, that's Mehta, that's Mehta Bren and he's, what is he doing—*

She backed into the living room, stumbling, scarcely able to breathe—

—and a hand clamped over her mouth, stifling the scream that leapt into her throat. She struggled wildly, but only for the second it took her to see the weapon held up in front of her rolling eyes.

Gard could feel the girl's rising panic in the flutter of her heart, in the tension that ran through her body and made it tremble against his own.

"Where's Dax?" He whispered against her ear. The girl shuddered violently, her breath coming in hot gusts against his fingers, her limbs twitching. She was too afraid, he had to calm her down or she'd start screaming the second he let her go.

"Listen to me," he whispered, doing his best to sound reassuring, aware that Joran could be moving toward them now, sliding through the dark with a weapon of his own, something much deadlier than a stunner. "You're in very real danger, and I'm here to help, but you have to *tell me where he is.*"

The girl seemed to understand. She nodded against his hand and he let her go, quickly scanning the room as she collected herself enough to respond.

"I don't think he's here," she said, her eyes wide and bright with tears. "I didn't—"

Across from them, an explosion, a black shape hurtling through the window with a thundering crash, the high squeak of splintering glass an assault in the whispered dark. Gard threw himself to the floor, pulling the girl down with him, doing his best to shield her from the rain of glass as the shape, Dax, fell across them both.

Gard tried to bring the stunner up and a sharp pain slashed across his wrist. Instantly, his fingers turned dumb, the weapon clattering away. Joran held a thick, daggerlike piece of glass in one bloody hand, as shining as the demented grin he wore.

"Nice work. Fast. Now you and the girl, and it's all over," Dax said, and slashed again with the glass. Gard reeled back, narrowly avoiding the cut, praying that Kov had heard, was coming, praying that the girl would survive.

Screaming wordlessly, Dax lunged forward, striking at Gard's throat—

—and the scream was cut short by the solid *thunk* of blunt instrument against skull. Dax crumpled forward, the girl standing behind him, the sharp end of his dropped *sh'uk* grasped in both of her hands.

"No!" Gard snatched at the monster, desperate to save him, to finally have the answers to the questions that he'd spent centuries following, *why*—

—as Dax fell against his own makeshift dagger, the weight of his body forcing the glass deep into his chest.

Gasping, Joran Dax rolled onto his back, resuscitated by the pain of his impalement. Dying.

The pain was everything. It was the world, and just like that, Joran felt something inside of him break.

Don't leave me, Dax . . .

"The circle's not finished," Joran rasped, not sure who he was talking to, not expecting an answer from the agent who'd orchestrated his death.

"It is for you."

Temzia was crying, somewhere. Joran couldn't see.

"I . . . still am . . . Dax," he whispered, and knew that it was true, that the circle *was* the truth. Never ending. Dax was alive, and he was part of Dax now, in harmony with the symbiont, forever.

That cool voice, from out of the dark. "No. You're Joran Belar, and you're dead, and no one will remember."

Joran felt a burst of fear, of terror, and it was the last thing he felt, the foul eulogy from the stranger the last sound he heard as the dark joined around him, taking him away from the eternal and into silence.

* * *

Gard wasn't in the mood to jog but he went to the park anyway; the sun was out, and although he was tired, the light felt good. Cleansing.

He wasn't a bit surprised to see Kov waiting for him by the path, even though the agent probably hadn't slept yet. Gard had had only a few hours himself, but he felt okay.

The younger man fell into step, and together, they walked slowly toward the woods.

"How's the wrist?" Kov asked.

Gard smiled. "Good as new. My fingers are a little numb still, but it should pass in a couple of days. Is that why you came to visit me?"

Kov smiled in turn, staring off into the distance as he spoke. "The procedure was successful; the new host has no memory of Joran. I thought you might like to know."

"What about the records?"

"There never was a Joran Dax. Joran Belar was killed yesterday while trying to escape the scene of a murder—"

"The murder of Dr. Hajan," Gard finished. "Because Hajan recommended his expulsion from the program."

Kov smiled a little, but said nothing.

"What about the pilot? What about Mehta?"

Kov shrugged. "There'll be questions for a while, but in the long run . . ."

He didn't need to finish. The TSC was all about handling the long run; Gard knew that as well as anyone. Better than most, in fact.

They walked for a few moments without speaking, and Gard decided that it was too nice a day for the discussion that could have been sparked by the events of the past few weeks, particularly of the past few hours. About what the

TSC was doing, and the apparent lack of feeling they had for the unjoined. About who they were helping by refusing to admit to the world that sometimes, even after all of their careful measuring and planning, things went wrong; the need for Gard's existence was proof of that.

But there's only one of me. Maybe that's it's own proof, that things are never as dark as they seem. Maybe.

"What's the new host's name?" He asked suddenly, not sure why he wanted to know.

"Curzon," Kov said. "He's going to be a diplomat."

For some reason, that made Gard laugh out loud. The two men continued their walk, enjoying the quiet, the park seeming fresh and new as it always did after a storm. Gard knew that he would remember Joran Dax, even if no one else would—and perhaps that was as much a reason for his existence as the rest of it.

After a few moments, Kov left him without saying good-bye; he never did.

CURZON

"I think one of the reasons I liked him so much was that he had more faults than the usual, socially acceptable Trill."

—Benjamin Sisko
"Dax"

Steven Barnes

Steven Barnes is a novelist, screenwriter, columnist, lecturer, and personal performance coach. He has written fifteen novels, including several in collaboration with award-winning science fiction writer Larry Niven. His television credits include *The Outer Limits, The New Twilight Zone, Baywatch,* and *Stargate;* his Emmy Award-winning episode of *The Outer Limits,* "A Stitch in Time," was also nominated for a Cable ACE Award. For five years he was a columnist for Black Belt magazine, and for three years host of the *Hour 25* radio show on KPFK in Los Angeles. For six years he was one of the most popular instructors at the prestigious UCLA Extension writing program.

Barnes created the acclaimed Lifewriting seminar and audio course to help writers at all levels improve both their writing and their lives by examining Joseph Campbell's model of the Hero's Journey. Visit his Web site at www.lifewrite.com. He can be reached at lifewrite@aol.com.

"The Music Between the Notes" marks Barnes's second foray into the *Star Trek* universe. His previous project was the novelization of the acclaimed *Star Trek: Deep Space Nine* episode, "Far Beyond the Stars."

Barnes lives in Longview, Washington, with his daughter and his wife, novelist Tananarive Due.

The Music Between the Notes

Steven Barnes

THE AZZIZ SHIP approached Pelios Station like a great, glowing diatom, a crystalline testament to a technology long rumored, but rarely seen in Federation space.

The shape was unmistakably organic, like something found in the depths of an ocean. It most resembled what it truly was: a construct extruded, not constructed. Grown, not built.

I was an ensign then, not yet graduated from the Academy, and adjunct to the great Curzon Dax, who stood beside me. I say great with the accuracy of memory, although that and other words ran through my mind at the time. Some of them were oddly contradictory: aged and ageless, pompous and frivolous, brilliant and oblivious.

My thoughts of him ran to dualisms, perhaps in part because of his symbiotic nature, which I admit confused and perhaps even repelled me at first.

At the moment we both stood at the greeting dock of the Federation's Pelios Station, a diplomatic and defensive satellite in the Pelian system, a double-star cluster home to several mining colonies and the planet Bactrica, a world friendly to the Federation but not yet within her fold. Bactrica, with just over two million arable square kilometers and a population of forty million souls, was governed by a hereditary theocracy.

A world of beauty, grace and wealth, four times within recent history Bactrica had been invaded by a mysterious people called the Tzenkethi, who in later years would launch a brief but bloody war against the Federation. Three times Bactrica had repulsed the Tzenkethi by her own efforts, and a unique energy-weapon technology. The most recent invasion had required Federation intercession. During it, Bactrica's reigning monarchs had died. The line of succession was clear, there was no crisis of leadership, but the Bactricans had finally decided that there was strength in numbers.

They were a species very similar to Asiatic humans in appearance, with a stolid, mildly androgynous grace of motion. The females were a bit shorter, but that was very nearly the only visible difference.

Our presence was officially neutral but de facto protective. Despite her recent near—disaster, Bactrica took the official position that her spiritual nature protected her from the need for membership in what they considered a militaristic Federation.

Privately, I thought this nonsense. The energy weapons were hardly spiritual. Although we had never obtained a sample, our analysts proposed that it actually disrupted matter in its most basic, sub-quark level, producing an effect our own theorists had considered to violate at least three basic laws of physics. The Bactricans quite understood our desire to understand the technology behind the weapon, which they simply called "God's Tooth," and were negotiating savagely. Those negotiations had been proceeding for months, the Federation team led by Curzon Dax, who was, although in the twilight of his illustrious career, still perhaps the most respected diplomat of his time.

I had watched him juggling arguments, concerns, and treaties with unquenchable energy, until it dizzied and drained me. The announcement of the approach of the Azziz ship was a welcome break from the negotiation table.

Glowing from within as if in greeting, the Azziz ship nosed her way to the dock, and then locked there.

The Azziz, unlike the Bactricans, wished to join the Federation, *wished* to exchange knowledge. For far too long they had been virtually alone, and they craved entrance to a larger community of worlds.

Curzon Dax barely seemed to breathe. "I have done this many times, young Sisko," he said, "but it always astonishes me how exciting it is."

"Please, sir. It's better you refer to me as 'Ensign.' "

"My apologies." Was that a glimmer of humor in his eye? "How exciting it is, Ensign."

"The contact, sir?"

"And what is to come."

I studied Dax, feeling more curiosity than I cared to admit. "What aspect do you find most exciting? If you don't mind the question."

"Not at all."

"Is it the new technology? The new languages and customs?"

Dax considered before answering. "Languages and customs. The important thing about a language is that it contains the *thoughts* of a people. Although one can think things which cannot be put into language. . . ."

I bristled, remembering endless late-night dormitory debates on this very subject. "I consider it axiomatic that language contains *all* that can be thought by a being. Deny the word, and you deny the thought."

"Well said, Ensign. Freshman philosophy one-oh-one, I believe. Be by the book, but not of it, young Sisko."

"There is more in heaven and Earth . . . ?" I asked respectfully, inwardly seething.

Dax didn't seem to notice my sarcasm. "Precisely. Language is invariably shaped by the philosophies and perceptions of the linguist. But while it tells us much about a people and the way they see the world, it doesn't tell everything."

I nodded silently. It was my place to assist, report, and learn, not to question or interfere. Or debate. I could understand why a joined Trill would believe in non-linguistic cognition, but the idea was, to me, anathema.

The tiled floor began to vibrate. The inner door slid open. The hallway beyond was good Federation tritanium and transparent aluminum, strong enough to contain a thousand atmospheres. Halfway down, the texture changed.

The pathway beyond midpoint was smooth, enameled, perhaps too slick, rather like a snail shell. On the wall at my side, I saw the point at which the Azziz docking "device" had joined with the Federation platform. It appeared to be some kind of dried, hardened sap. I pressed against it with my thumbnail. Somewhat to my surprise, it was not diamond hard. Rather, it depressed an eight of an inch and then held firm. When I removed my thumb the imprint healed almost instantly.

"Look." Dax pointed. Above us was something that looked much like a crab, hanging from the ceiling by a thick strand of that rubbery epoxy. "Imagine," he said with unfeigned respect. "A substance extruded by the living body of a creature, that would pass Federation standards for structural strength."

I had to admit, the idea was dazzling.

Dax stood before an opening that . . . well, looked like nothing so much as a mammalian sphincter muscle. It was dry, but glistened.

I reached out and touched it, felt it give beneath my touch—for perhaps two millimeters this time, and then hold firm.

Dax shook his head very subtly, and I dropped my hands back to my side.

"Nervous?" Dax said quietly.

"Yes, sir," I said. "This is my first 'first contact.' "

"Forget your theories, young Sisko."

I almost objected, but noted how excited Dax was himself: eyes bright, carriage erect. This was a Moment, and clearly, he had never tired of them.

With a tiny whiff of escaping atmosphere, the sphincter opened, and the Azziz ambassador stood before us.

The ambassador was four feet tall, vaguely humanoid, with vestigial featherlike bristles that made me think that, in earlier days, his folk had been avian. His skin and bristles were black, and he was cloaked in a stiff leather armor that flexed without joints. Interesting.

"Ambassador"—and here Curzon Dax said a word that I have never managed to pronounce, a tongue twister brimming with lethal fricatives—"we welcome you to Pelios Station."

The ambassador inhaled, and made a hissing sound. Somewhat to my surprise, a creature that looked rather like a flying amphibian, all wings and oversized head and a bullfrog throat, flew up and nestled on the ambassador's shoulder. Rather like a rubbery parrot, I thought. "We of the Azziz," the creature said, "extend our greetings in return."

Dax nodded sagely. "Would you care to come aboard?"

The bullfrog croaked in the Azziz tongue. The ambassador answered, and then the bullfrog spoke in English once again. "I would love to. My Poet will accompany me."

"Poet?" Dax asked politely.

Without translating into Azziz, the bullfrog spoke again. Its throat puffed out with unmistakable pride. "I am the Poet," it said. "May our Refrigeration Unit, and Grain Exchanger come aboard as well?"

Dax's expression betrayed momentary bafflement. I leaned over, whispering: "Sir, if we assume that the Azziz vehicle is entirely bio-synthetic, it follows that the vehicle itself is a colony. Each part: refrigeration unit, translation unit, 'grain exchanger,' etc., is a living, separate creature."

Dax smiled at me warmly. There was no guile there, and no condescension. "Indeed."

It was that smile that won me, made me want to know this Trill more deeply. The humor was there, some joke that I could not quite see. And Dax was inviting me to open my eyes, as if he had greater confidence in my potential than I did. In all likelihood there would be good conversation about this, later, over warm ale.

"Yes, please," Dax said, to the bullfrog Poet this time. "And to any of your colony would like to explore our station, we would be a happy to appoint a guide to answer all questions. How many . . . ah, members would this entail?"

The Poet croaked and whistled. The Azziz ambassador answered in kind. "We think that perhaps eight of us would care to see your station. It has been a very long trip."

Dax made swift, quiet comments into his communicator, and then smiled. "It will be done," he said.

"Would you and your companions care to inspect the ship?" the Poet said, without prompting from the Azziz.

"Very much." Dax turned to me. "Would you care to accompany us?"

The laughter was in his eyes again. I would rather have had my fingernails pulled out than miss such an opportunity. "Yes, sir."

I hadn't seen anything like the inside of the Azziz ship since the last time I attended an autopsy. It was moist but not wet, but everything seemed to glisten. The air was dry, but every surface seemed covered with a thin mucosa. The walls dilated to allow us to pass, and contracted behind us. I imagined that at times the ship could form a solid, organic knot with no extra space at all.

In its present mode, the interior of the ship itself rather

reminded me of the valves of a great heart, with wide open chambers surrounded by clusters of living tissue that fluttered, chittered and in general behaved like bats sleeping against the walls of a cave.

The Poet preened and buzzed to various of them. Several pieces of the walls and ceiling emerged, whole creatures where before there had seemed to a mosaic of tissue, patched together for some unified purpose.

There were no viewing screens in the craft as such, although the Azziz ambassador explained that its own nervous system joined with the creature which exuded the external shell, and that elements of that shell were sensitive to the entire electromagnetic and gravitational spectrum, that this information was passed to another creature whose brain could sort the information, from infrared to ultraviolet, into a coherent map.

"And the range of perception?" Dax asked politely.

The translator seemed momentarily confused.

"The range?" Dax pressed. "How many millions of miles, or light-years, or . . . ?"

"The entire range," the Azziz said, simply.

Dax nodded. My own head spun. The ambassador couldn't possibly have meant what he said.

Could he?

The entrance back into the station was quite the parade, with a procession of slithering, hopping curiosities bouncing after ten guides recruited from the diplomatic staff. The Bactricans seemed to resent the Azziz, for reasons I couldn't fathom. Perhaps they felt the newcomers distracted us from the formal negotiations. Perhaps their apparent frivolity offended them. Personally, I thought it was simply that the Bactricans felt most comfortable with their noses held firmly and stiffly in the air.

My Academy friend Cal Hudson was among the hapless guide recruits, and he smiled grimly as something that looked like a headless chimpanzee climbed up his legs and arms and hunched on his shoulders, ready for the tour.

"She looks just your type."

Headless hugged him around the neck and did something that was either a kiss or the gravest insult imaginable.

"You owe me," Cal said.

"It must be love."

"You're buying tonight." Cal made a face, and headed off down the corridor. "Pelios Station itself is a midsized platform," he began, "orbiting Pelios between her second and third planets, twelve light-minutes from the star. It maintains a stable crew of two hundred and fifty . . ." I didn't have the heart to tell him that Headless probably didn't understand a word.

The Azziz ambassador and his (its?) translator were as interested to examine our technology and mechanical innards as we had been to inspect the Azziz accomplishments. Through the Poet, it made the appropriate *ohh* and *ahh* sounds, and looked at the rivets, seals, and welds holding the steel and ceramics together. It touched, and perhaps most disconcertingly, *tasted* the seams.

Curzon Dax, ever the diplomat, remained carefully oblivious to the chaos, guiding them here and there, showing them the station taking all the time needed or desired to absorb the entirety.

It seemed forever before Dax turned the ambassador

over to Starfleet Admiral Janeway, who had arrived at Pelios
only an hour after the Azziz ship. Janeway was here for the
final negotiations with the Bactricans, and to assist in the rituals of initial contact, but the unflappable admiral's eyebrows
definitely raised at the spectacle.

I managed not to laugh aloud.

Finally, Dax and I were alone. "So, Ensign," he said.
"What did you see?"

"They're like a troop of trained monkeys," I said. "I'm
not at all certain that we're really dealing with the Azziz
brain. I think they sent this flock out as a test."

In the hall behind us, something that looked like a
leather beach ball with tongues for arms bounced down the
hall, stopping every few hops to sniff the feet and crotch of
passersby.

"Then you haven't seen enough yet. I heard you offer
young Hudson a drink."

He *would* have heard that. How a man can have such a
tolerance for the leaden rituals of diplomacy and simultaneously possess such an appetite for good ale, I will never know.
I enjoyed a drink now and then at the end of an excruciating
shift. It was dessert, if you will. For Dax, I sometimes thought
the dessert was the meal itself. "Come, Ensign," he said. "You
will buy me a drink, and I will tell you what your eyes do
not see."

Because of its position near two mining planets, exploration and transport ships paused at Pelios Station more often
than such a minor outpost would ordinarily require, and en-
trepreneurs of several kinds managed to establish a good living, providing for their varied tastes.

The most popular of the shops, not surprisingly, was a grogatorium, offering a variety of flavored ales and entertainments, most of them of the gypsy variety, but lately a new dancer had thickened the evening's crowd. I rarely missed a show when off duty.

Dax had the capacity to work through any normal creature's sleep cycles without losing focus or mental speed. That being said, just as he could focus himself utterly on any task at hand, he could concentrate just as impressively on a good glass of synthehol.

We sat at our usual table, in a corner dark enough to avoid the glare, but central enough to catch the eye of the overworked waitresses.

"So," I said as we waited for the next show to begin. "Exactly what is it that you think I missed?"

Dax leaned back against the wall. "You saw a conglomeration of creatures, engaged in an enterprise, and assumed that they were nonsentient, controlled by a central mind."

"They certainly behaved that way. They only allowed a few of them off the ship, and those behaved like children at best. I can only assume that those remaining behind were vegetative."

Dax's every word and gesture were carefully measured. He paused deliberately, listening to the music for a moment before continuing. He seemed to understand that good teachers and storytellers make the audience *want* the information.

"The mere fact of interaction in a group effort says nothing about the individual intelligence of the members, young Sisko. Each member of the Federation suppresses certain elements of its own will for the common good. Each member of a military unit forgoes certain personal liberties in exchange for a heightened efficiency of action."

"I hardly think that's the same thing. And even if it were, that's not my point."

"Isn't it?" Dax said with deceptive innocence. "And, regarding that theme, what would you say of our Bactrican brethren?"

I cocked my head sideways. "I fail to see how a bunch of—"

"Ah ah ah . . ." Dax reminded me. He was, as usual, right. I had to fight the urge to assume that those things I cannot understand are necessarily of a lower order.

"All right." I wrestled with my thoughts, seeking a better way to express myself. "I hardly see how the two situations are equivalent. One is a group of genetically engineered animals designed to replace machinery, the other is a highly evolved, cultivated world in which ideas of caste and duty have evolved to a level that would shame the sixteenth century Chinese court."

"And if I were to suggest that the two have much in common?"

"I might grant that," I said, "but still wouldn't understand your argument."

"You're learning, young Sisko. Only a month ago, you would have allowed me to ambush you. . . ."

Despite myself, I allowed myself to feel a touch of pride. He was right. I would have.

Cal Hudson appeared, and dropped himself into the seat at my side.

"Well, Ensign Hudson," Dax laughed, "Young Sisko tells me you might be engaged."

Cal muttered words I have never written down in my adult life. He grabbed my ale, telling me to order my own.

On the stage before us, the bar's Betazoid manager was quietly setting up a trio of chairs for their musicians. A moment later, three creatures of mismatched proportions emerged, and initiated a tuning-up process with strange instruments.

Dax leaned forward. "Mr. Hudson," he said. "We were debating whether a culture utilizing advanced language and symbolic logic is necessarily more advanced than a symbiotic form."

"Such as the Azziz?" Cal asked. "Or such as the Trill?"

Dax chuckled and sat back.

"I wasn't falling into that one, sir."

"Kudos, Mr. Hudson. Ahh," he said with vast satisfaction. "The evening's entertainment commences."

Cal actually felt more at home than I with verbal games, and I was glad that he had seen through Dax's question—although mortified that I had not. The waitress returned with a glass for me just in time for the lights to dim. The bar had gone mostly quiet now, in expectancy, and I felt the tension building even before she arrived.

And oh, yes, it was she. Unmistakably she, devastatingly *she*. As positively *she* as any creature I had ever seen. Behind the silver body makeup and the silver mask, it was difficult to tell what race she belonged to. Humanoid, certainly, but her dance motion was so fluid that I would have sworn her to be some manner of cat. She moved not exactly *to* the music but *with* it, using it, her muscles fluttering and writhing in a costume that fit more closely than a sheen of oil.

It was impossible to miss her animal sensuality, but there

was far more to her, a kind of purity, an almost religious ecstasy.

I had seen Sabbath Nile perform at least a dozen times, and every time, she wove me into her web. I saw Dax reach under the table for the slender contact wires. After a moment's hesitation, I pulled a set out and applied them to my temples.

And was lost. The contacts fed me her exertions, created the sensation that I was observer, the dancer, and the dance itself. As if Sabbath spun me, spun us in a web of exertion, skill, and pure spirit. I forced my eyes open, saw that most of the others in the bar had also donned the equipment, and that we were all joining together, all feeling what she felt. I felt what the others felt, a feedback that grew more intimate and intoxicating by the second.

I was drunken with her, touched by and reveling in the woman called Sabbath Nile. She called herself an Empath mime, one whose art consisted of the creation and projection of emotion. We not of her species needed some kind of artificial linkage to experience her art.

I could barely imagine its impact in native form.

Dax was connected as well, I could *feel* him on the web, feel his odd, doubled presence there next to me, but . . .

But where the rest of us were completely immersed in her performance, helpless in the hands of a master, Dax's eyes roamed the room, perhaps searching for something.

Was he studying the effect she had on others? Strange, because on the surface he was as attentive, as passionately silent as the rest of us.

And yet his attention was elsewhere, as well, no doubt a side effect of his symbiotic nature.

I saw where his eyes had roamed.

Today, for the first time, I saw a pair of Bactricans in the bar. Dour, dry creatures with no observable sense of humor, half the time I found myself hoping that the negotiations with them fell through, and that they never joined the Federation.

I had seen their thin tall males and short dusky females (at least that was what I assumed them to be). But the sight of them shuffling about Pelios Station in their robes, on their way to this meeting or that, had never meant anything beyond the need for another round of talks.

Now, they watched Sabbath like a hawk, and halfway through her performance, rose and stalked out, seething with hostility.

Jealousy, I thought. Simple jealousy.

There was a yearning quality in Sabbath's performance now. I felt her sadness pulsing in my temples, and her dance had ceased to be a thing of rhythm or spirit, but more personal, something of her own heart. Her aura literally flared, the light seeming to emanate from her pores like a glowing mist.

Every motion, every time she folded her waist like a flower bowing to the setting sun, triggered another whole spectrum of response from the room. The induction equipment fed it to us, and took a portion of our emotions and, doubtless, fed it back to her, taking us all higher and higher.

Except for Dax, whose attention remained on the departing Bactricans. I wondered if the man had any real feelings at all. Was everything just an exercise in diplomacy?

When the performance was over, and she took her bow to thunderous applause, whistling, nods, and body sounds that might have seemed rude in another species. Sabbath left the stage and approached our table.

"Hello, Benjamin, Cal" she said to us, but slid into the booth beside Dax. Cal made a disgusted clucking sound, and I felt a touch of heat simmering beneath my collar, but managed to repress it. She peeled off her silver mask. The face beneath was slightly flattened, rather like an Egyptian mask, but no less feminine or appealing for it. Her eyes changed color with the light, or her mood. She was a fabulous creature, to be sure.

"I don't get it," Cal whispered beneath his breath, sipping from his brew. "She could have either one of us—what does she want with . . . ?"

"At ease, Ensign," I muttered. "The battle is not the war."

I wanted to know Sabbath with an intensity I had never felt before, and would never again. It wasn't lust, exactly. Well, maybe it was, but it was much more than that. And the fact that she only seemed to have eyes for Dax was absolutely maddening.

Cal and I had vied for feminine attention since our earliest academy days, and despite an enviable record of success, I sensed our efforts were useless.

I wanted to smile, to dance, to sing, to quote poetry, but knew that Dax would merely smile one of his maddening smiles and undo any efforts either of us might make, revealing us as a clumsy and callow pair of boys in comparison. At that moment I hated and admired him.

So devoid of any meaningful choices, I drank my ale, afraid to speak, fearing that my clumsy mouth might betray me even further.

Curzon Dax seemed to treat her like a fond child, not

the devastating creature that she was. "An excellent performance, as always."

Sabbath inclined her head graciously.

"I've only been here two weeks," Cal said, "But just in that time I've seen your performance ripen, and mature." I'm sure Cal thought that that sounded *very* worldly.

She took her eyes from Dax for a minute, and regarded Cal seriously. "So many peoples. It is hard to weave the web."

Should I ask a question? Or not? I noticed that Dax was watching us, with something approaching amusement sparkling in his eyes. Oh, damn him.

"We were having a discussion," Dax said finally, effortlessly wresting control of the conversation. "About the role of the individual in the nurturance of the whole. We in the Federation have encountered everything from extreme individualism, which virtually precludes the creation of any society at all, to extreme submersion of individual identity. This last creates a society so stable that it remains unchanged for a million generations. Ensign Sisko: Would you care to present your own position?"

I knew I was on rocky ground here. Dax was probably trying to lure me into making some kind of callow, straight-out-of-the-academy comment, which he would use to prove I was incapable of individual thought. That, in turn, might reduce my chances with the lovely Sabbath.

On the other hand, if I said something that went *against* Academy philosophy, it would doubtless end up in my record. Permanently. Dax was doubtless studying me carefully with an eye to future promotions.

And also, doubtless, enjoying the position in which his young aide currently found himself. Damn him.

"I think," I said, "that a culture must deny individuality to the point that symbolic logic systems have developed. After that point, there should be sufficient divergence to encourage creativity. But after a time, the needs of the one must be subsumed into the needs of the many."

Cal rolled his eyes.

"In a cycle," Sabbath said quietly.

I almost clapped my hands. She agreed with me! Hah! One for the Earthling. I turned on Dax. I mean, *to* him. "And you, Ambassador. What do *you* think?"

"Your idea of a cycle presumes, I think, a 'group will' which cannot actually exist without constant communication. Not like the turning of the seasons. I think that there is a constant intermeshing of elements. Temporality is not part of the equation. A culture is symbiotic. The organ systems function in a manner simultaneously separate and collective. Evolution occurs when current behaviors and philosophies are challenged or proven inadequate. Unless protected by artificial barriers, such provings happen regularly. Individuality is overrated and immature."

Sabbath watched us both, with a smile as secretive as her true face. There seemed something sad behind the smile, something I could not quite grasp.

"And you, Sabbath?" I asked. "What do you believe?"

"My people have a saying." And here I listened eagerly. She had yet to answer a direct question about her people, although I assumed that she had come to the station with one of the gypsy groups that regularly traipsed through, perhaps stranding her here after an argument. "Serve the self, serve the group. Both are slaves to the flesh. Serve instead Spirit, and serve both."

Cal rubbed his temples. "My head hurts. I'm going to find a game of chess. If I don't have some logic today, my head is going to explode." He made his apologies, and left the table.

She laughed, a sound as musical as temple bells. "I am sorry." She turned to Dax. "Could we be together tonight?" she asked him.

I wanted to pound my head into the table. I had heard of Curzon Dax's legendary facility with females, but it was still difficult to believe, even when the evidence was as clear and indisputable as this.

Infuriatingly, Dax barely seemed to notice her overture. "Not tonight, my dear. But I may have time for you tomorrow."

She smiled eagerly, and I ground my teeth. I reached out and touched her wrist. The fur on her arm was very slightly electric. I remembered the sight of her aura, her electromagnetic field shifting into the spectrum of visible light, as she danced, and the urge to touch her more . . . *intensely* was almost overpowering. "I've managed to acquire two portions of Rellian beef," I said, trying to keep the eagerness from my voice. "I would love to prepare them for you tonight."

She touched my face, gazing into my eyes. Something like passion flared there, and my own rose to meet it. I felt myself drawn forward, leaning into what would have been the most intense kiss of my life. Then she pulled back. "You are very dear," she said. "And I think one day we will spend the time together that you seek. But it will not be when you think, and it will not be what you imagine."

Her skin crackled as she brushed it against me, and she stood. "I must prepare myself." And she went away.

I blinked several times, trying to get my mind back from the edge of overload. When the room stopped spinning, I had the distinct impression that Dax was laughing at me.

"Ensign Sisko," Dax said. "If you are to succeed with the opposite sex, you simply must stop drooling. Might I furnish you a bib?"

My ears flamed. "What was that all about?"

"Later, perhaps. And did the story about the Rellian beef have any veracity? It's been a long time since I have enjoyed that delicacy."

I squinted. "Allow me to understand you. You have no appointment tonight. You admit that the lady is incredible. . . ."

"Virtually a singularity."

"Then why postpone the inevitable? I assume that your symbiotic nature . . ." I brought myself up short, suddenly realizing I might be forgetting my place. "I'm sorry, Ambassador. I don't mean to presume."

"You presume, but are not presumptive, young Sisko," Dax said kindly. "My apparent reticence should not deceive you. Sabbath Nile is an extraordinary creature, and I eagerly anticipate the consummation of our relationship."

That, I decided, was more information than I actually needed. Nonetheless, I had opened the door and could not complain if Dax strolled through it.

"Ensign Sisko—are you familiar with the writing of your sixteenth century master swordsman, Miyamoto Musashi?"

"*A Book of Five Rings?* I read it, yes."

"Are you familiar with his nine core precepts?"

"Ah . . . 'Do not think dishonestly . . . '?"

"Yes. That was the first. But the sixth and seventh are the most interesting, I think. 'Perceive those things which cannot be seen,' and 'develop intuitive judgment and understanding for everything.' " If you have a weakness, it is not in your mind, which is strong and well-wrought. Neither is it in your body, which is quite well developed. It is in your intuition. You don't understand what you can't see and touch. And you don't trust what you don't understand."

I felt on slightly firmer footing now, and sipped my ale again. "And I should learn these things from a sixteenth century Japanese?"

"Or a twentieth century jazz artist. I forget his name. I believe that he said, 'Jazz is what happens between the notes.' "

"Between the notes," I repeated. "And what *exactly* does that mean?"

"It means, young Sisko," Dax said, pushing himself heavily from the table, "that it is time for me to find my way to bed. In the morning, then?"

I nodded, studying my sparkling ale. I couldn't help the sensation that some game more important than chess was being played out, right under my nose. "In the morning."

I awoke in the morning with my head splitting. That sparkling ale was definitely not as harmless as synthehol, and I made another of my periodic promises to confine myself to the more placid brew. I needed every erg of mental energy. Whatever game Dax was playing, I wanted to be a part of it. Currently, I couldn't even understand it.

My quarters aboard Pelios Station were modest but comfortable, enough room to sleep and wash, a tiny dining nook for private entertainment (I took most of my meals in the mess hall), and a desk.

Performing my morning ablutions, I caught sight of the time in time to curse, realizing I was late for the morning meeting.

The replicator coughed out the simplest possible meal that would satisfy my morning nutritive requirements, a chewy bar of enriched oatmeal fortified with everything a human body needed to survive a day of manual labor.

It tasted terrible, but those were the wages of oversleeping.

I was out the door, thinking of the reason I had overslept: the attempt to retrieve the fragments of a dream which swam just at the edges of consciousness as I awoke. In it, Sabbath and Dax were pruning a tree, a little bonsai tree, and commenting about the branches: how they appeared separate, but were actually part of the same trunk. The tree was trying to talk. It kept changing aspects, and the last one, held just before I was wrenched awake by the voice of the station computer, was a topiary which bore a suspicious resemblance to one Benjamin Sisko.

By implication I had granted Dax a free rein with the lovely lady, but had no intention of quitting so easily. There were still gambits to be played. Ambassador Dax might well have seniority on the station, and I had to defer to the old man in all such matters. But when it came to affairs of the heart, well, that was one arena where I knew it was fair to compete in any way I chose, including those which might be blatantly unfair.

By the time I entered the conference room, the next set of negotiations were already underway.

The Bactricans sat at one side of the table, Federation officials on the other. I understood some of the negotiation points, such as mutual defense treaties and access to Bactrican technology. Others were secretive, not spelled out explicitly in these meetings. Some codicils were in the memory of Ambassador Dax, and others remained in coded transmissions.

Bactrican mining rights were currently on the table, and the negotiations seemed to be going well.

Dax nodded his head in brief acknowledgment as I entered the room, and then returned to his intense conversation.

Again, I was struck by the drabness of the Bactricans, male and female. It was odd: Both seemed not only androgynous, but utterly bereft of the kind of mild and pleasurable tension one finds between members of most species. Perhaps they only mated at some set time of the year. On the other hand, it was certainly possible that the Bactricans treasured a low birth rate, and toned down their personal chemistry as an odd form of birth control.

A Bactrican rose to speak. "That leaves a final matter, recently brought to my attention by Co-councillor Y'men." He seemed familiar. Where had I seen him . . . oh, yes. The prude who had fled the bar the previous evening.

"The abomination. It must end. The ceremony of death is not to be violated, and must be completed, or the spirits cannot rest."

There was a buzz around the edge of the table, and Dax spread his hands flatly on its smooth surface. "I cannot promise that," he said. "Please remember that until you are officially a member of the Federation, you cannot make such demands, whereas our rules of sanctuary are very clear. I doubt if you wish to discuss this further in so open a venue."

"You blackmail us," the Bactrican ambassador said. "You know that we need this treaty. And yet our customs, strange as they seem to you, must be respected, or our peoples can never live in peace."

"I am quite certain," Dax said, "that we can find a resolution."

"We must," The Bactrican ambassador insisted. "The Prince Royal arrives later today, and all such matters must be resolved—or we will resolve them."

There was a moment of deadly silence. What was passing between this creature and Dax? What was the implicit threat, and what the transgression? Frankly, it was beyond me.

There followed a series of words which I could not understand, but when the translator caught up with it, he said, "—presence of the Azziz is offensive."

The Bactricans stood from the table and filed out, the drab, gray little creatures seeming to brighten the room by the mere fact of their departure.

"What is the enmity between Bactricans and Azziz?" I asked.

"The Bactricans are strict isolationists. To this day, they will not allow visitors to their planet's surface. If they didn't need Federation strength, they wouldn't be at the table now. The Azziz aren't part of the Federation—so the Bactricans don't need to be polite."

The level of emotional intensity at the table seemed to imply more than mere distaste. I wondered if Dax was lying to me. "The Azziz don't seem fazed."

Dax chuckled. "Not at all. They have technology, and knowledge, valuable to us, but nothing *we* have has ever really been more than an interesting oddity to them. Like a delicacy, not a necessity. They won't enter into any kind of diplomatic negotiation with us. They barely understand the concept."

"Because their connections are more basic than that?"

Dax smiled, temporarily lifted from his thoughts. "Yes, Ensign. That is apparently it. It would be like negotiating to be someone's liver."

I laughed. Then as casually as I could, I asked: "And what was all of that about 'the abomination'?"

Dax's face darkened again. "Well, that is a matter I can't discuss with you yet. It involves the most basic aspects of their culture. It seems we have offended them. It must be resolved before the treaty can move forward."

He sighed. "I was invited to meet with the Azziz, who are transferring their goods this afternoon. They will leave again tomorrow. I asked Sabbath if she would care to attend, but I will be detained. You might care to take my place."

I felt a jolt of surprise. "You'd trust me?"

"Young Sisko," Dax said kindly. "If I didn't, I would hardly have requested you as my adjunct."

Sabbath was surprised to see me when I appeared at her door. I hazarded that she was between shows, and resting. She was dressed in a wrap that was as sheer as a breath of spring, and yet somehow modest. The fine fur that covered her body was at rest, without the fine, rippling motion that was so appealing.

She greeted me with cautious pleasure. "Yes, Benjamin?" she said. "Can I help you?"

I felt much like a schoolboy, wishing that some of Dax's studied, confident manner would rub off on me. Little doubt why she preferred the old man. Be that as it may, if I lost the contest, at least I would lose fighting. "Ambassador Dax sent me to escort you to the Azziz ship."

Her stride was long and fluid, and although she was four centimeters the shorter, she easily matched speed with me. "You've never said much of yourself," I said, trying to open the conversation.

She smiled without answering.

"And Dax has said little about you. He implied once that on Earth you might have been thought of as a nun."

She cocked her head sideways, as if not recognizing the word.

"A nun. A celibate female practitioner of a religious discipline. Sometimes thought to be married to the spiritual head of the sect. Nunneries were often places to drain off the excess female population, a form of birth control."

Her smile was secretive, and maddening. "I would expect Dax to say something like that."

"Is he sworn to secrecy?"

"He is discreet."

I wanted to pound the walls. "For God's sake. Where are you from? What are your people? I've never seen anyone like you before."

She stopped, and gazed up at me. "I like you, Benjamin. I really do. But it is not proper for you to ask such questions."

I sighed, and nodded, and we went on. *God damn you, old man,* I said to myself. *What do you have that I don't have, and how long will I have to live before I have it?* Sabbath moved slightly ahead of me. I watched her body sway beneath the robe. Hypnotic, the most feminine thing I had ever seen in my life. I contrasted her with the Bactricans, the pale males and doughy females, and shuddered.

There was just no justice in this world, I thought, and then hurried to catch up.

The Federation bioengineer, a Vulcan named Sh'tan ushered us through the tunnel toward the Azziz ship. "I have modified our tricorders," he said, "so you will be able to see the input from the Azziz ship as interpreted by the station computers. This is a rare opportunity."

Apparently others on the station agreed. Admiral Janeway and two assistants accompanied us. Even Cal was there, although I suspected that he was more interested in Sabbath than Azziz technology.

"Since first contact with the Azziz almost two hundred years ago," Sh'tan said, "we have admired their bioengineering. But we never had anything to offer them. However, our own advances in these areas led us into some arenas where the Azziz themselves have not gone."

"Such as?" the admiral asked.

"Some of the genetic manipulation which has enabled crossbreeding and intermarriage between species has led to interesting avenues. When we demonstrated some of the results to the Azziz, it was as if they finally considered us to be civilized. Until now, they would make only minor trades with us. We believe that they found us amusing. Now . . . we think we have cause to be optimistic."

The dock's former incrustation had become more advanced, a crystalline shell over the initial weld. It matched the coloration of the station walkway. "As far as we can tell, this happened automatically," Sh'tan said. "What we thought was an exudate created by a living thing was instead a colony of polynucleic organisms regurgitated by a host. They spontaneously analyze any substance they come in contact with, and produce a matching composition." One of his arched eyebrows lifted. "Quite remarkable, considering that it is stable to a thousand atmospheres."

The sphincter dilated, and our group of eight entered the ship. It was warm, and the bullfrog Poet bounced ahead of us. It bounced up to a portion of the wall, stuck, and then burbled at us. Its English had grown surprisingly polished in its forty hours aboard the station. "Meet the Navigator," it said, "Its optic nerves permeate the entire outer shell. It is sensitive to the entire electromagnetic spectrum. It allows us to navigate by the stars."

Poet bounced to another wall. "This is the Refrigeration Unit," it said. A blue ball of what seemed to be glowing fluid oozed from beneath a bunch of cables that descended like living intestines. It extended a pseudopod toward me in what seemed a friendly gesture. Without thinking I reciprocated, and the Poet yelled something in a pitch far too high and fast to be intelligible. The pseudopod withdrew after the barest touch. Cold raced through my hand like electricity.

Poet had narrowly saved my fingers. The Refrigeration Unit had sensed my body heat, and responded by draining it off. I blew on my fingers to warm them.

The admiral asked several questions about the interaction of the Azziz ship components, some of which grew so technical and abstract that I had difficulty following. Sabbath listened intently to every question, and every answer.

One of the interesting surprises was the secondary propulsion system, something that apparently acted as a low-velocity steering system when the ship positioned itself. This was a creature whose digestive gasses apparently exited at a sufficient velocity to allow its primary "engine" to begin gathering interplanetary, and then interstellar hydrogen.

This primary creature would unfurl from the ship like a gauzy net, continuing to thin and expand and feed, gathering fuel and feeding it to the ship, which then accelerated to near light-speed. There was a living warp drive as well, but language failed our attempts to understand how such a being functioned.

It was magical. Why did all of these creatures work together? The more I saw of the ship, the more I realized the delicacy of their interdependence. The admiral seemed stunned at the implications of the Azziz ship, but curiously, Sabbath smiled, as if she understood something that we did not.

What was there about the Azziz ship that the Bactricans loathed so greatly?

I didn't know, but suspected that the clue was right in front of me. If I could read the secret codicils. If the Azziz had interacted with the Bactricans in previous years . . . but what was Dax hiding . . . ?

The tour ended, and the Poet continued to interact with the officials as Sabbath looked out through the ship's clear crystal shell, gazing out at the stars, her flat, beautiful, delicately furred face saddened.

"Is there something wrong?" I asked.

"They've come so far," she said. "And so far to go

home. You're wrong, you know. You think they want your technology."

"They don't?"

"No more than you want another arm. No. They want family. That is their great drive."

"And you understand them?"

"I think so." She was quiet for a time, her lovely face falling into repose. "I was trained for my dance, to weave my web, my—" and here she said a word that sounded like *shatharma*. Then she seemed startled that she had said it, and smiled ruefully. "I shouldn't have said that."

"Why not?"

She ignored me. "But it seems that the more we do what we must do, the further from ourselves we stray."

"What?" She was making no sense at all.

"The Azziz ship was constructed to leave home. Can you imagine what their home world is? One mass of organisms interacting for the common good. But the better such a ship is, the further it travels from all that it knows. Its excellence brings it pain."

"And that's what you understand?" I sensed that she was saying something of critical import, and strained to understand it.

She seemed to emerge from a self-inflicted trance. "I speak too much," she said. "Come. Let's join the others."

The next event of the Azziz itinerary took us past the Bactrican negotiation hall, where Dax joined us once again. He had just finished his round of negotiations and was, I am certain, quite ready to join the company of joyful creatures once again.

And it was quite a parade. There was virtually a procession of the little living components hopping and rolling down the hallway, in and out of the paths of the humanoids and humans who walked in their midst. Because of the confusion, I didn't see what was about to happen until it was too late.

A member of the Bactrican council stepped out of the corridor, and fired a narrow-beamed energy weapon. The beam was no brighter than a phaser's, and at first that's what I assumed it to be. But from the corner of my eye I saw it strike the Poet, bouncing just in front of Sabbath—and what happened then I didn't think about until moments later.

As disaster struck, Dax grabbed the little Azziz ambassador and moved him to relative safety, out of the line of fire.

Cal protected the admiral.

Reflexively, without thinking, I threw Sabbath to the ground and shielded her, then jumped up again. But Cal had already seized the offending weapon, and wrested it away from a Bactrican I had never seen before. He was tall, and feral, and wore jewel-encrusted chevrons on his shoulder, and I automatically assumed that this was the prince of whom the Bactrican ambassador had spoken.

I glanced at Sabbath. Her eyes met mine. She knew that I had placed my own life in jeopardy for her. Something profound and electric passed between us.

All was confusion, voices strident and frightened. "Was anyone hurt?" I looked again at where the Poet had been, and shuddered.

There was nothing left. And my memory, searching back over the last few seconds, remembered something that made no sense: the Poet had not "disintegrated." It looked as if he had been abstracted to angles, then impossibly folded and folded and folded again until there was nothing left, until he simply disappeared from our reality.

"God's Tooth."

The Bactrican writhed in Cal's grasp, hissing "The abomination! The abomination!" before collapsing in defeat. A team of security people arrived, circling the Azziz ambassador and the admiral.

Dax looked utterly ashen.

The entire group was hustled into a side room, while alarms blared throughout the station. Dax calmed the Azziz ambassador with gestures, then surprisingly, and quietly, spoke to Sabbath.

He turned to me. "This situation is very grave," he said. "Grave for all. Please, take charge here. You are my eyes and ears. I will call for you later."

Dax and Admiral Janeway hurried away. I was able to overhear only a little of what was said between them. A little was enough. My ears burned.

From diplomatic triumph, suddenly this one crazed act had destroyed everything. What worried me, and what I couldn't understand, was the way the Bactrican seemed to have completely deflated. There was no mistaking his body language. Alien or not, inhuman or not, the only possible message was one of naked, feral rage and betrayal.

And a promise of death.

The station was quiet again, and I had waited for the emergency to die down before relaxing my guard. I was completely wrung out, exhausted. The situation seemed clear cut, and yet impossibly complex at the same time. For reasons that I didn't understand, a Bactrican prince had attempted to assassinate the Azziz ambassador, and had instead killed the little translator. Had he acted alone? That seemed unlikely, considering that he had ranted of "the abomination", the same word used by their diplomatic mission. But as an act of policy, what if anything exactly did it mean?

My head was spinning.

Dax sent me a message to join him in his quarters. When I entered I was surprised that the room was so dark and gloomy. For a moment, I didn't see Dax at all, then finally spied him in a corner standing, gazing out through a wall-sized viewscreen that masqueraded as a window. He looked somber in a way I had never seen.

"Excuse me," I said, after standing for almost a minute with no sign of recognition. "Is this a bad time, sir?"

"Indeed it is, but not for the reasons that you might suspect."

I was silent, suspecting that Dax was about to tell me something I had been waiting to hear for weeks.

"Would you care to pour yourself a drink?" Dax asked and indicated the bar. I did, but this time gave myself a good synthehol-based brandy. I suspected that I was going to need all of my wits.

"Sir, you were nearly killed this afternoon. . . ." Dax waved me away, dismissing that concern. I tried again. "Does this destroy hopes of recruiting the Azziz for the Federation?"

Dax nodded. And then he sighed vastly, and began. "Ensign," he said. "I am going to tell you something that I should tell no one. But I have to have another mind share the information, or it is going to be impossible for me to think. Can you do that for me?"

I nodded, and approached a bit closer.

"You know that the situation here has been delicate. The Bactricans seek to join the Federation, but have cultural as well as economic considerations. We would like access to their null-beam technology, and they don't want to share it."

"Moot, now that we've seized a sample for ourselves," I said. "And the Poet, well, that is tragic, of course, sir. But the ambassador is safe."

Dax shook his head slowly. "No, young Sisko. I am afraid that there has been much here that you have not understood. Unfortunately, your contact with other species has primarily been through study. You have yet to make the adjustment to actually interacting with them. You see only what is shown."

The day had been entirely too stressful. I really didn't need to hear this. But I controlled myself. "Please," I said. "Educate me."

Dax sat, enough of his face in shadow that I still couldn't read it easily. "You saw the Azziz collective without intuiting the implication of such a body. You saw the Bactricans and felt some disdain for their drabness. . . ."

"I never said . . ."

"You didn't need to, Ensign. And lastly, you saw my interaction with Sabbath, and assumed that my interest in her was the same as yours."

That perked me up. "It isn't?"

"No, it is not. Let us progress down the line." He held out his hand and began to tick off fingers. "One. The role of the Poet was crucial. Each separate creature in the collective had its own dreams, its own needs, its own mind. They stay together because of the Poet. It was the job of the Poet to sing to them, to keep them in harmony."

I was sobered by the implications. "And without him?"

"Without him, the collective fails. The Azziz ambassador cannot return home."

"But . . . certainly one of our own ships can carry him . . ."

"Again, you don't understand. The entire *ship* is the 'ambassador,' as if a biosphere sample of every important lifeform on Earth were sent to another star for study. Remove a single major link, and the chain fails. We have no means of conveying the entire ship to its origin. We wouldn't even know where to begin."

This was bad. "All right. And where else have I presumed?"

"You presumed that the Bactricans tried to kill the Azziz ambassador."

"Didn't they?"

He shook his head. "No. The target was Sabbath."

My head spun. "Sabbath? Why? Have they a quarrel with her people?"

Dax turned and looked at me flatly. "They *are* her people."

"What?"

"That is the secret that they have fought so hard to keep, for which they very nearly ruined their entrance into the Federation. You have seen the 'male' and 'female' of their species. Sabbath is like a bee, a creature that lives to aid their pollination. There are not many of her kind, but they are necessary for reproduction. Their males and females cannot respond to each other sexually except in the presence of

such a creature. Sabbath's kind are raised and taught in nunneries, separate from the general population. And only the
ruling classes have them on permanent call: They form
bonded triads, betrothed at birth, and sealed until death."

My head spun. "Then the recent death of the royal
family . . ."

"Yes. Sabbath is a 'Third,' the third of the Triad. It was
her place to die with the king and queen, a custom that on
Earth I believe was called 'suttee' and ended by your British
in the India of the nineteenth century . . ."

"It was actually continued well into the twentieth," I
said. Dear God. Suddenly it became clear. Sabbath's unique
appeal . . . trained from childhood, bred for a thousand generations, there was only one downside: She was expected to
commit suicide when her "mates" died.

Instead, somehow, she had escaped to Pelios Station,
stowed away perhaps, and there she had found Curzon Dax.

"She supplied you with information about the Bactricans, and you fought to keep her alive," I said, finally understanding.

He nodded, silently.

"And you're going to give her passage from the station?"

"No. What I tried to do was force the Bactrican government to renounce their claim on her life. If she travels
from the station, they will hunt her down. Here, at least, I
could provide a modicum of protection."

What a nightmare. His attempts to protect her had led,
indirectly, to the death of the Poet necessary to return the
Azziz to their home world.

I shook my head. It hurt. "Why is Sabbath's existence
such a secret, for God's sake?"

"Multiple reasons—only the obvious one being the fact of the royal disgrace. Long ago they fought a terrible war over the 'Thirds.' Jealousy beyond anything we can imagine. It is impossible for them to imagine outsiders who do not desire the creatures of Sabbath's sect."

I saw the problem now, for the first time, and marveled that Dax had been able to hold it all in his head. The Azziz, who possessed a technology coveted by the Federation. The Bactricans, who enslaved an entire segment of their population, but might be induced to change their ways to gain the recognition they craved.

And a single creature named Sabbath. Certainly not male, but not truly female, either. Something else. Something *other,* that had touched me deeply, almost spiritually. Her life was in the balance, in a situation that now *had* no balance. The treaty would collapse, the Azziz were lost. Without the intercession of the Federation, Sabbath's people might endure another thousand years of reproductive subjugation.

And I had seen the look in Admiral Janeway's eye: This little problem could end Curzon Dax's career in disgrace, and kill mine before it had a chance to start.

The Academy had not prepared me for this.

I cradled my head in my hands. "Is there anything we can do at all?" I said.

He laid his broad hand on my back. It felt strangely comforting. One part of me wanted to kill him, and another wanted to praise him for attempting the impossible. If he had succeeded in pressuring the Bactricans into pardoning Sabbath, it would have created a cultural ripple that might have freed her kind.

Bless you, Dax.

Damn you, Dax.

"Nothing *we* can do, no," Dax said finally. I rose, still shaken, and left him. And it wasn't until I had left Dax's presence that I realized that I had heard an emphasis in that last sentence that I hadn't understood at all.

Sleep came slowly to me that night, and for a very long time I was certain that it wouldn't come at all.

I lay in my bed, staring at the ceiling, wondering what kind of creature Curzon Dax was, to weave so tangled a web.

Here there was despair, alienation, murder, perversity, miscommunication, technology beyond our imaginings, provincialism, and disaster on five or six different levels. Those were just the first problems that came to mind.

A single tragic error seemed to have collapsed the possibilities for success on two different fronts. I was horrified. If this was the life of the peacekeeper, give me the cold equations of an engineer. This was not for me.

I barely heard the door to my cabin opening.

I smelled her before I saw her, outlined there against dim night light. I held my breath, not believing. She bent over me, silencing my questions with a single finger to my lips.

"Do not ask from me," she said. "Do not try to take what I cannot give. But you risked your life for me, and it is right to share with you."

She bade me stand, and clumsily I obeyed. I seemed to have forgotten how to speak, or move. She took my hands, and smiled the saddest, gentlest smile I had ever seen.

We danced. Just danced. She performed for an audience of one. I didn't need the induction equipment. I wasn't a

Bactrican. But I understood then, what she meant to them. I understood why they would kill for her, would throw away their chances of peace and security to keep her kind a secret.

She opened my mind that night, opened my eyes there in the darkness of my room, and filled them with her own light.

The last thing I recall was her voice, soft as perfume in my ear. "Do not walk away from what you need, young Sisko," she said, almost as if she was someone else. "He cannot offer it. You must ask."

I tried to ask her what she meant, but her fingers stole my thoughts, my words, and left only song.

It was enough.

I awoke without ever realizing I had lain down to sleep. Of course, she was gone. I drew my knees up to my chest, shivering with the heat, wondering if I would ever belong to myself again.

I was afraid for her, knowing that her life was forfeit if she was found on the station. The princeling had tried to take revenge for the royals, but there would be others. I was not thinking clearly, and knew it, but could not help myself. There was only one thing to do. I would take her away. If it meant that abandoning my commission, so be it. Certainly there were things more important.

My vision narrowed down until it seemed I was staring down a tube, darkness at the edges. All I could see was Sabbath, all I could feel was the need to be with her again, on whatever terms. The thought of her performing in the cabaret one more night was more than I could endure.

It had to end, and I would end it.

I tapped my wall communicator, and called her quarters. There was no answer. "Computer," I said to the empty air, "locate Sabbath Nile."

"Sabbath Nile is no longer on Pelios Station."

I stood, staring at myself in the mirror, temporarily not seeing the man I was, the man I had always assumed myself to be. Suddenly it seemed that I was not there, that I was looking through myself, that I could see a man-shaped outline, with stars sparkling behind them, an odd illusion that persisted even when I blinked. Certainly I was sleeping. I could not see what I saw. Could not have heard what had just been said.

"Repeat that?" I heard myself say.

The reply came at once. *"Sabbath Nile is no longer on Pelios Station."*

I remembered opening and closing the door, but couldn't remember dressing. Couldn't remember running down my hall, couldn't remember how long it took me before I stood before Dax's door. I pounded my fist against the door, and it did not open. I drew stares from the people who passed in the hall, and whispers, and suddenly realized that I was a sight to behold.

I slowed, the stars no longer drawing me when I closed my eyes. I slapped my combadge. "Computer, locate Curzon Dax."

"Curzon Dax is in the main council room."

I took a deep breath, attempting to steady myself, and looked down at my clothing. I wouldn't have been surprised to discover myself naked, such a fever was I in. But I wore my uniform, and except for the fact that my creases were out of alignment, I looked fine. I straightened myself, thanking endless hours of practice for allowing my unconscious ablutions to be as polished as this.

I was still in a fever when I came to the council room door. It opened for me. Admiral Janeway and several Federation officials were congratulating Dax as I entered. I caught snatches of their conversation, and only a very tiny word that told me everything that I wanted to know.

"Sacrifice," the word had been.

I stared at Dax, suddenly understanding, not wanting to understand, but in some way needing to. Dax shook Janeway's hand as the admiral left, still speaking his congratulations.

Dax stood in the empty room, at the podium.

I felt the essence of the understanding Sabbath had imparted to me slipping away. "A celebration," I said numbly.

Dax nodded. "Yes, Ensign. There is cause to celebrate."

"The Azziz have left, haven't they?"

Again, Curzon Dax indicated the affirmative.

"And Sabbath Nile is with them."

"Sh'tan predicts a seventy percent chance that her nervous system can carry the load, can sustain them. Can get them home."

"But she'll never return."

"We do not know that. This opens a new era in our relationship with the Azziz. We don't understand enough about them to say."

"She may not survive the journey."

"None of us survive the journey, young Ensign."

Anger such as I had never felt, never known *existed* flooded up in me, coursed through me, strong as the love and the need, only inverted. Through it I heard Dax say:

"She came to you last night, didn't she?"

I nodded, miserably. In a moment, I would kill Dax for what he had done. In a moment, I would—

My legs were unsteady.

"She should not. What she shared with you was forbidden at the deepest levels imaginable. She gave you a gift, young Ensign. One she thought you strong enough to bear. Was she right?"

I couldn't see, couldn't hear. Knew only the great, great pain filling my heart.

"She could not stay. Could not go anywhere within the Federation. Assassins are inexpensive, and they would have considered it a matter of honor to kill her. She wished to live. We now have the treaties, and the technology we need. That her people need. The Azziz, in being joined to her, are joined to the Federation in a way that they can understand."

My entire body trembled, and I could no longer stand. I sat heavily on the table, arms hugging my stomach.

He was a monster. "So everything . . . is *fine* now?" I put as much acid in the word as I could.

"No, it is ill," and as he said that his officious manner slid aside for a moment, and I saw a very old, very tired man, a man who had, once again, made decisions and compromises lesser men could not even imagine. Sacrificing a splendid young woman. Or saving her. Capping his own career. Or damning himself. "But it was the best we could do. It was the only answer, once the violence occurred. Young Ensign, I see something in you, an urge to understand everything within the logic you love so dearly. But the last and greatest lesson of reason is to understand that there are things beyond its reach. I see this in you. As did Sabbath. Which is why she gave you the gift she did. Was she wrong?"

I gazed at Dax, every muscle in my body trembling, feeling the tide of my rage washing over me, clawing at me, demanding . . .

What?

Dax watched me with eyes that were old before my birth, eyes that were beyond compassion.

We are each so alone. We treasure what small joinings we may find. As the Azziz with their colonies. As Dax and his symbiont. As Sabbath and her Triad, even though she had chosen life.

And where did I belong, and to what?

My knees weakened beneath me and I felt a great wave break as the induced rage and rapture began to subside. I looked at my fingers and saw hands, not stars. Looked at Dax's face and saw a face. Dax touched my shoulder, and I stepped back, knowing that I did not understand the creature before me, and worse, that I did not understand myself.

And I had never understood Sabbath at all.

What was I doing here? As the wave broke I felt naked, exposed, like a child standing on a beach, staring at a tidal wave representing the knowledge of a universe vaster than all the seas, trying to contain that vastness in the plastic bucket at my side.

"Young Ensign," Dax said kindly. "There comes a time when we understand that our minds do not contain the firmament. But still, our hearts can grasp it. *Let go.*"

I turned away, the breaking of the wave unleashing a flood of grief so strong that I wanted to die, knew I must die, knew that I could not survive, and Dax's arm was around me, comfortingly, and I was ashamed—

And that passed as well.

I wiped my face, turning aside, composing myself, feeling Sabbath's presence receding away and away from me, even as the Azziz ship was accelerating toward its distant point of origin. Felt myself saying goodbye to someone who had broken vows to embrace life, had cheapened herself to display in a bar gifts that had once been the exclusive province of royalty. And due to a bizarre twist, had found a way to redeem herself, and before she had, had set my mind free in a way I couldn't have imagined.

And how much of this was Dax's doing? I gasped for air, unformed words catching in my throat. There was a tiny space open, Sabbath's gift, dwindling even as I examined it. Soon, if I did not fill it, it would close completely, and I would once again be thrust into a world of numbers and physics. Such a waste. There was more, so much more.

I looked at Dax with desperation, seeking words that wouldn't come.

"I know," Dax said.

"What do I do?"

"I cannot tell you that."

Desperate, feeling the insight vanishing, even as I could not place it into words, I said: "Be my mentor, Curzon Dax. Be my friend. Help me understand."

"You will never understand," Dax said, and watched me carefully.

So many things, so little time. That spark of light glowed within me for a final moment, and I said: "Then help me *see*. Help me hear the music between the notes."

His face broke into a small smile. "That I can do . . . Benjamin."

The world was not what I wished it to be. It was not what was represented in the text books, not what I thought or theorized or philosophized it to be. It just was.

And perhaps, just perhaps, that was not such a frightening thing. Tentatively, I extended my hand. He extended his, and for the first time, I truly felt the clasp of the greatest friend and teacher I have had in this life, the good and honorable Curzon Dax.

JADZIA

"Don't mistake a new face for a new soul, Kang."

—Jadzia Dax
"Blood Oath"

L. A. Graf

L. A. Graf is herself a conjoined species, collectively possessing degrees in geochemistry, biology, and neuromuscular therapy, as well as two dogs, four snakes, six cats, and a breeding leopard gecko colony whose population fluctuates seasonally between twelve and forty animals. Individually, she is: Karen Rose Cercone, university geoscience professor, author of the Helen Sorby–Milo Kachigan historical mystery series, and owner of half the dogs and cats and all of the snakes; and Julia Ecklar, author of the popular Noah's Ark science fiction series originally published in Analog magazine, professional animal trainer, and owner of the other half of the dogs and cats, as well as all the geckos.

Reflections

L. A. Graf

T
HE SYMBIONT INSIDE her stirred.

Not physical movement, not really. After joining, the soft-bodied packet of neurons and wetware that was the soul of Trill immortality fell quiescent among its bed of living organs until its host finally died decades later. So Jadzia knew, intellectually at least, that her reservoir of living memory didn't squirm about inside her, didn't spasm with her fear or twist with her pangs of guilt. But another part of her—the part that struggled to wrap words and images around the river of sensations poured into her awareness by her symbiont—that part insisted on fabricating tactile impulses where none could possibly exist. When Jadzia "felt" Dax tremble and huddle closer to her heart, she knew it was only a phantom reflection of their shared despair.

Still, her stomach clenched around that pulse of apparent movement, and she knotted her fist against the pouch in her belly without caring whether the sensation was real.

"Ziranne?"

She'd made her voice as soft as possible, but the woman at the window still jerked around as though she'd been slapped on the shoulder. Fear shadowed her gray eyes almost to black, like a broken owl's wing spread across polished river stone. *Stranger's eyes,* Jadzia thought with another subtle tremor. *Stranger's eyes in a sister's face.*

"Can we go home now?" Ziranne asked plaintively. "I don't want to be here anymore. Whatever happened, I'm really sorry. I just want to go home now."

Jadzia tried on a reassuring smile. It felt stiff and unconvincing on her lips. "We can't go home just yet. The doctor will tell us when." Maybe later. Maybe never.

"But I said I was sorry." Ziranne plucked at the bandaging that swathed her forearm to the elbow. "I never meant to hurt anybody. I was only trying to help." Long, precise incisions carved parallel tracks down the length of her forearm, revealed inch-by-inch with each unwinding turn of bandage. Her voice hardened, becoming more adult and less familiar to Jadzia's ears. "Any Trill who wasn't already joined would have done the same thing I did."

Jadzia swallowed dryly to release her voice. "But you *are* joined now. Aren't you?"

The sound that burst from Ziranne might have been a

laugh. She turned to face the darkening sky outside the window, her back to Jadzia, and her not-quite laugh abruptly dissolved into tears. Jadzia watched her run trembling fingers over the ridges left in her arm by what the doctor said might have been a knife blade, was probably a piece of glass.

"How did you become joined, Ziranne?" She hated that she sounded so distant, so cool. But she was also afraid of what might happen if she were to weaken her guard. "Whose symbiont is inside you now?"

That was the question. Its elusive answer was why the Symbiosis Commission had sent for her, and why Benjamin Sisko had rerouted the *Defiant* from returning to Deep Space 9 following its near disastrous recent visit to Earth. After he'd successfully thwarted a plot to overthrow the Federation government by a group of renegade Starfleet officers—officers who'd been his friends—Dax knew that a new crisis was the last thing Sisko needed right now. But he'd brought them here just the same. That was the kind of friend he was.

So the questions hung in the air. How does a Trill preschool teacher who has never requested joining acquire a symbiont without stealing it from the subterranean pools? Had she killed the previous host? If so, who had the victim been . . . and why had she done it?

Ziranne answered that question the way she had a half-dozen times before. With a flinch, as though some painful specter rushed up and stabbed her from behind, followed by a frightened, childlike question of her own: "How did I get here? Why don't I remember it?"

Jadzia knotted her hands together in her lap. "You walked into a hospital in Gheryzan, in Trill's eastern hemisphere. You were frightened, incoherent. When the doctors checked your medical records, they realized that you weren't—that you shouldn't have been—joined. They tried to find out where your symbiont came from, and that's when you . . . hurt yourself." No—lying, no matter how well intentioned, would get them nowhere. Lifting her chin, Jadzia continued, more bravely, "You tried to kill yourself. Everyone was worried that you didn't feel safe with all the strangers around you, so they brought you here to the Symbiosis Commission and asked me to come and stay with you."

Whether Ziranne drifted or stumbled, it was hard to tell. Within a few steps, she'd settled to the edge of the room's only bed, one hand still clasped around her wrist as though holding back blood that no longer flowed. "And they asked you . . . why?"

This time, the pain rushed in before Jadzia could distance herself and ward it away. "Because I'm your sister." Something felt odd about that assertion, so she clarified it by saying, "Jadzia is Ziranne's sister. Don't you remember?"

Ziranne rolled onto the bed in a single sluggish collapse, hands fluttering up to shield her eyes from things Jadzia couldn't see. "I'm tired of remembering," she whispered. "All I ever do anymore is remember. And I don't even know whose memories they are." She dropped her hands and stared back at Jadzia with those dark and alien eyes. "If you're really my sister . . . you remember. Remember it for me."

Jadzia sucked in a deep breath, not sure if her sister meant that as a challenge or a plea for help. Over the past hours, she had tried every conversational gambit she knew to reach through the tangled knot of illicit symbiont and unprepared host to reach the real Ziranne. This was the closest thing to a breakthrough she had managed to achieve. Another shiver, a real one this time, shook through Jadzia as she tried to decide what part of their shared past could call Ziranne's own personality out of hiding. It was her symbiont, not herself, who calmly processed that reaction and extracted from it a strand of her personal history, saved and stored in its neural tissues now as well as her own. The memory came to her with such force that Jadzia was almost surprised not to see her breath turn to frost in the air.

"Do you remember the summer we got to play in the snow?" Nothing flickered in those shadowed eyes, but at least a little of the tension seemed to seep away from Ziranne's pale face. "We were eleven, and we spent our vacation on Uncle Koal's farm. . . ."

It was already midsummer, and it had finally snowed on their uncle's plantation in Trill's southern hemisphere. They swathed themselves in identical yellow snowsuits, stamped their feet into identical bloodred boots, and squealed off into the snow as though these few months in another climate somehow extended their entire year. Summer was their favorite season, but they did so love the snow.

Separated in age by only ten months, it was during the dull, muggy summers when they gloried in their temporary sameness. Sharing an age, even if only for a couple of months, seemed almost the same as sharing a soul. They told strangers they were twins, laced and twined their hair the same, looked at themselves in the glass of still summer ponds and speculated as to whether it was necessary for twins to arrive in the world at the very same time, or if twinness was something more than that, something that still blessed them despite the months separating their respective births. Spending their "twin season" this year in a southern winter somehow seemed to cement their bond, promising to extend its warmth and giddiness year-round. They were too young to really appreciate how it would be later, when they returned to the north feeling as though they'd never had a summer at all.

Jadzia was technically oldest. That meant very little when they weren't in school, but it was something about which adults would meticulously remind them. Even when they *were* in school, their general sameness in age, looks, and temperament opened up a delightful array of options for mischief. Jadzia excelled in mathematics; Ziranne had a natural flair for art. Jadzia attended two years of math classes (one of them in Ziranne's name), while Ziranne produced an impressive collection of cybersculpture all signed in Jadzia's distinctive hand.

When they were eleven, they didn't realize yet how the change from children into young women would shatter their illusion of sameness. It was the last year in which the shape of their faces would be so exact, the lean wisp of their bodies so featureless. By the very next summer, Jadzia would have begun the irreversible bolt toward statuesque; the year after, Ziranne's voice would deepen and her form fill out toward plumpness. They would forever carry the family mark that said "sister," but no one would ever again mistake them for twins.

So in retrospect, that summer-turned-winter was in many ways the last of their childhood. Jadzia often wondered if they would have spent it differently, done things differently, if they'd had some inkling of the different directions in which they'd soon go. Seven lifetimes of experience said no. That was part of the joy of childhood—every day seemed eternal, the whole of the universe spread out before you. By the time you could truly appreciate the fearful impermanence of life—even seven times over—it was already too late to go back and make better use of your misspent youth. So instead of cherishing each moment by constructing loving holopics of all the childish pleasures they shared, they galloped heedlessly through that vacation time, squandering their days in countless undocumented snowball battles and skating contests. They made silhouetted tableaux by flinging themselves into the snow, and dared each other to stick their tongues to icicles.

Surfacing from yet another collapsed burrow in the snowy blanket, Jadzia blinked through the sparkle of frost on her eyelashes at the escarpment bordering the *lida* orchard. "Hey, Ziranne," she announced, "I'll bet we could slide down that."

Ziranne didn't look up, distracted by the detailed work of scooping the slush out of her snowsuit sleeves. "We could if we got up to the top." She yanked off one glove and shook it fiercely. "I don't feel like climbing, Jadzia."

"Sissy."

An angry blush steamed across her cheeks. "I'm not a sissy. I'm cold."

"It's *winter.*" Jadzia scooped up a double handful of snow, twisting to cram it down the back of her sister's collar. But Ziranne, as always, knew what she was thinking, and flung herself backward with a squeak to avoid the attack. "Everybody's cold in winter. *You're* a sissy!" Hauling one foot then the other loose from the rucked up snow, Jadzia trooped off toward the hillside with big, stomping strides. She felt like she had to pick her feet up to her shoulders to crunch her way through the drifts. "I'm gonna go sliding."

She heard Ziranne flounder upright behind her, but didn't expect to see her mirror sister barrel past at an awkward run until Ziranne was already in the lead, arms pumping, snow-wet hair flapping in her wake. Yelping a wordless objection, Jadzia gulped a lungful of air and galumphed off in pursuit.

They reached the foot of the hill almost together—Ziranne got her foot on the slope first of all, but Jadzia let herself fall forward so that her hands hit only a bare heartbeat after. Their eyes sparkled with tears from their running, their cheeks red and glowing, and steam blasted out on the sound of their laughter as they collapsed atop each other, panting.

"So how do we get up?" Ziranne asked at last, rolling to her back to peruse the hill from this new perspective.

Jadzia propped herself up on her elbows and took a serious look. "Uncle Koal has a path that he climbs up to spray the trees in the spring." She only knew this because she'd heard him talk about it, not because she'd ever been here in the spring. "It's got to be under the snow someplace. All we have to do is find it."

Which, under almost a meter of windswept powder, was much easier to contemplate than do. They finally found the first weathered stone close up against where the rocky slope jutted straight skyward. Jadzia used the full length of her arm to sweep one step, then the next, and the next, climbing the carved path as she cleared it. Ziranne followed behind, kicking loose whatever snowpack was left with the heel of one thick-soled boot. By the time they crested the top, Jadzia shrugged against a trickle of clammy sweat between her shoulder blades, and Ziranne was forced to plop to the ground and dig snow out of her boot tops as well as her sleeves.

The view more than made up for any discomfort. The

whole of Uncle Koal's plantation stretched out beneath them, a fluffy quilt of patchwork white, brown, and silver where snow, roads, and ponds intersected. Jadzia imagined she'd scaled Bes Manev in the far east of Trill, the world's tallest mountain. She squinted against the fierce Manevri sunlight, shielded her eyes from the stinging wind that had blown many a previous explorer from this exalted height. *When I'm joined,* she thought, *I'm going to explore all the places and do all the things I've ever dreamed I could.* She might even bond with a symbiont who already possessed all those experiences and more, memories ripe for the living. She found the thought exhilarating.

"Jadzia, look! It's already got a slide built in!" Ziranne ducked across Jadzia's view, interrupting her reverie. Tugging at the arm of her sister's snowsuit, Ziranne shook a soggy mitten at the narrow downward sweep clearly visible in the contours of the snow.

It wasn't really a snow-slide, of course—it was the run-off channel Uncle Koal had installed to keep the *lida* trees from flooding when the spring rains came so often and hard. This became apparent as they rolled and slid and scooted their way down the curving track. It took three or four passes to finally pack enough snow against the synthrock to form an acceptable chute. When they'd succeeded, the trip from top to bottom was wild and fast, and Jadzia had to close her eyes so that the thrilling rush of the world flying by didn't distract her from her screaming.

It was on her third trip down, after she'd thudded into the wall of snow at the bottom and rolled, that she craned a look back up the slide to greet her sister—

—And found no one there.

"Ziranne?"

A thin little sound that might have been a voice, might have been the wind. Lurching to her feet, Jadzia gulped two deep breaths to fill her lungs and clawed partway back up the bottom of the slide. *"Ziranne!"*

This time her sister's shriek was unmistakable.

She aborted her first instinct to struggle back up the way she came, and instead flung herself down the rest of the chute to hit the ground running. They'd used their own bodies to plow a crumbling trench from the foot of the slide to the foot of Uncle Koal's hand-carved stairs. Jadzia stumbled through it now with her knees knocking against the too-close sides, her feet catching on lumps and bumps she'd somehow never noticed in her previous passings. The trail stretched suddenly endless and labrynthine. She skidded to round the last bit of curve before the stairs, and her eyes clapped on a splash of sun yellow suspended from the hill only a few steps from the very top.

Jadzia was up the narrow flight and on her knees above her sister without clearly remembering how she got there.

"Jadzia!" Ziranne had lost one scarlet mitten; the fingers of that hand made a claw between chinks of stone and had already gone from pink to white in the cold. Her mittened fist balled around a handhold Jadzia couldn't even see. "Jadzia, I'm stuck! I slipped and I'm stuck!" She glanced up at her sister for barely an instant, sensing perhaps some dangerous shift of weight Jadzia could only imagine. The trembling in her narrow frame kept knocking one foot off its perch, forcing her to fight all over again for that purchase.

"Hold still!" Jadzia commanded. She felt suddenly cold herself, her belly all liquid and sick. "Stop shaking, Ziranne, or you're gonna fall." She tried to straddle two steps, a knee on either, and lean over to take hold of Ziranne's wrists. But even before she could put a hand on her sister, she knew she didn't have the leverage, didn't have the room to drag her back up to safety. She straightened without ever grabbing her. "I can't pull you up—"

"Jadzia!" Ziranne jerked with sudden movement, as though frantic to lessen the distance between them. "Jadzia, don't leave me!"

Jadzia let herself thump a few steps farther down the stairway, afraid she'd reach out to Ziranne on frightened impulse and cause them both to fall. "Ziranne, hold on. I'm just going down the stairs, but I'm not leaving. I'm gonna fix things. Okay?"

Ziranne might have nodded, Jadzia wasn't sure. "Just hold on," she said again. Then she turned decisively away and rode the stairs down on her bottom. Suddenly, the thought of standing up on that narrow descent was too unnerving.

At the bottom, she rounded the slope to stand beneath her sister. From above she'd harbored some vague plan to go below and catch her—to stand on something, maybe, and reach up and let Ziranne drop down into her hug. But there was nothing there to boost her taller, and Ziranne was higher than she'd seemed from the stairs. They'd even shouldered away whatever snow had shrouded the foot of the slope to make their path from the slide, which left only packed ice and frozen ground to catch her sister's body. Jadzia felt frustrated tears burn at the backs of her eyes and blinked them angrily away.

Ziranne's wail floated down from above, a lace cloth dropped from a great height. "My feet are slipping!" That same foot, pawing at the rockface, slipping off, flailing in the air for a moment until it found its place again. "I'm gonna fall!"

"No, you're not!" The assertion burst out of Jadzia sounding more like anger than the desperation she felt. "I told you, hold on! Don't let go 'til I tell you to!"

She said it without quite knowing what she meant. But as soon as the words were in the air between them, Jadzia knew what she needed to do.

Slim, child-arms could only shovel up so big a load of snow, and the whole width of a child's shoulders could only bulldoze a tiny bit better. She ended up turning her back to the target she'd mentally drawn on the ground beneath her sister, and bent over to dig two-handed like a *mreker*, throwing snow between her legs in a rapid shower. She dug out everything within a body length of ground zero, then moved another length away and starting digging some more. Her back ached by the time she moved inward to redistribute the new circle of snow onto the rest of the pile. First with bent-over digging, then an armload at a time when her hands wouldn't dig anymore, she built up a bed of snow almost as tall as her head. She could hear Ziranne crying high above her and realized even before her sister did that if this cushion wasn't good enough, they didn't have time to make it any better.

"Okay!" she called upward, stumbling back from the pile. "It's okay now, Ziranne—let go!"

Ziranne was falling before Jadzia's voice had even faded from the air.

She hit the pile with a breathy, heavy *whump!* Snow billowed up like smoke, splashed outward in a wave. Jadzia ducked her face away only enough to avoid being blinded by the shower, then rushed forward to scale the mini-mountain and grab at her sister's hand.

"Are you all right?" she demanded breathlessly. She crawled on top of Ziranne, patting at her fearfully, trying to read the wide-eyed expression on her face. "Are you hurt?"

Ziranne raised her head up to look from side to side. Her bare hand patted at the snow her fall had packed, and she blinked as though not sure what she was seeing. "You piled up the snow." Looking squarely at Jadzia, she repeated, as though amazed, "Jadzia, you piled up the snow to catch me!"

Jadzia's heart lodged in her throat. "You didn't know?" When Ziranne only shook her head, Jadzia hit her on the shoulder, hit her again as fear and anger all came to a head inside her. "Then why did you let go, you idiot? If you didn't know I had the snow pile down here, why did you just let go like that?"

Ziranne seemed amazed the question even had to be asked. "Because you told me to." She laid back against the snow and gazed up at her sister with a trust Jadzia had never recognized before and would never misunderstand again. "I knew you wouldn't tell me to let go if it wouldn't be okay. I knew you'd take care of me, Jadzia. You always do."

Not this time, Jadzia thought as she watched Bashir carefully repack his medical kit at Ziranne's bedside. It pained her to admit that she'd failed so miserably at her age-old job as sister's keeper. *This time there's not snow enough in the world to cushion your fall, Ziranne.*

None of Jadzia's recollections had seemed to connect with her sister, and she'd finally given up when Bashir had come in to do another round of tests in an attempt to identify the symbiont biochemically. She didn't know whether to be reassured or worried that chemically induced sleep could erase so much more of the turmoil from Ziranne's face than the most important shared memory of their young lives.

"How are you holding up, Old Man?"

She flashed Sisko a quick, automatic smile. "I'll be all right." She crossed her arms and hugged herself against another phantom shiver. "I just wish I could say the same about my sister."

"We're certainly not making the progress I'd hoped for," Duhan Vos admitted. Jadzia thought she detected a surprising impatience in the Symbiosis Commissioner's voice. He'd been elected to the Commission less than six months ago. A late arrival from a backwater colony world, he'd entered the running with promises to revolutionize how the Commission dealt with unjoined Trill and abuses of power. Now, the possibility of making good on all his campaign promises apparently took precedence over whatever empathy the man had once possessed. Or maybe it was just his newness to a position of power that left him feeling he had to prove his worth by solving this mystery single-handedly.

Whatever his reasons, Jadzia didn't need Duhan Vos to tell her that if she failed to find out how Ziranne had come to be joined, the only alternative was to take the symbiont from its unauthorized host and place it directly into the subterranan pools to regenerate. She fiercely pushed that thought out of her own mind, although she couldn't keep its shadow from darkening the cascade of Dax's memories. Duhan was right—this would all have been so much easier if the traumatized symbiont inside Ziranne had been able to communicate with the unjoined symbionts in the pools when Ziranne was immersed in their waters. Instead, they'd detected only chaos in that ancient mind.

"What about your end?" she asked Sisko, abruptly. If she thought too long and closely about all the odds arrayed against them, it only served to distract her. "Have you managed to track down any hosts who could have lost their symbiont without the Commission being informed?"

Her old friend shook his head. "We've checked all of Starfleet's sources. There still haven't been any reports of a dead or dying Trill host, on-world or off." His dark glance slanted over to Bashir, who was running more diagnostics over the slow rise and fall of Ziranne's diaphragm. "So far, all Julian's tests have been able to do is help narrow the search to symbionts between two- and three-hundred years old. That still leaves us with hundreds of possible joinings to check up on."

"Some of which," Duhan said with an edge of frost in his voice, "the Symbiosis Commission has already made contact with. Captain Sisko, I've already told you that we're going through the list of joined Trill as fast as we possibly can."

"The *whole* list," Sisko reminded him. "I'm sure your overworked assistants won't mind us continuing our efforts to narrow down the number of Trill they have to call or visit. After all, Starfleet has put us at your disposal until this matter is resolved."

"It wasn't my idea to call Starfleet." Duhan looked as if he wished he could call the words back once they were released, tightening his lips until his teeth dug into them. After a moment's thought, he continued, "I don't feel it's appropriate to involve outsiders in what has always been a most private and sacred affair for Trills." He didn't have to elaborate for them to know he meant the passing of symbionts from host to host. "Yes, the Commission has heard rumors that a sort of . . . 'black market' exists for unjoined Trill symbionts.

The theft of symbionts from their legitimate hosts is a crime so heinous that most Trills could never consider such a thing. But for others . . ." His voice trailed away, and he turned away from Ziranne as though suddenly unable to look at her. "Well, Captain, you simply can't imagine what it's like to be denied something every aspect of your native society insists you want to have."

Sisko might not be able to, but Jadzia certainly could. For a handful of hours, Dax had been nested in just such a symbiont thief—a sad, desperate communications worker named Verad who had been willing to risk as many lives as it took to obtain the symbiont he wanted. Dax had been Verad for the duration of their joining—hours that the symbiont, and, through it, Jadzia, still remembered with an eerie, pitiful clarity. The feelings of self-hatred and rage that seemed to boil out of those brief memories were so alien, so horrible, that Jadzia touched on them as rarely as possible. Dax had seemed perfectly content to bury them as deeply as any symbiont's memories could be, although they were never truly gone.

Could Ziranne have felt that same crushing self-hatred? What kind of sister did that make Jadzia Dax, to have never noticed Ziranne's agony?

Duhan Vos saved her from further recrimination by reaching out to draw the blinds on the room's only window. "I'm sorry, but as soon as we finish this questioning session, I'm going to recommend—"

"We may not be able to finish it." Bashir snapped off his medical tricorder and swung around to join them. His somber face warned Jadzia that the news wouldn't be good. "Your sister needs more than just bed rest. Her neurotransmitter and endocrine levels are all over the map, and I'm seeing evidence of peritoneal inflammatory in the connective tissue surrounding the pouch."

"She's rejecting the symbiont," Duhan said sadly. "It appears it no longer matters—"

Jadzia opened her mouth to protest, but Bashir forestalled her. "Normally I'd agree, Commissioner. But there are also signs of iscemic necrosis in the symbiont itself. That generally means the symbiont hasn't established the vascular connections it needs for life-support."

"And it's also a sign of even more advanced rejection." Duhan looked truly alarmed now, not just unsettled by the intrusion of Starfleet into Commission affairs. "We have to act. Jadzia Dax, I'm sorry, but if the choice must be between your sister's life and the life of a symbiont, you know the Commission must protect the symbiont."

Jadzia glanced over her shoulder at the still form on the bed behind them. She felt more than saw Benjamin Sisko's reassuringly solid presence come a step closer to her. "Yes," she said quietly. "I know."

Bashir surprised her with a loud sigh. When she shot a startled glance at him, she could tell from the twist of his mouth that it was himself he was irritated with. "Excuse me if I was unclear, Commissioner. *Ziranne* has begun forming the appropriate capillary network to support the symbiont. It's not complete, of course, since implantation was so recent. But the necrotic tissue I'm seeing is from some previous implantation trauma. Something of a much greater duration than the normal host–symbiont bonding period."

Jadzia frowned. "You're saying the previous host kept the symbiont despite ongoing rejection problems? For a long time?"

"Impossible." Duhan shook his head, hands smoothing the air in front of him as though chasing out the wrinkles in a quilt. "The Commission would never allow—"

Benjamin Sisko frowned him into silence. Sisko might have no official standing here, but the cloak of moral authority he wore as a Starfleet captain seemed to carry as much weight in the Trill Symbiosis Commission as it did on Deep Space 9.

"Doctor, is there anything about the symbiont's condition that the host would be able to feel physically? Could Ziranne have known something was the matter if a doctor didn't tell her?"

"I'd need to run more tests to be absolutely sure." Bashir opened his tricorder to consult whatever notes he'd made there. "There are some anomalous protein and enzyme traces I'm not sure how to interpret, but I think they're contributing to the symbiont's inability to establish a correct neurological bond with its host. And when you add that to the previous damage—I don't think Ziranne can be consciously aware of very much concerning this symbiont."

"Other than being overwhelmed by its memories, which she can't organize or control." After that long first session with her sister, it was still the only thing Jadzia was sure of. "She can't sort any of her own memories out of that flood, not even the most basic childhood facts."

Bashir followed her gaze to the bed and its restless occupant. "She may not have access to her own memories. She's been sedated in one form or another since showing up in Gheryzan. With a majority of her higher neurological functions suppressed, she can't possibly be processing speech on her own. Anything we're hearing has to be from the symbiont." And its inability to communicate in the pools—as well as Jadzia's repeated failures to reach through it to Ziranne—proved just how addled and unreliable it had become.

"Maybe we don't need Ziranne's memories." Sisko leaned back against the windowsill, fists clenching in thought. "Maybe all we need is what we already know."

Jadzia took a deep breath, hearing the undertone of realization in her old friend's voice. "What are you thinking, Benjamin?"

Sisko took a step as if to begin pacing, then brought himself up short, glancing across at Ziranne's fragile suspension into sleep. "According to the other teachers at her school, your sister took a leave of absence a week ago. Before she left, she told several of them she was concerned about the grandfather of one of her students, and intended to go off planet. We've found records of her having booked a shuttle to Shal Tul, but no records of her return to Trill."

"That was all in the message we sent to Starfleet," Duhan said tiredly. "And I don't see what any of it has to do with the symbiont's current state of health."

Sisko ignored the comment, turning instead to look directly at Jadzia. "We all assumed Ziranne wandered into that hospital in Gheryzan because she knew she needed help—she knew the symbiont and she were in danger. But what if that wasn't the case? Gheryzan is half a planet away from Ziranne's home. What if she went there, to that particular hospital, because she was looking for someone?"

"Her student's grandfather?" Bashir guessed.

Jadzia frowned. "You mean she never went to Shal Tul? But it's not like Ziranne to lie." That was assuming she was still Ziranne then, that she hadn't yet become the not-quite-joined thing she was now.

Sisko shrugged. "Maybe she did go to Shal Tul first—and whatever she found there sent her surreptitiously back to Trill. Back to that hospital in Gheryzan."

This time, it was Duhan's turn to pace. "Captain, I'm afraid there's nothing special about the hospital in Gheryzan."

"Except for the mental ward." Jadzia was rewarded with puzzled looks from Sisko and Bashir, and a startled, but suddenly thoughtful, frown from Duhan Vos. Curzon Dax's cynical memories reminded her that even up-and-coming Trill politicians didn't get appointed to the Symbiosis Commission by being stupid. "Unlike humans, Benjamin, there are Trills who still suffer from some brain disorders that don't respond to even the most advanced Federation medicines. Our neural chemistry is complicated by our ability to join—"

"So the same characteristics that let you bond with your symbionts also leave you susceptible to debilitating brain disease." Bashir sounded satisfied rather than surprised, as if this confirmed something he'd long suspected. Duhan's scowl told Jadzia this was another matter the Symbiosis commission preferred not be discussed among non-Trills. If Bashir noticed the Commissioner's discomfort, he gave no sign. He was already striding over to punch a new request into the computer terminal at the corner of the room. "That means the symbiont could have come from someone whose own brain-damage in turn gradually damaged the symbiont—"

"—and who was a permanant resident of the hospital in Gheryzan," Sisko finished.

"No!" Jadzia couldn't tell if the distress in Duhan's voice reflected his agitation at the disclosure of so many intimacies regarding the Trill symbiont-host relationship, or merely his growing anxiety about the damaged symbiont itself. It didn't help that Ziranne looked more pale and fragile with each straining breath. "This is all a waste of time!" the commissioner insisted. "Even if you locate a former host at that hospital—even if the host is still somehow alive—we can't risk putting the symbiont back into a brain-damaged Trill. Look how much damage has already been done! What we need to do is return this symbiont to the pools so it can heal."

"If we do that, my sister will die!" Jadzia heard her own voice scale upward, but didn't care anymore how much fear it revealed. She was fighting for a life as important to her as her own. "I won't let you take the symbiont until we've exhausted every other possible—"

"Verad."

The name seemed to echo between the white walls like the dying rumble of the avalanche of shock it triggered. Duhan spun around to stare at the human doctor in what looked like horror, as if Bashir had sprouted wings. Jadzia simply stared at Bashir, stillness the only possible lid she put on the cold, unwanted flood of memories her symbiont could not help but offer. It was left to Sisko to ask the obvious question.

"What about Verad, Doctor?"

Julian Bashir turned away from the computer, his dark eyes looking as stunned as Jadzia felt. "That's who's at Gheryzan. The Trill who tried to steal the Dax symbiont over a year ago—he was sentenced to permanent residence in the mental ward at Gheryzan."

It made a certain amount of sense that he'd be there, Jadzia realized. Verad certainly hadn't been stable when he'd appeared at Deep Space 9 to announce that, despite the Symbiosis Commission's opinion otherwise, he was the perfect host for Dax. Yet the last she'd heard was that he'd spent one year and a day at a Trill rehabilitation facility, only to emigrate to an offworld job after being declared cured of his pathological insecurity and envy of the joined. Jadzia had magnanimously allowed that she'd probably have wanted to move someplace where nobody knew her, too, if she'd committed the crimes he had.

"Don't expect him to be too communicative," Bashir had warned them, paging through the documents on his computer screen more rapidly than any human had a right to. "His medical record states that he's currently suffering from dissociative catatonia. That's just a few steps up from a persistent vegetative state. Not surprising, really—dissociative disorders are apparently the most common facultative disorder among Trills." He looked up from his reading, the blue-green light from the touchscreen reflecting faintly in his eyes. "If this is right, he'll be in a worse state than your sister. She at least has a stolen symbiont to give her some semblance of a voice."

Crossing the Symbiosis Commission's central garden, Jadzia tried to focus her thoughts on something other than the image of her sister as a silent, fragile mannequin. So, instead, she thought about how the Trill sunlight felt almost alien on her skin after all her time in the artificial light of Deep Space 9.

It always unsettled Jadzia when she came home—this feeling that her home planet had become less familiar to her than a Cardassian-built orbital pile of steel and duranium. For reassurance, she reached as she always did for Dax's memories of Curzon's reaction to the same feeling. Her immediate predecessor had enjoyed the intellectual stimulation of seeing his homeworld with fresh eyes after every diplomatic mission, and Jadzia could usually soothe her uneasiness by dipping into his remembered delight. This time, however, all she felt was her buffeting fear that the Trill homeworld would never be the same after this visit, and neither would she.

"I'll try to talk to the symbiont while you're gone," Bashir had promised softly, just before Jadzia slipped from her sister's room to follow Sisko to Gheryzan and whatever answers waited there. "I think I can adjust the sedative balance enough to completely neutralize Ziranne's input while leaving the symbiont coherent. Commissioner Duhan can help me try to make contact with it. I actually think it may work better if you aren't here to spark an emotional response."

Jadzia nodded, not trusting her voice by then. After coming so many light-years, it felt strange to be told her best chances of saving her sister involved simply walking away.

"What are you thinking, Old Man?" Sisko held the door that led out of the garden and through the Symbiosis Commission's teaching halls to its transporter station. He'd already alerted Chief O'Brien back on the *Defiant* to coordinate their transport to the Gheryzan mental hospital, although for politeness sake they'd use the hospital's own pad. Now that they knew Verad might somehow be involved in this mess, Sisko had said grimly, there was no sense taking chances. Jadzia wasn't sure if she should feel vindicated that Sisko took the Verad threat more seriously than Bashir, or if she should just suspect her captain of humoring her.

"I'm really worried, Benjamin." Jadzia took a deep breath, trying to sort through the emotional worries she knew were hers and the logical concerns that belonged to her inner self. "Ziranne wouldn't have any reason to get in touch with Verad on her own. Any connection she has to him has to have been initiated from his end. What if Verad's not catatonic, and this is all his idea of getting revenge on me—on Jadzia—for being the one who got to keep Dax?"

Sisko shook his head, but she knew him well enough to recognize disbelief rather than disagreement in the gesture. "Don't jump to conclusions, Old Man. We still don't know for sure that Verad had anything to do with what's happened to your sister. After all, part of the agreement Starfleet had with the Symbiosis Commission when we returned Verad was that they'd never let him endanger another symbiont, especially yours. His presence in Gheryzan might just be a coincidence."

Jadzia stepped onto the transport platform before him, her own headshake as crisp as Emony could have made it. "If there's one thing I've learned in seven lifetimes, Benjamin, it's that even coincidences don't come out of nowhere. I can't ignore the fact that my sister ended up practically on the doorstep of the man who once stole my symbiont, only days after she apparently stole a symbiont of her own."

Sisko sighed softly, as though carefully considering what he was planning to say. "Maybe you want to believe Verad's involved in this because you can't believe Ziranne would do it to herself." He caught Dax's hand in midair, stopping her before she could end the conversation by signaling O'Brien. "Old Man, I was there, too, when Verad came to Deep Space 9. I saw his pain, and I saw how readily Dax adapted to Verad's conviction that he'd been wronged once they were joined." He shook his head. "Are you absolutely sure your sister didn't feel that same frustration? That she didn't decide, all by herself, that joining was worth any price she might have to pay?"

"Benjamin, I know my sister as well as I know myself. And in all her life she never lied to me." Or, if she had, she had lied so well that even Jadzia couldn't pierce the deception. That thought was intolerable. As intolerable as the possibility that Ziranne had refused joining only because Jadzia had achieved it first, thus sacrificing her own happiness in some misguided loyalty to her sister. "She wasn't the sort to steal someone else's symbiont," Jadzia said carefully, her hand moving reflexively toward her abdomen. "There isn't much else I'm sure of lately, but I have to be sure of that."

"So," Ziranne asked, her face alight with mischief, "what's he like?" The late spring breeze through the windows tied her hair into macramé knots, tossing the ends playfully over her shoulders as she shook out another of Jadzia's wrinkled shirts. "Have they let you talk to him yet? Is he nice?"

Jadzia sighed somewhat dramatically, and bent to rearrange the contents of her small suitcase in an effort to hide her blush. "I wished you'd stop calling the symbiont 'he.' " She tried to sound cool and precise, but had a feeling she merely sounded prissy. "It makes me feel like I'm getting married, or signing up for a sex change or something."

"Well, calling him 'it' makes me feel like you're buying a hovercraft." Plucking a pair of trousers from the suitcase, Ziranne lifted a skeptical eyebrow and turned to rehang the slacks in the closet. "Come on, Jadzia. Half its hosts have been men, including the last two. It isn't *wrong* to call your symbiont 'he.' "

A little taste of discomfort twisted Jadzia's mouth. "If you have to call it something, call it Dax."

"All right." Content with her new choice from Jadzia's modest wardrobe, Ziranne turned back to the staging area that used to be her sister's bed and resumed her folding. "But you still didn't answer my question."

It seemed somehow unfair that her younger sister could be more balanced and mature than Jadzia so much of the time. She bought herself some time by sorting through her toiletries, counting the last few doses of the medicine that would help ease her transition, then having to count them again when the number simply flew out of her head. "I've met Curzon lots of times," she said at last, quite calmly. "That's kind of like meeting Dax."

"And?"

She shrugged, was suddenly afraid that would look too sulky, and sighed a little as she dumped the toiletries back into their bag. "Curzon used to be an ambassador for the Federation. He worked a lot with the Klingons, even lived on *Qo'noS* for a time." That last thought made her stomach pinch. While she'd studied the structure of Klingons in comparative biology, she'd never actually met one. She wasn't sure she wanted to adopt a lot of intimate encounters with a species she wasn't even sure she liked. "Before that, Dax was joined with a pilot, and before that, the scientist who headed the Symbiosis Commission." She glanced up at Ziranne a little shyly. "There's a lot of math and science in Dax's background." As well as a craving for strangeness and new experience. *The need to understand,* her Symbiosis advisor had called it. It was what got her picked for this symbiont over hundreds of other applicants.

Ziranne stepped back to let Jadzia finish patting down the contents of her suitcase. Teaching preschool had imbued her with a patience Jadzia sorely envied. So few things seemed to frustrate her, not even a sister who couldn't articulate what made her want to run and hide on the eve of her joining. They'd grown so different, not just in height and figure, yet remained so much the same that Jadzia knew her thoughts still leapt straight from her brain into Ziranne's.

"This is a wonderful thing for you," Ziranne said gently. "You can't know how proud I am." She let a moment of silence grow between them, then finished, "So why don't you seem happy?"

Jadzia closed her case with a bang, crying out in frustration, "Curzon doesn't like me!"

It didn't help that Ziranne's first reaction was to laugh.

"I'm serious, Ziranne!" She swept up her suitcase and swung it to the floor. "He really, really hates me! I think he tried to stop me from getting any symbiont at all."

"That sounds just a little paranoid."

"But it's true." She sat on the bed hard enough to jounce it, and leaned forward to catch at her sister's knees. "Do you know what it's like to have your symbiont's last host hate you?"

Ziranne twined her fingers with Jadzia's and gave her a little shake. "Maybe it's not about you. Maybe he's not ready to give up Dax just yet."

"No." Jadzia shook her head, frowning with sincerity. "He's been ill a long time, and after that heart attack on Risa, he's been deteriorating rapidly. I think he means it when he says he doesn't want the symbiont to be damaged as his health fails." Besides, there must be a certain complacency about your own death when you knew that, in a sense, you wouldn't really die. A certain aspect of your awareness would remain within the symbiont forever. The possibility of who-knew-how-many more lifetimes of exploration and challenge was more exciting than any fear of death could be.

The fear that nibbled at Jadzia, however, couldn't be so easily addressed. "What if it isn't Curzon?" Her voice came out all quiet and small. "What if even after Curzon is gone, it still doesn't like me? What if it's *Dax?*"

A sister's value lay in her ability to judge when to laugh and when to take a foolish fear as seriously as its presenter. "How can it be?" Ziranne wanted to know. "Doesn't the symbiont become one with the host after joining? In a sense, won't Dax essentially *become* you?"

Or the two of them become something else. Still, the end result was the same.

"Then how can you hate yourself, Jadzia? You've worked so long and hard for this. You know what it means to accept joining, and you *know* that you'll be good for this symbiont, and for Trill." She smiled and reached up to tuck Jadzia's hair back behind her ear. "You can't hate yourself as Jadzia Dax when you don't hate yourself now."

"I might hate myself for leaving you," Jadzia said, very softly.

"But you're not leaving." Ziranne pulled her into a fierce hug, and Jadzia clung to her with a strange feeling that she was never going to see her again. Not precisely like this. Not in exactly this way, with these eyes. "If symbiosis is really right for the Trill," Ziranne insisted in her ear, "then it's because there are people who are made greater by joining, who make the Trill greater by sacrificing a little of themselves to carry the legacy of all that knowledge and power." Separating them, Ziranne gazed deep into her sister's eyes. "You're one of those people, Jadzia. You were *made* for this."

Jadzia tightened her hands on Ziranne's shoulders. "So were you. You passed all the tests—the Commission said you'd make a wonderful host."

But Ziranne only shook her head. "No, I wouldn't. I know I wouldn't because I don't want to be joined." She laughed a little at Jadzia's disbelieving blink. "Honestly, Jadzia. I have never wanted this. I went with you to take the tests because—" She shrugged a bit self-consciously and squeezed her sister's hand. "Because I always followed you everywhere. When I did things with you, it was fun, and exciting, and so different from any of the things I do by myself. But I never pictured me as anything but who I am, and I never pictured you as anything but joined."

Standing, she hefted the small suitcase and thrust it playfully into Jadzia's arms. "Go have this adventure for us."

Jadzia blinked back tears, the love between them pushing against her heart so hard she knew even a million lifetimes couldn't weaken it or wear it away. "I'm glad you're my sister."

"So am I." Ziranne smiled and took her by the arm. "I'm really looking forward to all the fascinating conversations I'm going to have with Jadzia Dax."

"Are you sure he's a criminal? He doesn't look like one to me."

Jadzia's heart felt squeezed inside her chest as they made their way down Gheryzan Hospital's quiet halls. Memory wasn't supposed to have this effect on a Trill. Not even the memory of the man who tried to kill you and steal the very essence of what you were. She could almost smell Verad in the cool green walls.

She let Sisko answer the medic who'd walked with them since the main gate. "A kidnapper and a thief," the captain explained in a voice much calmer and more pleasant than Jadzia could have managed. He made no effort to clarify that the object of Verad's attempted theft had been a symbiont. Perhaps he thought that information something the other patients in Gheryzan didn't need to know, like never telling the inmates in a prison colony that one of their number had murdered babies.

The hospital medic shook his head in disbelief. "You'd never guess he had such a colorful past from what he's like in here. Especially if they've been declared rehabilitated, their criminal records are sealed and we never even know they did anything." He sighed, then surprised Dax with an almost affectionate smile. "Well, whatever he did before he came, he's the easiest client we've got nowadays. Some of these dissociative disorders, they're outwardly violent, or self-damaging, at least every once in a while. Verad just watches holovids all day." He gave a little laugh as he pushed open the door to the sunroom ahead of them. "I think the most trouble we've ever had with him is over *syto* beans at dinner. He really hates *syto* beans."

It was a strangely intimate detail, one Jadzia wasn't sure she wanted to share. "How did he end up here?" she heard herself ask. She didn't mean to pry, yet her thoughts kept circling back to that off-world job, and wondering how it led him back to Gheryzan.

"Slipped into catatonia while on the job." Their guide wove his way neatly and gently through a sunroom not even half-filled by perhaps two dozen quiet, blue-gowned

"clients." Except for the disparity in their ages, they could
have been residents at one of the many communities for el-
derly Trill who no longer had families to look after them.
"Most Federation outposts these days don't have anything
passing for long-term care for mental patients, so Shal Tul
was forced to ship him home. He's been here ever since."

Jadzia exchanged a look with Sisko. He nodded without speaking, letting her know he remembered Ziranne's
shuttle passage to Shal Tul without committing himself to
any other interpretations.

Few of the patients in the sunroom seemed interested
by the trio's passing. They continued with their reading, or
worked with computers; others slept on mats rolled out in
the nicer sunspots, and still others sat in little groups and
talked or worked on puzzles. In most cases, it wasn't easy to
see what about their behavior made them unable to live in
the general flow of Trill society.

In other cases, the difficulties suffered became more obvious. A row of chairs, padded and draped with colorful
quilts, faced a large holoscreen that ran a lively video track
with no sound. It was among this group that Jadzia saw the
unconscious gestures and slack, sightless eyes that she associated with the severely mentally ill. Her heart went out to
them all, even Verad, wherever he might be. To be of a people
that valued mind and memory so much, only to end your
days locked away inside yourself like this . . . It was a too
horrible a fate to consider.

The medic singled out a dark-haired man of middle
years, and smiled down at him as he pulled his chair out of
the line. "You've got company." As he swung the chair
smoothly to face Jadzia and Sisko, he announced cheerfully,

"He'll have been with us four months next week. Like I said, a good guy, as far as these things go."

Jadzia wasn't sure what to say. Glancing uncertainly at Sisko, she knelt to stare into eyes as pale and blind as brushed silver. "This is Verad?"

"Sure." The medic sounded surprised. "Isn't that who you asked for?"

Indeed they had. But the man staring back at Jadzia from the bottom of a well so deep he couldn't climb out wasn't familiar because of buried memories from Ops on Deep Space 9. He was familiar because of the arguments she'd had with him—or with a man who looked exactly like him—less than two hours ago in her sister's room at the Symbiosis Commission.

The man staring slackly from the chair in front of them was Commissioner Duhan Vos.

Even the long moments needed to fully materialize seemed too long. Jadzia willed her legs to *run!* before the transporter had a chance to release her, wanted to shout with rage at the delay between her thought and when her muscles obeyed. She heard Sisko trying again to raise Bashir via combadge, but burst through the door separating the transporter station from the rest of the hospital without waiting to hear if he received an answer this time.

The sunshine that had warmed her so well on her way to Gheryzan was merely blinding now. She squinted hard against the shards of brightness, and told herself the tears flooding into her eyes were from that pain and not her own helpless fear.

A quick records check via the *Defiant* had given them enough information to create at least a sketchy image of the horror Verad had committed. Duhan and Vos had been joined more than twenty years before, when Duhan had been a very young man, eager to take his first off-world job as a chemical engineer. Now, the real Duhan sat, dead-faced and dull-eyed, in the last Trill asylum, and there was no sign of Vos within him. Verad had found a way to have the symbiont he desired without having to flee the quadrant after his theft—by taking over the life, even the face, of an already existing joined Trill. There was no need to explain how Verad came by a symbiont; he became Duhan Vos, not Verad Vos, and Duhan Vos was the legitimate version of everything Verad wanted to be.

Jadzia shuddered to think of what he intended to accomplish as a member of the Symbiosis Commission.

Sisko grabbed at her arm to slow her as she skidded around the doorway to Ziranne's room. "Easy, Old Man." Whether he'd somehow known to suspect what they found or simply saw the tableau a moment sooner than her own fear-blinded eyes, she'd never know. But Dax's trust of the man let Jadzia be stopped, and she would forever be grateful for that instinct.

Ziranne didn't turn, didn't even so much as cock her head when the two Starfleet officers froze a few meters away. Her face was so pale, Jadzia could almost see the yellow of her skull through the flesh, her spots faded almost transparent by shock and system imbalances Jadzia could only guess at. She had backed Verad/Duhan against the window, the electromagnetic blade of one of Bashir's laser scalpels glowing greenly against his throat. The doctor himself was nowhere to be seen.

The commissioner slid a panicked glance toward the doorway. "Help me," he whispered. "We've been here . . ." He swallowed thickly, took a shuddering breath. "She's sedated—the woman is gone. Your doctor was able to waken the symbiont, but . . . it's ruined, it's gone completely mad—"

"Stop lying." Ziranne's voice sounded clotted, blurred and rounded by drugs and—Jadzia suspected—a certain unfamiliarity with producing language minus the help of an appropriately suited brain. Nothing else about her body moved, as though the act of creating speech made it impossible to move any other muscles. "If we're ruined, it was you who ruined us. Tell them what you did to me. Tell them why I'm going to kill you."

Verad's eyes reached for Jadzia across the distance. Frightened, defiant, he wouldn't back down, she knew. Not for her, not for Ziranne, not for anyone. "I don't know what she's talking about. You've got to stop her before she does something no one can forgive."

"It's over, Verad." Sisko tightened his hand on Jadzia's arm, ever so slightly, and took a step closer to Ziranne. "We've been to Gheryzan. We know what you've done."

There was a moment when Jadzia thought he'd try to extend the ruse. Then Verad stared yearningly at Ziranne, and the naked desperation on his face made him look suddenly more like Jadzia remembered. "I only wanted a symbiont," he said, in a very tiny voice. His eyes looked at Ziranne, but his words reached deeper, toward the life-form she carried inside her. "Just one symbiont. For myself."

"And he followed the rumors to Shal Tul," the symbiont took up. "To Bethan Roa, the old man whose failing mind led him to the greatest madness of all." The host's head twisted slightly to direct the words toward the officers in the doorway, but Ziranne didn't precisely turn away from Verad. "He wanted to hide his brain's infirmity from the Symbiosis Commission. He took drugs that the humans said could knit his fractured thoughts back into order. Except the price he paid for clear thinking was ours. His mind rebounded to its youthful brilliance, but the drugs began to dissolve the bond he shared with us. Thus a new and bitter vice was born."

"I only wanted a symbiont." That mantra seemed to sustain Verad. *A lack of empathy toward others,* Bashir had said. Perhaps this was how Verad justified it all to himself. "Bethan Roa sold me a perfected version of the drug, which I used on Duhan Vos. The drug makes it possible to extract a joined symbiont without killing the host. Bethan knew of doctors who could help, who could transfer the symbiont once the bond was broken, and dispose of the old host. They gave me his symbiont and his face. I made my own life for myself."

At the expense of a man who had never done Verad even a moment's harm.

"He won't recover." Jadzia couldn't keep the anger and anguish from her tone. "Whatever your drug did to him, it's destroyed his mind forever."

As sincerely as could be imagined, Verad said only, "I'm sorry." The same answer he'd given on Deep Space 9 when told his theft of the Dax symbiont would kill an innocent young woman. Old men on distant colonies were less well defended than Starfleet science officers, but apparently no more valuable.

Jadzia met her sister's eyes, but saw someone else in the anguished face. "You're Roa, aren't you?"

Slowly, as though with extreme conscious effort, Ziranne blinked and took a breath, nodding. "The trace chemicals your doctor found in this host's system were from the drug set Bethan developed. His success with Verad convinced him he could use it to exploit others like him—unjoined Trills who would do anything to be joined. The drug would

make it possible to give them a taste of what they wanted—
for a fee. One symbiont could be passed among many—a
month in one, two weeks in another. When Verad learned of
Bethan's plans to use Vos, he used the drug on Bethan first.
He killed Bethan, and made me a *commodity*. But Verad gave
no thought to the damage Bethan's drug was doing to me, or
to my hosts. Then this host found out, and paid to be the
next in line, in order to bring me back to Trill."

Jadzia was too horrified to speak. Sisko asked, "So
you—and Ziranne—never intended to remain joined?"

The joined thing that was neither entirely symbiont
nor entirely host shook its head. "There was no intent involved. This host and I stole the drug before running, to use
them once we were back on Trill, so that I could return to
the pools. This host gave of itself to rescue me. This host offered of itself the gift of movement and form. But we were
too damaged to continue functioning for as long as we had
hoped, and the drug was lost."

Jadzia's complete revulsion at the atrocity being de-
scribed was absolute. Bond, dissolve the bond, pass the symbiont along to the next host in line with no regard for its
mental health or stability. Her stomach turned sour at the
prospect. In the past, when there weren't enough homes for
individuals on an overpopulated planet, whole families
learned to live in a single apartment, people who would
never otherwise know each other chose to pool their funds
to purchase housing. But a symbiont was not a house. Neither Jadzia nor Dax could imagine the damage wreaked—on
both symbiont and host—by something so barbaric as treat-
ing a fragile life-form like a summer house that many different owners could share. Yet it stood here in front of them, in

the form of a beloved sister who no longer knew her own name.

"Ziranne . . ." Jadzia took a few careful steps into the room. The remnant of her sister didn't even turn to look. "Ziranne, you can't kill him."

"She doesn't have to," the stranger's voice said. "There is no part of her consciousness involved in what's happening here. As soon as we have forced him to confess his part, I will kill him for us all."

Fear flooded her eyes briefly with tears. Jadzia blinked them back, retreating to Dax's steadier perspective. "You can't kill him either, Roa." This time Ziranne's head swivelled, slowly, dreamily. "The symbiont inside him doesn't deserve punishment anymore than you did. If you kill Verad, you risk killing the symbiont he carries—the symbiont he stole."

She thought she saw just the slightest hesitation in Ziranne's eyes. "You could remove it before he perishes—"

"We can do that anyway."

Realization blossomed between Roa and Verad at almost the same moment. The horror and anguish on Verad's face almost balanced the satisfaction that crept into Ziranne's expression.

"The drug set Bethan developed gives us that ability," Jadzia continued. "You may have lost the sample, but you were once Bethan, too—you know what's needed to synthesize more. We can use it to remove you from Ziranne, and Vos from Verad. You can both return to the pools and find some peace. With the information you can give us, the Commission will find Verad's other 'customers' and make sure this never happens again. And Verad will be punished as he deserves."

"More carefully than last time." Roa angled a pleading look over Ziranne's shoulder.

Jadzia nodded solemnly. "More carefully." Although she didn't know that this was a promise she needed to make. The loss of life in Verad's eyes almost matched what she'd seen in Duhan's back at Gheryzan. They had no idea how long Verad had carried this symbiont, how complete their mutual bond had become. Or how much like Duhan he would finally be when this was over. Even if he retained his sanity, to face the rest of existence after having your symbiont extracted from your being, and no chance that death would mercifully release you from that future—that seemed a greater punishment than anything Jadzia or anyone else could devise.

Evidently, the Roa symbiont agreed. With a slow blink, and then a sigh, Ziranne's body took an unsteady step back from the hunched-over form of the erstwhile commissioner—then crumpled into Jadzia's outstretched arms.

Holding her sister's cool hand in both her own, Jadzia watched the ghostly movements of Ziranne's eyes behind their lids. Even in sleep, she smiled now. Once, when her eyes flickered open at the sound of a bird caroling outside the window, she'd focused hazily on Jadzia and whispered, "I knew you'd come. I knew you'd make everything okay."

Jadzia leaned down close, resting her forehead against Ziranne's. "Have I?" The not knowing for certain frightened her. "Ziranne, the symbiont is gone."

"Roa." Ziranne nodded sleepily. "I know. I can . . . tell." She smiled with amazing peacefulness. "I was so afraid they wouldn't call you. That no one would believe me when I said I wanted it removed. But I knew you'd remember. I knew you'd know what to do."

It seemed like such a big risk to take. "Was Bethan Roa your student's grandfather?"

Again the drowsy nod. "Lyrrin was so upset when her grandfather died. So I took her to the pools to see Roa, to show that her grandfather would never be completely gone. When Roa wasn't there, and when I couldn't find any information about a new host, I knew something was wrong."

"Why didn't you just tell someone?"

"I didn't know what to tell them. I thought maybe Lyrrin's family had heard wrong. I wanted to make sure I did the right thing, so I just asked myself, 'What would Jadzia do?' " She squeezed Jadzia's hand, her eyes drifting closed again toward restful slumber. "And I knew you'd find the missing symbiont and make sure it got back home. You'd find out what went wrong, and you'd fix things—you always do."

Jadzia didn't answer. Being anyone's hero was always a huge undertaking. Being the hero of the person who mattered almost more to you than yourself was a fearfully powerful thought.

"Is your doctor okay?" Ziranne asked.

"Recovering." They'd found him nearly a half-hour after Roa surrendered Ziranne's body, locked into a storage closet after being nearly overdosed on sedatives. "I don't know whether to scold you or Roa for taking advantage of his good nature."

Ziranne managed a sleepy, lopsided smile. "I'm not sure who to blame, either. It was so strange, knowing and wanting things that somehow weren't my own, but which felt so much like mine. I knew when I—we—it—drugged the doctor, that we meant to get him out of the way so we could kill Verad. Yet I kept thinking how I would never do that, how I could never kill anybody." She laced her fingers with Jadzia's, her grip loving and strong despite the lingering anesthetic in her system. "Thank you for helping me rescue him without having to become him. Thank you for letting me be just me."

Jadzia smoothed a hand across her sister's cool cheek, smiling, then let Ziranne slip into whatever private dreams would soothe her now that she was alone with herself again, the way she wanted to be. Although it might not be very important to her sister, Jadzia was comforted to know that at least a little of Ziranne's life would be remembered by one of Trill's symbionts, and shared with all the others resting in the pools. She wanted the joined of the future to know what she knew now: that many, maybe even most, of the unjoined people of Trill felt no less a part of their complex species than those who hosted the symbionts. And that at least one of them, with no desire to be part of the continuum of joined memory, would still risk her own life to bring a symbiont safely home.

EZRI

"We're part of something bigger than any of us."

—Torias Dax
"Facets"

" . . . and straight on 'til morning."

Judith & Garfield Reeves-Stevens

"ALL THAT," VIC said, "*all* of it . . . and it hit you . . . *pow!* . . . Just like that?"

"All of it," Ezri said. "And more. So much more. I . . . I couldn't even tell Brinner what it was like. And he had had the preliminary courses."

"Brinner? He was okay?"

Ezri nodded, experiencing the sadness and the awkwardness of her reunion with Brinner Finok once more. He was safe, unhurt, but what they'd had together could never be the same again. Not when she had been given what he had so desperately wanted and worked for all his life. "The changeling didn't kill him. It just put him into medical stasis and hid him in a medical supply room."

"Kinda odd thing for a changeling to do, don't you think?"

Ezri sat up from where she had been leaning against Vic's shoulder. "I suppose. No one ever figured out what that changeling was really trying to do. We don't think there's any way it could have joined with Dax. Maybe it could have linked minds somehow. Accessed Dax's Starfleet secrets. Maybe even have kept Dax alive long enough to get back to the Founders' homeworld and . . . who knows what could've happened then?"

"Which is why you couldn't tell anyone what happened," Vic concluded.

"Not while the war was on," Ezri confirmed. "In most sectors, especially on the front lines, it was Starfleet policy to withhold reports of changeling impersonations. To keep up morale. And to keep other changelings from finding out which ones had been caught. I think the policy's changing now. But it still comes down to the same thing. At the time, I *was* the only Trill on board."

"And that changeling in the Bajoran uniform?" Vic asked. "The one that brought Dax onto the *Destiny?* Odo, right?"

"Odo," Ezri said. "I realized that later. But he was so upset, I don't think he even remembers seeing me. At least, he's never mentioned it."

"Strangers in the night," Vic said.

Ezri let Vic's sports coat slip from her shoulders. Somehow, the night felt warmer. Maybe it was the heat from the lights on the improbable giant slipper. Or maybe she was just getting used to the night air.

Vic stretched out the arm he had kept around her, as if a simulated cramp had formed in his simulated muscles.

Ezri narrowed her eyes at him as he rubbed his arm, thinking about all the theories she had heard to explain his behavior. "Are you *really* a hologram?" she asked.

Vic's only answer was to give her a sly wink and a friendly punch on the shoulder. "Funny thing about those stories," he said.

Ezri decided he was trying to change the subject. Someday, she'd make a point of asking to hear all of Vic's stories. She suspected he had more than a few surprises of his own. But that was a question for another day. Or for a timeless desert night. "What's funny?" she asked.

"They're all so different. I mean, same worm, right? But there's Lela Dax loving politics and mixing it up with a crowd. But Tobin Dax sounds like he would've been happy living by himself in the middle of Death Valley. Torias Dax wanted to win everything for himself. Curzon Dax wanted to help everyone else win. And Joran Dax . . ." Vic paused as he seemed to understand the sudden flash of warning in Ezri's eyes. "Well, enough said about that cat."

Ezri couldn't have agreed more. Having all of Joran's memories restored was one of the hardest adjustments Jadzia had been forced to make, and they proved no easier for Ezri to live with.

She stood up and stretched herself. She had no idea how long she had been sitting with Vic. "Your point?" she asked.

"Hey, I'm a crooner not a counselor."

A hologram with false modesty, Ezri thought. *What a uni-*

verse. "You're not 'crooning' now," she reminded him. "But you do look like you have something to say." She folded her arms as she faced him. "Am I right? Or am I right?"

Vic laughed. "Seems to me that you didn't want to get joined because you were afraid of losing yourself. But from what I can tell, none of Dax's previous hosts lost anything from being joined. They just got more."

Ezri had never thought of it that way. "More of what?"

Vic pursed his lips, shook his head. "More of . . . I don't know . . . maybe more of whatever it is that . . . that makes us human."

Ezri stared at the hologram until he lost his stage performer's grin. She didn't care what anyone else said. She was certain there was something more to Vic Fontaine than holoemitters and microforcefields.

"I told you what I was doing out here," she said at last.

"Checking out the place for Julian. For one of his lost causes."

Ezri nodded. "So tell me, what were *you* doing out here, in the middle of nowhere?"

"It's my night off."

"No," Ezri insisted. "I mean, really, why were you out here?"

Vic put his hands in his pockets, and for once his expression was serious. "Really? It's a big simulation, doll. I like to make sure my friends don't get . . . lost." But then he grinned again, erasing whatever moment of connection Ezri felt she might have just established with him. "It's bad for business when the tourists start turning up in the sand dunes, if you catch my drift."

"Yeah," Ezri agreed, "I suppose it is."

Vic picked up his sports coat from the electrical box, gave it a shake, then brushed some dust from it. "So how about it, doll? Need an escort back to the bright lights and big city? Maybe check up on that boyfriend of yours?"

Ezri looked up, past the glowing shoe, past the jumbled, waiting signs no longer pointing the way to anywhere, to the stars above.

And with a start, for the first time that night, she realized they were not alien stars after all.

"Emony was on Earth," she said, the memories of those days and those adventures rushing through her consciousness even as she said the words, sparked by the stories she had told.

"You mentioned that," Vic said.

Ezri was suddenly overcome by the knowledge that the tapestry of lights above, nothing more than random patterns to Ezri Tigan, were old familiar friends to Ezri Dax.

"Orion," she said softly as the patterns coalesced. "And Taurus. Ursa Major."

"You sound like you're on to something," Vic said encouragingly.

Ezri sighted from those stars and pointed into the darkness. "Due east," she said. "The Strip is three kilometers in that direction."

"No holding you back, dollface."

Ezri smiled in agreement, even as she tried to find some hint of what Vic was actually thinking, what he really meant. But the hologram, the nightclub singer . . . her *friend,* gave no clue to the depths that lay hidden deep beneath his surface. If, indeed, there were depths there to be explored or comprehended.

"No," Ezri said, because she did understand the truth of what Vic meant. "No holding me back. Not now."

"For my money, doll, not ever."

For no reason at all that would ever make sense to her, Ezri suddenly stepped forward and kissed Vic on the cheek, hologram or not.

He actually blushed.

"Whoa, what was that for, doll?"

Ezri straightened his tie. "You know." She sighed and the sigh turned into a yawn. "I'd better be going."

Vic checked his watch, as if a hologram could have someplace else to go. "Me, too."

"See you," she said.

Vic cocked a finger at her, as if to shoot her with an imaginary phaser.

"And thanks," Ezri added. Then, her earlier fatigue a thing of the past, like so many other things, she started to walk from the clearing, into the thicket of signs.

"Hey!" Vic called out from behind her, "it's two miles to town! You could just say, End program."

Ezri looked back over her shoulder. "I know where I'm going."

"You know something, doll? You always did."

Ezri couldn't resist. She gave Vic his own parting shot with an imaginary phaser. "Badda bing," she said.

Vic laughed, threw his sports coat over his shoulder, and started off in another direction, wherever it was that holograms went when there was no one around to see them.

Ezri turned back to the east, saw the sky brightening with dawn, or, at least, a reasonable facsimile thereof.

This should be interesting, she thought. Not even Emony had seen Las Vegas by day.

No longer lost, Ezri Dax set off on her own journey, sure at last of her own destination, but, like every Dax before her, curious to see what she might find along the way.

From the shadows of the signs, Vic watched her go, and allowed himself a smile. A real one, this time, and not a simulation.

Then he turned and hurried off on his own journey, secure in the knowledge that there were many more stories still to be told by his friends on Deep Space Nine, and that he'd be able to hear them all.

Because he knew that he'd be back—they *all* would be back.

Just like Dax.

Bajor is in flames. The corridors of Terok Nor echo with the sounds of battle. It is the end of the Cardassian Occupation—and the beginning of the greatest epic adventure in the saga of Deep Space 9. . . .

Six years later, with the Federation losing ground in its war against the Dominion, the galaxy's greatest smugglers—including the beautiful and enigmatic Vash—rendezvous on Deep Space 9. Their objective: a fabled lost Orb of the Prophets unlike any other, rumored to be the key to unlocking a second wormhole in Bajoran space—a second Celestial Temple.

Almost immediately, mysterious events plague the station: Odo arrests Quark for murder; Jake and Nog lead Chief O'Brien to an eerie holosuite in a section of the station that's not on any schematic; and a Cardassian scientist whom even the Obsidian Order once feared makes an unexpected appearance. With all these events tied to a never-before-told story of the Cardassian withdrawal, Captain Benjamin Sisko faces the most dangerous challenge of his career: Unless he can uncover the secret of the lost Orb, what began with the fall of Terok Nor will end with the destruction of Deep Space 9 . . . or worse.

In March and April 2000 the untold story of the fabled red orbs is revealed in

STAR TREK: DEEP SPACE NINE®
MILLENNIUM

A three-book series from the authors
Judith & Garfield Reeves-Stevens.
Turn the page for a preview of Book I:

The Fall of Terok Nor

Lieutenant Commander Jadzia Dax stood on the deck of the *Starship Enterprise* with her back to the captain's chair, and because it was the first *Enterprise,* there was only one direction from which the final attack could come.

The turbolift.

Five minutes ago, when she had hurriedly studied the ship's schematics on the desktop viewer in the briefing room, she had found it difficult to believe that the most critical command center on the entire ship was serviced by only one 'lift. But in the memories of her third host, Emony, was the explanation. The more-than-century-old *Constitution*-class to which the original *Enterprise* belonged had been designed primarily as a vessel of scientific exploration. The engineers of the twenty-fourth century might perceive its design idiosyncrasies, such as a single turbolift serving the bridge, or fixed-phaser emitters, as design flaws. Dax's third host, however, considered such features to be the last echoes of the twenty-second century's charmingly naïve optimism toward space travel inspired by the end of the Romulan Wars and the resulting birth of the Federation a mere two years later.

As a joined Trill possessing the memories of eight lifetimes, more or less, that spanned the past two centuries, Jadzia Dax understood she was more attuned than most beings to the similarities of every age. And the truth was that while the technology might change, human hearts and minds seldom did. It definitely wasn't the case that life was simpler or that human nature was less sophisticated in the past.

But in the case of this *ship,* Jadzia couldn't help thinking, *the designers were behind the curve. They really should have known better.* After all, the first *Enterprise* had been launched a full twenty-seven years after the first contact with the Klingon

Empire, a disastrous meeting that clearly proved that not everyone in the quadrant shared the Federation's belief in co-existence. And right now, the proof of that was about to face her in a life-and-death confrontation.

Jadzia heard the distant rush of a turbolift car approaching the bridge. She hefted the sword in her hand and with one quick step vaulted over the stairs to the upper deck of the bridge. She reflexively tugged down on the ridiculously short skirt of her blue sciences uniform, changing her balance to be prepared to spring forward the instant the doors opened. *If*, that is, she *could* spring forward in the awkward, knee-height, high-heeled black boots that were also part of her uniform.

The turbolift stopped. She held her breath as she faced the doors with only one thought in her mind—*Klingons . . . can't live with them, can't*—

The red doors slid open. The 'lift was empty! Then a sudden crash made her spin to see a violently dislodged wall panel beside the main viewer fly into the center well of the bridge. The wall panel had covered the opening of an emergency-access tunnel, and from its darkness emerged her enemy, resplendent in the glittering antique uniform of the Imperial Navy, a blood-dripping *bat'leth* held aloft, ready for use again.

Jadzia straightened up, unimpressed. "Worf, that wasn't on the schematics."

Lieutenant Commander Worf leapt down from the upper deck and moved warily around the central helm console, eyes afire. "I am not Worf. I am Kang, captain of the *Thousand-Taloned Death*. And you are my prey!"

Worf lunged past the elevated captain's chair, swinging for Jadzia's legs with a savage upsweep of his *bat'leth*.

Jadzia expertly deflected the ascending crescent blade with her sword as she flipped through the air to land behind the safety railing that ringed the upper deck to her right. Although he had missed his target, Worf's momentum forced him to continue his spin until his *bat'leth* plunged deep into the captain's chair behind him, shorting the communications relays in its shattered arm and causing a spectacular burst of sparks to shoot into the air.

"Worf, I'm serious," Jadzia complained testily. "I was just in the briefing room. I specifically called up the bridge schematics."

Worf grunted as he struggled to tug his weapon free of the chair. "You should not be talking. You should be running for your life."

He turned away from her to give the stubborn *bat'leth* one final pull.

Jadzia saw her opportunity and took it. She leaned over the railing and swatted Worf's backside with the flat of her sword.

Worf wheeled around in shock. "That was *not* a death-blow!"

"I said, I checked the schematics. There *is* no emergency tunnel beside the viewscreen. You're cheating."

Worf flashed a triumphant grin at her, his weapon finally free. "If you did not see the tunnel on the deck plans, it means you did not use the proper command codes to access them. To the computer, you might have been an enemy, and so you were not shown the correct configuration."

"What?!"

"Defend yourself!" Worf shouted. He swung down to slice the safety railing in two, directly in front of Jadzia.

But Jadzia lashed out with her boot to slam Worf on

the side of his head, at the same time she swung her sword against his *bat'leth* to send it spinning out of his grip to shatter the holographic viewer on Mr. Spock's science station.

"You never told me about needing command codes!" she protested.

Worf put one huge hand to the side of his head, looked at the pink blood on his fingers, flared his nostrils in what Jadzia, sighing, knew all too well was a sign of intense pleasure. There was nothing a Klingon liked better than a caring, loving mate who knew how to play rough. "You did not ask," he said, breathing hard, then leapt over the twisted railing to land heavily on the upper deck two meters from Jadzia.

"You're not playing fair," Jadzia told him.

Worf shot a glance upward at the center of the bridge's domed ceiling. "That is not the opinion of the Beta Entity," he growled.

Jadzia risked a sudden look at the ceiling as well. It was maddening to admit, but Worf was right. The amorphous energy beast that fed on the psychic energy of hatred and conflict grew brighter as she watched.

Worf took a step closer. Jadzia took a step back.

"Do not attempt to delay the inevitable. Escape is impossible."

Jadzia stood her ground, raised her sword. "Who said I wanted to escape?"

Worf took another step, arms reaching out to either side, eyes absolutely fixed on his quarry. "Ah, knowing you must lose, you choose to attempt to take your enemy with you. The *w'Han Do*. A warrior's strategy." Worf threw back his massive head and roared approvingly.

"Even better, I have no intention of losing, either."

Then Jadzia slashed her sword back and forth in an intricate display of *k'Thatic* ritual disembowelment which had taken her past host Audrid more than eight years to master, and finished the motion by unexpectedly launching the sword across the bridge where it crashed into an auxiliary life-support station.

Worf, who had been transfixed by Jadzia's dazzling swordplay, appeared shocked by what could only have been a careless mistake. He stared at her sword as it twanged back and forth in a shower of sparks from a shattered display screen.

The diversion worked exactly as Jadzia had planned it. As Worf puzzled over the sword, she slammed into him, shoulder first, elbow in the stomach, driving him back until he collided with a station chair and pitched backward, falling flat on his back.

In an instant, Jadzia was astride him, hands raised, fingers scooped in the strike position for a Romulan *deeth mok* blow to crush the larynx.

Worf fought for breath, the air in his lungs knocked out of him by the violence of his impact. The sweat and blood that covered his face gleamed as the energy beast pulsated above them.

". . . you can not defeat a Klingon with a pitiful *deeth mok* . . ." Worf wheezed defiantly.

"There's more than one way to skin a Klingon," Jadzia said.

Worf's eyes widened in alarm at the thought—and also, Jadzia thought, more than a touch of anticipatory excitement.

And then she swiftly brought both hands down to the sides of Worf's enormous ribcage and—

Worf howled with laughter. He frantically wriggled under Jadzia, ineffectually trying to slap her hands away as he gasped for breath.

"Give up?" Jadzia asked.

Worf's eyes teared as he snorted, "I will not surrender! I am Kang!"

"Ha! I knew Kang," Jadzia said as she dug in, effortlessly repelling his futile attempts to stop her. "Kang was a friend of mine. And *you* are no Kang!"

By now, Worf was totally incapable of speech. Any intelligent sound he attempted to make was overwhelmed by convulsive laughter.

Jadzia went for the kill. "Say *'rumtag,'* " she demanded as she drove home her attack, running her fingers over Worf's ribs at warp nine. "Say it!"

The word erupted from Worf like a volcanic explosion. *"Rumtag! Rumtag!"*

With a whoop of victory, Jadzia rolled off her husband and stretched out on the floor beside him, holding her head up on one elbow as she watched him struggle to catch his breath and regain his dignity.

His pitiful attempt to glare at her as he said, "You tickled me," made even Worf burst out laughing again. After a few more aborted tries, he took a deep breath and blurted out, suddenly deeply serious, "Now we are both in danger."

"Something else you didn't tell me?" Jadzia asked lightly.

She was suddenly aware of the light from the Beta Entity getting brighter, and then, the creature was all around them both. She felt a mild electrical tingle over her body and tugged down on her short skirt again. Then the light winked out as the energy creature disappeared.

"What happens next?" she asked, curious more than alarmed.

Worf took an even deeper breath, in an obvious attempt to restore his warrior's concentration. "Nothing. We are both"—he fought to stifle an incipient giggle—"dead." He snorted again and rubbed his ribcage.

"Say that again."

"The Beta Entity was not pleased with the change in our emotional mood. Thus, it enveloped us and drained us of our life energy."

Jadzia screwed up her face in confusion. "That's not right. I studied this mission at the Academy. The energy creature that captured Kirk and Kang and made their crews keep fighting to the death on the *Enterprise* fed on hate. When Kirk convinced everyone to stop fighting and to laugh, to express joyful emotions, the creature didn't kill anyone. It just . . . left."

Worf had finally regained his appropriately stern expression. "This is the Klingon version of the holosimulation. And besides, it was Kang who convinced the others to stop fighting."

Jadzia raised an eyebrow and playfully placed a single finger against Worf's side. "It was who?"

Worf smiled. "It was . . . your *rumtag!*" And then he was on her, running his fingers up and down her sides, until this time it was Jadzia who was reduced to inarticulate laughter.

Finally, exhausted, breathless, they both collapsed together on the lip of the upper deck, Jadzia sitting up, leaning against Worf's broad chest, Worf's fingers gently untangling the intricate weaving of her twenty-third-century hairstyle.

The bridge of the *Enterprise* was silent, filled with a soft haze colorfully lit by the shifting display screens that ringed the Trill and the Klingon, a ship out of time.

"It's almost romantic," Jadzia said softly, sighing. She remembered being on this same bridge, in reality, when she and Captain Sisko had taken a trip into the past. She thought of the legendary Spock again, how close she had actually come to him. She sighed again.

Worf ran a finger along the spots that trailed from her temple. "Perhaps we should return to our quarters."

Jadzia looked up at Worf and smiled teasingly. "Actually, I was thinking that maybe we could slip down to the captain's quarters. Imagine, James T. Kirk's bedroom. Think of the history."

Worf frowned. "I would rather not. Besides, we only have the holosuite for another five minutes."

Jadzia considered the possibilities of the bridge for a moment, but five minutes was more of a challenge than she was in the mood for right now. She ran a finger along Worf's sexily rippled brow. "There's an arboretum a few decks down. Call Quark and book another hour."

"That is not possible, Jadzia. Odo has requested all the holosuites beginning at oh-seven hundred."

"All of them?" Jadzia sat up, away from Worf. "He's having a party and he didn't invite us?"

"It is for his investigation of the Andorian's murder."

"Ahh," Jadzia said, understanding. Once highly-detailed scans had been made of crime scenes, they could be flawlessly recreated with holotechnology, and the computers could be used to call out various anomalies with great precision. "Does he have any new leads?"

Worf blinked at his wife. "Why would he need new ones?"

It took a moment for Jadzia to realize what Worf was actually saying. "Worf, Quark didn't kill the Andorian."

"All the evidence points to him."

"All the *circumstantial* evidence."

Worf got to his feet. "It is my understanding that the evidence is more than circumstantial." He adjusted his old-fashioned gold-fabric sash, then turned in the direction of the turbolift.

Jadzia jumped to her feet and grabbed his arm to stop him. "Not so fast, Kang." She forced her groom to turn to face her. "What evidence does Odo have?"

Worf rolled his eyes, replying like a five-year-old asked to recite logarithmic tables. "The Andorian businessman—"

"Dal Nortron," Jadzia said. "Let's concentrate on the facts."

"The Andorian businessman, *Dal Nortron,* arrived on DS9 last Sunday afternoon. Sunday evening, he won more than a hundred bars of—"

"One hundred twenty-two bars."

Worf glowered at Jadzia. "One hundred, *twenty-two* bars of gold-pressed latinum—after *three consecutive wins* at dabo. That fact alone is enough to suggest that Quark had arranged to pay off the Andorian—Dal Nortron—through rigged winnings."

"Dabo's a popular game in this quadrant. There are two documented cases of gamblers winning seven consecutive dabos, which is within the statistical realm of probability."

"Not at Quark's," Worf said.

"Come on, Worf. Odo inspects the table every week. Quark doesn't rig it."

Worf let his opinion be known with a grunt.

Jadzia shrugged. "Go on."

"Two hours after Nortron left Quark's, he was found dead and the latinum was missing."

"Stop right there. There's no logic to what you're saying." Jadzia waited for Worf to interrupt, surprised when he didn't. "If Quark had arranged to pay off Nortron with rigged dabo winnings, then why would he *kill* Nortron to get those winnings back?"

Worf shifted his considerable weight from one foot to the other. "Perhaps Nortron took advantage of the table once too often. Perhaps Quark wanted people to think he had settled a debt to Nortron, and when he had done so, *then* steal back his latinum. Perhaps he did not like the way Nortron was dressed."

"Oh, well, now that is motivation for murder."

"Jadzia, Quark is a Ferengi. Ferengi do not think the way other civilized beings do."

Even though Worf's sternly-delivered pronouncement told Jadzia that her new husband was reaching the limits of his patience, she persisted. "Worf—this is the twenty-fourth century! That kind of stereotype belongs in the dark ages."

"The Andorian was found dead near the reactor cores in the lower levels. Security monitoring is limited there. Who else would know that better than Quark?"

"*You,* for one. Maybe we should suspect you. That makes about as much sense as suspecting Quark."

Clearly upset by her lack of wifely loyalty, Worf glowered at Jadzia. "I am DS9's Strategic Operations Officer. It is my job to know the station's security weaknesses. Just it is in Quark's interest to know them because of his long involvement in smuggling operations."

Jadzia softened her tone and affectionately reached up to straighten Worf's sash. "There's a difference between smuggling and murder, Worf. Especially since some of Quark's smuggling operations benefited the Bajoran resistance as well as the Federation."

Mollified but only slightly by her touch, Worf regarded her gravely. "He cares only for profit."

"Granted. But not enough to kill for it."

Worf brushed aside Jadzia's hand. "This conversation is useless. You have not listened to me at all. You have already made up your mind about the Ferengi's innocence."

"Me? How about you? You've already made up your mind he's guilty."

Worf stared at Jadzia as if he really didn't understand what she was talking about. "Of course I have. Because he is."

"Worf! We don't even know if it *was* a murder!"

Worf's heavy brow wrinkled and Jadzia could see he was waging an internal debate. She decided that he knew something that she didn't, and he was wondering if he should tell her. Jadzia decided to help him make the right decision. There were better ways to defeat a Klingon than through combat.

She stepped closer to him, slipping her hand beneath his sash this time. The old Klingon uniforms had no armor and the thin cloth of his shirt did little to interfere with the contact of her flesh against his. "Worf . . ." she whispered into his ear, "I'm your wife. We have no secrets from each other, remember?" Then she bit his ear lobe. Hard.

Worf took a quick breath, then spoke quickly, as if he was worried that he would change his mind. "Odo showed me Dr. Bashir's preliminary autopsy report. Dal Nortron was killed by an energy-discharge weapon. Odo believes such a weapon would be too primitive to show up on the station's automatic scanning system."

"How primitive?" Jadzia asked, stilling her hand on his chest.

"Microwave radiation. Extremely intense. It . . . overheated every cell in his body. A weapon without honor."

Jadzia swiftly reviewed everything she knew about microwave radiation. In this case, it was her own experiences as a science specialist which took precedence over the memories of Dax's previous hosts.

Microwaves were part of the electromagnetic spectrum, one of at least seven energy spectrums known to exist in normal spacetime. In pre-subspace, EM-based civilizations—those converging toward rating C-451–45018–3 on Richter's scale of culture—the primary applications of microwave radiation were line-of-sight radio communications and nonmetallic industrial welding, typically with some half-hearted attempts to create first-generation beamed-energy weapons. On Earth, it had even been used for cooking food. Primitive was not the word for it. Prehistoric was more like it, right alongside stone knives and bear skins.

Jadzia took her hand from Worf's chest, amused in spite of the situation to see her groom only then resume easy breathing. "Be reasonable, Worf. Why would Quark use an old-fashioned microwave weapon when he could have disintegrated Nortron with a phaser?"

Worf glanced over his shoulder at the turbolift doors, as if worried someone was about to join them. He took a step back from her. "Phaser residue can be detected for hours after a disintegration."

But Jadzia curled one finger under his gold sash to gently pull him back to her. "Who would have know he was missing?"

Worf smoothed his sash again, trying to dislodge

Jadzia's grip. "Perhaps Quark didn't want to put the latinum at risk."

"So . . . stun Nortron, take the latinum, *then* disintegrate him."

"Just because I believe Quark is a criminal does not mean I believe he is a *smart* criminal. And would you please stop that!"

Jadzia was about to raise the stakes when she was interrupted by an announcement from hidden speakers.

"Ladies and gentlemen, boys and girls and morphs, this simulation will end in thirty seconds. Thank you for choosing Quark's for your entertainment needs. Be sure to enquire about our half-price drink specials for holosuite customers when you turn in your memory rods. Now, please gather your personal belongings and take small children by the appropriate grasping appendage. And remember, Quark's is not responsible for lost or stolen articles, or for damage caused by micro-forcefield fluctuations. Five . . . four . . . three . . ."

The bridge of the *Enterprise* melted from around Jadzia and Worf, retreating back into history. Now they stood in a simple, unadorned room, its lower walls studded with the glowing green emitters of a compact holoprojector system.

"Please exit through the doors to the rear of the holosuite, and thank you for visiting Quark's—the happiest place in the Bajoran Sector."

Jadzia and Worf exchanged a look of shared puzzlement.

"That voice sounded like Leeta," Jadzia said.

"I have heard that Rom is introducing new policies during Quark's . . . incarceration."

"If Rom is next in line for the bar, I'm surprised you don't start suspecting him of setting up his brother."

The holosuite door slipped open to reveal Odo and two security officers.

"Commanders, I trust I'm not interrupting," the constable said.

"We have finished," Worf said brusquely. He started for the door.

"No, we haven't," Jadzia countered.

"I'm sorry," Odo said, "but I do require the holosuites for assembling—"

"That's not what I meant," Jadzia interrupted. "Odo, Worf told me that Dal Nortron died of exposure to microwave radiation."

Odo frowned. "That is privileged information. At least," he added gruffly as he looked at Worf, "it was."

"Worf was conferring with me, Security Operations Officer to Science Officer."

Odo did not look convinced. But then, he rarely did. "Go on."

"A microwave weapon seems such an unlikely choice to commit a murder, I was wondering if there might be another explanation."

"I am open to suggestions."

"Well, if the body was found near the reactor levels, have you ruled out energy leaks or power modulations coming from the power transfer-conduit linkages?"

Odo blinked. "I was not aware that fusion power-conduits could generate microwave radiation."

Jadzia shrugged. "Not directly. But there's so much other equipment on those levels, a fusion power surge could set up rapid oscillations in various circuits. That's all you'd need to generate an electromagnetic field. And if the field was strong enough or close enough to something that might function as a waveguide, it could reach microwave levels."

Odo looked off to the side as if reprocessing the data she had just provided. "Could traces of such a field be detected after the fact?"

Jadzia ignored her husband's disapproving frown. "Absolutely. You'd need to examine everything in the area for magnetic realignment, heat damage, even signs of electrical sparking between conductive materials.

"Electrical?" Odo made a sound in the back of his throat, then nodded. "Very well. I'll send a forensics team down at once. If they find evidence of anomalous energy discharges, I'll let you know."

"And if they don't?" Jadzia asked.

Odo gave her a grim smile, as if he had successfully led her on. "Then it will be additional evidence that the murder was committed with a microwave weapon."

Jadzia was surprised when Worf suddenly grunted. "Unless," he said, and Jadzia could sense his reluctance, "the Andorian was killed by an anomalous power discharge somewhere else on the station and his body was taken to the lower levels to confuse the investigation."

Jadzia was pleased that Worf had offered some support for her theory, despite his conviction that the guilty party was already in custody.

But Odo rendered Worf's suggestion unnecessary. "We can rule that possibility out, Commander. I do have enough security tapes and computer logs to establish that Dal Nortron took a turbolift to the lower levels approximately twenty minutes before he was killed."

"Before he died," Jadzia corrected.

"He was murdered, Commander. Of that I have no doubt."

Jadzia ignored Odo's increasing air of formality. "Do your security tapes and computer logs show that anyone else was in that area at the same time?" she asked.

Odo's hesitation answered the question for her.

"I didn't think so," Jadzia said.

"There's no such thing as a perfect crime," Odo said bluntly. "I've already connected Quark to Nortron. They were involved in a business dealing together. They had a falling out. Quark killed him. Accidentally, more likely than not. But it is definitely murder."

Jadzia studied Odo closely. She had seldom heard such emotion in the Changeling's voice. Almost as if he were personally involved in this case.

"Odo, did *you* know Dal Nortron?" Jadzia asked.

"Of course not. Why would you even ask such a thing?"

Eight lifetimes of experience told Jadzia she was on to something. "No reason. But I'd find someone who did know him," she said. "Someone who can tell you why he came to DS9, and why he went down to the lower levels."

Now it was Odo who was losing his patience. "To meet Quark."

"But your own records say Quark *wasn't* down there."

"Records can be altered, Commander."

Jadzia smiled sweetly. Now she had led *him* on. "Exactly. Altered to take someone out. Or to put someone in. And if the records could be altered so easily, Quark and Dal Nortron could have met *anywhere* on the station without you knowing about it. And if they could have met anywhere, then why did they choose the lower levels?"

Odo exhaled in frustration, but said nothing.

Worf tugged on Jadzia's arm. "We should let the constable get on with his duties."

"What's down there?" Jadzia asked again as she left with her husband. "You answer that question, Odo, and you'll solve the crime."

Odo did not respond, but Jadzia didn't care.

Eight lifetimes of experience gave her the answer she knew the constable didn't want to admit.

Somehow, in some way, whatever had happened to Dal Nortron, Odo *was* involved.

And the answer to *that* mystery was somewhere in the lower levels.